BING

BANGED

MY LULA

BING
BANGED
MY LULA

Frankie Park

ORION

An Orion Paperback

First published in Great Britain
in 2000 by Orion
A division of Orion Books Ltd
Orion House, 5 Upper St Martin's Lane,
London WC2H 9EA

A CIP catalogue record for this book
is available from the British Library

Typeset by Deltatype Ltd, Birkenhead, Merseyside
Printed in Great Britain by
The Guernsey Press Co. Ltd, Guernsey, C.I.

Grateful acknowledgement is made for permission to quote from
'Roll With It' written by Noel Gallagher, by kind permission Oasis Music,
Creations Songs Ltd. & Sony / ATV Music Publishing (UK) Ltd

for Marlon

Acknowledgements

I can't believe I've finally got to the stage where my editor asks for my list of acknowledgements. How cool is that? Everyone is going to have to be really nice to me now, just to make sure they get their mention. I could enjoy dangling this carrot – I've never had a carrot like this before – but I resist, especially as there are certain people who I'd like to thank anyway for their untiring interest and support.

So: a big sloshy thank you to the inspirational P-girl who listened and laughed; to the nutty T-bird who told me about Charles Bukowski; to my big sister and big brother who told my dad my book was great; to my old friends S.B. and J.M.; to my fab agent M.D.; to my rigorous but brilliant editors at Orion; and, of course, to Nigel. Big thanks also to others not mentioned, but you know who you are.

I think I'll go away and have a little cry now. It's so touching – thank you, thank you . . .

Contents

Part One

New School, New Friends and a Headbutt or Two

1

It began one Easter term, when my son first started school. That's where I first met Conka: her daughter was starting too. It was at the school that I began to fully appreciate the *them* and *us* situation, the complete picture. I knew the others already. Tasha was actually a pre-kid friend – not many saw me all the way through. She soon caught up though, kid-wise, a couple of years later, when she had Daniella. I'd originally met Tasha in the students' coffee bar when we were doing Art Foundation, years ago. Tasha had always loved coffee too. Her skin even looked like coffee, a soft milky brown – with two sugars. We had love of art, music and coffee in common – it wasn't just the kids.

Sarah and Sharon were other single mothers, post giving birth, pre-school friends. Sarah was the oldest of us, in her late forties. She was the original Single Earth Mother. Sarah had three kids by three different men, in three different decades. She'd been through three big disappointments, and at the time was still occasionally involved with the last of the three. She didn't live with him any more, but she sometimes let him stay when he visited their youngest. We thought of Sarah as someone responsible: it was she we turned to as a source of strength and stability.

Sharon was yer babe: a completely scatty, unreliable, air-head, Wonderbra'd, peroxide-haired doll. She was basically drop-dead, but she was a pain. She had really long legs and nice plump tits. She even had a cheeky but sexy gap between her front top teeth – I've always liked that, maybe because my teeth are all so greedily squashed together. But you really needed patience with Sharon. Sarah had patience in buckets, but I think I was just taken in by her incredible sex appeal – and she was funny. I suppose I sympathised with Sharon. She was in a love-mess I recognised. She had a crap relationship and I felt I could save her. I didn't mind shouting the coffee and fags. I felt like Jesus on a mission, I *wanted* to save her. I think Sarah felt the same way about me. Everyone needs somebody, I suppose.

Sharon and I had very similar relationships with Sarah. We both hated Sarah's husband and enjoyed her mothering. She understood us, had *suffered* more than us: she *knew*.

Sharon met Sarah a few years ago in London Zoo. They'd gone there to escape reality and distract their kids. The two mums, out on their own with their kids, stared at the animals, wrapped up in their dire domestics. They stayed out – even though it was the middle of winter, freezing cold and the kids were whingeing – rather than go home. Sharon reckoned that the caged monkeys had smirked ironically at them. I always argued that monkeys don't know the meaning of 'irony'.

Anyway, Sharon and Sarah recognised each other's distant look. They needed to talk and went for a nice cup of zoo tea. They have been good friends ever since.

I met Sarah in much the same way, except not in the zoo, in the park by the sandpit. I hate sand, especially on my feet and even more so in the middle of the city miles away from any kind of beach. I soon drifted off, dreaming about another life, not paying much attention to my boy Luke – he seemed happy enough playing with this other mum and her kid. I was so involved in my dream existence that I failed to notice Sarah pack up and try to leave. Luke had attached himself to them so strongly, he started crying and making a fuss when they said goodbye. Unfortunately, I didn't notice any of this – I didn't even hear him cry. Sarah had to come over to ask if I was Luke's mother. I couldn't deny it, I *am* his mother. Some flipping *on it* mother I was, poor kid. Luke wasn't much more than a baby then and I felt terrible. I was so embarrassed, I started crying too. How awful – a couple of crying strangers, I'd hate that, but not Sarah. She calmed us down. She pulled out the wet wipes. Luke wet himself and I bawled louder. Still unruffled, Sarah understood: she'd been there and knew how hard coping with a toddler was, especially when his father was breaking your heart *and* your wallet. She pulled out a spare pair of trousers (oh, to be more organised) for Luke to borrow, I mumbled eternal gratitude, we exchanged numbers and became friends.

4

Once Sarah had moved to her relatively big house in the country – well, the 'burbs actually – Twickenham just seemed like the country compared to Shepherd's Bush – she often babysat for Sharon and me, over whole weekends. She recognised in us the anguish she had struggled with, when she was about our age and a twenty-something single mother. She was a lifesaver. She'd have the children to stay as much as we wanted.

Sarah's home was comfortable. Every room carpeted with thousands of toys, the garden littered with rabbits and their hutches, swings, slides and footballs. She even had a incredibly cool cat, and I'm a dog person. The kids loved it there. Going to Sarah's was like going to a health farm as far as destressing goes, only not so healthy on the lung front. As payment for looking after Luke now and then, I'd buy her a big lump of dope, which we'd proceed to make rather a large dent in while drinking tea and comparing horror stories.

When Sharon and I became friends we would go to see Sarah together and I soon introduced them to Tasha, whose spookily vast knowledge of herbal remedies and Jung-meets-Jong philosophy amused Sarah for ages. Tasha was someone new for her to convert to the teachings of the Liberal Democrats – she'd already converted Sharon and me. She was quite a politico, was Sarah.

Sharon hit it off with Tasha, who was fresh ears for the drama queen of the century. Not that *everything* Sharon said was daft – some of it really helped me, especially about the school. That first day was pretty daunting. By the time Luke started, Sharon had been going to and fro for two years – her son Liam was seven.

We got there early. Outside the tall iron gate, Sharon gave me the low-down on most of the not-so-bland characters and the so-bland-that-they're-practically-milk characters: the dreaded *other parents*. She noted that we'd be seeing them all the time – five days a week, at nine in the morning and at three thirty in the afternoon, for the next six years. Awesome. Sharon hated it. Her advice was to keep your head down and your mouth shut: that way they *wouldn't know*. Wouldn't know what? I wasn't quite sure. As it was all new to me, I let her carry on while I listened attentively and observed.

She pointed out the hairy-armpitted I-don't-believe-in-television-but-if-I-did-it-would-be-Channel-4, no makeup, test-tube-mother dyke, the cute widower who all the women find really sweet, the teacher with acne, the ex-television soap extra. She showed me her friend Conka's ex, Edwin – the man with the knife collection, the Manson tapes, a man apparently rather partial to extreme violence. He had loved to use Conka's head as a duster for his baseball bat. Edwin, infidelity personified, had a son and another daughter at the school all with different mothers. Sharon reckoned he'd make a play for me: he liked variation and adored fresh blood.

Of course, Sharon had already told me about Conka. She was *rough, very rough*. Sharon was such a gossipy snob, I never took anything she said that seriously and I wasn't about to now. *Rough!* Sharon had had some kind of run-in with Conka years ago, when Conka was still under the anvil thumb of her ex. Apparently Conka had told her where to shove her advice and I couldn't exactly blame her – more often than not Sharon's advice just pissed you off. Anyway, since their argy-bargy, Sharon hadn't spoken to Conka, but that was her problem, not mine. If anything, Sharon's warning just made me even more curious to meet the rough, tough bird. Sharon really cracked me up, she played on her patheticness. She loved a scene. She hinted that Conka might try to beat her up – hilarious. I'd watch.

Sharon and I leant on the rail opposite the gates watching all the arrivals. I hated it already. I didn't remember my mum coming to school with me. I'm sure she probably did for the first couple of days, you know, to show me the way. But *six* years? I hoped Sharon was wrong when she'd said that as these parents had started to annoy me and it was only day one. I'm sure they all stared at me, especially the square, married-looking ones – the ones who reminded me of what a parent should look like.

There were the harried-marrieds too, I suppose. But you kind of ignored them. They were too close to what you'd be like if you were in a relationship, and they just made you jealous. Bastards! It was the terribly organised, shove-it-in-your-face-marrieds who pissed me off.

You see, it's kind of like being two different breeds. *They* stand

6

there all tidy and organised – and they say, 'Oh, *single mum*, are you? Never mind, dear . . . What? He doesn't help you out at all? Oh, I see.' I could just hear it.

They don't 'see' at all. Then they give you that warm, understanding smirk – you know, the one that makes you want to shout, 'No, *actually*, I bloody well left him, you overweight nerd.' But you don't say that. You say nothing or you manage a feeble, 'Hey, perhaps we're better off without them, eh?' And at the same time you're thinking, If you only knew what that smarmy, lairy, slimy bastard of a husband you call your better half was really like, you'd hang yourself with your boring flouncy scarf.

Hmm, if only. Funny how our kids turned out not to be so popular with those from the allegedly functional families. It's like they're a gang. In fact, just one married mum can make you feel as if she's an entire gang. I think they suffered too, though, you know, the married mums, mainly from husbanditis, a non-definable virus. The symptoms run to tight lips, swollen ankles, varicose veins, too much foundation, frizzy hair and general absence of character. The kind of men that cause this are often spotted trying to pull off a ring or band. They have leering faces and stinking breath, they like their kids in public, but forget their names in private. They call their kids names you'd forget anyway: John Jr of John Jenkins Sr of Jerksville. And they tell their wives what to do, who to be. Shame.

Sharon was tugging at me to go *into* the school. Dropping the kids off at the gates was not all you did. No, you walk them right into the school building and you take them all the way to their classroom. I'm positive my mum never did that. Turned out to be quite a distance from the gates. All on your first day. All on your own, unless you're lucky enough to know another single mother.

We spotted her in the school building. Conka – what a sight. All fit five foot-Amazon-ten of her comes steaming down the corridor with her Walkman blaring loudly, shades on, giving the tidy married mums something to fear. I liked her instantly. I liked the way she strode – her athletic gait made no compromises for any male oglers. She was sexy in her cockiness. I liked the haphazard way she dressed. She didn't care. She was wearing a red, Spanish-looking, knee-length A-line skirt with orange socks and white trainers. A long pastel green jumper fell loosely from her strong, broad shoulders. The wire from the Walkman divided her generous breasts. Her short dark hair was pulled tightly back with mad pointy bits escaping all over the place. Her face was fresh and unmade-up. Her Mediterranean skin laughed at us pasties around her. She shone. She rebelled against the expected, the anticipated, the conforming, the many squares.

Conka. Conka the Conqueror. Well, you can imagine, she was like a breath of fresh air. She was another single mum and I wanted her in my army.

2

As soon as we saw each other, we felt an affinity – it was as if we already had some private joke. She came straight up for an introduction. Sharon, expecting Conka to hit her, froze. I grinned. Conka asked Sharon if the cat had got her tongue. Visibly relieved, Sharon introduced us before slinking away discreetly.

We had a quick and funny conversion. She was very blunt, but I loved her honesty and I sensed that she was a bit intrigued by me. Conka was one of those Londoners with an answer for everything. Brusque and brash, she seemed the type to speak her mind, however inappropriate and I liked that. She was immediate, in yer face, take it or bleeding well leave it, mate. Exuberant, alive, spirited. Within five minutes she'd ascertained that I'd come by car and had got me to agree to drop her off at her mum's house, where I'd duly return, six hours later, to take her back to the school. It soon became the norm.

It made sense for Conka and me to do the afternoon pick-up together. Her daughter was in the same reception class as Luke so they finished at the same time. We'd go back to mine, roll a big fat one then play the sort of inventive games that my mum was certainly never stoned enough to play with me. Then the kids would go off on their own peculiar tangent and we'd be left in peace to have that cup of tea and conversation – we'd contrast our grim pasts with our imagined futures.

We wanted somehow to improve our lives – make them easier, entertain fatter wallets, buy a few bits. We'd discuss ways to raise some money, what work we'd do, what business we'd start. We'd get so far on our dream excursion, but inevitably return to the same conclusion – after paying for a child-minder, blah, blah, blah, we'd still end up with next to nothing . . .

We'd smoke another joint. Conka would pick up her guitar, which soon lived at my house, and then she would make up ridiculous songs about our – actually, mainly mine – disastrous but funny sex lives. She was free with her music and had a good voice. She encouraged me whenever I joined in. I only hummed at first – I had been told unceremoniously, aged seven, that I sounded like a bat and should never sing, so I never had until then. Conka's spirit eased my inhibitions.

Then we'd debate men. That was our game, I suppose, our version of Trivial Pursuit. Criteria and categories: he'd have to be at least financially sound, if not extremely well off; he should give good massage, always arrive with presents, etc. Well, Conka's crits and cats were pretty silly: he should be an expert in origami; he should excel in soufflés and rise to the occasion both in baking and in the sack; he should deliver an occasional smattering of Oriental love poetry in Cantonese; he should read her mind.

She had reason to create these virtually impossible and impenetrable barriers. Conka had been through the lot. Not only did she know the inside of the casualty ward like the back of her hand, she had also suffered a bad case of *ripped-off-itis* (possibly related to *husbanditis*). When she'd got shot of Edwin and convinced herself of her own recovery, she'd met another wanker and fallen for that old tart called 'love' again. Love, darling, love? Idiot or what? Anyway, Mr Fucking Fabulous moves in and sure enough, six weeks later, she's back to smoking herself stupid, falling asleep swearing and making herself promises. But some things take time. A long time. Back then, Conka, with one hand in the proverbial cookie jar, still succumbed to that old horizontal jogging number and fell hook, line and sinker.

It went like this. Dude moves in, Dude is very nice, Dude makes excellent coffee, Dude gives even better head. Conka is loving it. Everything is hunkadelic. Blissville. Conka has to go away for a few days. Dude moves out, Dude takes everything with him, I mean *everything*, right down to the last sodding lightbulb. No wonder she's a little reticent about the opposite sex. A damned double whammy. The first man beats her blue, the second robs her silly. What a fan-fucking-tastic way to treat a lovely lady, eh? That was the last time, though, I'll give her that. No guy will ever get near her now – unless he takes her to Paris for dinner at least three times in one week. No guy is allowed to pass through her front door – unless he's armed with six numbers on that evening's lottery ticket, and then he's lucky if he gets to massage her stinky feet. Tricky when the gas man calls, but a vow is a vow, especially the ones you make to yourself.

Conka had a load of music equipment that Dude-shitbrains took with him, the whole tuneful lot, all gone. It's not as if Conka had much. What can you get when you're forced to depend on the quicksand of benefits, car-boot sales, backs of lorries and natural cheek? Conka had lashings of that, though – cheek, I mean. But she didn't have any other kind of back-up. Not like me, with a well-off dad (handy), and a talent in the art of makeup. Well, I'm all right . . .

So over the weeks, I learnt a lot about Conka. She has a black and white philosophy, an if-you-don't-like-it-change-it attitude. Her body is her temple and is to be listened to. She's found an answer and she likes it. Her fanny is her pot of gold, her treasure trove, her epicentre which she controls from within. She tells her brain which man she fancies at that particular moment, whether it be a Wimbledon star or the guy next door, then she gets them to do all these horny things to her, in her dreams, and wakes up totally satiated. Marvellous.

We had a laugh. I wanted to be her, she was strong and sorted. She'd gone past the emotional, vulnerable, insecure, pathetic stage that you seem to have to go through after a major gut-gashing split, and had bounced boldly back into the land of confidence and positivity. The land I was aiming for – I just hadn't quite got there yet. I was more like Sharon: weak.

My wounds from Shit-relationship City were still fresh, although healing. It wasn't very long ago that I had been rudely awakened to love's shortcomings by the bailiffs banging on my door. Those fairy-tale walls had been blasted, Sleeping-I don't mind if you freaking snore-Beauty, and Snow White and the seven little liars were piles of crap. My knight in shining shell suit was telling me that everything I did was wrong, while making a competitive mark on the 'Spendolympics', with muggins here being the sole sponsor. Makeup artistry earned me some money but not enough to keep up with him.

But Conka had been stung harder and I was learning fast. I suppose I kind of had a crush on her about three weeks into the term, although it was in a strictly adoring way. I watched the way she had the guts to bare her pearly whites in the face of the kids' monster teacher – the teacher who terrified me, the teacher who always demanded notes: absence notes, permission notes, lunch notes, music notes, school photo notes, bank notes. Conka didn't flinch and that made me breathe deep. Phew.

Sharon was useless in comparison. I reintroduced her to Conka, alongside promises that I wouldn't allow any beatings, although fuck knows what I would have done if Conka had ever let off. Not wanting to be left out, Conka made Sharon promise not to talk about the past. Once past these minor hurdles, we were away. I can proudly say that I neutralised their mutually cagey opinions of each other, and soon the three of us began to spend quite a bit of time together.

I suppose it was the computer course that really bonded us. Tasha didn't do it, but she only ever does weird courses like Afghanistanese magic with shakra kalm or something. I had to force myself to go as it was. It didn't really sound like me.

The course was Conka's idea. I had been frightened of computers and anything vaguely technical all my life. I thought I could survive being an old-fashioned sort who'd never get a mobile phone, never play computer games, never own a microwave or dishwasher – certainly never know how to operate a computer. I'd survive quite adequately in my long-hand, pen-and-paper, backgammon, log-fire, spring-water and simple-arith-metic world, thank you very much. Conka was more forward-thinking and keen to learn.

This was an age of Internet, modems, sites, bytes, rams, bams, bebs and webs. I didn't have a clue, I was rapidly understanding less and less of my native lingo. If I was to live the sex life of a nineties woman (which I was trying to do), then I'd also have to overcome some of my old-fashioned fears in other areas in my life. The technical side definitely needed a rethink. It was more than likely I wouldn't even be able to help five-year-old Luke with his homework.

Conka felt the same way, fed up with taking on menial jobs when she needed extra cash. We realised we'd have to be more clued up, or miss out. I thought of it as just getting a little bit more up-to-date, not as acquiring skills for a secretarial post – or any kind of office job, come to think of it. Hopefully I'd carry on with my stunning makeup career.

At that time Sharon was also talking about brushing up on her typing skills, so we persuaded her to join us. It was held at a strange little adult-education centre near to where we lived, which offered free courses to those who were unemployed. We signed up for two, which loosely covered skills in office management, word processing, typing and database – four hours a day, twice a week. Plus, we could come into the centre at other times and get free use of the computers.

We went regularly, practising touch-typing and various other computer skills. Another regular was a Down's syndrome woman called Homer, whose hearing-aid was often so badly adjusted that it squealed a horrible high-pitched sound. You had to yell at her to turn it down. Homer's reply would be, 'Shut up, piss off and leave 'lone.' She was pretty funny. I quite envied her: Homer said what she wanted when she wanted. Although she shouted a lot, she generally seemed to have a content and independent life – something the three of us were striving for.

Conka began to go so frequently that the staff asked her if she felt like running the canteen. Not being one to turn down an opportunity to make easy money doing tea and coffee, alongside typing and database, she accepted. She roped her friend Elsa into doing it with her. They kept the menu simple: greasy breakfast, or lentil soup for the health fanatics, tea and coffee served all day and baked potatoes cooked on special request. That way she could whip from the kitchen to the computer room, burning her eggs, while she did an accuracy test on the computer tutorial. Blue smoke would slowly waft in and hang above Conka, waiting for her to realise that Elsa wasn't paying any attention either and that the kitchen might be on fire. It was pretty hectic.

The enterprising duo only ever made about a tenner a day between them, but as they were using all the educational benefits of the place, they remained lighthearted and spent most of the time singing. Between bacon butties, cover versions of 'Waterloo' and a selection of Marvin Gaye classics, Conka worked her way through each and every typing lesson until she was fast and accurate. I was impressed.

Sharon was more slack. She made the excuse that the place was depressing. I admit it was underused and underfunded and we did bring the average age down by about twenty-five years. I didn't mind, though. Most of the other users were in there to type out the church news or write their latest letter of complaint to their landlord, or just for the warmth and company. They were not writing up their CVs, or seeking help in filling out job applications. Mind you, Conka was probably the only one of us using the centre 'properly'. When Sharon bothered going, she just typed out a load of poetry. She was quite good, although a touch dark maybe. I never got beyond SALAD.

3

After dropping the kids off in the mornings, Sharon and I began to stay longer at the nearby café than Conka, who was immune to scalding coffee and keen to get typing. She'd call it our 'coffee-cum-moans'. I just couldn't be that lively so early in the morning, and certainly not technical. Sharon was never remotely lively at that time of day (unless she was still up from the night before), so I can't blame Conka for wanting to keep it brief.

Initially I quite enjoyed Sharon's morning moans as my insight into the diseased state of her fucked-up relationship grew. Her incredible, demanding hunger for information concerning Trevor's whereabouts and whatabouts gave her endless moan material. I happened to be shagging a friend of his at the time, which led her to believe that, maybe, I could shed some light on Trevor's questionable fidelity.

My shag Rob wasn't much better than Trevor, and probably worse than him in bed. Sharon was always going on about what an Adonis Trevor was. Rob certainly wasn't that. He and Trevor were basically a couple of lads. And as my relationship with Rob was based on the bi-weekly, booze and bed theory, and not a lot else, I didn't really have any angle on what the lads got up to between our sessions.

Sharon insisted I knew otherwise. I became the object of her childlike interrogations. She became like a woman possessed and it soon began to get dull. I spent hours trying to convince her that there was a hell of a lot more to life than wondering where your man lays his one-eyed trouser-snake, but she'd just gaze at me for a few moments, wondering aloud where I could have found the strength to leave my ex and be so independent. Then she'd ask me if I thought Trevor was seeing Diana from the pub. It became very frustrating as she didn't seem to hear me, although I suppose I couldn't hear my mum when she'd said, 'He's sucking all the sunshine out of you, darling. Don't let him treat you like that.'

Sharon couldn't hear, couldn't care. I knew it, but it didn't stop me from trying. I thought that maybe I could say it more clearly than it had been said to me. I decided on one last blast and launched into my preaching tone.

'Leave that twat. You deserve better than this. Think of your son. Do you want him to grow up thinking that it's kosher [Sharon's Jewish] for men to treat women like this? He's got to learn to respect women and that starts at home.'

Sharon ignored me. I could tell she was planning something else. 'Hey, let's go out. We haven't been out in ages. What do you think?' she suggested.

I knew Trevor hated Sharon going out with me. But I enjoyed the odd night out with her even though she was extremely irritating.

'Okay. Let's go out,' I said.

Sharon's face lit up. 'Brilliant,' she said, grinning.

Fortunately, Trevor was nowhere to be seen when I arrived. I'd brought a bottle of brandy with me and Sharon had a can of Coke. I found a couple of grimy glasses, washed them up and poured the drinks.

Sharon was prancing around, with her long legs all over the place, in a miniskirt and Wonderbra, insisting that she looked dreadful – not the adjective I would have picked.

'Fuck off, Shassa! You look amazing!' I told her.

'Fuckable' was what I would have said if I'd been a bloke. I gulped back some more drink. This was going to take a while. She always needed so much reassuring. After she'd insisted she looked 'dreadful' in about seven outfits, she eventually decided on the one she'd had on right at the beginning. She'd looked absolutely stunning in all of them.

I didn't normally have to drive when I went out with Sharon and tonight was no exception. She always wanted to go out locally, *'just in case we bump into Trevor'*, and then she'd *'know once and for all'*. So we'd walk – or should I say, roam?

We were pretty sloshed by the time we left Sharon's place, but that was cool as we could only afford to buy straight Coke in the pub. We'd lace it ourselves, using the remainder of the brandy secreted in my coat pocket.

As usual we roamed from one pub to the next checking out who was there. Sharon Trevor-searching, immune to her many male admirers – sometimes not even staying for one drink. I was just beginning to wonder how I was going to manage being a mother the following day when Sharon dragged me into a private drinking club.

'Just smile at the doorman and walk in,' she hissed in my ear as she pushed me past the queue. 'Hi, Reg,' she cooed to the wiry bouncer as we wafted in.

I felt a hand on my shoulder but kept walking until we got to the bar. Sharon was doing her usual scan when Rob came up from behind.

'Is Trev with you?' Sharon shouted at him, above the music.

'Can't hear you!' Rob yelled back, giggling to me.

Uh-oh, that meant Trevor was here. Rob pointed upstairs and Sharon disappeared.

'How are you, then, Charlie?'

'All right!' I shouted. 'Pissed!'

'See ya, then.' He patted me on the shoulder as he walked towards a girl in the corner.

Luckily, I'd already chucked him. Unluckily, I'd forgotten that and followed him. He turned round just in time to stop me from lunging at his frigging new girlfriend. It was only then that I remembered he was a crap shag anyway.

'It's *over*, Charlie. You just don't get it, do you?' Quickly he ushered the poor girl out of the bar.

Fucking humiliating, when you think about it. He thought he'd been talking to Meryl Streep in one of those really emotional films.

'I don't think so, sunshine!' I screamed after him, trying to keep up the movie dialogue.

But he was long gone. I was left contemplating the beer rings on the table and the fellow drinkers. There was no sign of Sharon or Trevor. I watched all the sad people. Why are they always sad in late-night drinking bars? Some of them, like me, were contemplating all the other revellers, waiting for something interesting to happen. Others, providing the entertainment we were all so desperately seeking, were lurching from one stable-looking object to another. Sure enough, in the only place where I wasn't looking, some guy couldn't uncross his legs and did an amazing tantric yoga fall. I always miss what everyone else always sees – it's really irritating.

I was drifting off, bored and drunk, drunk and bored, when Sharon, her face on fire with excitement, ran down the stairs.

'I've just head-butted Trevor!' she squealed at me.

'Fantastic!' I replied.

Looking at her exhilarated face, I noticed a big fruity shiner developing on her forehead.

'He looks worse!' she continued, laughing. 'He's got a bloody nosebleed!'

Howling would be putting it mildly. I could not believe it. I loved this woman. She'd blinkered and bounced her bleeding fella!

Then came the bad bit. 'Well, he head-butted me first.'

That dampened my ardour somewhat. Maybe Sharon had

been badly hurt and was delirious. But then in he walked, handkerchief wrapped around his hand and nose, blood everywhere. It was back to howling for me, until I realised that Sharon had left the table and was following Trevor up the stairs – again. They'd end up shagging, as usual. Sharon was well up for it, no doubt about that.

That was enough for me. I left behind my humiliation, Sharon and her bloody mess and lurched home. It was too late to call anyone, the babysitter was fast asleep and too young to talk to anyway, so I lay awake thinking and spinning. I thought of Luke, my son, my one and only. I knew I ought to make more of an effort with him.

I woke up the next morning, freezing cold and fully dressed, on Luke's floor. Some frigging example I am. Thank God it was Sunday.

4

Luke had been on at me since Easter when he first started school to go on one of those school outings with his class. It was now nearing the end of the summer term. I had hoped to make it outings-free all the way until the autumn but he was piling on the pressure.

I tried to like the school, but couldn't help reverting to childish behaviour whenever I went near it. However, I was beginning to feel bad about being one of those parents who never helps at the fête, one of those parents who forgets to bring in old books for the book fair, one of those unreliable mums who doesn't get asked to do anything because they're so useless. I knew that if I started out being all keen and helpful, and there with armfuls of milk-bottle tops or whatever the equivalent is these days, then they'd never leave me alone. I wanted to be let off the hook at some point. I needed time for my own life and school created a natural break; my only break. Stupidly, I hadn't reckoned on Luke forcing me to get involved.

Of course, I had felt guilty about my slackness on some occasions – like when I saw the recent school newsletter. It read,

'And a huge thank you from all the staff for all the wonderful gifts and cards at the end of last term.' Cards? Gifts? Where do these mums get their money from?

I felt worse when I went to Luke's class assembly and the headmistress did her usual school-news bit at the end. 'Finally, I would like to thank all those very hard-working *few* – and it always seems to be the same *small* handful of parents *each* and *every* time – that make such a *valuable* difference to our little school,' she said, all smiles and nods aimed in the direction of the pocket of perfect parents in one corner, followed by a scanning scowl and arched eyebrow across the rest of the room.

Well, I for one couldn't look up when she did that. I coughed instead. Not a good tactic.

'If we could *all* make the same *supreme* effort in our Bumble Bee project as those of us who always do,' she went on, 'then I think we will rocket *above* our humble, but necessary target...' Meaningful pause and looks. I held my breath. 'Thank you. Now if we can let the children out first, I think that'd be easier for the mums and dads.'

An appreciative murmur of 'Absolutely,' sounded through the hall from the perfect, sycophantic, goody-goody lot.

I tutted. I'd done my bit: I'd seen my kid do nothing in his class assembly. All the girls did everything. The boys were too thick – or perhaps just further behind on their reading skills than the girls – and spent most of their time waving at their mums while the girls stole the show. I'd clapped when everyone else did. I'd shut my eyes when the headmistress said her little prayer and now I wanted to get the poo out of there.

I didn't feel much like a grown-up. When I was little, I couldn't wait to be a grown-up. Now I wasn't so sure. Mind you, I wasn't sure of much, these days. I started to question everything I did then compare it with what Conka would have done. For example, school assemblies: Conka had that one well under control. She showed up looking polished: a bit of makeup, hair neatly swept back and co-ordinated clothes for a change – amazing. At least she looked in control. I'm sure I would feel better if I didn't turn up looking such a mess. I'd have to smarten myself up. Conka had school trips pretty much sewn up as well. She always got out of them. She was smart. I was useless.

Luke's teacher Miss Clifton terrifies me. She's thin and wrinkled, with nicotine-stained fingers, hair and mouth. She really puts me off smoking. She has deeply set small dark eyes that peer at you from beneath heavy lids and bold brown eyebrows, which aggravate her permanent frown. I can't recall ever seeing her smile. Her rounded shoulders exaggerate her thinness, and when she speaks, you get glimpses of her black teeth. Her chest rattles louder than an old VW Beetle, and her scrawny witch hands rub and clutch each other nervously. She's yer traditional spinster monster.

Today, class RC was going to the Science Museum, and I didn't have any reasonable excuses that I could genuinely make to Luke to get myself out of it. I was hoping Miss Clifton would tell me they didn't need me and that there wasn't enough room on the bus. Unlucky. Another mother, that bastard Conka in fact, had dropped out at the last minute. Anyway, the bus was massive. Shit.

I was allocated four children, Luke being one of them. All I had to do was make sure they got safely on and off the bus, and to and from the museum. I already thought my child was in danger and wanted him reallocated, but instead asked which four children it was again, deliberately forgetting Luke every time. Luke thought it was funny. Miss Clifton was losing her patience and gave me a very stern stare. She seemed pretty relieved to be able to have a sneaky fag and was the last to board the bus. She'd made some lame excuse about forgetting the tickets, but I could smell it on her. I tried to give her a stare back that said *I know ya liddle secret, baby*, but she ignored me.

I enjoyed the bus journey, the children were sweet and excited by the trip. I talked to them to avoid too much conversation with the other mums, in particular one married mum who, I felt, was looking down her nose at me. I listened to the kids' conversations. They are all so competitive and brag their heads off. Or they slip into Pretend Land, where they spend the whole time telling each other what they were going to pretend to say and do. I loved it.

When we got into the museum, we were shown into an empty

room. We were asked to sit down on the bright blue, scratchy Brillo pad of a carpet, under the watchful eyes of 'Miriam', our 'host' for the morning. She was a young, enthusiastic, bouncy Australian girl, with bad skin and a big smile. She wore a sweatshirt in the same blue as the carpet with a Science Museum cartoon logo. She was geeky and goofy.

'Hi! How are y'll doing?' she greeted us. 'My name's Miriam and I'm here to welcome you today, to tell you a few things about our wonderful museum and to answer any questions you may have.'

Fantastic. She said the museum wanted the children to take an active part: to climb, to build, to play etc., etc., with all the exhibits in all the rooms that had the same bright blue carpet. She said we weren't to go anywhere that didn't have this carpet. We would have forty-five minutes to explore, after which the name of our school would be announced over the tannoy and we were to meet back in this room. We were all pretty clear on that and shortly afterwards were let loose on the exhibition and its lovely blue carpet.

I instantly lost my four charges. I tried not to panic – we were in an enclosed area. I noticed the other parents watching non-allocated children so I thought I'd do the same. I'd just make sure to be on the lookout for any different-coloured carpet.

Carefully staying on the bright blue Brillo, I wandered purposefully around, making a bit of a show of keeping an eye on things. I found myself thinking about Conka. She would have loved it here. It was an interesting place, exploring ideas about gravity, weight, balance, very educational. She would have been climbing all over the place. I wanted to have a go on some of the gadgets, but was too self-conscious. Instead, I forced myself on to a couple of kids from Luke's class and insisted they let me help them with a ball machine. They soon walked off, so I decided to find Luke. I'd rather muck about on this lot with him, anyway.

He was playing with a train track, weight and pulley exhibit. He'd always loved trains ever since he was a baby. We played with the trains for a while then moved on to this thing that spins you really fast. When Luke stopped feeling dizzy, we walked together, hand in hand, looking at all the fascinating mechanisms, pulls and wobbly glass baubles. It felt nice. I was glad to have come. I thought it was a real 'good mum' thing to do. We then went on to the bridge-building blocks. You had to work out how to build your own bridge with the blocks provided. If you did it right, it would be strong enough to hold a small child, the perfect category for our Luke. So we set about the task of bridge building.

After what seemed to be only a few minutes, I looked up to check that I could still see children from Luke's school. The place seemed to have filled up a bit. My eyesight is pretty appalling, but I thought I recognised a couple of girls from his class. My hearing is good, though, and I hadn't yet heard the school's name over the Tannoy.

I decided to keep my ears open extra wide but, even so, I thought it must be about time to go. Luke would hopefully have just about long enough to finish his bridge. Proudly, I watched him work out where to put the last couple of bricks.

'Well done, Luke,' I said. 'Go on. You can cross it now. It's strong enough to hold you.'

Luke began his walk. I saw the excitement in his face as, cautiously, he climbed the first few steps. The bridge was firm. He smiled a broad, happy smile and began marching across it. I couldn't watch any more. I thought the bridge was not meant to be stamped on quite so heavily and would collapse. I also thought I should look for other members of the class again. I hadn't spotted any for quite some time now.

I looked up into the face of Mrs Goody-Married-Two-Shoes.

'Oh, hello. We've been making a bridge,' I told her. 'It's really fantastic in here, isn't it? I'm glad I've seen you. I was just wondering where everyone was. Have you seen any of the others?'

Before she could answer me I heard the anticipated, almighty crash, 'Oh, no. Excuse me.' I turned and helped Luke climb out of the debris.

Madam was still staring at me. 'Didn't you know? We've all been waiting in the other room.'

'What? They've already called us?'

'Three times, and once addressed personally to Luke and his mother.'

'No way! I swear I didn't hear a thing.'

God! This was so embarrassing. How could I have missed that? What a turd.

'How long have you been waiting?'

'Oh, *only* about ten minutes.'

Sarky now too, I thought. I grabbed Luke and followed Teacher's Pet back to the room. Irrepressible giggles began to bubble inside and I stuttered apologies as I dived on to the carpet, causing minor abrasions and burns to my elbow and legs. I decided to keep my eyes well down. I could feel Miss Clifton's stare burn right into me. I was dying to laugh out loud, but knew that everything I did from now on would only make matters worse. And the worse it got, the more I wanted to giggle. I'd totally fucked up again, and all I could flipping well do was laugh. I let slip one uncontainable gulp of mirth, badly disguised in a sneeze, then urged myself to be more controlled.

'Now that we are *all* here, we will make our way in twos back to the bus.'

Luke and I held our hot hands together. I squeezed his. I spotted my other three charges and we walked silently to the bus. So much for me doing the good-mum thing. Luke seemed happy, though. He even let me kiss him goodbye at the gate.

'See you after school, darling.'

I waved goodbye, then got the hell out of there before Miss Clifton could collar me.

5

Sharon felt strangely excited about the computer course. It wound Trevor up, but since their head-butting scene, anything wound Trevor up. Maybe it wasn't the course itself that excited her so much. In fact, Sharon hated going. She applied a fresh coat of lippy right in front of Trevor before she left. She knew it was childish, but couldn't resist it. He sneered at her. Ha! He was the childish one, getting so jealous. If only he'd seen the people who went to the centre. *Tree-man*, for example – nicknamed Tree-man because his head had a flipping tree growing out of it. Trevor didn't have a bleeding clue. Tree-man was about the only male who ever went to the centre and he was disgusting – an old Jamaican Rasta with matted, dirty locks so badly glued together that they could only be removed with a saw. He always sat next to the radiator, drinking tea, shaking his head and laughing to himself. Conka gave him free pieces of cake. Still, no charity could stop him from putting enormous amounts of garlic salt in his tea and on his cakes, which helped maintain his high standard of genuine 'bad tramp pong'.

Today was no exception, Sharon could smell him from outside the building. She hesitated. It was going to be very hard facing this educational sewer.

Charlie and Conka, already there and obviously in their stupid-schoolgirl mode, spotted her and called her over. They had saved a place for her, even though there were about five seats per person – the room was hardly crowded. As soon as Maggie, the tutor, turned her back to roll the blackboard down, Charlie started poking Conka. Two minutes later, Conka pulled Charlie's chair away and she crashed to the floor.

Sharon wasn't in the mood for any of this. She wanted to get back early and surprise Trevor. She feigned a migraine and left.

Tasha felt the warm sun pour in through her window. The crystals spun a pink, orange and purple web of light around her bedroom. She whispered hello to her plants, which stood on a table next to her bed. She'd have to check her feng-shui book. They weren't thriving and she had a feeling they were in the wrong place. Daniella hadn't woken up yet, so Tasha had time to say her daily affirmations. She was ready for a good man to come into her life.

'I'm open to receive a warm and caring relationship,' she began.

Ten minutes later, affirmed and ready for the day, Tasha woke her little girl. But Daniella wasn't in such a tranquil mood. She was not ready to be dragged off to nursery.

'I don' go.'

'Yes, you are, darling. You'll see Zac and Felia and all your friends. You'd have such a boring time with Mummy.'

Daniella started to cry. *'No go!'* she screamed.

'Oh, come on, Daniella. Don't be like that.' Tasha pulled Daniella's pyjamas off over her head.

Daniella continued with her liquidiser sound effects. Tasha was beginning to lose her rag. Maybe she didn't feel like being a mother either, but so what? Daddy wasn't anywhere nearby now. Yeah, he was great at weekends and the occasional afternoon, but these morning brouhahas that Tasha had to deal with were hard work on her own. She felt that she'd learnt all she could from this particular lesson in life: the one where you struggle with everything on your lonesome.

Now, she was ready for a bit of permanent company. She felt that she had fully discovered who she was. Before she had had Daniella, she had jumped from one relationship straight into the next, but since parting company with Daniella's father, she'd been by herself and just picked and shagged, not getting close to anyone. She'd spent enough time on her own – she'd had a great time, but enough was enough.

Tasha had enjoyed her shags. She reckoned she could pretty much pick up who she wanted when she wanted. She picked purely on shagability. There was the chef at the local Italian – a stallion of a man. They had moonlight sonatas whenever Tasha clicked her fingers. And then there was Dean from the sports shop. Conveniently positioned opposite the Italian. Dean was really nice – massive dick – but he was married. Yeah, not good, too shallow. She was definitely through with that bonkorama. Tasha was ready to share a lot more now, more of her actual existence, her essential being – Daniella's wailing continued – real ready.

After shovelling in the last mouthful of soggy Weetabix and soya milk, Tasha put on Daniella's shoes and took her to the nursery down the road. She felt like getting together with Sharon today.

Tasha was surprised when Trevor answered the buzzer. She'd only met him once before so she was even more surprised when he asked her up, especially when she discovered that Sharon wasn't in.

'So how come you're not doing the computer course, Tasha?' he asked, once she'd sat down.

Tasha laughed nervously, not understanding what he meant. He was staring at her pretty intensely.

'You guys have got a really great vibe here, you know,' she began. 'Do you know about feng shui?'

'Feng shui? Yeah. Turns out I'm allergic to the stuff.'

'Ah.' Tasha didn't notice his sarcasm. 'Do you know when Sharon'll be back at all?'

Trevor smiled at her, a big broad smile. 'No.' He shrugged his shoulders.

Tasha stood up. She'd better get to the post office. 'I'll be off then, Trevor. Thanks.'

'Okay. Say hi to Sharon, when you see her.'

Sharon was just quick enough to get behind a tree. What the hell had Tasha been doing with Trevor? She looked up to her kitchen window. The light was on. She knew he was there. She glanced down the road, just in time to catch Tasha going into the post office. Hoping Trevor hadn't been watching from above, she followed her.

Tasha was at the front of a long queue. 'Sharon! Over here,' she said brightly.

'Hi,' Sharon said, causing a string of tuts as she passed the bellyaching queue.

'I *knew* I was going to see you today. I had a feeling.'

'Look, he's free.' Sharon motioned towards one of the windows.

Tasha cashed her child benefit and decided to splash out at the nice Portuguese café.

Sharon was pretty quiet as she ordered their coffee and they sat down.

'Are you doing a computer course, Sharon?'

Sharon didn't answer. She was waiting for Tasha to come straight out with it. If Tasha didn't say anything about meeting up with Trevor, then her guilt would be proved.

'Sharon? Are you okay? Was it really bad?' Tasha asked, looking concerned.

'Was what really bad, Tasha?' Sharon snapped.

'The computer course. Trevor said you'd gone to one.'

'Oh. You did speak to Trevor, then?' Sharon said, trying to be cool and casual.

'Yeah, yeah, I stopped by to see if you wanted to come for a coffee.'

'Oh, right,' Sharon tried to say lightly. 'Did you go up?'

'Yeah.' Tasha noticed Sharon's jaw tighten. 'Only briefly, so don't worry . . .'

'No, no. It's fine, Tash,' Sharon interrupted. 'It's just that . . . It's Trevor . . . just wasn't expecting . . .'

Tasha put her hand on Sharon's arm. 'I was in and out in five minutes, honestly, Sharon. Oh, I don't mean *in* and *out*, shit, I just popped in to –'

Sharon saw suddenly how off-centre she was getting. Tasha wouldn't lie.

The brawny waiter brought their coffees; Tasha eyed him up. 'I always look at their hands, I don't think you can tell by the feet – certainly not the nose,' she confided.

'Oh, I know. Tell me about it. I fancied this guy ages ago, and he had huge feet and a huge nose – and he was really tall. Well, you can imagine, I thought it was a dead cert.'

'Uh-oh.'

'It really was "uh-oh". It took about three weeks of heavy petting before I got to undo his trousers, so you can imagine how gutted I was. Tasha, it was *so* small.'

'What? In three weeks you hadn't even felt it?'

'God, no. It wasn't all in proportion with the rest of him. His little finger was bigger – no, *my* little finger was bigger.'

'What did you do?'

'Well, I laughed.'

'Oh, no!'

'I couldn't help it, Tash. There'd been such a big build-up. He talked as if it was massive.'

'So . . . you didn't do it?'

Sharon was shocked. 'No way! I legged it out of there and ignored his phone calls.'

'Man, he must have a real complex now.'

'So he bloody well should. You haven't got a ciggie, have you, Tash?'

'You know, I've had enough. Daniella was being a real pain in the arse this morning. Don't you have days when you don't want to be a mother any more? . . . I really want to meet someone who's gonna treat me like I deserve, not just fuck me.' Tasha sighed, getting out her cigarettes.

'Yeah, but we're sitting ducks, aren't we? Men love going out with single mothers.' Sharon lit her fag.

'Oh, I don't know. I haven't been out with anyone in ages, not properly. I don't know any men who love going out with mothers.'

'Think about it, Tasha. They know that we're always at home in the evenings. They know that we always have food in the house – or, at least, should have. They know we're stuck indoors and grateful of any adult contact we can get after eight at night. Basically, Tash, they know that they can come in after the pubs shut, get a bite to eat and a shag. And what more does a man want? Certainly not conversation.'

'But that's what I want. Someone who I can really communicate with – maybe another Aquarius?'

6

On her way back from the computer centre, Conka popped in to see her mother, to show off a bit. But when she arrived, she found Marge, champion hoarder of the century, having a turn-out.

Conka was stumped. 'What's happened to you?' she asked, kissing her mother.

'You read *The Celestine Prophecy*, you'll see,' Marge replied, with a glint in her eye.

Conka had too much energy and there was plenty to do, so she took off her ski-jacket, pushed up her sleeves and started opening doors. There were four tall cupboards in the living room – they stretched from the floor to the high ceiling – plus countless other bureaux and drawers downstairs. Every one was loaded with antique treasures ranging from Belgian lace 1940s dresses to avant-garde knick-knacks. All of it would be perfect for Conka's stall on Sunday and all of it would have to go. Her mother, a retired seamstress, had been living there for years, stuffing her cupboards fuller and fuller.

'This one's gorgeous, Marge. One for Christie's, I reckon.' Conka wiped a porcelain figurine clean. 'I'll sell this lot for you and then get you a ticket to Spain. What do you think, eh?'

Conka looked up when her mother didn't answer and saw Carlos, one of her least favourite bulky brothers.

'She doesn't want to go to Spain,' he said, in his dead-pan drone.

Conka watched his hugeness turn his fat arse round and lower it into the dent in the sofa that had housed his enormity for the last thirty years. Marge must have snuck off downstairs when her back was turned. Carlos wrestled with his daily tabloid and grunted a few times. The only reason their mother wouldn't be going to Spain was him. She still spoilt him, dinner on the table, ready for when he walked in, every day. He was thirty-flipping-three.

Conka looked at him with disgust. 'You know what? I feel sorry for your girlfriend, man. You're a fucking peasant. Anyway, *Carlost*, what makes you so sure that Marge don't want to go Spain? It'll do her the world of good.'

'Fuck-off, druggo.'

Conka laughed before carrying on with her noisy excavation. Everything was wrapped in tissues or plastic bags or both. Carlos grunted again, probably wanting an argument, but Conka couldn't be arsed. He was too fat to argue with. She couldn't understand how two people from the same parents could be so different. Sure she liked to smoke weed but that was it, and it was much less harmful than the amount of alcohol he consumed. 'Druggo'. What a prat. He didn't have a clue.

She pulled out a beautiful beaded black dress. It was stunning. Why didn't people wear clothes like this these days? She thought maybe Charlie would wear it, it would definitely fit her. Conka reckoned it was about time they got dolled up and had a night out.

I was just beginning to get depressed about my dire finances when Conka showed up.

'All right, babes? Come on, we're going out. Here.' She thrust a carrier-bag into my hands. 'Have you got any splidge?'

'Yeah, in the pot.' But she was already rolling. 'Wow, Conks, this is beautiful.'

For some reason it wasn't the type of present I would have expected from Conka. It wasn't that she wasn't stylish, I just hadn't expected her to come across something so amazing then to give it to me, out of the blue, for no apparent reason. It was the type of dress you saw in the movies and Conka thought I should have it. I was very, very touched. I tried it on.

'Wow! Fits you like a bleeding glove!' Conka said, as I paraded in.

'This is what I shall wear for my Grammy award, dear.'

'You look amazing. Wear it tonight,' she said, passing me the spliff.

'What's all this about going out? And where did you buy this gorgeous garment?' I blew out the heavy-duty smoke. She certainly rolled them strong.

Conka laughed. 'I didn't buy it! But I'll sell it to you. I've been clearing out Marge's cupboards. She's got tons of this shit.'

'How come?'

'How come, up yer bum! Never mind how come. D'you fancy a night out, or what? I've asked Marge to have Luke for you, 'cos I thought we should go to town, you know – go out somewhere we haven't been before. We should get all dressed up. Let's go out as other people.'

'What do you mean?'

But she was already opening my makeup box, looking for ideas. I put my depression *re* finances on hold. Time for my little plastic friend. After all, going out would help me let go.

I had a couple of top-quality Afro wigs, stolen from a video promo I did the makeup for years ago. As soon as Conka put one on, Brazilian Sex Goddesses became our theme. By the time we'd finished we looked more like overtanned transvestites, a bit embarrassing considering my line of work. Conka's accent alone cracked me up. Her father is Hungarian and her mother Spanish, which has absolutely nothing to do with the fact that she normally has a rather rasping Norf London accent. But it does mean that she can adopt a fascinating cross-cultural nuance. Her Brazilian-cum-Bindi made me wet my knickers, or it could have been the smoke we had before we left.

We were heading for a popular London nightclub when we realised we were out of fags. I pulled up outside the local all-night shop, and refused to go in alone. As soon as we walked into the cruel neon lights, highlighting the smeary brown makeup and wonky false eyelashes, we began to giggle. I felt like I was fourteen again. I wondered why it was that when you grew up you're not supposed to do stupid things. By the time we were almost controlled enough to ask for twenty Marlboro Lights, the worst thing to happen when stoned happened, the reason why you're not supposed to do stupid things when you're a grown-up. The head mistress from the kids' school walked in.

Childline sprang to mind. 'You've got to go and stay with Auntie Social for a while, pet,' was one of the many thoughts ambling around my soggy brain.

Hiding in a small all-night shop ain't no easy thing to do, especially if you're over five foot nine and in Afro wigs. Conka got hers caught in a pineapple while I, paralysed with hilarity, merely rocked in the middle of the crisp boxes, looking like a laughing policeman going to one of those funny balls. However, Lady Luck must have been on our side, as the headmistress turned either a blind or uninterested eye on our innocent fantasy world, or the social workers hadn't got to that tray yet. We hadn't even got to the club and I had already cried off my eyelashes.

Once there, we found being Brazilian trannies wasn't such an unusual thing in London. We had a great liberating dance, and took the piss out of just about everyone. Conka was a great mover. Sexy too. We danced well together. The second time we got asked to leave the last port of call – we were accused of being threatening – we grooved home, unimpressed by the general lack of humour in central London nightclubs.

I'd never been called threatening before. Conka had. Sharon had described Conka as threatening – or was it terrifying? Either way, I went to bed that night feeling I'd achieved something. Conka was cool.

The following Monday Sharon was looking puffy-eyed and in need of a treble espresso. It was one of those rare occasions that I had a makeup booking, so I had to rush off. Sharon persuaded Conka to come to Mario's with effusive promises of buying her a sweet cappuccino. I happily left them to it. Well, actually, happy, I wasn't: I was on my way to the morgue so it was far more 'begrudgingly'. Even so, I didn't want to be late. This was the first job I'd had in quite a while.

Although Conka was not one for shoulder tears, she was still a single mother and, in Sharon's eyes, that meant empathy. She dragged Conka inside the poky café.

'Look, Shassa, I'm not coming if you're gonna talk 'bout Sweaty Pig.'

'Don't call me Shassa. Christ, Sharon's bad enough.'

She slumped on to one of the narrow shiny wooden benches and allowed Conka to order the coffees.

'Ciao, mon amigos, duo cappucinque, prego.'

Conka's Italian was rusty in a Spanish sort of way, but Mario seemed to love her effort. She took off her ski jacket, nearly knocking over two neighbouring cups of tea in the process, then sat down opposite Sharon. 'Where was Charlie off to so smart this moron, then?' she asked.

'God. When are you going to get some elocution lessons, Conka?'

'When you get some electrocution ones, babes.'

Mario brought their cappuccinos and gave the table a skim with a dirty-looking rag.

'Cheers, mate.' Conka saw how down Sharon appeared. 'C'mon, cheer up, gal. Why don't you get a job today?'

'Oh, I don't know. I'm so tired. Trevor kept me awake.'

'Where was Charlie off to, anyways?' Conka interrupted, before Sharon could get started on that one.

Sharon stared glumly into her coffee.

'Well?'

'Oh, she's doing the makeup for some poor girl's funeral.'

'What? I never knew she did that. No wonder she was in bleeding black. We were out all night at the weekend and she never mentioned it. Why is she so secretive about it?' Sharon was silent. 'So she's going to make up some dead chick?' Conka grinned at her.

'Look, Conka, there's no need to get all morbid and funny about it. Okay?' Sharon took a moment to light her fag. 'Some people have an open casket, and this one . . . this one fell off a high-rise.' She pulled a drag from her cigarette, making the shock-horror suspended moment linger.

'What? You're telling me not to be "all morbid and funny" when our mate has gone off to make up some dead woman. Not only that, but a dead 'un who flung herself off some flipping high-rise –'

'Who told you she committed suicide?'

'Believe it or not, Sharon, no one's told *me* nothing, *nada*. Well, did she, or what?' Conka was leaning over the table, trying to see into Sharon's brain.

'Look, all Charlie told me was that she had to go and put the finishing touches on this woman at the funeral home. God, imagine how depressed she must have been.'

'She looked all right this morning.'

'Not Charlie! That poor woman. Apparently she was a mother. Charlie didn't have time to tell me all the details, but it sounds like this woman had everything – nice home, fantastic husband and a beautiful little baby girl –'

Sharon gazed out of the window, choked by her own words. She allowed a tear to tumble down her cheek. Her thoughts were racing between Trevor's latest performance – the shoe had caught her eyebrow and the fucker was now throbbing – but this seemed so petty in comparison to the woman in the open casket.

'I think it's selfish,' Conka said.

'What?'

'The woman, you know, leaving a baby an' all that. What's the kid gonna feel like when she grows up?'

Sharon stared at her.

'That's one big one to fucking get over, innit? I mean, imagine knowing your mother killed herself when you was a baby? It's fucking terrible.'

'Charlie didn't know if it was an accident or suicide –'

'Oh, come on, Sharon. You don't accidentally fall off a fucking high-rise. I just wonder what state her face is in – I mean Charlie's good, but she ain't no plastic surgeon. Anyways, I didn't even know she did dead people.'

'Well, she doesn't usually. It's just that she knows them at the funeral director's and they, you know, give her jobs once in a while. She'd like to be doing more magazines and that kind of stuff – you know, through an agency. Oh, sorry, I forgot – you've not known her quite as long as I have.'

'Well, I knew she did Brazilian sex goddesses and weddings. That made me laugh. But dead people too – mar-vel-liscious!'

'How can you find it funny, Conka? God, you are *so* sick sometimes.'

They stared at each other. Conka noticed a bruise on Sharon's eyebrow. She couldn't understand why she was still with Trevor. He wasn't even Liam's dad. Still, that was her picnic and the silly cow could eat it.

'Anyway, while Charlie was busy telling you the gruesome details of Mrs I-forgot-the-elastic Bungee, she told *me* that she's gonna get me some socks for my birthday. I think she thinks I should change my socks more often. Cheeky poncy makeup artist.'

'I wonder what Charlie will have to do, though. I mean, which way up would she have landed?' Sharon's imagination was beginning to gain the upper hand again. 'The base of the skull is the heaviest. God, it's awful. Her face must've collapsed – poor unhappy woman. How easy one can die, how fragile . . . God it must have – Oh dear, I know I wouldn't like to see that first thing in the morning . . .'

'Well, Sweaty Pig ain't far off it, darling.' Conka gulped back the rest of her still hot coffee, put a pound on the table and got up to go.

'You going already, Conka?'

'Yeah, you're boring the knickers off me, and I've got things to do.' Conka reached for her jacket while Sharon fumbled around for her purse.

'Conka! Conka, hang on a second.'

Conka put her hand in her pocket, knowing what was coming.

'You haven't got another pound, have you, Conks? I can't seem to find my purse.'

'You should sort that eye out, my friend, before it turns really ugly,' Conka said as she put another pound on the table.

As she left, she knew that Sharon was crying. Conka had been there years ago when Edwin – argh, this was boring old shit. She just couldn't be bothered to deal with all that crap, not right now.

7

Today was parents' day. Cue school-phobia *extraordinaire*. Add that to a generous helping of depression (provided by the morgue – my latest mission had been a real test of guts) and you're left with a fragile husk of a parent. I had to remind myself that, even as a husk, I was still Luke's only functional parent residing in the country. So, with summer holidays ahead, I had to brace myself and get it over with. And yes, I had to go it alone.

I had to control my fits of rage-cum-envy while waiting in the little anteroom where you're advised to peruse your child's stack of books before seeing the teacher. I sat there perusing with the backlog of other parents, all stuffed in this room, squashed and embarrassed, each sneaking curious looks at each other and every so often having polite, hushed little chit-chats. Everyone tries to compare their child's efforts with yours while accidentally holding their kid's books in a hidden, protective way, so you can't quite see them – well, at least, that's what I do. Anyway, the atmosphere was totally uncomfortable and I was feeling more and more nervous.

Then, of course, I started noticing the other fathers and immediately felt bad for Luke. One child had as many as four parents waiting to go in all together on his lone behalf: the real dad and his new wife, the real mum and her new man. I was feeling unbearably jealous of the other children for having such an abundance of loving parents. I envied the 'thirty-something' attitude these parents had. They'd all been very grown-up about their separations and new unions. They had discussed, debated and agreed upon what would be best for their child. How did they manage to agree? They all seemed to be so damned cool about the whole parent thing, so good at it.

Then there was me, sniffing and sweating in the corner, looking at my lovely little boy's sweet but pretty poor attempts and hiding my giggles at his mistakes. I was confident he'd get there in the end.

I could tell when he'd reached his boredom threshold and when he simply couldn't be bothered by the way his handwriting went. I could tell that school bored the pants off him. His work reminded me of mine when I was his age – it was crap. I was a day-dreamer and so was he. There was no pinning me down for a stint of concentration, and it was the same with Luke. Oh, well, I survived. So can he.

The fantastic four went in together, which cleared the anteroom considerably. I breathed a sigh of relief. If we'd sat out there much longer, I might have asked them to adopt Luke. He might have more of a chance with them. I spent a few bitter moments sending hate vibes to my ex. Thanks, mate, for being so *on it.*

As I leafed again through Luke's work, I looked for any signs in his drawings. You know, indications of serious mental and emotional problems, such as a painting of a black cloud entitled 'Mummy' or something. However, I got distracted by the teacher's scrawling comments. Some of them really upset me. *Luke was really too tired to concentrate today.* Too tired? That must be my failing – why can't it have said too bored? *Luke must be encouraged more at home to become more interested in this work!* Exclamation mark? Home? How dare she! *More encouraged?* I wasn't going to stand over him cheering the whole time, but I'm sure I did encourage him – a bit. What had Luke been saying to her? This was going to be hard.

The gang of parents finally emerged, all jolly smiles and chatting with Miss Clifton. I think I even heard one of them call her by her Christian name. This was too much.

I could feel my hands getting clammy, as my turn came closer. I was convinced that my breath stank as well. I don't know why. I hadn't recently been eating much garlic or anything else of a similar breath-defying nature. It was all nerves.

'Hello. Luke's mother?' The monster had spoken.

I jumped to attention, nodding. She walked into her room. I followed, carrying Luke's work under my arm.

'Sit down, please.'

She motioned to the scabby armchair, specially reserved for parent meetings and supply teachers in the staffroom. I sank down and fumbled with Luke's work before setting it on the low table in front of me. I felt her stare at me all the while – I almost heard the judgements she made about me – as she figured out why Luke was like he was.

'Right. Are we ready now?'

I squirmed beneath her patronising tone. 'Yes, thanks.'

Boy, oh *boy*, this was going to be hard. She took me through the general curriculum, showing me examples from his work, all the time pointing out Luke's failings and mistakes. I answered her by saying that I was exactly the same as him as a child, I wasn't worried and that I knew he'd get there in the end, I knew he was an intelligent boy.

Miss Clifton didn't seem quite so convinced of that. I asked if she knew that Luke was the fastest runner in the class. She didn't, which was lucky, because neither did I. But I wasn't happy with the sporting facilities at the school. I had walked passed the assembly hall when some ten-year-olds were having a gym lesson and they looked more like they were doing a stretch-and-tone class for the upper arms – the sort of exercise designed by Age Concern for the over-seventies. Miss C explained that the curriculum was set by the Government and there simply wasn't enough time to do any more sports. So what I wasn't happy with wasn't up for debate or discussion. Great. Glad I came.

Then we got to the part I really objected to. She got out some kind of official-looking form and wrote down my answers to her pointed questions.

'Does Luke watch television in the mornings before school?' she croaked.

36

She glared at me, in me, looking for any faltering, any tell-tale signs that I might be lying.

I squirmed. 'Well, sometimes he does. But I really don't like the television in the mornings. So . . . not much.'

Miss C went ahead and ticked the *yes* box. Why hadn't I just said no? I could tell I was going to look pretty bad by the end of this. But I couldn't paint the best mother in the world picture about myself either. Miss C had recently seen me in action on the school trip, so there'd be no pulling of any wool over her eyes.

'Do you read to him every day?'

Argh! Another loaded missile. Oh, hell, recently I hadn't read to him every *single* night, but I read to him a lot. Oh, shit, I suppose we had slacked off a bit over the past few days. Oh, Christ, this was going to be tricky.

'Well, over the past couple of weeks I haven't had the time *every* night, but I do read to him a lot. Just not recently. We get so waylaid doing other things, like skateboarding and blading, you know . . .'

I trickled to an embarrassed end. God, that sounded terrible – I was really fucking things up, big time. There she goes – Go on, Adolf, tick the *no* box. The social services will definitely be coming round now. Not only do I let my son spend all his waking moments transfixed by the television, but I never read to the poor little blighter either.

My answers to the questions sounded progressively worse. I couldn't understand how she felt she had the right to be so goddamned nosy. I mean, I know they had to be on the look-out for lunatic parents and all that, but she was making me feel like the worst kind of mother, and I'd volunteered to come to the school. I had believed they'd be informing *me* about my child's progress, telling *me* how well he could now write his name.

She asked me to sign the summary she'd made of our meeting. I read it through. It sounded terrible but I signed it anyway. I couldn't start arguing with her, I just needed to get the fuck out of there and fast. With every relieved step I took, I chose to write off her negativity as her own problem and nothing to do with Luke's lack of concentration, or bad habit of answering the register in annoying voices. She'd been pretty critical and pretty scary, but it

37

was over now and I couldn't help it if the poor woman had never had a decent shag in her whole life.

As I was leaving Conka was coming in. She wasn't nervous at all. She had no fear, that girl. I felt ashamed. If Conka could pull it off then so could I. Luke was a great kid and I'd let him down. Conka's daughter, Helena, was quite a hard worker, so her report would at least be reasonable. Conka might get some flak about Helena listening – she wasn't so good at that – but Conka would handle it alone, no problem. Edwin was going in later. Even though he'd been behaving himself recently, Conka still couldn't sit in the same room as him for more than about twenty seconds and was on her way to her half of the appointment now.

I watched her disappear into the school. She looked really smart in her office outfit. She had a confident air that suited her strong body and energetic stride. She had no problems with Miss Clifton. They'd probably share a little joke.

Once Conka was out of sight, I wandered down the road to the bookshop, where I could hang around for free until it was time to go back to the school and collect Luke. It pissed me off that I didn't even have enough money to get a stinking coffee from Mario's.

I sat in the play section, leafing through a David Mamet – he always cheered me up – half reading and half feeling sorry for myself. These teacher-parent meeting things really got to me. I'd have to overcome it though – preferably before Luke reached school-leaving age.

On my way out, I bought three books with my credit card, two for me and one for Luke. The term was ending in two days' time and we'd have a literary summer holiday. Ha! That would show 'em, I thought, as I marched proudly back to the school. Fuck poverty.

8

Three weeks into the summer holidays and the days were dragging like sacks of sand shackled to my ankles. Suddenly I loved the school. I needed it. Why did it ever have to shut? Luke was driving me crazy. I felt like torching his fucking toys which had totally taken over. I would have been happier in a Japanese endurance test. I was plonk-pissed and pissed off. I decided to call Conka in the morning. She might have a couple of bright, sexy ideas.

She didn't let me down. She instructed me to pack my bikini and come over straight away. Having spent a few minutes making some calls, we found a camp-site with a caravan available to rent. We piled in the car and felt very *Thelma and Louise* as we drove down the A21 to somewhere near Hastings. We told the kids we were going to China – well, they asked where we were going, we asked where they wanted to go and they said China, so China it was. What's the difference when you're five? People who say they remember a foreign country they visited when they were five are liars, as far as I'm concerned.

It was the first time that we'd be spending more than a few hours together. Although Conka was ahead of me on the controlling of the old emotions front, we were at the same stage materially. I'd finally got a permanent roof over my head; Conka had replaced a lot of her musical equipment; we were rediscovering what it was we wanted out of life and that anything was possible. We hated men but were still optimistic that there was a chance there'd be someone out there who was all right. We knew we could laugh. We wanted to. We were out to make up for lost time, and were going to enjoy ourselves wherever we went. We couldn't possibly be anything other than glorious because we were free. We were *free* and it felt fantastic.

We arrived around ten thirty at night and everything was pitch black. As city-dwellers, our eyes were not used to seeing in such darkness. This made it spooky and exciting even though, in the cold light of day, nearly all caravan sites are totally boring. After driving around with the headlights on full beam, trying to find number eleven, we eventually found the place we were going to be calling home for the next few days. We found the key in the prearranged hiding spot under the doormat and let ourselves in.

The kids immediately went crazy, chasing around the place. We unpacked our supplies, put the kettle on and had a look about. There was a tiny kitchen, a living area with a television and a couple of built in sofa-cum-cupboard-cum-bed things, a miniature bathroom, a small room with bunk beds and a larger room with one smallish double bed. I caught Conka's eye when looking at the double room. I was sure she was up to something. She seemed as if she might be giving me the come-on. I know we got on great, but this was something else. The kids declared their territory and, needless to say, chose the bunk beds.

'We can share the double, if you want,' Conka suggested.

I looked at the sofa. 'We can toss for it – with a coin, I mean,' I stuttered, nodding at the sofa.

'I don't mind sharing, but if you do, I'll take the double and you can have the sofa.'

She wants me, I thought. How funny – she's scared me on to the frigging sofa. Not that I was completely averse to sexual relations with another woman, I just wasn't *that* into it either. Although, of course, it was just as likely to have been a clever ploy by the Artful Dodger to get the nice bed to herself, and I was being paranoid.

Eventually the kids settled in their den, and Conka and I were able to spoil ourselves with a facial steam, a chat, a squeeze and a mask. It was quite chilly sitting in the caravan, especially as we'd stripped down to our vests and knickers – Conka had suggested 'getting comfortable', so I followed suit. Getting undressed seemed the natural thing to do. I was definitely quite cold, though: the windows were steaming up from the hot water. Our nipples were poking our vests with unabashed temerity, especially Conka's. It was definitely cold. Hot and cold.

'You know what?' Conka began, speaking carefully, so as not to crack her mask. 'I'd love to come with you to the morgue, one day.'

'Oh, no, it's horrible. Well, it's a job, but – Nah.' I trailed off.

'It's good money, though, innit?'

I shrugged.

'I reckon Sharon should get a job.' Conka must have realised I wasn't up for morgue chat. 'It'd do her the world of good to get off her lazy arse and cut down the hours in the day available for analysing her love life.'

'She did get a job,' I said, slightly too defensively. 'Well she did, once – for a bit. Babe Sharoness got all hoity-toity, Wonderbra in place, and did a barmaid stint at the Albert.'

'Oo-er, missus, I didn't know that. I bet the blokes loved her down there.'

'Oh, yeah. She pulled in bucketloads of male punters.'

'Bucketloads?' Conka grinned, causing a couple of forked cracks to appear.

'Bucketloads.' I could feel my mask crack now. 'But it was the usual story. The pub rings up at the last minute asking Sharon to work that night. Of course she can't – Trevor would never babysit – so her lack of impromptu babysitters immediately loses her the job.'

'Fucking sucks, don' it?'

'Infuriates the poo out of me.' A lump of mud fell off my chin. 'She was almost getting a life of her own, albeit a crap one.' Crumbs were dropping with every word now. 'And, through pigging lack of organisation and understanding, she was given the push. Pissed her off, pissed me off too. Means she can complain again.'

'Yeah it didn't take long for her to go back to full time moaning.'

'And part time job surfing.'

'Yeah, right.' Conka said sarcastically, but it seemed to me she was already thinking of something else.

Suddenly there was an almighty clap of thunder. The kids screamed, ran out of their room, and screamed even louder when they saw us. The noise from the rain was tremendous. It was belting down so hard on the thin roof, we had to shout to be heard above it.

'IT'S OKAY, HELENA. I'M YOUR MOTHER! SHUT UP!' Conka shouted.

Once the kids realised who we were they yelled harder. Conka and I joined in, it became very noisy and the green mud from our face masks flew everywhere. The caravan site was lit up eerily for seconds from the bright flashes of sheet lightning. The kids loved it. We grabbed our jumpers and huddled together, feeling cosy inside while Mr Weather had a right carry-on out in the dark night of China.

By the time the storm died down, we were all tired. I was on the sofa and it was freezing. Conka had the warm, fluffy double bed – and apparently slept like a baby. I hardly slept at all.

The next morning, bright sunshine poured in and we woke up early. I decided against asking Conka who she'd had dirty dreams with, secretly wondering if it'd been me.

She soon put together an impressive fry-up, having persuaded the kids to go and make friends with the neighbouring caravans, especially the two nearest, who looked like they could be going home today and shouldn't be chucking out all that food.

Eggs, bacon, sausages and beans later, we were ready to explore the site. It didn't take long and we soon realised that you were supposed to go and do things away from base camp and that this required looking at a map.

Back to number eleven, compasses out. Dungeness power station was looking painfully close. Then it started raining, or rather pouring, again. The bikini would not be going on today.

'Bollocks to the map. Let's just get in the car and drive towards the blue sky,' Conka suggested.

'Good thinking, Batman. Okay, kids. *Let's go!*' I shouted. All I got was groans in response.

The kids were miserable. The drive, the late night and the early morning were now catching up on them, and bitching was their speciality. We shoved them into the car, ignoring their moans and answering with the radio on full volume. Gradually they quietened down as we sang raucously along to the music.

'You've got a good voice, mate,' Conka said, after a particularly good effort at Bob Marley's 'I Shot the Sheriff'.

Nevertheless I was shocked. I can't sing! I had always been told that I was the stupid but pretty one, my brother had the brains, and my sister the voice. I had never even considered singing to be part of my earthly life. The one and only time I'd sung a lullaby to Luke, his dad had rugby-tackled me to the floor, shouting at me to stop torturing our baby. But Luke was five now, so to drown their moans singing became an option. Even so, I was touched by Conka's complimentary remarks. I hoped she wasn't joking.

'Trade you singing lessons for driving lessons?'

Now, Conka *knew* how to sing. My driving was fairly formula too, but this sounded like fun. I found the idea of me singing funny, but funny is good in my book and if Conka thought I could do it then why not? I also liked the idea of giving Conka something really useful. I knew I could teach her how to drive. My worry was the car: would it take to Conka's brute force? I doubted it somehow.

'Are you serious?' I said.

'Yeah. I'd bloody love it if I could get some practice with you.'

'I mean, about my singing.'

'What? Will you teach me to drive if I teach you to sing?' I noticed that she was avoiding answering my question *re* the quality of my voice.

'Do you think you could? I'd love to be a singer.'

'Everybody is a singer, my friend. Everybody has a voice,' she said slowly. Conka was very wise.

We arrived at a car-boot sale, of all stupid things. But that seemed to be the only place with blue sky above it, and, hey, they weren't London prices. I normally hate car-boot sales. I hate junk and that's precisely what I thought they sold. Some people have the knack of delving around in these shit-heaps and finding the most amazing things. I'm just not like that. I haven't got the eye. Still, I knew that Conka was a bit of a fanatic and I reminded myself that it wasn't just me on holiday. We'd have to get back to the big singing question later.

Five minutes later I'd finished and was ready to go, but Conka was rapidly becoming more laden with God knows what. It looked like we were going to be here a while. I decided I should try and get over my phobia about buying other people's unwanted crap and make the blinking effort to find something good to take home.

Right at the back there was an old man, all on his tod, so I headed over, humming softly to myself. He had some very bizarre-looking gear: an old pencil sharpener disguised as an elephant, an old elephant disguised as a pencil sharpener and hundreds of packets of that hard toilet paper. No wonder the locals were ignoring him.

I walked further down the field, gazing casually at the wares neatly laid out on one of those gingham tablecloths. Then I saw it. I had found my bargain! I had actually found something that I wanted and I wasn't even trying. There were a few pieces of that terribly English blue and white stripy crockery. Two or three plates, three cups and two saucers. I knew that in Habitat these would have cost a small fortune. I asked the price and nearly laughed out loud when she told me. Fifty pence for the lot! I wanted to hug her. I couldn't understand what she was doing there selling the occasional object for fifty pence, let alone a bulk buy. How could she possibly cover her costs? I wanted to stay and talk her through a bit of a financial plan, but it looked like Conka had finally bought enough.

Five miles down the road, we could see the sea beyond some fields so we parked and took a shortcut on foot. I was brought up in the country and was therefore used to cows, cow-pats and flies. The others, including my city-boy son, were somewhat flustered by the frisky young cattle, curious about our presence. As the others fled, a small herd gathered around me. Turning to face them, I realised they weren't lady cows and, as with all males, they didn't seem to want me in their field. 'Shoo' wasn't a very effective deterrent – the bullocks merely snorted at me. Legging it was my only option.

Out of breath and enthusiasm for country strolls, we decided on some light refreshments at a nearby village. The traditional tea-room was traditionally full of fat Americans. We squeezed in and ordered. By the time we'd finished it was raining again. Pouring. The car was about two miles away, and that was taking the shortcut across the danger field. The Americans had already left in their luxury coach and it wasn't the kind of place where you'd find a taxi.

As we stood in the doorway wondering what to do, a local ran past.

'Enjoying the weather, eh?'

Conka and I were contemplating murdering him for having such a naff sense of humour when we saw him getting into his car. 'Give us a lift!' we shouted in unison.

We pushed the children on to the pavement, so he could appreciate how sad and wet we were.

'Okey-dokey. Hop in!'

We rushed over and clambered in.

'Not afraid of dogs, are we?'

Well, we're not normally, but we don't normally get in their owners' cars. This dog wasn't happy and the short journey seemed to take for ever.

'As a Christian, I couldn't exactly leave you young ladies out in all this weather, eh?'

As a Christian, how could he have the devil himself, cunningly disguised as a foaming black evangelical Labrador, cushing it in the front seat? I asked myself.

'You lovely ladies on your holidays, then?'

Was he ever going to shut up? We had told him where we needed to get to, the rest was fucking obvious. I knew Conka was dying to throw a sarcasm sandwich at him, so I nudged her.

'Do you live here?' I asked, before Conka could get us chucked out. But, of course, I may as well have said, 'You've got a mile and a half left in which to tell us your entire boring life story, starting now!'

He certainly got a lot in. His wife died five years ago and he'd lived around there ever since – immediately I started thinking that he was a murderer. He was in the forces – those thoughts ain't going away; then, he spent twenty-seven years in the police force. That dog could probably smell the ganja that always lingers, and was probably telling his master right now in coded growl language that we were massive drug-dealers, wanted all over the country for loads of offences. At that point, I had to remind myself that chronic paranoia was a side-effect of smoking pot first thing in the morning. I glanced over at Conka. She looked totally mad. I wouldn't have given us lot a lift even if I *was* a murderer.

Thankfully the car park was in sight. He wasn't going to kidnap us and torture us with talk for hours on end; or murder us and destroy our bodies along with his wife's; or even turn us in at the nick, having previously planted some smack on us. Our journey was over.

We drove back to base via a supermarket and cooked some dinner. After whiling away a bottle of cheap red wine, we were all tired and cosy in the caravan. We sat around playing cards with the children until they got tired of losing all the time. We were feeling fairly wiped out and gradually everyone wandered off to bed.

Conka didn't make any suggestions that night about singing, driving, double beds or lesbian activities. Maybe I had read more into her lingering looks than was warranted. She probably hadn't even been staring at me. She was just stoned and her eyes had glazed over.

I was freezing all night again, and had a weird dream about the cows and Conka. Conka was in with the cows and they were all laughing at me. It was really horrible. I was woken by it and couldn't get back to sleep. This holiday was turning out to be pretty gruelling.

The next day was going-home day. It was sunny, but the caravan site had turned into a quagmire. We sent the kids outside to go and jump in some puddles while Conka and I tidied up and packed the car. We paid the man, found the sodden children, said goodbye to our little box and set off.

It was a nice drive back. We had a sing-song and Conka reiterated how pleasant-sounding she thought my voice was. She hadn't been joking before – amazing! She said I had a good tone; no one had ever mentioned tone before, and I reckoned she might just know what she was talking about. She even suggested we formed a band. We could record on her four-track and it would make us a lot of money. Conka had vision. Perhaps we could turn our lives right round. I felt great and got on everyone's nerves singing 'Blue Sky'. It was a very pleasant drive indeed.

By Tooting I shut up, mainly because I realised that I'd gone drastically wrong and probably added another hour to the journey. By the time we crossed the river, Helena and Luke were fast asleep with contented muddy faces, looking every inch like two little adventurers who'd travelled to China and back, twitching every time they jumped a puddle, still living the holiday. It filled me up seeing them like that.

Conka was deep in thought and quiet, too, for once. We were soon in home territory, West London, which for the first time in years felt warm and good to come back to. I wasn't nervous about what kind of mood or sulk would be waiting for me. I had no one to justify myself to and I loved it.

I was just getting a little romantic about this when we turned into Conka's mum's road, and saw Edwin's van double-parked right outside. With Edwin sitting in it.

Conka immediately reverted to being noisy. 'What the fuck is that rat doing dirtying my mum's front yard?'

I've never seen anyone flare up quite as quickly as Conka did then. She changed in an instant from totally relaxed to raging mad. Her pupils were doing weird things. Even her hair looked angry. I now saw where the writer for *The Incredible Hulk* got his ideas from – Conka's muscles were twitching through her T-shirt.

I pulled up fifty yards from the house so that we could decide what to do. Conka didn't wait for the car to come to a standstill before she leapt out. People do dangerous things when they're angry.

I looked in my rear-view mirror and watched her charge up the road towards Edwin's parked van, rolling up her sleeves as she went. I thought I'd stay right where I was, you know, for the children's sake.

I watched Conka with something close to adoration – her industrial strength, her lack of fear, as she came face to face with her ex. An avalanche of verbal poison came pouring from her suddenly enormous mouth. He started winding up his window, but not quickly enough.

Then she did it. The thump. She saw red and threw a splendid right hook clean through the gap right into his cheesy face. Triumphantly, she turned her back on him and started marching back towards us. The ever-so-funny Edwin yanked the van into reverse and tried to run her over. But Conka was quick enough to see it coming, turned round and kicked the van so hard that she left her footprint in it.

Edwin drove off and a shaking Conka got back into the car.

47

9

Sharon couldn't understand it. She'd left it there last Friday, and now it had gone. The street looked the same, although it all seemed cleaner than she'd remembered but then everything had seemed terrible, dirty and disgusting a week ago. Ever since their summer holiday in Wales things had been wrong, *really* wrong, and she had not been able to shift that sickness. Her stomach was permanently clenched.

She'd thought that she'd be able to eat at her mum's when she dropped Liam there, but she'd lost even more weight. Trevor, no doubt, had managed to eat like a pig in her absence. He'd revolted her so much the weekend before that she had finally given him an ultimatum: money by the next Wednesday for the phone – well, for fucking everything, like the sack of potatoes and the crate of milk he must have consumed at her cost over the past month – or he could go, and go for good.

Anyway, he didn't come back with any money. In fact, he didn't come back at all. He said he was popping to the shop. Sharon *knew* he was lying. She was ready for it. They'd played this game before. He never gave her any money, he'd be really nasty, then disappear for a couple of days. Sharon's green monster would rear its spectacular horns and take the driving seat. Loneliness would take hold, she'd forget about the bad times, he'd return, and she'd be grateful – apologetic even.

But she wasn't going to let it happen this time, not after Wales. She had followed him to the shop. He didn't look back once, so she hardly had to hide. But that made her want him to see her. Why the fuck didn't he turn round? Before she knew it she was virtually treading on his heels. She was just about to say something when he went down some steps into a basement. A young girl – she couldn't have been more than seventeen – opened the door and he walked into her flat like he'd lived there all his life. Well, Sharon couldn't just stand out there not knowing – she had to knock. She knew she shouldn't, but she had to. She watched her hand bang on the door, she saw her knuckles split and bleed, but she couldn't stop it – banging and banging. They had to answer. They didn't want to. He knew who it was, all right, but eventually he came to the door. He said he didn't know her 'personally'. He said *that*? How could he? How did he keep his face so cold?

Sharon could hear his words: 'Don't worry, Tiffany. She's the local loony. I'll get rid of her.' Get rid of her? Local loony? Tiffany? What kind of jerk-off name was that? And then the foul profanities he hissed in her ear as he marched her up the steps, pushing his legs against her from behind, with his big hands half lifting her by her elbows, occasionally brushing against her tits. Finally he gave her arse a boot in a fucking vicious way.

But something about it had turned her on. That's what really freaked her out. Would she want him to rape her next? Fuck! She'd always enjoyed rough sex, but the last few times he'd hurt her and she was getting pissed off with her underwear getting ripped the whole time. It'd be all right if he went out and bought her some new stuff, or even just gave her some fucking money. Back to that one. Money. Trevor expected everything for free.

Sharon paced up and down where she thought her house used to be, vaguely looking for it but too lost in thoughts of her own madness to look at the house numbers. Losing your house? How could you lose your house? It was ridiculous. Back to madness, back to grotty Shepherd's Bush, back to hell. Back home. *Home?* Fuck. Would he be there? Where was the fucking house, anyway? It was here before. Surely Trevor couldn't be right after all. He'd always said she was mad. He couldn't be right – could he? At least Sharon knew which way she swung.

'Where the FUCK is it?' she shouted. 'Where is MY HOUSE?'

An old couple crossed the road away from her. Sharon flapped her hands around and started laughing. 'This is FUCKING RIDICULOUS!'

She took a closer look at a door. 'Well, that's number twenty . . .' She walked and counted. It wasn't far. She'd been practically there for ages.

I'd never witnessed a woman punching a man before. Unfortunately I'd just missed Sharon headbutting Trevor. But a *punch* was something else. I'd loved to have punched my ex. I had planned to, the last time I thought I'd see him, but typically he didn't show up. However, I'd not thoroughly considered the inevitable adrenaline explosion that was now charging Conka to maximum capacity.

Her body was shaking and shuddering. Her face was contorted. She was still spitting profanities under her breath. I tried to calm her down, worried that she might self-combust. The kids were awake and I didn't think Helena should see her mother like this. But with Luke prodding her persistently, Helena was watching her mum, probably building up quite a case for therapy when she reached twenty-five.

We turned into the street where I park my car. Unfortunately it's also where Edwin often parks. The thought of running into him five minutes after Conka had punched him made me a bit panicky and nervous. Still, I tried to hide my fears.

'Right, kids! When I park, I want you both to get out of the car as quickly as you can. Okay?'

They ignored me. I parked and they got out slowly while I stood screaming at them to hurry, thinking that in any second Edwin was going to come screeching around the corner. Finally disembarked, we ran, dragging the kids like rag dolls, to the safety of my front door. I fumbled with the keys. The doors had never been harder to open. I have a security wrought-iron gate and another front door with three locks, so there were keys all over the place. Once inside, I locked the cage behind us. We were safe, for now.

I sent the children out to play in the garden, which seemed to have shrunk while we'd been away, and made some drinks. Conka, still angry, lit a cigarette and smoked the whole thing in one puff.

Conka was brought up in this area, had lived here all her life and it was the same story for Edwin, so they had the difficulty of seeing each other every so often, hearing each other's business and tittle-tattle gossip through mutual enemies. In small commun-ities, it seems that taking sides is encouraged and remaining above this is hard. Conka tried, but since Helena had started school, third parties were becoming involved. I was one of them.

'I have tried bloody everything with him, Charlie, but he's a psychopath. He can't seem to stick to any kind of agreement we make,' Conka blurted out. 'He shouldn't have been anywhere near my mum's street, let alone her house. Bastard!'

'That sucks. You should really get a solicitor and let them sort it out, you know.'

'I've got one and she's great, but what can they flipping well do? I'm fed up with the verbal shit I get from him and, if that's not enough, Helena comes back from his gaff with nits every time.'

'That's so disgusting. That's grounds to stop access altogether.'

'She has to sleep in a bed with all her half-sisters and -brothers and probably the pet fucking hamster. There must be nits jumping about all over the place. He should open the Royal Nit Ballet – every day a new crop of lively bouncy nits is born.'

It was nice to see Conka regain her dynamite sense of humour. We were just beginning to relax when the doorbell rang. We knew it was Edwin. He'd seen Conka get in my car and, although not a brain surgeon, he did have the ability to deduce that we'd come here and he wasn't one to let sleeping dogs lie. Another ring.

'Shit! Are you here?'

'Absolutely not,' Conka replied, with a smile that said, 'Over to you, girlfriend.'

I took a deep breath, which was interrupted by the doorbell yet again. This was intense. Another breath and I was opening the first door. I explained rapidly that I couldn't find the keys to open the cage. I don't think he believed me. His face had the contorted anger I'd seen written on Conka's, except he had a black eye to add to the drama of it all. I couldn't stop staring at it – the eye. I acted as natural as possible, but Edwin wasn't about to start discussing the weather on my doorstep. I was smiling inanely at him when he asked if Conka was in. I told him that, unfortunately, he'd just missed her but I'd pass on a message – if he wanted. He didn't. He stomped away while I waved goodbye, still being the friendly neighbour. I should be an actress, I thought.

Back inside, Conka had heard the whole thing. 'Did he have Fat Slag with him?' she asked, meaning Edwin's third woman.

'No, just a load of nits in tutus jumping all over the place.'

Conka humphed, vaguely aware of my attempt at humour. 'Wrap one up, will you?'

Well, then I knew I had something that would bring a smile to her face. I rolled an extra-strength green one, put the guitar in Conka's hands and assured her that one day things would be calmer and easier.

'That was a fantastic punch, you know,' I stated. 'Impressed the crap out of me.'

'Fucking hurt my knuckles. I'm not going to be able to play that for a few days.' She gave the guitar back to me.

'Oh, I'm sorry.' I felt like an idiot.

'This latest act of revolting testosterone maleness has succeeded in putting me right off men,' she said, looking at me very seriously. 'Right off.'

'Um,' I said.

By the time Sharon had found her house and put the key in the door, she had almost forgotten her fears about whether Trevor was going to be there or not. She was simply relieved that she'd found her home and that she wasn't going mad after all. As she climbed the last flight of stairs, laughing to herself, she looked up and saw him standing in the open doorway. She was shocked, but still smiling. She prayed he'd smile back: she just couldn't deal with any heavy shit, and wanted her bath. She had always loved hot, candle-lit baths. Thankfully, he smiled back, Sharon's smile broadened in return.

'You're mad, you are,' Trevor said, laughing too.

Sharon's heart sank. She brushed past him and walked into the flat. He followed close behind, grabbing her arse – God, he knew how to turn her on. She stopped walking and tried to remember her anger and the money. But he had this power, this irritating fucking control. She would try to stop him, but instead would get turned on by his persistence.

He saw the glint in her eye and pulled her closer. As he slid his hand down her bum – down, through, and between her legs – he kissed her neck. 'You know I was watching you from up here. Why didn't you just come straight in?'

'Oh, go away –'

He gripped her arm with one large hand while his other moved up her belly, underneath her T-shirt – she was hot and sweaty – over her bra, then inside it. He lifted her breast out and pinched her nipple. Their breath quickened. He let go of her arm, took her hand and dropped it down with his. She felt him stroke and grope his way up her thigh, lifting her loose summer skirt with every movement, until his fingers finally slithered through the side of her knickers, taking her fingers with his, making hers play with his as he explored her. She was already wet.

He bit her shoulder gently, while pushing his finger inside her. He cupped her breast, then squeezed. 'I really love you, Sharon. God I missed you –'

Trevor's hands and kisses coupled with his few insincere words were enough to obliterate his obscene behaviour on their Welsh trip, and Sharon turned to face him. They kissed passionately, like their first kiss. Her hand felt his belt buckle and pulled it free. Her thumbnail scratched him as she undid his jeans button. She could feel him pushing to come out. He was hard, very hard, big and throbbing.

'You fucking pig. You missed me, didn't you?' Sharon said, as she pulled him free of his boxers.

His dick was beautiful, so big, so hard, so perfect. She had missed him too, she thought, as she fell to her knees. She couldn't wait to get him in her mouth. As she licked and played he undressed her. She enjoyed his dick. It was the only thing about him that was perfect – huge, but she liked the fact that it was so big he sometimes had to force it in. Thoughts of money, Wales, Tiffany, dissipated with every thrust. Sex was the *only* thing he did well.

An hour later, Sharon looked up to see if Trevor was awake. She noticed saliva dribble down his jaw – he was definitely asleep. She fumbled around the table looking for a cigarette. Fuck it, she'd have to get up. There was a packet in the kitchen. She had just enough time for a quick coffee and a fag before she had to pick up Liam. The bath would have to wait.

She sat on the stool and looked out of the window. It must have been from here that Trevor had watched her pace up and down. She laughed at the thought. Everything seemed all right again – brighter, nicer. She decided to ring Tasha. She fancied hanging out in Holland Park with the kids, and didn't want Liam waking Trevor. She wanted to keep him in a good mood.

As we smoked the joint, Conka calmed down and began to strum the guitar tentatively, even though her hand still hurt. In too much pain to be raucous and rocky, she became quite graceful and soft.

She caught me staring admiringly at her and started to hum along to her romantic riff. I wondered if she was serenading me. She seemed to lose herself for moments with her eyes closed and her body swaying. Then she'd sway around to me, opening her eyes like a fluttering *señorita*, luring me into her rhythm. She nodded to me to join her on the sofa, still humming and strumming. I slowly stood, silently clicking my fingers and swinging my hips, as I danced nearer in musical appreciation. Suddenly nervous, I closed my eyes. Conka was making like the enchantress with me the hypnotised snake rising to the occasion.

It was all about to get too much when the doorbell rang. We froze: please don't let it be him again, I thought. It rang a second time. I decided to brave it. Well, it was either that or get down on one knee and prostrate myself, so the door seemed the safer option.

I was greeted through the cage with a marijuana plant. Another of my neighbours stood behind it.

'It's okay, Conka!' I shouted as I opened the door. 'It's only George.'

George is a very laid-back bloke in his forties. He and I feed each other every so often, tell each other our worries and generally have a mutual interest in class B drugs.

'Hello, gorgeous,' he said, offering me his lips and screwing up his eyes in his usual cheeky way. He was the type of bloke you wanted to slap and hug all at the same time.

'Come in, come in, and bring your friend with you.'

George followed me, eyeing up my bum. He always cheers up the women, not that his eyeing up my bum cheered me all that much. He was just a little bit of light relief after Edwin.

George wanted to plant his medium-sized marijuana plant in my garden, which seldom got any sunlight. I didn't mind. It wasn't much of a risk. It was a male plant and my defence was going to be exactly that: it's male, and what could I possibly get out of him, females being the stronger and more potent? George explained that his mum was coming to stay with him for a week and he knew that she was even more likely to kill it off than me. I let George in and through to the garden, and while he dug, he told us that he'd just seen Sharon behaving like a lunatic.

He'd been driving along the road when he noticed a mad woman pacing up and down waving her hands all over the place, shouting at innocent bystanders. As he got closer, he realised it was Sharon. This sounded bad. Even worse, George hadn't stopped to find out what the hell was going on. Fucking typical.

I was getting quite concerned about Sharon: she was going around in circles, and now verging on the downward spiral. Liam didn't make it any easier, but I reckoned that git Trevor was her major problem.

It seemed obvious to me: Trevor was in her life, therefore nothing was going to be right. No one can make anyone happy, as far as I'm concerned. You have to find your own happiness, rely on yourself. That way you only have yourself to blame if things go wrong.

Perhaps she enjoyed the on-going saga of Trevor abusing her. Maybe she was frightened of what kind of life she'd be left with if she got him out of her life for good. Maybe it was purely a sexual thing, or she was scared of letting a bad thing go. And now this. Still it had taken Conka's mind off the big fight and that cheered me up. I reminded her that, as the long, hot days were nearly over and the kids would shortly be back at school, everyone's tempers would soon be that helpful bit cooler. Conka, calm enough to go back to her mum's, then left with Helena and George.

I, however, was not calm. George had put a bastardly annoying bee in my bonnet, and I wanted to find out exactly what had been happening. I tried phoning Sharon, but the stupid machine picked up and I decided against leaving a message – just in case she had told Trevor she was out with me.

I rang Tasha. She wasn't in either. There was therefore a high probability that the two sexy mothers would be in the park where the kids could roam around safely, leaving them free to talk. So, to the park Luke and I were headed.

10

Holland Park was a fresh little lung in smelly, asthmatic London and it was always a pleasant place for Luke and me. It was early September: Luke would return to school in two days' time, so long warm evenings lolling around licking orange lollipops would have to end. It was a bit of green relief to go to a park so extremely well kept, with its ever-changing array of colourful flowers and stretches of freshly cut lawns. Luke loved it there.

The children were adequately catered for too, with an adventure playground and sandpit for the little ones. There were a couple of ponds with enormous goldfish in them. There was even a toilet for the dogs. There were hundreds of different trees, filling the air with that very green, ferny kind of smell. I loved that. But there were way too many signs which really annoyed me after a while: *no* skating, *no* roller blading, dogs *must be* kept on the lead, *no* entry, *no* unauthorised vehicles, *no* walking on the grass, *no* talking, *no* cycling, *no* farting . . . And I'd *always* see at least one policeman wandering around in an offensive, unthreatening, chatty, bobby-on-the-beat bleeding way.

But this hadn't stopped Luke and me from spending days, weeks, probably months in this park, right from when he was a baby. I used to take him there by myself, angry that his father wouldn't play happy families with me. I used to look at all the dads that came out, seemingly happily, with their kids and wives every Saturday and Sunday with envy, anger and deep sadness. I was always alone with my beautiful little boy, wondering why I had chosen someone so fucking unsociable and awkward.

Then we split up and Luke and I continued to come to the park. Only now I was no longer pining for the 'happy family', no longer angry when I saw all the dads. I looked at them differently then. I could see behind their external smiles, beyond the token sandcastles and into their lives that, to my mind, had to be fucked up because these dads were men. They were bound to be having affairs or be crap in bed or really boring and set in their ways. If they weren't grumpily reading the Sundays, they were all bloody new-age smiles and giggles and their kids were probably faking enjoying themselves with Daddykins just to avoid full-blown molestation later on. Okay, I was still a tad bitter. But, hey, at least by then these dad-creatures had ceased inspiring anger and sadness in me – almost.

We got to the park and headed for the café. Both Sharon and Tasha were coffee fiends, and I thought they might be there. But they weren't. On to the big green lawn.

Sure enough, I spotted the two bombshells strewn comfortably in our usual spot. Tasha, cross-legged with her guitar in her lap, her thousands of long, thin plaits falling gracefully around her face, and Sharon lying on her belly, jangling her ankles like a fidgety schoolgirl, smoking a cigarette. At least she wasn't roaming around shouting at anyone, which was quite a relief, given what George had said.

Luke ran ahead and joined Liam and Daniella, who were playing with fairies on a makeshift forest floor. Tasha saw me and waved hello. Sharon looked thinner than usual. Dying to find out if George's malicious rumour was true, I interrupted the pleasantries. 'What *were* you doing today, Sharon?'

Tasha and Sharon burst out laughing. Tasha was obviously in the know.

'George said you were pacing up and down shouting at innocent bystanders.'

Tasha laughed all the louder. 'You must have looked ridiculous!' she said.

'*What* then?' I asked, getting impatient.

'You're not going to believe this,' Tasha began, 'but Sharon lost her house!'

'No way! The housing association found out you over-claimed?'

'God, no! I went away for a week, but I'll tell you about that in a minute. Trevor is such an arsehole, you won't believe what he bloody did –'

I had to interrupt her. Sharon was such a spinner. She loved it when she had a story, and she was very funny. 'Come on. What about the house?'

She lit her cigarette slowly. 'Oh, yes. Well, I went away for the week . . .'

'Yes, yes,' I said, nodding.

'Well, when I came back, I couldn't find my house.'

'What? You forgot where you lived?'

'No. I *know* where I live, but I did think that maybe I had totally gone mad, because I just couldn't see it anywhere.

'What did you do?' I was fascinated.

'The housing association painted the bloody outside of the building while I was away and I just couldn't see the house. It sounds mad, I know. They probably sent one of those letters warning everyone, but I never read them and I had no idea that they were going to give the building a fucking face-lift, so I just couldn't see it.'

This was brilliant. I could imagine Sharon pacing up and down, frantically looking for her house and questioning her sanity instead of just looking at the door numbers like any normal human being.

'It looked so different, I couldn't believe it.'

The panic I imagined Sharon to have endured cracked me up. I wouldn't fancy a wound-up, hysterical blonde confronting me with a lost-house situation.

'Oh, stop it, I did look at the door numbers, you know.'

'George was right. You are raving mad.'

I could understand Sharon's reasoning to some degree. I think I'd probably doubt my little grey cells too if it'd happened to me. But I'm pretty certain that I would keep it to myself a fraction more than Sharon probably had.

To shut me up and change the subject, Sharon launched into what she really wanted to talk about. She and Trevor had gone away for a week to South Wales to stay with a good friend of Trevor's. Liam was holidaying with Sharon's parents, so they had some oh-so-precious time on their own. They were all getting on very well and having a healthy out-of-doorsy time, going on lots of beautiful walks and writing poetry and all that shit, and Sharon recognised the Trevor that she had initially fallen in love with. Everything was gorgeous – she got on well with his mate, they had good food and good wine – until the fifth night. Sharon had declared her undying love to Prat Features and they had decided to have a little party.

Peter, Trevor's mate, went and got a few mind-bending drugs. The three of them swallowed their goodies, drank a few jars and put on some loud music.

Later on, Sharon had felt a bit heady and went outside to get a breath of fresh air. When she came back in they were *snogging*. Eyuck! Her macho fella was licking his best mate's tonsils. How rough is that? Especially when you know they've been 'best buddies' for years and that homosexuality has always been stoutly denied. They didn't stop when she came in. She was supposed to flipping well join in. She'd rushed outside to throw up – her stomach's not been right since. No one came out to see if she was all right, especially not Trevor. Stuck in the middle of South Wales, with his tongue doing aerobics in Peter's mouth, there was no moving him to Sharon's side. She was miles away from home and anyone she knew, and Trevor knew it. Just as he knew that it wouldn't take long to get round her. Besides, right now, he was busy.

Caring chap, I thought.

At that point I got a bit cross. They'd cajoled me into listening to yet another Trevor saga, telling me they wanted my opinion. I mean, what did they expect me to say? 'Oh, don't worry about a thing, sweetie. I'm sure he uses condoms and there is no chance of HIV. After all, what's a little snog between a couple of happy campers?'

Enjoying the attention, Sharon attempted to tell me yet another jealousy story, involving some girl called Tiffany.

I cut her short. 'Yeah, yeah, Sharon. You don't know anything for sure. It's all bollocks. What I want to know is whether or not he's actually gone?'

'Course he hasn't. Can't you tell by the just shagged senseless look written all over her face?' Tasha said.

She had a point. Sharon looked like she'd been fucked so much that she should really pong. She didn't – but she should have. She gave me a stupid lovey-dovey grin. This Peter, Tiffany, whatever thing wasn't enough for Sharon. I tried to tell her to look at the signs, and these were really big flashing neon signs. They weren't just little indications that something could be slightly amiss. The signs to me were in capital letters, spelling it out, loud and clear, GET HIM OUT OF YOUR LIFE. It was that simple. 'Change the locks and refuse to ever see him again,' I told her.

Yet Sharon thought she'd re-fallen in love with this walrus while playing Cathy and Heathcliff on the rolling hills, she merely had to be a little more nineties about the whole thing and to understand Trevor better. She explained that she'd be happier competing against a member of the opposite sex than another woman (she wished she could somehow find out if Trevor was telling the truth or not about Tiffany). At least then she'd know that she was probably the only woman in his life. Well, what a result that was. Whoopie-doo!

She had an answer for everything: 'He was on drugs', 'He was really shy about telling me'. Sounds to me like he'd got over the shy thing all right.

Tasha was more interested in the male bottoms walking past. 'Check out the arse on that, girls,' she said, nodding towards two young men. 'Now, that is what I call seriously sexy. What d'you think, Charlie?'

'Nah, not my cup of tea, thanks. A bit old.'

I decided to go and buy some ice-creams for the kids, hoping that by the time I got back Sharon and Tasha would be wrapped up in a discussion to do with something else – anything other than Trevor. During the entire time it took me – to go there, choose ice-creams and pay – I couldn't think of anything else that Sharon talks about, apart from the occasional little anecdote like the house-painting story. I was sure that she wasn't quite as bad as this when I first met her. She did have a creative, fascinating side to her – didn't she?

*

Sharon lit another cigarette as she watched Charlie and the kids wander off. 'Do you think Charlie really is anti-bisexual and she's slagging Trevor off because he snogged a bloke, Tash? Or is she after him?'

Tasha laughed. 'You're mad. You really think Charlie would be after Trevor?'

Sharon's response was to drag harder on her fag.

'Charlie isn't interested in Trevor at all, honestly. She wants the best for you and thinks he's no good, that's all.' Tasha sighed, as she saw the mouths belonging to the cute little arses meet in a full-on frenchie. 'Shit. I should really be better at spotting them by now.'

'Are you sure?'

'I'd say a snog is pretty conclusive, Sharon.'

'No, I mean about Charlie.'

'Yes!' Tasha rolled her eyes at her.

'Okay!' Sharon conceded. 'So she's not after Trev and she's not bisexist. I've got it. She wants me to split with Trev because she's after me!'

'You *are* nuts!' Tasha said, grinning.

'Oh, I don't know. You never know, you know.'

'Shut up! She needs a man, stupid!'

'Don't we bloody all. And then when you think you've got one – well, say no more. Here, pass me the pen.'

Liam was being a right royal pain in the arse. He wasn't that good at playing with kids younger than him. After a while, he'd get bored with baby games, trick them into doing things they didn't really want to do, they'd get upset and then he'd call them names. Luke wasn't an idiot and – knowing that I didn't really like Liam – was a bit of a snitch and told tales. To stop Luke from telling on him, Liam went one step further and 'accidentally' pushed him over. Being a bit of a hypochondriac (even though he *is* my son but, hey, I was a hypo too at his age, I try and be forgiving), Luke totally overreacted, and they both started crying and hollering. By the time I'd paid for the ice-creams, I felt like shoving them in their faces. I resisted, and we went back to the lawn.

I found Sharon playing bongos with a biro on two empty Coke

cans and Tasha plucking her guitar. They sounded terrible, but at least they'd shut up about men for five seconds.

'Hey, Tasha, don't you think we should form a band?' I suggested.

'Who?' Tasha asked.

'You, me, Sharon and Conka.'

Sharon started laughing. 'That's ridiculous.'

'You can play the bass, Tasha and Conka the guitar – Come on, it could be brilliant.'

'Yeah, right.'

'I think it's a great idea,' Tasha said.

'Tasha, you're forgetting that I'm five years older than you and probably past it. Besides, I've done all that before.' Sharon sounded despondent.

'Yeah, and had to stop when you had Liam. Life can carry on you know. You've got to follow your destiny. It's important to have something in your life for you. Something you enjoy and that gives you self-worth.'

Tasha was right on that one. Sharon was in dire need of something to do apart from complaining.

I joined in: 'You're not too old. I'm happy enough doing the occasional makeup job, although I'd prefer more hot fashion work and less of the freezing dead, but imagine how much money we could earn.'

'Poor Charlie, I heard about your high-rise. How awful,' Tasha cooed.

'That was ages ago now,' I mumbled glumly.

'But aren't all the funeral jobs horrible? You get dressed in black and it takes you a week to recover.'

I nodded.

'And you're cynical about weddings. You can't be working for *Vogue* when you've got a child in tow. A band would be perfect for you. You're craving the high life. Music is where it's at.'

Tasha was trying to convince me now. This was getting silly.

'I know, Tasha. I want to do it – it was my idea. Well, actually, it was Conka's. It's Sharon you need to convince. She plays the bass. The problem is, I can't play anything.'

'Charlie's craving the high life,' Sharon teased.

We were about to argue that one out, when the clouds loomed over and it was suddenly quite dark.

I stood up and jangled my keys. 'Come on. I'll give you a lift home.'

11

I couldn't sleep. Sharon had struck a nerve. I didn't like to think of myself 'craving the high life', but Tasha was right about my makeup career. I was finding it more and more difficult to do the dead, even though it had been my forte, ever since that high-rise suicide number. I couldn't even find it slightly funny any more. Not only that, the magazine work hadn't happened in months. People seemed to shy away from us mums in the fashion world, especially when you had to tell them that you couldn't do that other gramme after work 'cause the babysitter was about to run out. They'd laugh and say, 'Ho, ho, *sweetness*. Just like the parking meters, eh?'

That response always cracked me up: 'Fucking hilarious,' I'd say, knowing that I'd never work with them again.

Luke was well worth it. I never got love from a parking meter like the love I got from Luke. And he made me feel needed. But that night I felt horribly lonely. I craved for someone to put their arms around me and tell me that everything was going to be fine. I was fed up with coping with life in general and the daily fight to make ends meet. I'd had enough of doing it alone. I wanted some relief, any relief, from anyone. Conka maybe, maybe a band, maybe singing *would* help. I wanted my mum. Fuck this. Fuck all of this. What I needed was a man to shag me senseless to take my mind off things for a minute.

I hated myself for thinking like this as I was determined not to make the same mistake twice. I had to earn my own worth and adulation. I wasn't going to rely on a man again – not for anything. That was just asking for disappointment.

But I was so horny and masturbating was no good. I had finished with Rob shortly after I became good friends with Sharon. Nearly six months ago. And Rob was shit in bed. So I hadn't had sex, not even *bad* sex, recently enough to convince my fanny that my cold fingers really were a big, throbbing, hot dick. That was it – dick – I needed one of those. I didn't want the whole package. I didn't want a relationship. I couldn't get wrapped up in another man's ego and insecurities. I didn't want my sexual needs resulting in another man intruding in Luke's life. Not that I was against men being in his life, he has met and enjoyed boyfriends I've been with since his dad, I just didn't want him to get any ideas about surrogate fathers. If I was ever going to have another more permanent relationship (unlikely), then I wanted to select a partner when I was a little more coherent and a lot less troubled about getting laid, then slowly introduce him to Luke, maybe. With a quickie, Luke needn't even know.

Fuck it. I didn't want to be one of those women who leaves it so long that they forget how enjoyable sex really is and then forget about it altogether. 'Oh, no, I don't miss it at all. You stop thinking about it after a while you know – you really do.' Fan-fucking-tastic!

If men can go out of an evening, feeling pretty basic and in touch with their animal instincts, then why not women? If I could check out the guys, pick one who was at least mildly attractive and suggest a quick roll in the hay – no questions asked and no repercussions guaranteed – it would be ideal. I could get a *lurve injection*, without all the crap that goes with it. It'd be great. I would still be a free woman, whole but without the need for love which inevitably seemed to result in weakness.

It was just a question of who.

I lay awake, a little less depressed as I started working my way through all the men I knew, looking for that perfect candidate. There had to be someone I could pick 'n 'lay. I soon got depressed again. They were all revolting. I didn't 'do' ex-boyfriends on principle and every other male I could think of seemed either too short, too unfit, too married or too related. I couldn't think of one bleeding possibility. Shag it, shag it, shag it! This was so frustrating. I went back to wanting my mum. Who flipping well thought of the sex drive in the first place?

The clock said a quarter to four, I had to get up at ten to eight to take Luke to school. He had to be at school at nine and I'd got it down to a fine art, maximising my lie-in as much as possible. But now I'd be buggered for the whole day. This made me even more depressed. I stared at the clock, feeling tragic, trying to work out what it was that was eating away at me apart from the lack of rumpy-pumpy.

Maybe a band wasn't such a bad idea. But me in a band? Well, Conka seemed to think I could sing. If it worked, it might be a way of getting away from our financial restrictions – none of us ever had enough money. It might be fun too. So what if three out of four of us were over twenty-five? We'd get to travel a bit. It'd be hard with the kids but it would be the ultimate kick in the teeth to my ex, if I was successful in the one thing he'd professed to be so great at. *Sweet revenge.*

It doesn't seem to matter that much if you aren't particularly talented. My ex was a great guitarist, but no one could stand being around him and his ego, so no wonder he never got anywhere. At least we mums all had a good laugh together, and we were all *people* people. Conka and Sharon were reasonably talented and they were certainly sexy. Tasha looked cool, but wasn't that great on the guitar. I didn't know what I'd be doing. I guessed singing, and I could do their makeup. It wasn't an entirely insane idea. But I'd be a fraud unless Conka could teach me to sing.

I finally fell asleep imagining the 'single mother' band on tour in a luxury coach.

We didn't get very far. About a second later the alarm went off.

After the school run Sharon and I went for our usual coffee. I had a double espresso – I'm so glad we're finally in Europe: the coffee situation has improved so much. Sharon was about to launch into last night's events, merely a phone call she'd overheard Trevor make but it would have taken at least an hour to dissect, when I decided I'd complain to her instead. I related my dreadful night's sleep, my decision to stop waiting for the most ideologically sound partner and, in the meantime, just go for the straight shag. I wondered if she had any suggestions.

'Have you seen the football teacher? He's pretty tasty – at least, he's tall, and probably got a big 'un. He's got nice eyes,' she suggested.

Liam and Luke had coaching after school with him on Tuesdays, Wednesdays and Fridays. Shit! Today was Monday. He always seemed pleasant enough and was over six foot, which I always find attractive.

'Yeah. I'll check him out.'

'It's not really a good idea to get involved with someone from the school, though –'

'Look, Sharon, I don't want to get involved, I just want to get laid, no strings attached. Okay?'

'What about Bing? You know, the guy we bumped into by the frozen fish in Tesco's the other day.'

'But, Sharon, he's got red hair!'

'Look, I thought you just wanted to get laid. What does it matter if he's got red hair or blue hair? He's pretty tall. It's nice to be with a big guy.'

'I don't think I could. What else have you got?'

'Well, I don't think you should rule him out. He's in a band, you know.'

'I'm trying to avoid that type. Anyway, what about our band?'

'I thought you said you didn't want to get involved. At least he's fun, and I can't see you shagging a banker.'

Sharon was remarkably adept at avoiding questions she didn't like.

'No, me neither – especially with my overdraft in its current state. Okay, so we'll make Bing a possibility. I suppose he was quite funny about the cod and parsley sauce. There must be someone else you know. Come on, think – you've lived around here for long enough.'

'What about Paul?'

'Your ex?'

'Yeah. He was *great* in bed. I mean he really knew how to –' She tried to show me – gesticulating and mouthing – what she was pretending she was too delicate to say aloud.

'Oh, really? Sounds good.'

'It felt fucking fantastic and he's got one of the biggest.' Again she used her hands to make the point.

'No fucking way!'

'Yes!'

'You are such a size queen! Give him my number.'

'Oh, shit, Charlie, I forgot. Sor-ree, he's moved to Spain.'

'Bollocks! Mind you, I don't know that I'd be that keen to sample your seconds, but if I'm going for the straight shag at least I wouldn't waste any time trying to find out whether he's well endowed or not. Have you had Bing?'

'Sorry, love. I hate redheads.'

God, Sharon was annoying. 'Oh, well, it's all pretty futile anyway. You know what else I was thinking last night?'

Strangely enough, she didn't.

'I was thinking about the *band* idea.' I stared at her. There'd be no getting away from it this time.

'Oh, no. Tasha's put a spell on you. She's given you some herbal tea that makes you believe you're Madonna.'

'Don't be so silly! And answer the question: why don't we form a band?'

'Talking of herbal remedies, I've got to get that recipe from Tasha for Sarah.'

'What are you talking about?'

'Sarah thinks she's pregnant,' Sharon continued. 'She's not sure, and can't think how it possibly could have happened.'

'How comes she's not sure?'

'Well, she thought she was going through the change.'

'She's not old enough, surely?'

'No one really knows with Sarah. I mean, she's always telling us she looks great for her age . . .'

Sharon was such a gossip. She loved to make everyone appear mysterious or sneaky in some way or other.

'Anyway, she's old enough to know better, and now she's up the duff and needs some of Tasha's contra-indicative suggestions. It worked for me that time my period was late.'

'Oh, she'll be all right,' I said, knowing how often Sharon got it wrong. 'What about the band, Sharon?'

'So it's a choice between Bing and the football teacher, right?'

Once home, I went back to contemplating my life and the ever-increasing itch between my legs. I knew that leaving it too long would inevitably result in 'lost lib', and as sex is the one thing in life that is both enjoyable and free, I wanted to hang on to my libido. The itch was there and it was there for a reason. It was not to be ignored.

Sharon had mentioned a couple of possibilities: the football teacher was good looking and he had flirted with me a couple of times, and Bing seemed to have a good sense of humour, and we all know how a good laugh helps to get the knickers down. I decided to be open to both, to test the water, to try out my new-found philosophy – why focus on one or the other? I knew I'd get a more speedy result if I didn't put all my fingers in one pie, so to speak.

I also thought more about the band idea. Sex wasn't the only unsatisfactory part of my life – it was just the most pressing. I still had ambitions, didn't I? Conka inspired me so much. It would be great to do something in a group as well. I decided I'd pick her up early to see exactly how serious she was about exchanging singing lessons for driving lessons.

12

I was excited to see Conka and tell her about my grand plan. I knew she'd be up for it. She was the one who thought I could sing, and she was gagging to learn how to drive.

Carlos showed me in and Conka looked up. She was glowing.

'All right, Conks?'

'You're early, Chas.'

'Yeah. C'mon, I've got a proposition. Bring your provisional licence with you.'

'Ye-ha!' Conka said. "Bye, Carlos – I'm having a driving lesson.'

'Fuck off, druggo.'

'I want to learn to sing,' I said, as we piled into my car.

We stopped at the nearest garage and bought some stick-on L-plates. I stuck the buggers on the car and drove to a quiet area, while explaining her first lesson; that is, if she didn't listen and respond to what I said immediately, then I would kill her; at no time should she think she could judge a situation better than me; that driving a car was no picnic and required concentration.

Conka was only slightly taller than me, which was lucky as the driving seat was bolted to the floor and could not be adjusted. She checked the mirrors and, having found them all there, set off. Not a bad pupil, Conka. I found myself breathing in only a couple of times and, apart from the odd close shave, we survived the first ten minutes. I was experimenting. I thought if I exuded calm and trust, she would gain confidence and relax. I told her in the most serious of voices when she was doing well, but that she should 'LOOK AT THE FUCKING ROAD!' I remained stoical and pleasant – 'BRAKE!' Finally I decided it'd be better (and healthier) to give her the next ten minutes of the driving lesson with yours truly behind the wheel. We would have to build it up slowly.

On the way to the school, I detailed my intentions concerning Mr Cullen, the football teacher, and Bing.

'You see, Conks, you've just got to get selective. I think of it like catalogue shopping. Look at the picture, not the rest of it. Take it home and try it on. Try a couple, change the size. Simple. I need servicing, you see. Not everyone can get horny dreams whenever they feel like it. I think I've only ever had one. So my back's against the wall on this one, Con. I'm gonna give it a go.'

Conka was very encouraging. She even suggested one of her bulky bruvs – not fat Carlos – as a back-up. I told her I was open to offers and she gave me a sneaky sideways glance.

'The only thing is,' I confided, 'Bing has red hair.'

Despite our parental criticisms, it had to be said that Sharon was always at the school early to pick up Liam, almost as persistently as she was late in the mornings. In some ways she was a typical Jewish mother: worried to death that if she wasn't standing right outside the classroom at twenty-five past three Liam would run out of school straight into the arms of a mass paedophile who'd sling him in front of a juggernaut. She was terribly protective of him. Worried that the bus would crash or he'd get lost, she hardly ever let him go away on school outings, let alone trips.

She waved as soon as she saw us and started flapping her *Evening Standard* all over the place. 'Look what the stars have to say for you today,' she said, pointing to the astrology page. 'It's Bing!'

The most sceptical of Virgos would have been surprised by this. A change in some planet or other meant a drastic change in my mount Venus. But I couldn't read it properly as Sharon was jumping up and down. 'It's Bing, can't you see? You'll never guess who rang me today –'

I was just about to wander off in the direction of Luke's class, when she grabbed my arm.

'Not Trevor, silly.' She had read my mind. '*Bing!*'

My plan was coming to fruition, first base had been touched, the eagle had farted, a go-between established. Things were looking up, indeed.

We got the kids and made a plan. Sharon was in a good mood and was in her 'go out and get totally pissed, have a larf' mode. She knew the pub Bing and his motley crew hung out in at night and suggested we got a babysitter between us and went out ASAP.

Trevor had heard through the vine that the revamped King's Arms needed bar staff and today he had every intention of scoring that job. He and Sharon had been getting on all right and he wanted a fresh start. But, even when she wasn't around, Sharon somehow managed to hold him back.

The first battle was getting through the kitchen, the next was finding a clean cup. The blocked sink made clearing up impossible: there was no way he was sticking his hand into the cold, murky, greasy water to remove the tea bag or whatever it was. He found a cleanish cup, which he rinsed hurriedly, then discovered there wasn't any coffee. He hated Sharon's inability to throw away even an empty jar. Feeling well fucked over by the kitchen, Trevor decided to have a bath. That, too, was disgusting, full of grime and hair. She really knew how to piss him off.

Having given up on the bath, he decided to get dressed. Another wind-up. When he eventually found his blue jumper under a pile of Sharon's dirty fucking clothes he was extremely vexed. And when he saw the coffee stain, like a map of Africa, all over the front, he punched the wall, knocked his shin against the bastard coffee table, grabbed his leather jacket and went out. He couldn't take another second of Sharon's shit. She could moan to and crap on someone else. He needed a drink. Fuck the job.

When Sharon gets an idea in her head, she usually does something about it immediately.

She rang me that night. 'Little Alison said she'd do it for a tenner – for both of them – but you'd have to bring Luke here.'

'Tonight?' I asked.

Luke was already in bed, although still awake.

'Yeah. Now. Come on, Trevor's not back yet. I really want to get out. Please, Charlie' Sharon begged. 'You know you want to –'

'I really can't. It's too late.'

We spent about an hour arguing, and finally agreed that we'd go out to the local that Thursday. I was just about to hang up, when Sharon muttered, 'I gave Bing your number, I hope you don't mind –'

'What?'

I heard a muffled "Bye', followed with a click.

I put down the phone and, before I had time to decide whether I should be angry or not, it rang again.

'Hiya,' the drawl said. 'It's me. All right, are ya?'

Well, I knew who it was. I've always been very proficient at recognising voices.

'Who is this, please?' I inquired, in my best telephone voice. Play it cool, I thought. The arrogance of the man, anticipating that I'd recognise his voice. I mean to say, was I to know Bing had my number?

'It's me – Bing.'

'Oh?' Sod it. So it was time to play that game. Let's pretend I don't have a frigging clue who you are – I have so many male callers.

'Yeah, you know. We met with Shassa the other day – you know, in Tesco's,' he continued.

'Ah, I see, was it you by the frozen veg, then?'

'Fish.'

'I'm sorry?'

'Fish, darling. I met you by the frozen fish.'

I think he was beginning to get a little impatient with my feigned memory lapse. It was my way of flirting, but I thought that maybe he was beginning to think I was the frozen fish. 'Oh, *hello*, Bing. How are you?' I said quickly.

'I'm all right, fanks.' Pause.

I hate it when blokes ring you up and then expect you to make conversation, so I remained silent.

Another pause. 'How are you, Charlie?'

I had to remind myself that I was looking for a straight shag and not mind-blowing conversation.

'Fine.' Pause. 'Thank you, Bing.' Still in my best, huskiest voice. I waited for him to make the next move.

'Sharon gave me your number . . . Didn't she tell you?'

'Oh, I see. No, she didn't,' I lied.

'She probably thought you'd bite her head off.'

I realised that maybe I did come across as a tad aggressive. 'Now why would I do that?'

'I don't know. Perhaps you might be hungry.' Now he was flirting.

'Nah. I don't fancy her head, thank you very much.'

'What about her biting your head?'

'You filthy bastard!' I had to act all brusque to regain my icy exterior, after all, it was going to take some serious persuading for me to get over his challenging colour scheme.

'I dunno what you're talking about. You're the filthy one, thinking like that. I dunno.'

'Clever sod, aren't you? Turning things right round, eh?'

'Look, I just rang to see if you wanted to go out for a drink some time.'

'Actually, I was planning to go out with Sharon on Thursday to the poetry night at the K.'

'Well, maybe I'll join you.' Now *he* was being cool.

'But I don't know if I can get a babysitter or not – yet.'

'Why don't you give me a bell when you know?'

'Okay then. 'Bye.'

He hung up. The cheek of it! He expects me not only to get his number from someone else, but to ring him and ask *him* to join *me*. Maybe I should go and do an adult education course in flirting. There should be one – they listed every goddamned other subject in that *Floodlight* book.

I fell asleep that night trying to imagine Bing in the nude. Instead, I found myself thinking about all the things I hate that are red; tomatoes, current account, steak tartare, phone bill, nail varnish, Bloody Marys, Father Christmas, Rudolf's stupid nose, traffic-lights, tonsils, tampons – yuck, violence, strawberry jam, screams, Jesus's anus . . . What? Surely that would be brown. Madness – that seemed red. Maybe these were signs that shags weren't that easy to come by. This straight shag thing was beginning to turn into more of a nightmare.

Before I knew it, the alarm clock went off. That was sodding red too.

Part Two

Warm Dates and
Strange Flirtations

13

Today was football day. Operation Mr C.

Luke had woken up in the night complaining of tummyache. He was still a bit under the weather at breakfast, but there was no way he was getting out of school. At least Mr Cullen had brown hair.

I managed to bump into the man himself at the school. I used Luke's tummyache as an excuse to talk to him. '. . . so if he does seem a bit ill, perhaps you could give me a ring?'

Thinking, it works for Sharon Stone, why not for me, I smiled at him, raising my eyebrows and licking my lips.

'No problem. I'm sorry, I only know you as Luke's mum?' he said, offering his hand.

'My name's Charlie, Mr Cullen.'

I allowed our handshake to linger while I looked him right in the eye. I liked the *size* of his hands. He was picking up on all my signals, but I was behaving like a bitch on heat. I was half expecting a dozen randy stray dogs to come charging up the corridor at any moment, sniffing me out. You'd have to have really bad sinuses not to clock on to the potent waft of my sexual deprivation.

'Please call me Nigel.'

Was he a sucker for punishment, or was this his real name? 'Nigel?'

'Aye, pleased to meet you.'

We took this opportunity to have another firm handshake – the size of his hands! Maybe I should just grab him now and lead him back to my place, putting my fingers on his lips if he tries to say anything, while I undress him and . . .

'Charlie? Charlie?'

. . . roll my tongue down his torso, kissing my way to his *monster* . . .

'Charlie?'

. . . licking and undressing, kissing and – Shit! God! I'd lost it, and I was still holding his hand.

'Are you all right, Charlie?'

Embarrassed, I pulled my hand away. 'Yes, yes. I'm sorry. I just feel a bit dizzy all of a sudden.'

'Sit down, Charlie, sit down. Let me get you a glass of water.'

Wow, chivalrous, I thought. Point in his favour.

He was looking very intently into my eyes. I wanted to laugh at his ridiculous puppy eagerness. He was so keen, it was disturbing. I had to get out of there.

'I've got to go. See you later.'

'Ta-ra, then, Charlie. See you later.'

''Bye.' I started to walk away.

'Oh, Charlie.' Oh, no. Now I've told him my name he's going to wear it bleeding well out.

'Charlie?'

I turned around.

'Don't worry. I'll call you [wink] if we have any more tummyaches. Okay [wink, wink]?'

'Okay. 'Bye.' Why do they have to always open their mouths? And wink?

'Oh, Charlie? I hope you feel better.'

I think he was still saying, 'Nice to meet you,' as I left the school. Well, he may be good-looking and *big*, but we certainly were not clicking mentally. Perhaps he was just outrageously shy and nervous, or perhaps he really was a total prat. I decided I'd investigate further, if only to compete in Tasha's and Sharon's size competition.

That afternoon, thanks to much encouragement and daring from Conka, I decided to try to make a date: phase two in Operation Mr C.

I arrived early at the school to watch the tail end of football practice. Mr C gave me a winning smile as soon as I walked in. About five seconds later Luke was made captain. Woah, Teacher *was* keen. To start the flirtation as my kid's hero was a very flattering effort. I quite enjoyed watching all six foot six of him lollop around; the kids ripped him to pieces, though. He had zero control – not attractive. There again, I won't be asking him to teach me football, I suppose.

I wished I had the balls simply to go up to him and say, 'Fancy a no-strings-attached, no-repercussions, no-questions-asked, low-expense shag?' I wouldn't want him to go around claiming he was my 'boyfriend'; nor would I want him to ask me any questions. I would have to get him to understand that it would be merely a stop-gap, a temporary post, although an enjoyable one for both parties (one would hope). This was going to be difficult.

'Afternoon, Charlie!'

Mr C lolloped over. I decided to count how many times he said my name. One.

'Hello, Nigel.'

Launch into it, girl, start with the no-repercussions angle. But it was too scary. If I was in Brazil, I'd say whatever the fuck I felt like saying. I just couldn't do it in real life, in the grotty Bush.

'Are you all right, Charlie?'

Two.

'I'm fine, thanks.'

'We don't want any slo[wink]-mo[wink] replays of this morning's action, eh, Charlie?'

Three. More winking. And a bad joke – slo-mo. I had to shut him up, before all was lost.

'No, we don't. How are you, then?'

I tried to repeat my overtly effective Sharon Stone smile of this morning's magnitude, but only got as far as a Bet Lynch grimace.

'Er, Charlie . . .'

Four.

'. . . I'm fine. Er, would you, er, Charlie, er, like to come out for a drink tonight?'

Blimey! I wasn't anticipating that. I had to act quickly. I looked at his hands.

Five. 'Yes, thanks.' I hadn't felt so stupid in years, what was I doing? This was ridiculous.

'I'll meet you in the Bull and Muffin at nine o'clock, okay?'

'Or – d'you have a car?'

'No, but I've got me bike, so I'll meet you there, all right?'

There'll be no shagging in the back of any cars, then.

'Fine, see you,' I muttered, before making my hasty exit.

Of course he had only chosen the most nerdy pub in the whole area. Still, if we started off there, I wouldn't bump into anyone who knew me.

I got to Conka's house at warp speed. I needed to spill my story immediately. She cracked up. She couldn't believe I'd done it.

'You've gone and got yourself a bleeding date with Mr C! You nutter!'

'What do you mean? You encouraged me!'

'Yeah, but I didn't think you'd go through with it.' Conka was almost crying with laughter.

'Yeah, but why not, Conks?'

She merely snorted more giggles. I continued to try to convince myself, 'I mean, he's a *nice* guy.'

Conka laughed louder.

'He's a teacher, a good man. He's got no form.'

Conka whooped and even I started laughing when I said that. I looked at her then and realised it was her I'd much rather go out with. It was piss easy having a laugh with Conka, and dead tricky even talking to that Mr C, let alone laughing. I guess I'd lost my nerve, you know, to go it alone. Besides, I wondered if all the encouragement and laughter were hiding other feelings – perhaps of jealousy.

'Bollocks. Conks, you're coming with me. I'll pick you up at nine.'

'I'd love to, but I've got to get Helena from her grandad's. She's having dinner with him tonight.'

'I don't care. We'll go together to pick her up.'

'You're on. I'll do anything for a lift.'

I could always rely on Conka for that essential nutty ingredient. I went home and started phoning around for a babysitter. I still couldn't believe I was going to be dating a hand-picked, prospective shag. This could be the beginning of my new-found enjoyment-of-life theory. It also could be disastrous and completely embarrassing.

*

I picked up Conka dead on nine, having pre-rolled a mildy. Conka's laughter had been resounding through my head every time I'd tried to think of Mr C in any saucy way. Nope, he hadn't flicked my switch. But one must persevere, I told myself. However, I acknowledged that there was absolutely no way I'd be able to hold down a private conversation with him. I decided that I wasn't going to go anywhere alone with him.

He looked surprised to see Conka stroll in with me. I told him to drink up and come with us if he wanted, or we'd see him around. As he chose not to be ditched immediately, I feel no remorse about what happened next.

We made all six foot six of him fold up and squeeze into the back seat of my small Citroën. He had those massive, over-developed, footballer thighs, so it wasn't easy. He looked very oversized and squashed in the seat usually occupied by two three-stone children. I asked him not to talk for the duration of the journey, as I would be giving Conka a driving lesson. He was a natural anti-women-driverist, but he took this opportunity to really shit himself. We couldn't resist it.

He mumbled something about putting the front seat forward, but I ignored him. There was nothing I could do anyway, the seats being bolted in place. It was when he whinged about the broken rear seat-belt that I lost my rag.

'Can't you be quiet for a minute? Conka is trying to concentrate,' I snapped.

It had begun to drizzle and the car was steaming up rapidly. Nigel clambered around trying to wipe his great big hands all over the windows, but again we had to stop him. Conka's rear-view mirror was getting severely obscured.

'Nigel, can you crouch down, please, and stop fussing with the flaming windows?' I barked, smirking at Conka. She was loving it. 'Conka can't see.'

The oaf mumbled something before trying to reduce himself by burying his chin in his chest. It didn't work. He was still just a great big annoying glumph. It was fucking hard not to laugh.

'Conka, open your window,' I instructed, opening mine all the way. We'd blast the bastard now – you always got it worse in the back. 'There you go, Nigel. That's getting rid of the steam, eh? You're not getting too wet, I hope?'

If he answered me I didn't hear him, the noise from the car, wind and rain meant you had to shout to be heard. That'll teach him to go by sodding bike, I thought.

Although laughing for the large part, Conka, unfortunately, drove very well – it must have been the mildy. Until we came to parking. She kept confusing reverse and first.

Mr C joined in at that point. '*Look out!* You're heading straight for the – Oh, my God! Crikey!'

'Crikey' was about the only interesting thing he ever said. But until then, his face was frozen, he was holding his breath, just waiting for that crash to happen, anticipating disaster at every gear-change. He made me seem incredibly laid back in comparison.

Eventually we clambered out of the haphazardly parked car and walked to this strange little family hotel in Bayswater where Conka's old man worked. All three of us crammed into the front reception area, with Papa offering us – the young people – cups of tea. It wasn't a simple run-in-and-grab Helena situation. I had to remind myself I was supposed to be sizing up Nigel for a shag. Surely he couldn't be as bad as I'd found him in the car? I tried to smile at him, but was really smiling at my surroundings – I couldn't recall Sharon Stone doing this.

14

Sharon wasn't going to wait in yet another night. She had to go out. There was no way she could hang on until Thursday – tomorrow – when she'd be playing gooseberry to bloody Bing and Charlie anyway. She lit a ciggie. She'd stayed in last night and not slept a wink. Trevor had done his disappearing trick again. He'd rung, but not spoken – she knew it was him, checking she was in. He hadn't walked past her house. She'd spent virtually the entire previous night staring down to the street below from behind her tatty curtain. She would have seen him if he had. She could spot Trevor anywhere, day or night. His walk gave him away – he was so cumbersome. She lit another fag without realising the last one was still smoking itself in the ashtray.

She wondered about Tiffany, about the band, about lost ambitions. It was like being forced into a room full of video screens, each showing her something she really wanted to see, but couldn't watch. There was Tiffany, there was that Diana from the pub, Dad, her, there was Trevor – Trevor. But it was patchy, she couldn't concentrate on any one screen, it was all too frantic and fast, a bad music video. She'd lost something, something'd gone and she couldn't put her finger on it. It wasn't Trevor, nor her home. It was something else. Loss, loser, losing.

'*Christ!*' Sharon screamed aloud.

'*Mum!*' Liam yelled. 'You made me lose the goal!' He threw his control pad in her direction.

'*Oh, stop it, Liam!*' Sharon screamed back.

It would drive her mad to stay in tonight. She rang little Alison – thankfully she was free to sit Liam – and then she rang Tasha.

When Sharon called round Tasha was nowhere near ready. Sharon couldn't see any sign of a babysitter either. While Tasha was talking to her from her bedroom, she counted the numerous incense sticks that littered the living room, paying no attention to whatever it was that Tasha was saying. She had no idea why Tasha burnt those dreadful hippy things. There was nothing worse than going out stinking of bloody patchouli oil.

'Do you fancy going to the Half Moon, Tash?' Sharon shouted, as she opened the large sash window and breathed in the stale London air. She didn't know which smell was worse.

Tasha walked in, tying the waist of her loose silk trousers. 'I thought maybe we could go to the Gas Station,' she suggested.

'No way. I hate that place.' Besides, Sharon thought to herself, Trevor wouldn't go there. 'What's wrong with the Half Moon?'

'Well, nothing's wrong with it. There's just not a lot right with it, that's all.'

Tasha sat down and rolled a joint. Coping with Sharon was much easier when stoned.

Sharon went to have a dig in Tasha's kitchen. As usual it was full of brown rice, organic sodding lentils, rice cakes and soya bleeding butter. No wonder Tasha was looking more and more like the innards of a kitchen roll. 'Got any vodka, Tash?' she shouted.

'Yeah, in the freezer.'

Sharon fixed them both a frosty frozen voddy. 'I would lurve some cocaine,' she said, as she floated back.

'Here. Have a puff on that, instead.' Tasha passed her the joint. 'You need to slow down, not speed up, babe.'

'Yeah, right.' Sharon took a deep drag on the spliff, as she slumped down on the sofa. 'Jesus, this is strong stuff.' If she had too much of this she'd be getting to know Tasha's sofa in intimate detail tonight and not a lot else.

'God, life is weird.' She turned to face Tasha.

Sharon's eyes were suffering from the skunk. She squinted and blinked trying to focus on her friend.

'You know what, Tash? Over the last few days, I felt like I've been going mad, but everything I see around me *is* mad. Do you see what I mean? I'm normal to think that a man walking down the road dressed in black bin-liners is mad, right?'

Tasha finished plucking her eyebrow and did her lips before answering. 'You know what,' she said, staring at her perfect lip line in her small mirror, 'there's been a lot of very strange planetary activity over the past week. Mars is in retrograde,' she smacked her lips together loudly, signifying the end of the astronomical lipstick application, 'all hell breaks loose for all communications, travel and all that kind of thing. You know, you're not the only one.'

Sharon thought Tasha must be mad as well. What the fuck was all that about? Either that or the pot was even stronger than she'd thought. Thankfully the bell rang. Tasha's mum, aka the babysitter, had finally arrived.

Tasha passed her mum the rest of the joint as the two of them left for the Half Moon.

Conka disappeared with her papa, and Mr C and I made awkwardly fragmented conversation. Not liking his voice, I was soon drifting off, taking in my surroundings. The walls of the hotel reception area were covered with tacky religious pictures.

Numerous postcards, with bright blue oceans and luxury palm trees were shoved in the corners of every frame. Ornaments and letters packed the mantelpiece. As I looked around at my bizarre situation, they came back with the tea.

Conka's father was light years away from her. He was lost in his world – an old Hungarian keeping traditional in his recipes, songs and tales. We drank our tea and left giggling with Helena.

I drove back, amused that Mr C still hadn't jumped out. We dropped Helena off with Conka's mum and went back to my house, ostensibly for a spliff, but really because I couldn't risk being out with him in public a moment longer. He could seriously damage my reputation. I also thought it might be easier for me to try to fancy him in my own home. Wrong! Everything he said made me wince. I'd wanted to like a nice guy and Mr C hadn't been nasty in any way. What the fuck was wrong with me? Why did I have to find him so repellent? I watched him glug back his glass of warm, cloudy London tap water – I hadn't even let the tap run when I'd got it for him. He still looked as if he flipping enjoyed it. A glass of dodgy water – yuck! His organic wholesomeness was a real turn-off.

There was no doubt about it: this guy was one hell of a turnip. Even his size was getting on my nerves now. I didn't want to know how flipping big it was any more. Imagine if it was small, after all this? The risk was simply not worth taking. Red hair was becoming more and more attractive. Conka and I behaved as if he wasn't there, except when he went out of the room. Then we'd slag him off and try to work out how we were going to get rid of him.

An hour later, after a bathroom visit, he gave me the ammunition to fire him out of my house.

'I see you've got a dirty toilet. It could do with a good scrub you know,' he said in his broadest northern accent.

'Well, do feel free to clean it then,' I snapped back. I made my face tight and mean. I pursed my lips so tightly they ceased to be lips. I wanted him to believe that he'd deeply offended me by daring to criticise my household hygiene.

'It's late now. I think you'd better leave.' I ushered him to the door, still keeping my lips well disguised as a cat's arse.

'Thanks for the drink. See you soon.' He bent down to kiss me. Quickly I turned my face, to avoid full-on lip collision. He got me in the ear, and it was really flipping loud. That announced the end to that particular straight-shag effort.

Operation Mr C was declared utterly unsuccessful.

15

Morning. Coffee with Sharon. A quick breakdown of the previous night's events gave her hysterics. She found it hard to believe that I'd even attempted a date with Thunder Thighs. Thanks, Sharon. We then had more discussions *re* red hair, leading me further along the Bing trail. Today was Wednesday and I already had a babysitter lined up for poetry-cum-Bing night. Maybe tomorrow I'd hit the jackpot.

Sharon had bumped into Bing in the Half Moon last night, and thought I should ring him to make sure of meeting him. Trevor had pissed her off and she wanted revenge. I was the perfect accomplice; he hated her going out with me. She was needy, and the mercenary, shag-searching me took advantage.

'You call him,' I suggested.

'I can't bloody call him! What should I call him for?'

'You know him, he's your friend.'

'I'm not going to bloody well call him, Charlie. He'll go there anyway. He's always there on a Thursday.'

'Oh, I don't know if I wanna go or not . . .'

'Oh, come on, Charlie, you promised. All right, all right, I'll bloody ring him. But you better not let me down.'

Great. The eagle was really coming along nicely. Bing had begun to get under my skin. I started to plan what I'd wear. During the day, I drank litres of water. That evening, I shaved my legs and trimmed my Mary. I went to bed ridiculously early to minimise bags. I was still gagging for it and Bing was looking like bonk material. Let's just say, there was a wiggle in my walk. The girl from Ipanema would have been proud.

Thursday. I actually had a live job, which always made me feel good, even though it was a wedding and I hate doing those. The bride's mother *always* wants more makeup than the bride. It gets on my nerves.

It was a register-office affair, fairly small. I put loads of black eyeliner on the unsuspecting mother to shut her up right from the word go. I felt a bit guilty, though, when she went and washed it all off. I made the girl look nice, soft and natural. She had a gentle face. It didn't go late either. It's always the same with register-office weddings: they're always too para to get there late. If they miss their turn they're stuffed. There's always poor suckers queuing up outside. So I packed mother and daughter off early, having gone on about the dreadful traffic non-stop since I arrived.

I got home early and indulged myself getting ready. I took hours. My makeup was perfect and I was happy with my outfit: tight and titty T-shirt, showing my belly-ring and a favourite pair of boot-kick-bottom trousers. I didn't want to over-glamour, try too hard, look stupid. I put my favourite big blue jumper on top. That way I had protection.

The babysitter arrived on time and I was hot to trot. I went to Sharon's, and once we'd gone through the usual palaver about her wardrobe and demolished the compulsory bottle of brandy, we sashayed along in the direction of the pub. Sharon had done her duty and had rung Bing to confirm. She'd said we would meet him around eight thirty and it was already a significant nine fifteen. There was no doubt in my mind that he'd be at the K-Kafe already.

The K, as we called it, was one of those places pretending to be something other than the pub that it was. It had that pretentious New York vibe to it. Edward Hopper would have painted it. It had a swooping high bar near one wall with a dark mirror backing it and spiky bits of stripped bark in proud, tall glass vases at each end, which softly reflected dapples of light from the occasional small lamps. Dark blue velveteen high-backed sofas lined the other three long walls, which were lit at intervals with warm red lights glowing gently down on the shiny tables. They served small amounts of sour curly lettuce, decorated with a suggestion of chewy fish or an eighth of lamb, all dressed in exotic, designer sauces, delicately served on massive plates. It was an anorexic's paradise.

The drinks were that touch more expensive, and the bar staff looked like sulky models. They all wore black. They would never acknowledge you, or even show that they vaguely recognised you, even if you'd been going and sitting on the same lofty bar stool every single goddamn night of the year. I could never get a free drink out of any of the buggers and they never got any of my jokes.

There were stairs near the far end of the bar, leading down to the low-ceilinged 'poetry room', which was little more than a converted cellar – not great for really tall or claustrophobic people.

We *strutted* in. The warm smoky air pinked my cheeks as I sensed the feast of faces study us up and down. Sharon's eyes darted around, like a frightened myxomatosis rabbit, looking for Trevor. I tried to sneak a look here and there. As I am virtually blind in one eye, I had to hope Bing would spot me. I was really ready for a long vodka and orange.

'All right, darling?'

The drawl from behind surprised me.

'A bit jumpy aren't you, Charlie? Do I make you nervous, darling?'

He was already flirting with me – what a good, refreshing start. He was dressed funkily with a hint of American retro, fifties style, and, in this light, his hair didn't look too bad. I found him surprisingly dashing but, there again, I was in a desperate situation. I noted the possibility that I might be hallucinating and reminded myself that we were, after all, in flattering light.

Bing bought some drinks, and for the first time ever, I saw one of the girls behind the bar smile. This guy must have charm. So far so pretty damned good. Buying drinks with zero hesitation was a big plus as far as I'm concerned. I'd bought enough drinks for my ex in the past, and now it was payback time.

We drank the first round at Mansell pace. Our conversations were more like sparring matches and Bing certainly gave good bounce. I wondered if he'd also been in a bonk-free zone for ages. He was pretty charged up. We certainly seemed to be doing a lot more clicking mentally than I had with his pratness Thunder Thighs. In fact, we were verging on verbal tap-dancing; this felt *good*. Sharon, feeling a little like a gooseberry no doubt, started knocking back shorts at a pace I found hard to keep up with. She began to behave a bit irrationally – roaming around the bar, stopping every once in a while in no specific spot, motionless, her eyes glazing over. She really was in another world. Still, she gave Bing and me something to talk about. He thought she was hilarious and scoffed at me when I voiced my vague concerns.

'Don't you worry about that old tart, darling. She's been a raving loony for years, ever since I've known her.'

This absurd statement reassured me enough for now. Bing and Sharon had known each other for a lot longer than I'd known either of them. Besides, I wanted to concentrate on the all-important Bing-flirting to be done. We got yet another round of drinks, grabbed Sharon and entered the seedier zone on the lower level. The low ceiling, bad ventilation and softer lights all added to the sexiness of the moment. It was pretty rammed as well, which gave Bing the excuse to stand dangerously close.

Sharon spotted Trevor and disappeared into a dim corner with him. That'll be the end of them for a while, I thought. One of our gregarious hosts announced the next act, the lights became even dimmer and the Irishman sang passionately along to his acoustic guitar. Boy, this was turning out nicely.

I became aware of Bing's breath hot on my neck. Yikes! I allowed myself to drift gently back, so I was slightly leaning on him. God, it felt good, especially as standing without swaying was becoming increasingly difficult. As I closed my eyes in romantic appreciation, he slipped his hand around my waist and gently fiddled with my belly ring. I put my hand on his and started massaging his fingers. He responded with a kiss on my neck. I squeezed his hand, he nibbled. I squeezed some more. He nibbled slightly harder. I squeezed again and he turned me around and gave me the biggest snog I'd had in donkeys. He held my face and looked at me wickedly, directly into my eyes. I was turned on by his cheek. I kissed him again, exploring his mouth with my tongue, hungry for more. He'd hit the switch and there was only one thing that was going to turn it off.

The Irishman finished his act, the light's became slightly brighter and I flinched momentarily at Bing's hair. I looked at his eyes and they definitely had the devil in them. Fuck the hair. We bought another couple of drinks and fondled each other during another couple of acts. I vaguely debated whether or not I should go home with this guy. I briefly considered that don't-give-it-away-too-easily theory, then chastised myself for not being a true nineties woman. This guy was turning me on and I'd already gone long enough without, I decided I'd go back if he invited me.

He invited me.

I went back.

Bing lived nearby and his pad had that same kind of American retro style that seemed to suit him so well. The hallway was a cold, flat, peach colour, dotted with black and white photos of him in various guises. I knew why the pictures were in black and white. I followed him into the bachelor's lounge, which had the compulsory black leather sofa. Records dominated this room and Bing was quick to get the turntable turning.

'Aw, you can't beat vinyl,' he drawled.

'No, I suppose not,' I agreed, lying. I way prefer the convenience of CDs any day.

He left me for a few minutes' snoop, while he fixed some drinks, went to the loo and hopefully checked himself for any unwanted vile smells. I took off my jumper and had a look round. He had a few nice unobtrusive bits: a collection of cactuses, a couple of unusual candlesticks, that kind of thing. There were loads of bits of paper with telephone numbers scrawled all over the place by the phone. I was just looking for mine when he came back in to the room.

''Ere. Get that down you,' he said, handing me a long cold glass and staring at me, while remaining unnervingly close.

I felt hot. I gulped back the vodka and allowed him to launch into another tonsil attack.

The record stopped and he went to change it. Jazz, modern jazz. Very sexy, I thought, very French Art Movie House. Nice.

We snogged some more and I fell into lust heaven. His hands felt big on my body, his kisses had the perfect balance of aggression and care. He'd stop and look at me with that devilish expression every so often. I knew 'it' was coming.

'Shall we go to the bedroom?'

I looked at him for a moment – to make him believe that I had to think about it. 'Yeah. C'mon.'

I was barely audible. As I walked the five or so metres along the corridor behind Bing, I suddenly felt extremely weird and lost. I didn't know this guy. I seemed to like him, and now I was going to fuck him. As if Bing intercepted my thoughts, he turned around and kissed me passionately.

Then he grabbed my bum and gave it a slap. 'Get in there and get your clothes off, you dirty bitch!'

He had broken my dark thoughts, and we were laughing, undressing and playing. He turned me on. Soon we were both naked and getting steamier by the second. I was on my back, he was eating his way down my neck.

'Have you got a condom?' I whispered in his ear.

He jolted off me immediately and threw me an incredibly disdainful glance. I propped myself up on my elbows and looked him right in the eye, trying to return the disdainful look. You've got me *really* going so you'd better not let me down now, you bastard, I thought.

He grinned. 'I might have one.'

'*Garrn*, get it, you dirty bastard. I ain't letting that thing get anywhere near me without one, you know.'

I began playing with myself – looking at him, challenging him to 'do' me senseless. He reached to his bedside table and opened a Durex, while playing with himself with his other hand. I looked at his willy. I've never seen one that colour before. I didn't really like it.

Bing caught me staring at it and started to go really floppy. Bing was banging it like mad, but it was just getting worse. I was drying up fast. I didn't want to look at it any more and yet I couldn't drag myself away. That thing, that cock, was what had led me to this hell-hole in the first place. Why? Fucking why? I'd have been better off rolling up a piece of flaccid smoked salmon. The result would've been much the same, except that I could have genuinely enjoyed eating it.

Bing was getting angry and began fumbling around with his boxer shorts. I was feeling like getting the fuck out of there. My head was pounding, I felt so sick. I jumped up and ran to the bathroom. I needed cold water on my head – even my ears were on fire. What the fuck was going on? After dunking my spinning head in heaven-sent cold water, I regained my composure, got my jumper and went back to the bedroom. I didn't know what to say. Bing was giving me a vibe of pure hate. Red hate. Nonchalantly, he watched me from beneath his torrid sheets, smoking a fucking cigarette, while I dressed. As I tied my trainers, I looked at him. He looked disgusting and disgusted.

'I guess I'll see you around,' I said politely. I made my way to the door.

'Not if I see you first!' he shouted, in his annoying drawl.

I rolled my eyes and walked slowly back to the bedroom. Leaning against the door-frame, half trying to look cool and half out of necessity, I stared at the mess of my warped fantasy. He was truly revolting.

'If I was you, I'd keep that thing well hidden – in the dark – at all times,' I spat. 'That's if you ever expect it to go anywhere near a pussy. In fact, even if you don't,' I slurred, now pointing at him, 'it's the most – repulsive, ugly, pink, pathetic attempt at a dick that I've ever seen. Get a Porsche, Flopsy-dear. You're gonna need it.'

I felt myself retch, I wanted to throw up there and then – on him – but my sick was too good for that ponce. I turned and made my way out. I decided to leave his front door wide open, instead of the traditional slam. That way the pig would have to get up off his putrid pink arse to shut it himself.

Once outside, I threw up. I hated men and their stupid cocks. '*Tosser!*' I shouted, to the world.

Somehow I managed to regain enough strength to march home through the cold, deserted streets. I felt so fucking angry. Unwanted hot tears fought with the cold rain beating in my face. Bing. Ha – another sodding sham! I would have to rethink my tactics. I felt more alone than ever. Why was everything so fucking difficult? I got home and washed a couple of aspirins down with some water, looked at myself in the bathroom mirror, smiled and collapsed.

16

Sharon grinned knowingly at me as she mistook my sunglasses for a good sign, until I took them off. She took one look at my puffy red eyes and realised things hadn't gone as planned. We had a subdued conversation that morning. My head was pounding and I found any noise above a whisper agony. Focusing was impossible. She ranted on about men being fucking useless for ten minutes, then cottoned on to my totally decrepit state. 'I think you should go and lie down for an hour or so. Listen, we'll go to Sarah's tonight and recuperate. I could definitely do with a visit. Besides, I need you to get better so I can tell you what happened to me and Trevor last night –'

I held out my hand, giving her the stop signal and, for once, she shut up. We walked out of the café, sunglasses on, like a couple of old women, arm in arm and very slowly.

I took her advice and went back to bed. The thought of going to Sarah's was a comforting one, even though she was in a highly hormoronic state, what with her being preggers an' all. I knew she'd still be able to throw together at least one great meal. She always brought me back down to earth and is the only friend who doesn't mind if we don't talk to each other. I can be completely silent around her without feeling guilty. Everything and anything is always cool with Sarah. She's been through so much that it takes one hell of a lot to rock her boat.

When I woke up, I began to see the funny side of last night's events. 'Bing banged my lula,' I sang to myself. Hey, we were not only going to Sarah's to administer the herbs, we were going for a band practice as well.

I ran myself a hot bath filled with soothing oils, jammed the extractor fan closed for maximum steam and indulged. I felt I deserved it. A few potential lyrics wormed their way around my head. 'Bing went wrong, with a big bong! I said goodbye and thought it was strange . . .'

Sing away my troubles, what could be better therapy?

Out of the bath, and in altogether better spirits, I rang around the others to make a plan. Sharon had decided to come with Conka on Saturday morning. She made up some lame excuse – as if I didn't know that she was planning some Trevor escapade or other. Tasha would come with me and bring her herbs.

We left straight after school, the worst time traffic-wise, and ended up being stuck in jams for hours. Still, I was desperate to get out of town, to run away from my life, to turn my back on all my silly troubles. The sooner I could forget about last night's fiasco the better.

Eventually we plopped out of the boiling pot of pollution into the freer, greener roads towards Sarah's. It was just getting dark when I finally switched off the engine and took my first breath of sweet country air – delicious.

Sarah greeted us with open arms and, sure enough, I could smell the preparations for an excellent dinner.

Tasha went straight to the kitchen and began to brew her broth. It was a concoction she had invented, using her vast mental store of flower remedies, Chinese herbal medicine and homeopathy all with potential contra-indicative qualities, to bring on one's period. The revolting tea 'induces the womb to cleanse itself, thus relinquishing one's conception naturally,' she intoned. Well, put like that, it sounded much more reasonable than t' 'termination' in t' clinic.

I had experienced Tasha's remedies myself. On one occasion my period had been a few days late and she gave me this very tea. It tasted just as revolting too. Sixteen hours later, my womb wasn't just cleansing itself, it was having a bleeding fireworks display. Anyway, I'd much rather do it that way than have to go to hospital and get depressed and all that. But I was never sure whether my period was just a few days late or if I was actually pregnant.

On another occasion I was suffering from a strange jittery condition. I assumed it was combination of too much coffee and a dire lack of sex. Tasha, however, pointed out that it could be an 'aura-contamination' situation. She prescribed eight drops of crabapple oil in a hot bath, in which I should remain for exactly eight minutes. After total immersion I had to ensure that I was totally out of the bath before I removed the plug, so that aura re-contamination was avoided. I got a bit worried at that point, as my plug had lost its chain. However, I followed witch Tasha's advice and, apart from getting a little overexcited about the time-keeping, which resulted in me dropping my non-waterproof watch in the bath several times, it was very relaxing. Eight minutes in the bath turned out to be quite a long time. Afterwards, I really did feel less jittery, my aura seemed marvellously clean and, I'd say, another success. I had great faith in Tasha's remedies. They had worked for me.

I helped persuade Sarah to gulp back this piss-awful stuff. She pulled her face around with every mouthful, so much so that she began to remind me of a Mervyn Peake drawing. But this hallucination was probably exaggerated by the quality of the Northern Lights we were smoking. I killed myself as I watched her drink: she turned the corners of her mouth down so far they practically fell off her face; her eyes were screwed up so tightly that her bags disappeared; and she did this strange Riverdance jig round the room, flinging her head from side to side, and sounding like an elephant being fist-fucked by his mate. I cried, and Tasha lectured her in an attempted soothing voice. I was feeling so much better.

Once the first dose of tea had been consumed, Sarah quietened down a bit and we all finished preparing dinner; or, rather, Sarah did, while Tasha got the kids' drinks and I got the adults'.

Dinner was delicious – a pasta sensation. Sarah wasn't well off and, for some reason, at dinner times I was always reminded of that biblical story in which a few cod and loaves of bread went miles. I loved Sarah's cooking. During dinner the boys got it into their heads that they wanted to sleep in the tent in the garden that night. I recalled doing exactly that with my sister when we were small – it was always a good crack. So Supermum Sarah organised all that. I flopped on the sofa and drifted off, again being the victim of my hangover. I really should remember that I couldn't handle drink.

*

95

It was the sleepy, casual mornings that I particularly loved at Sarah's. The warm morning sun shone brightly through the large french windows that opened on to the back garden. The smell of the rich green lawn soaking up its morning dew wafted through the air. The rabbit nibbled playfully at the still sleepy cat. Everyone mushed around in their sleeping attire taking cups of sweet tea to one another, snuggling under the cosy duvets, chatting or watching morning telly.

By about eleven everyone had had breakfast and we were all getting dressed – except for Tasha and Sarah. Tasha was trying to persuade Sarah to have her second, all-important dose. As I dressed, I knew she had succeeded because I heard the now familiar sound of Sarah's elephant impersonation.

At twelve, the noise of a car crunching along the driveway came resonating into the kitchen, where us mums were drinking coffee and smoking. The three of us made a beeline to the small kitchen window, straining to see who it was. We saw a manky yellow Cortina kangaroo up the drive. As we didn't recognise the car, we thought it must have the wrong place but, as it got nearer, we realised that it contained none other than Conka the Conqueror and Sharon the Shambles.

'My God!' I exclaimed. 'I gave her one lesson and now she's driving with another non-driver. What the fuck is going on?'

'It looks to me like they're having a bit of a barney,' Sarah remarked.

The car was nearly at the house, but not yet parked, when it jerked to a standstill. We giggled as we watched the pair of them waggle their fingers at each other, obviously arguing intently.

'You pair of evil cows. Making them come in the same car!'

'We didn't,' Tasha and I sang in unison.

Sarah knew of the friction between Sharon and Conka. She'd witnessed them arguing before, and responded by giggling quietly to herself, every so often muttering a refusal to get involved.

'What's Conka getting all that stuff out for?' Sarah asked.

No one had actually bothered to run the band-practice idea past Sarah, but she'd be cool. Conka had parked and was unloading the tatty second-hand and borrowed amps, leads and dodgy guitars that vaguely resembled the band equipment.

'And why is Sharon staying in the car?'

'Conka probably told her she was stopping for petrol.'

'Charlie!' Sarah scolded me, as Conka came steaming into the kitchen.

'Hey, Conka, you've left one of your bags in the car.'

'Charlie!'

Mrs Diplomat, Tasha wandered off to entice the stubborn, sulking Sharon out of the car. Liam and Helena wasted no time and had already disappeared into the garden to find the other kids. I wanted to discover exactly how Conka had got behind the wheel of this strange Cortina.

'Who's car is it, then, eh?'

Conka gave me that, 'What-can-I-say? What-can-I-do?' kind of face, smiling at me all the time. Instead of answering me, she turned her attention to Sarah. 'How's Sarah, then?'

She gave her a powerful hug. Sarah yelped like a small dog whose paw has just been smashed. Conka's automatic, self-defensive reflex to this was to fling Sarah away from her almost as violently as she'd hugged her in the first place.

'Blimey! Steady on, Conks. You don't know your own strength sometimes. Sarah's very fragile at the moment.'

Sarah regained her balance, sat down and held her stomach. Conka was leaping around her not knowing what to do.

'Oh, Sarah, I forgot. I'm sorry.'

'It's not your fault. I just had a really sharp pain in my stomach, but it seems to have gone now.' Although she looked pale, she stood up and started moving around.

'Are you sure, Sarah? Are you all right?' I asked.

'Yeah. Strange, though. Maybe it's the herbs beginning to work. Let's have some more coffee.'

Sarah began busying around the kitchen and seemed as right as rain again, although I don't know what's so bleeding right about rain in the first place. I pursued my line of inquiry. 'So, Con, where did you get the car?'

'I bought it, din' I? I thought Stewart – you know, my driving instructor, well, actually, ex-instructor – was really taking the piss charging me twelve quid a bleeding lesson, then having the bleeding cheek to tell me I need at least twelve. That's nearly a hundred and fifty quid. That's a flight to Spain, my friend. So I told him he was a crap teacher if he needed that bloody long to teach me how to drive. Anyways, I thought as I needed the practice, I'd get a car of my own. Then I can drive around as much as I want, take me test and Bob's yer uncle. Get it?'

Having offered her explanation, Conka hurried out of the room to finish unloading the car and avoid any further interrogation. Oh, yes, I got it all right. Money for those driving lessons added up to a hell of a lot in Conka's financial agenda. She was never flush enough on the ole spondoolicks front to be able to let go of a whole ton and a half too quick, that's for sure. Plus she always had itchy feet and saw everything in terms of flight tickets. This was just another of her short-cuts.

'What if you have an accident?' I shouted, as she was rushing out of earshot.

She heard me, but pretended she hadn't. Typical.

Tasha finally convinced Sharon to get out of the car. It turned out that Trevor hadn't wanted Sharon spending a couple of nights with the all-single-mum gang. He knew we'd slag him off big-time and he was right. He had convinced Sharon that we were sexually obsessed with him. He was wrong on that one, though. Very wrong.

Conka, apparently, had upset Sharon when she picked her up. The first thing Conka said to her was to leave the Trevor-fucker, if only 'cause he was giving her 'bad eye bags'. This struck a nerve, as only that night Trevor had been saying that Conka, specifically, had been flirting with him. Astounding! It would be easier to imagine Conka ice-skating naked in a firestorm than flirting with him. But Sharon refused to believe that anyone could not find him attractive. It sounded to me like he painted a pretty glamorous picture of himself. Evidently, they had been up all night arguing and probably shagging as well. Sharon looked like shite and Conka had merely pointed out the obvious.

'Oh, Charlie, it's so hard. I hate fucking men,' Sharon moaned.

'Huh, you hate men! Look what happened to me,' I said.

'Oh, come on, Charlie. That was a bit different. That was a one-nighter.'

'So? I had a man go for me like a flaming bee on dung, he gets me as horny as hell and when I mention condoms, he goes floppy, angry, bright red and freaky, and behaves as if I'm a piece of shit, like it was my fault. Fucker.'

Sarah laughed. Conka came back in and winked.

'You see, it's totally different for you, Charlie,' Sharon whined.

'Why? When I try and pull, I fuck up and don't even get shagged,' I protested. Conka giggled. I ignored her. 'Whereas you at least get shagged.'

'Yeah, but what if he doesn't love me and is having an affair? Anyway you've got your makeup work. At least you get to meet some interesting people.'

'Fuck off, Sharon. You know most of the work I do is with stiffs.'

Conka threw me a glance.

'I thought you said he'd gone floppy,' Sarah said.

'Very funny, Sarah. Sharon's trying to make out she's worse off than me.'

'I'm not!' Sharon shouted.

'Well, start appreciating your shags, then, and stop whingeing,' I snapped.

I'd had enough. We had to try and pull ourselves out of this rut and, so far, forming a band seemed the sanest suggestion.

I walked off, practising some scales. Much to my chagrin, the cat fucking ran away from me when I started.

17

'Okay, guys,' I hooted enthusiastically. 'Let's have a brainstorming session!'

We had accumulated once more in the kitchen. Everyone had calmed down a bit, this morning's adventures having been well and truly dissected and discussed, mainly by Tasha and Sharon. I was dying to get rehearsing.

'Okay, guys. Let's go!' I tried again.

I think I would have felt better if they'd pretended they hadn't heard me rather than get the reaction I got. They stopped chatting momentarily, looked at me as if I was completely mad, then carried on exactly where they had left off.

I looked at Conka for help. She was pretending to listen to Tasha's predictions of the bodily pains that Sarah would be feeling over the next day or so. She knew I was watching her. Sharon was telling Sarah about the time she went in for a termination and ended up coming out of hospital with all kinds of non-specific viruses.

I could tell Conka wasn't interested in any of this and was itching to play. Or itching for something. She looked at me from over Tasha's shoulder, and I thought how terribly foxy she was. The adrenaline rush she'd got from driving all the way in the new car had left her cheeks flushed and her eyes sparkling. I guess I was just giving her a searching, pupil-dilating look when we were distracted by another loud, pained yelp from Sarah.

Although Conka had clocked my stare, we both looked at Sarah, who seemed embarrassed. 'What? I'm sorry. It was just another one of those really sharp pains ... they seem to go as quickly as they come. I only make that noise 'cause they really take me by surprise –'

Tasha realised that she had to qualify this symptom. 'Yes. I think that seems pretty normal. I had quite sharp pains when I used this remedy once.'

We all breathed again, including Sarah, who didn't like being the focus of everyone's attention. Wanting to give Sarah a break, and never being one to miss an opportunity, I suggested song-writing again. This time Conka clapped her hands together, thrust a pen and paper in mine and picked up the guitar. As she fingered the strings, the others listened while we went over a few of the lyrics we'd written about my recent fling-flop with Bing. They were pretty silly, really.

Bing Bang, Bing banged my lula,
Bing Bang, Bing banged my lula,
I met Bing, he said he give me a ring,
He called me Joan, and thought it was funny,
We had some fun talking 'bout sausages and honey,
Shut up! Slow down and spend ya money!

Ooe lala, ooe lala, Bing bang, Bing banged my lula.
Bing went wrong with a big bong,
I said goodbye and thought it was strange,
I was on my own thinking 'bout
The birds and the bees and all that honey,
Get up! Go down! And kiss me funny!
Ooe lala, ooe lala. Bing bang. Bing banged my lula.
I was dead, my face was red,
Close to tears, I pierced my ears,
I got my life. He left his wife,
Stone me. Kiss me.
But I was eating the honey . . .

We threw lines in randomly. Conka picked out some kind of tune and somehow we got quite a rocking chorus going. Tasha kept singing in harmony, though, which would have sounded great if I'd stayed in tune but she really put me off. I could tell this was going to be a complicated hurdle to jump. Conka was a good teacher and guided us through our parts – she was in her element – being by far the most experienced. Sharon found instructions from Conka difficult to take and was fluffing all over the place – so much so you'd never have guessed she'd ever played the bass before.

We stopped for lunch at around three thirty. The kids, all starving from rushing around like lorries all morning, stuffed their faces furiously. It was good to see Luke away from the city smog, breathing freely again and eating like a pig. I wished I could move away and give him this suburban lifestyle, get him a puppy and all that.

Everyone began to be excited: Sharon was planning major outfits, Conka was talking of huge record deals and Tasha was busy telling us how amazingly good for you it was to have an organised creative outlet. I felt brilliant. I'd always wanted a group and now I had one. After smoking a couple more joints, we'd convinced ourselves we were the Four Tops of the future. We left Sarah in the kitchen and regrouped in the adjoining garage.

Mayhem would be putting it mildly. As soon as we walked in,

Sharon knocked over a load of metal shelves, sending thousands of little model men flying all over the place. I stopped Sarah from coming in, while everyone else scrambled around on all fours picking them up.

We got the electric guitars strapped on or wired up, or whatever the technical term for it is, miked up and everything. Then it was even louder mayhem. Tasha started picking out 'Stairway to Heaven', and Sharon was responding with a thrash version of 'London's Calling'; I think she was still a bit angry about something. Conka was shouting to everyone to shut up and get it together and I'm afraid my fart-cum-Schwarzenegger impersonations into the microphone weren't really helping. Finally we simmered down and attempted to go through a few numbers.

Although I say it myself, as first attempts go, my voice was sounding pretty fruity. Sharon remembered something at last and worked out a funky bass line to 'Bing Banged' and Tasha did a bit on the keyboards. Conka and I sang. We were even doing a bit of a dance routine. This was looking like it really could work. We were going noisily through it when an amp blew. While Conka was trying to fix things, the rest of us sat silently worn out from our little outburst.

We all heard it at the same time.

The blood rushed away from my face as we froze. A second later, we heard it again. It was Sarah: she sounded like she was being knifed.

I ran into the kitchen, not knowing what to expect. It was horrible. I've never seen anyone look so white, ever. Her lips looked like they'd been painted with white zinc. Her eyes, which were red and flooded with tears, looked as if dark brown eye shadow had been dusted thickly underneath. She was hunched up in the corner, like a terrified wild animal. As I looked down to her hands – away from her haunting stare – I saw the bright, sumptuous, sticky, rich red of fresh blood, and loads of it. Trembling, she pointed beneath her skirt where a lumpy load of blood rested amongst the cat litter. Sarah had miscarried messily – in the fucking cat tray! I picked her up gently and held her thin, frail body as it shook with sobs against mine.

Conka instantly took control: she sent Sharon to fetch a blanket, she rang the hospital to tell them we were coming, she even had the foresight to scoop up everything she thought the doctors would want to see – which also stopped Sarah's hysterics about the cat eating it. She told me to drive Sarah to the hospital with Tasha, as the doctors would want to know exactly what was in the 'tea', while she and Sharon would stay and look after the kids.

Tasha and I virtually carried Sarah, who was still crying and bending over in more spasms of pain, to the car.

I was feeling horribly guilty: I had persuaded Sarah to drink the tea. Tasha felt worse, and kept going on about never seeing a reaction like this before – I think she was secretly shitting herself. Sarah was silent all the way there, except for once when I nearly took the wrong turning, and then she only mumbled. She looked as if she was using all her remaining energy to stop the pain.

Casualty reception was surprisingly empty for a Saturday night. 'Emergency' programmes like *ER* and *Casualty* had led me to believe this was the worst and busiest time. There were certainly no handsome doctors charging through double doors shouting 'Clear!' or 'fifty-eight sillylitres amondionicane, twenty-four flori-flo-biactolene!' Maybe we were still a bit early – the action might start after the pubs shut. Empty or not, it still took about half a frigging hour for the receptionist to look up and acknowledge our presence, let alone send for medical help. After asking us a few essential deeply relevant questions, such as Sarah's National Insurance number – as if she was gonna know that – twit-head-receptionist-bitch-brains then nodded in the direction of some extremely uncomfortable brown plastic chairs, that you wouldn't want to sit on even if you hadn't had a miscarriage – they were haemorrhoid-hell. She then told us to wait until a doctor was available.

I folded and puffed my coat into a makeshift cushion: my pathetic attempt to ease Sarah's pain. I couldn't believe how long we had to wait. There weren't even any other patients to speak of except for the odd drunk coughing, sleeping, spluttering and swearing every so often. Sarah had real recent blood all over herself and fresh stuff was coming by the second. I made her open the blanket she'd cocooned herself in and sat her directly opposite Twit head Dogbreath. Should she ever look up from her Boyzone fanzine, she'd be forced into more of a reaction than we were currently getting.

Sarah couldn't have been paler. I kept leaping up to try to hurry things along, only to be held back by her not wanting to cause a fuss. She said I was embarrassing her enough already and to shut it because with every expletive she laughed, which hurt her. I was just glad to see Sarah laugh again, no matter how much it hurt.

Tasha kept going on about how much she hated hospitals. After I'd ranted on for half an hour, I decided to assume that Sarah was no longer 'compost Memphis' or 'compass mental' (or whatever the expression is), had lost a serious amount of blood, and I made it my business to find out what the fudge was going on.

The overly made-up tart of a receptionist looked at me defiantly while deliberately chewing gum. I leapt up and down and loudly demanded, '*A Doctor!*'

'You'll have to wait like everybody else.'

'What? You mean like those piss-heads over there, who are only in for the free heating? Or are there thousands of other patients here suffering from a strange infuckingvisible disease that only you *can see*?!'

She popped her gum in her mouth, giving me that hugely irritating 'have-you-quite-finished look. I wanted to head-butt her.

'I thought this was where you came in emergencies. There's absolutely nothing *emergent* about *you* what-so-fucking-ever! I haven't seen you ring anyone, apart from your mate Doreen. I haven't seen you do anything at all to aid my friend's agonising pain. I WANT A DOCTOR!'

She popped her gum. 'I think you should calm down,' she said coolly.

'*I want a doctor!*' I shouted, slamming my fist on her table.

She wasn't even looking at me now. I followed her stare around to the others and saw a young doctor talking quietly to Tasha and Sarah. God knows how long he'd been there.

'I'm afraid you'll have to wait,' he told me.

'I'm not the patient, for Chrissake!'

'She's with me,' Sarah muttered. She was obviously too embarrassed to have told him before. He looked terrified of me, but tried a brief smile. I sat down and felt like a complete neuron for a few moments – but not for long, as I started observing Dr Gorgelove.

He really *was* tasty, and didn't Tasha know it? Things were beginning to resemble the TV dramas after all, which would mean that this gorgeous one should be a paediatrician. Tasha turned on the old Bambi eyes and allowed her short skirt to ride even higher. She began to explain the contents of the tea to the doctor, pouting between every double edged word, 'Well, the pennyroyal and rue are particularly known for stimulating the *womb.*'

She nearly kissed him when she said 'womb'. She sounded kind of French and allowed the pout to linger that weeny, naughty bit longer. Her eyes were undressing him, and he was loving it. He had far more interest in what was in Tasha's knickers than in Sarah's, that was for sure.

Meanwhile, Sarah was doubled over in her chair – in the only comfortable position that she could find – with her mop of straggly, streaky hair tumbling down and hiding her face. Tired of waiting for any more appropriate painkiller, she was attempting to light a fag. I thought she was going to burn her hair. I was also convinced that there was absolutely no smoking, for real, in medical establishments. But the doctor didn't seem to be objecting – I don't think he even noticed.

He had lovely hands, though. I find so many doctors do. His were strong and elegant, with long, slender fingers that made generous motions when he spoke. His voice was gentle and deep, with an occasional stutter. He had thick brown wavy hair, slightly too long, which he allowed to fall across his dark eyes. He was about my height (five foot nine), and had good, broad shoulders. He was sitting with his legs crossed, resting his bony elbow on his knee and his carved Superman chin in his hand. I noticed he wrote with his left hand – both Tasha and I are left-handed – and I liked that. He'd peer from under his fringe, gazing at this seductress, falling under her potent spell, losing himself in Tasha's clear amber eyes.

'But, Doctor, I've taken this tea *myself*, you know . . .'

I couldn't believe it. My – sorry, *our* – friend was about to faint, Tasha was hitting on the doctor big time, and all he could do was stare at her. I had to intervene.

'Doctor! Hello! Are you going to do anything? Or would you and Tasha care for a couple of vodka-oranges and some condoms instead?'

'*Charlie!* Ow!'

'Now look what's happened!'

Sarah had laughed so violently when I mentioned the condoms that she'd fallen off her chair. At least Adonis had now jumped into action. Tasha caught my eye. I winked and gave her the thumbs-up. He was pretty damned hot in his white coat and stethoscope.

'It doesn't look like the porter's going to make it with the wheelchair. Do you think you can manage to walk a bit?'

Sarah nodded. The doctor took her cigarette and stubbed it out on the floor. He and I took one arm each while Tasha walked behind – dangerously close to him.

After a giggle-repressing lift journey, where I really did think I was going to wet myself as Tasha kept miming blow-jobs behind the doc's back, we finally entered a ward. The doctor laid Sarah on a bed and pulled the curtain round.

'If you could just put this on,' he said, 'I'll get my chart.'

'What's he reading his star signs now for?' I whispered, in mock-horror.

'He didn't mean that kind of chart, Charlie,' Tasha retorted defensively.

Wow! Already Tasha was so wrapped up in him that she couldn't tell when I was joking. This was serious. And that was a bad joke. We helped Sarah out of her clothes and into one of those ridiculous hospital gowns that shows your arse.

'What are you doing?' I whispered to Tasha.

She merely sighed and grinned, lost in dirty-doctor thoughts.

'Can you believe her, Sarah? She wants to do the doc! She'll want to become a nurse next.'

Tasha looked at me like that wasn't such a bad idea. Oh dear.

'*Shh!* These curtains don't block out sound as well, you know,' Sarah croaked.

Tasha left me to sort Sarah out while she checked her mascara and did her lips. Here was a girl always prepared.

'Reckon he's got a big'un, then, Tasha?'

'Shut up, Charlie! You're making Sarah laugh,' Tasha said, but all the time vigorously nodding.

'Yeah, me too. He's got a massive nose,' I said.

The doc came back in, walking pretty tall. Who cared if he'd heard us?

'I think you two young ladies should go and wait in Reception now. I'll call you if I need you . . . Actually, maybe you should stay.' He nodded to Tasha. 'I may need some more info on those herbs.'

Great. Tasha gets to stay 'cause he may need some more info – like her phone number. And I get to go and play psychopath ping-pong with my new friend on Reception. On my own.

'Well, maybe I should stay and hold Sarah's hand,' I pleaded.

'That's okay, thanks. I think we've got someone here who'll be more than able to do that,' he said, staring intensely at Tasha.

I might as well not have been there.

'Isn't she going to be holding yours?' I asked.

He answered with a nod to the gap in the curtains.

'I meant your hand,' I quipped, as I backed off. 'See you later, Sarah.'

Back on the hard brown plastic I fidgeted for the next couple of hours, waiting for their return. The day's string of events had definitely taken my mind off my worries. Fuck Bing backwards.

I waited and waited. I rang Conka, everything was A okay over there. I sat down again. The hateful receptionist had been relieved by a nice one. She was older, didn't wear so much makeup and seemed infinitely more caring than the other. She showed me the coffee machine. I was grateful and up for a chat, but she seemed pretty engrossed in her work. I guess she had a lot of catching up to get on with, what with going on duty after Dim Brains and all. I left her alone and stared at the ceiling. I thought about my old schoolfriend who's a nurse and then nothing much at all. I craved a joint, or at least I craved sharing one with Conks. After that, I suppose I just felt lonely again.

Eventually Tasha appeared. Sarah was going to stay the night, she was fine now and could probably go home but, for safety's sake, the doc would rather we picked her up in the morning.

We were tired, so didn't really talk much. Tasha had made some definite headway (so to speak) with the doc. He was gorgeous and she was falling in love. I gave her my bog-standard all-doctors-are-arseholes-even-if-they-do-have-nice-hands speech, but apart from that, it was a silent journey.

By the time we got back, Sharon had left, the kids were in bed and Conka was playing the guitar. She made us tea, got some biscuits and rolled a joint. It wasn't long before everybody headed wearily off to bed. I cuddled my warm, sleeping Luke. He was someone whose love for me was assured and that made me feel good. Then he farted – fantastic.

18

Sharon had intended to stay the whole weekend at Sarah's but when she found herself alone with Conka again, she couldn't wait to get the hell out of there. The journey back to Shepherd's Bush was torture. She didn't know which was worse: Conka's dangerous driving or England's public-transport system. Plus it was freezing: the October wind had a February bite, announcing the beginning of dark, cold evenings and fucking heating bills. She hated herself for it, but by the time the eighth bus had gone past Conka won. At least her crap Cortina had heating. By the time the twelfth bus passed, Sharon was ready to go back to Sarah's. It was only then that she realised they'd been standing at the wrong bus stop, although this was hardly surprising, with Liam going on at her the whole time.

'*Liam!*' she shouted. 'Will you STOP IT! How can you expect me to get us home with you *pulling at my bloody sleeve*?'

She yanked his arm off hers, causing her sleeve to rip. 'Now look what you've done! You *idiot*!' She went to slap him, but he ducked.

'I hate you!' Liam screamed, as he threw a strong punch at her arm.

'*Ow! Liam! Stop it!*' She grabbed hold of his wrists and was about to lunge a verbal sword at him, when she saw a number 151 come around the corner.

'Oh, I'm sorry, darling. Come on, Peanut, eh?' She held his face close to hers and gave him a cheeky smile, 'Come on. Let's make a run for it. That must be the stop – down there.'

She grabbed the bags and started racing down the road, with Liam running excitedly after her. They were both long-legged runners and it was a fair way, but Liam loved sprinting. One day he'd be faster than his mother and when she was fifteen she had run for the county. They were flying.

Liam and Sharon just made it before the doors closed. London bus drivers are terrorists: they can see you running, frantically waving at them, but if your foot ain't on that step after they've given the last person their ticket, the doors close – even if you're banging on the side of the vehicle. Sharon wasn't taking any chances. They weren't *that* far out of central London and she wasn't going to be fooled by any happy-looking green buses. Liam knew the routine and was on it like a whippet out of a trap.

'That was some run, eh, Peanut?'

'Yeah,' Liam answered, not knowing whether he was still in trouble about his mum's shirt or not.

'It warmed me up,' Sharon said, wiping her forehead.

Liam wasn't saying anything.

'Look, I'm sorry, Peanut, I didn't mean to shout at you. If I buy you some football stickers later, will you promise to be a good boy when we get home?'

'I don't want to go home, Mum. I thought we were going to stay at Sarah's. What am I going to do now?' He stared angrily out the window. 'Mum, I'm hungry.'

'Oh, Liam.' She rummaged around in her bag and pulled out a half-eaten, manky bar of chocolate.

'I don't want that!' Liam snapped, when she offered it to him. 'It's that weird chocolate.'

Sharon looked at it and noticed it was for diabetics. Why the fuck had she bought that? 'Well, you'll just have to wait until we get home. I can't exactly go and get a pizza or something right now, can I?'

'Oh, yes! Pizza! I love pizza! Can we get it as soon as we get off the bus?'

'Liam, I didn't say we were going to have pizza.'

'Oh, Mum –' Liam looked as if he was about to cry. Sharon couldn't afford to splash out on pizza, but she didn't know what there was at home – probably nothing as usual. She'd even run out of her small emergency stock of pastas and beans. She'd decided not to do any big shops until Trevor gave her her money. He was the one who ate everything anyway.

'MUM!' Liam interrupted her thoughts. 'I'm hungry.'

'I know.' She looked at him. She knew he was a pain in the arse but he had the sweetest face. 'Okay, we'll get pizza.'

Liam threw his arms around Sharon's neck. 'Can we get ice-cream as well?'

'All right, all right.'

'Yes, yes!'

For the remainder of the journey back they had a laugh together. A couple of old ladies were sitting directly in front of them, and Liam stuck torn-off pieces of his bus ticket in their overly sprayed bluish hair. Sharon began to mimic their voices – they were talking nonsense about someone's nephew anyway.

Once off the bus, Sharon bought the promised pizza but didn't have enough money for ice-cream as well. Liam was miserable. They argued during the short walk to the flat, by which time Sharon had promised to go out again and get him some ice-cream with some of the electricity money from the jar – as long as he was good.

When they walked in they got a shock. Trevor had totally redecorated the living room and it looked fantastic.

'Wow!' Sharon stammered. 'Hi, Trev. What have you done?'

As he walked over to kiss them, she noticed flecks of paint on his cheeks. He looked remarkably handsome.

'You're back. I didn't expect you until at least tomorrow night – I wanted to finish the whole place.' He picked Liam up. 'Hi there. Is that *pizza* I smell?'

Liam giggled and wriggled until Trevor finally let him go.

Then, after giving Sharon a quick hug, he chased Liam around in his mock grisly giant mode, incredibly hungry for little boys and *pizza*! Sharon looked on in awe. She loved Trevor when he was like this, Liam loved him too, and the flat looked beautiful. He'd moved a couple of mirrors around and, with the pale lilac paint, the place seemed a lot bigger, certainly fresher. Maybe things would be all right again.

I woke up to Luke and Sarah's boy Arthur playing *Husky and Touch*, their variation of *Starsky and Hutch*. This involved a lot of rolling around on the floor and not a lot else. Neither of them seemed quite sure of what they were supposed to be doing and, when they asked me, I confused them even more by suggesting they wrote a crass pop song, just like the original Hutch.

Tasha was already up and had got the coffee on. I could smell it. I shouted for a cup. A couple of minutes later, Conka shouted down for one. About ten minutes later I gave up waiting, got up and fetched my own goddamned coffee. Tasha was putting the finishing touches to her delicate makeup near the kitchen window, right next to the coffee. She was looking bright-eyed, bonny and ready to go.

'God, what time did you get up, then?' I inquired.

'Oh, I woke really early this morning.'

'Thanks for the coffee.'

'Do you like these trousers with this top?' she asked me, ignoring my sarcasm.

She twirled round, then posed, giving me the look over her shoulder, a sticking-out-the-bum-up-on-tippytoes number. Then a view from the right side. Then straight on, with her head always cocked to one side. I tried to think about the top and trousers, but instead thought that Tasha was way too thin, and should stick to baggier clothes or, better still, put on a bit of weight.

'You look great,' I told her. 'Except you need to put on some weight.'

Tasha stuck out her pathetic attempt of a tummy as far as possible. 'God – I think I look *really* bloated.'

It was still too early for me to be polite and pleasant, so I got a coffee for me and Conka, as Madam was still shouting for it, and went upstairs. She always managed to wangle her own way, somehow, even if it meant waiting half an hour. The cocky bastard was lying on her back staring at the ceiling with her hands folded behind her head, looking deep in thought, patient and pensive. She knew I'd turn up soon enough with nice hot coffee.

'Your coffee, Madam.'

Conka looked pretty good in the mornings, even though her hair was greasy and sticking up everywhere. Her skin looked shiny and fresh, and mine never did first thing. Sometimes she really annoyed me.

She took the cup. 'Cheers, darlin'. You know, you'd make someone a lovely husband one day.'

I gave her an insincere grimace back, feeling more like the downtrodden wife than any lovely husband. I didn't even know those two words could go together. Conka was more like the cheesy, bossy husband, largeing it in her plush double bed waiting to be served. She slurped her coffee and ignored my hurt look. 'What do you think about this, then? Why don't we do a slot down the K on a Thursday night?'

I walked off. I couldn't believe she was planning gigs when we hadn't even got one song done. 'Ha!' I shouted back.

She hadn't even thanked me for the coffee.

'We'd only have to do two songs!' Conka called down to me.

'Tuh! Men!' I huffed, under my breath.

I couldn't believe that she was thinking about the band at all, that early in the morning, let alone planning gigs. And there was me, about to iron her shirt, playing the role of a fifties housewife, for fuck's sake. What a flaming bunch of lunatics!

I found Tasha still in the kitchen, having an eyebrow-plucking session.

'We should go and pick up Sarah, Charlie.'

'Did you phone the hospital?'

'Yeah. She's fine and ready to go.'

'Okay. I'll just get dressed, and then I'll go and get her.'

I knew Tasha was dying to come to the hospital so she could see her fancy man.

'I'll come with you.'

'No, don't worry. Sarah won't need both of us now. You relax.'

Tasha cocked her head to one side and looked me straight in the eye, watching for a sign that I was mucking around.

'Maybe you could do the kids' breakfast?' I suggested helpfully.

Tasha screwed up her eyes even more, still not saying anything. I looked at her and started smiling. I couldn't keep this up for ever, although part of me wanted her to restrain herself a little. She had the habit of falling too far, too quickly; of spending too much time wondering about the man in view then getting badly let down. Let the guy call you up and find you, I wanted to tell her. Let him make the effort. Then you know that he is attracted to you enough to make some kind of giving gesture (unless of course, you're going for the straight-shag thing).

'You really like the doc, don't you? You crazy dirty mother!' I accused her.

A broad grin grew across Tasha's face.

'Okay, okay, you can come, as long as you break the news to Conka that she's left with the kids – again.'

'Oh, thanks, Charlie. Conka will be fine.'

I got dressed, and Tasha skipped off.

'I am ready to receive a warm and caring relationship,' Tasha said, to her reflection in the bathroom mirror. 'I am open and caring. I am beautiful and loving. I am open to receive a warm and caring relationship.'

She stretched her arms up and exhaled loudly as she brought her hands down, all the while concentrating on that thought, the doctor and herself as one, all the while staring into her reflected eyes. She had known the minute she had seen Dr Gorgelove that good things were coming her way. He had had an excellent aura. She wondered if they'd known each other in a past life.

'Come on, Tasha!' Charlie shouted.

'Coming!' she replied. Oh, yes, she was definitely coming. Her new life was just beginning.

Ten minutes later we were nearly at the hossie. Tasha was fidgeting like mad all the way there. She always does when she's on maximum horny-warp drive, mega-thrust city; a condition she works herself into whenever there's a specific target for her desires – a potential plug for her socket.

'Calm down, Tasha. He might not even be there, you know. I'm sure they'll have swapped shifts by now.'

Tasha looked at me in complete horror. She had reckoned on him being there for sure.

'Doctors aren't nine-to-fivers. You know that, Tash.'

She was still looking a bit distraught. Blimey! This was exactly why she should slow down and not marry them mentally and have three kids all on a first meeting.

I tried to distract her. 'I'm hoping to see that bitch-face receptionist being wheeled into casualty and no-one paying her attention, so that I could say something highly annoying like "Bad karma, man." '

By the time we got to the ward Tasha was positively depressed. We'd got lost deliberately at least three times – in case the doctor was in another part of the hospital – and had covered pretty much the whole place. I drew the line at the morgue. I'd had enough of those. It's where I'd look if Tasha *had* shagged him – she was so voracious – but she hadn't yet. There was no sign of him anywhere. In fact, I didn't recognise anyone at all. Everyone looked completely different. Even Sarah was rosier in the cheeks and I could see her eyes again, so she must have stopped crying and slept at some point.

'I didn't know the patients did shifts as well. You're looking like an altogether different woman, Sarah.'

I bent over and kissed her cheek. Although she still looked tired, I could tell she was almost ready to have a good laugh about the whole thing.

'Hi, girls. Well, Tasha, you're off the hook as far as attempted poison goes.'

'I knew those herbs alone couldn't have done that. What did he say?'

Tasha went a bit dreamy when she said 'he'. She was dying to talk about *him*, to find out if *he* had said *anything* at all that would suggest he was up for it with her.

Sarah smiled. 'Apparently I had some kind of sticking ovaries and a rupture or something,' she explained, 'and it must have been bad before I took the herbs, as this sort of thing doesn't usually happen overnight. If anything, they may have helped a bit.'

'Where is the doctor?' Tasha asked, pacing up and down the length of the bed.

Sarah stood up slowly and put on her clean clothes. 'Do you mean Dr Gorgelove? Or should I say Largeglove?' Sarah said, wiggling her tongue at me.

'Is he here or not?' Even I was getting excited at the prospect of ogling at him again.

Tasha was practically delirious, still poncing and pacing around, unable to keep still; she could probably smell reminders of him everywhere.

'He's gone now. He *was* here, until about five minutes ago. Then he gave up waiting.'

Ashen would be the word to describe her face. I really thought Tasha was about to keel over on hearing this.

Sarah noticed too. 'Don't worry, Tasha, he's got my number. He lives nearby and when he heard you were staying with me for the next day or so – you know you can't leave the hospital unless you've got another adult to look after you – he offered to do my home visit himself. It all seems remarkably efficient for the NHS, but I think it's got something to do with wanting to see you again . . .'

Tasha's face came back to life. 'What else did he say, Sarah? Sarah? What time did he say he was coming?'

Sarah was now fully dressed, and as we headed for the car park she just laughed with every question. She'd given Tasha enough information for now and really didn't have the inclination to go on about the doctor any more.

'I can't stop laughing because your beau has been medically doing things to me and *mine* that you would love in a non-medical way,' she said, wiggling her index finger, eyebrows raised.

'You – lucky – bitch!' was all Tasha could say, in between gulps and coughs mixed with hysterical laughter. She obviously hadn't thought of it like that before.

19

I could tell by the look on Conka's face that a mini disaster had happened while we were gone. I took a quick look round to try to see what she'd broken. 'Everything all right, Conks?' I asked.

She grinned at me then turned her attention to the patient. 'How's Sarah?'

She gave her a gentle hug, sat her down in the living room and went to make some tea. I followed her into the kitchen.

'What happened?' I whispered to her, once out of ear shot.

Conka bit her bottom lip to keep her giggles at bay. 'Well, let's just say, I suffered a seizure at the time and thought I'd be coming to the hospital myself – for shock treatment, you know.'

She let me take over the tea-making, while she rolled a joint to accompany her story. I was already grinning – whenever Conka used the 'seizure' word, it was always mad. She licked a cigarette open, tipped the tobacco into the papers and giggled again. 'I pulled the gerbil's tail off.'

'What?' I spluttered.

'Not deliberately! It was an accident, weren' it?' She looked at me, shaking her head, unable to go on explaining this recent nightmare while she rolled the spliff.

This was a first for me. I'd never heard of someone pulling off a gerbil's tail before. While Sarah's away, the gerbil plays and gets his tail chopped off by the sitter. I was beginning to see a Bobbit-style reconstruction. 'How'd it happen, Conks?'

Conka was losing herself in the memory of it all, taking serious pulls on the joint she was now smoking – or should that be vacuuming, she was sucking so hard? She blew out smoke for about five minutes – boy, did she have some lung capacity – engulfing the room in clouds of the familiar pungent smoke.

'Well, I thought I'd do Sarah a good turn, you know, and clean out all the pets. It's a lot for her, what with the rabbits, the cat, the fish, the booboos and the gaggas. I thought it'd be nice 'n' helpful.'

I nodded at her to go on, noting that I was standing with my legs crossed, just in case there was a possibility that I was going to wet myself.

'Anyway, when I was doing the gerbil's cage, for some reason the gerbil was scared of me and shot into the kitchen-roll tube. Well, I thought I could help it out . . .'

She was cracking up, shaking the hand that had been left with a tail in it, as if she could still feel it on her palm.

'What did you *do* with it?' I asked.

I was beginning to squirm. I've never been big on rodents and the thought of touching the tail of one was revolting enough, let alone have it come off in my hand. Yuck!

'I thought it'd just slip out. It got in there swiftly enough.' She looked at me, still shaking her head and raising her eyebrows. 'But the bloody thing was well and truly stuck. I couldn't believe it. So, anyways, I pull a bit harder but not very hard. I mean, you would have thought the tail was just Sellotaped on, the way it came off so easily. It was suddenly in my hand – on its own!'

I couldn't hold back the howls of laughter any longer.

'And the bloody thing was still stuck in the tube, so I had to cut it out. That's why there's kitchen bloody roll everywhere. I had to unravel all the paper. Well, I couldn't cut through it, could I?'

'You didn't give it the old Cleopatra roll across the room, did you?'

I could tell by her giggles that that was exactly what she'd done. She wouldn't want to waste a load of Sarah's kitchen roll. She'd probably convinced herself that the gerbil would enjoy it, and that it might spin out in the process.

'Once I'd got the paper off, I had to try and cut the tube, so I could get the rat out. The tube was a really hard one as well. It must have been one of those double-recycled-megadon things or something. Anyways, in the process I accidentally gave Gerby-babe a bit of a trim.'

Well, this would surely take Sarah's mind off any post-miscarriage blues. Sure enough, Sarah and Tasha heard us laughing and were calling for us to hurry up with the tea and tell them what it was all about.

'What did you do with the tail?' I whispered, desperate to hear the end of the story.

'Ate it, mate.'

'You are *revolting*! Is the gerbil all right?'

'The gerbil's fine, better than ever. It just falls over a lot.'

'Oh, no! Conka . . .'

But she was already making her way out of the kitchen, to join the others.

As anticipated, the gerbil story facilitated Sarah's recovery, although she did go slightly pale now and then. That story and others, the tea, the smoke and the jokes between the four of us took us through that afternoon and gave Sarah the rest and love she needed. Though I never did find out what Conka did with Gerby-babe's tail.

It was nearing Dr Gorgelove's call time, and Tasha had begun her tribal horn dance. She begged Conka and me to go out man-hunting for ourselves. She wanted rid of us, knowing that we'd blow her cool in front of the doc.

We didn't go far; it never really mattered much where we went. Drink, combined with being free from childcare, resulted in me feeling naughty but fruity and guilty, as if I were skiving. I'm sure I've been subliminally brought up Catholic, maybe Jewish, I feel guilty so often. Still, now we were out, we were going to enjoy ourselves, so we went down the road to the local pub, where we knew they had a skittles table.

We ordered a couple of drinks, while everybody stared at us. It was one of those pubs, slightly off the beaten track, where only the same twenty-five people ever go. If, by some fluke, someone different walks in, then, brother, does that give some waves. If I'd been in America I'd have called them rednecks, but as we were in Middlesex even that seemed too flattering. We opted for pink-throats, after debating quietly for a couple of minutes and going through some names that would have *really* suited them – the kind that get you into sticky situations if overheard.

Most of the customers, locals or regulars, or whatever you call them, were male. There were only two or three other women in the pub: one extremely fat lady who dribbled from her shiny bottom lip and drank pints, and one younger skinny woman with long, greasy brown hair, who smoked roll-ups and played pool. The men were no better: they were either grossly overweight in the protruding-belly region, or stick thin with sloping shoulders and no bums. They all looked unhealthy and smelly, although we didn't get near enough to any of them to have a conclusive sniff.

'Fucking fantastic hunting ground this is, innit, Conks?'

'They could do with a good scrub down, a hair wash, and a clean set of nicely pressed clothes. Then some of them wouldn't seem half as bad, you know, Charlie.'

It was true. Normal guys, these days, English guys anyway, really don't seem to give a shit about how they present themselves. If they were half-way ugly in the first place, their total lack of style polished them off a treat.

'They could at least pull their jeans up,' I said.

'Maybe we should quickly whip round and pull 'em all up for them. What do you think, Charl?'

'I think you could have a valid point, Conks.'

We surveyed the room. Giving them all a grand wedgie would certainly entertain us for a bit.

'But there's so much more that needs doing.'

'Yeah, Chas. I know what you mean.' Conka shook her head despairingly as she looked around. 'Even if we gave them a shave and introduced them to modern-day things like deodorant, we'd still have a long way to go . . .'

'I was thinking more along the lines of brain surgery for the whole bloody lot of them, Con.'

'I hear you, Cha.'

After we'd slagged them all off again, we played a game of skittles. We chatted about the band and the chances of it ever really happening. Conka was more optimistic than me, although she pointed out the importance of enjoying it at the time rather than worrying too much about the future. 'Enjoy the journey and don't worry about the destination,' she said wisely.

But I felt a need to be independent. I didn't like having to scavenge around and watch what I was spending the whole frigging time. I wanted to be in as much control as possible, materialistically; to allow room for the creative, spiritual and emotional sides of me to grow. Until I was in a comfortable safe position, I felt I couldn't be completely happy. But, then, maybe you're never completely happy.

Conka was forever ducking and diving, but she seemed happy. Things weren't any easier for her, except that her mum helped her out with Helena now and then but, unlike me, she never seemed fazed or panicked by any of it.

'You remind me a bit of Thighs Lightning, or whatever she's called – you know from *Gladiators*,' I told her.

'Oh yeah, why's that, then?'

Conka looked me right in the eye. She was strong but relaxed in her tracksuit bottoms and skinny blue T-shirt. You could see her toned arm muscles and, through her tracksuit, the shape of her legs. She had strong thighs and sharp knees, and you could just see a small area of belly, tanned and flat – everything was toned. She continued to smile at me. She made me a little nervous.

'It's your combined mental and physical strength, I suppose, which adds up to something representative of a gladiator,' I answered, grinning.

'I tell you what, them girls d'in' 'arf 'ave big biceps.'

'So do you, Conka. So do you.'

'Well, you're pretty strong yourself, Charl.'

As she made a space on the table I realised an arm-wrestle was in the offing.

'Come on, then, Charbar. Let's see whose got ze muscles zen.'

Now, I'm strong. I used to swim a lot, carry heavy weights, and other things all add to my strength, which leaves me confident that I ain't no weed. Conka is a slightly heavier build than me, but I knew this would be a red-faced contest. I took off my jacket, positioned myself opposite Conka and planted my elbow carefully on the table. Conka did the same. I could feel all the eyes in the bar concentrate on us. Our hands struggled to find the correct grip, while we stared at each other.

'Gladiator ready?' I asked.

'Gladiator ready,' Conka answered.

I firmed my grip and went for the short sharp shock, but Conka was ready and held my hand in place. She was an inch away from losing, but managed to hold it there.

'Have you started?' she asked me and tightened her grip.

'Don't ask me that. That's what my arrogant dad always says . . .' My strength was beginning to wane. 'It really annoys me.'

'Well, have you started or not?'

Our hands were now vertical again. I could feel the butterfly of a giggle begin to work its way up from my belly – that meant I'd quickly get floppier and weaker. I had to distract her.

'Look, Edwin's just come in!' I said.

She tightened her grip. Oops! I'd said the one thing that gave her more strength and she didn't fall for it for a second. I was getting weaker, the butterflies were getting closer to explosion point, and my hand was losing ground, 'Conka, I love you!' I blurted out.

Ah! That slowed her down. I managed to regain some strength and got vertical again.

'Not really! Ha ha!'

She glanced at me, then slowly pushed my hand all the way down and gave my knuckles a triumphant little bang – just to make sure.

'Well done,' I conceded grudgingly. 'Okay, left hands now.'

I had a hope of beating her with that arm. It had been pretty close with the right, and I knew she'd be weaker with the left. But Conka was sitting with her arms crossed, not making any moves to fight on.

'Come on, Conks. Left hands now, eh?'

'Nah, I'm all right, thanks. How about another drink?'

'Oh, come on, you're winding me up.'

Conka just grinned. She liked to be in control. Maybe she wanted to be the male in our relationship. Or maybe the drink was encouraging me to get carried away and I was thinking crap. Anyway, she wasn't moving, and our glasses were empty.

'Okay, I'll get some more drinks then.' I skulked off to get a couple more vodkas.

While waiting for the barman, I could feel Conka's eyes on me. The skinny woman sidled up. 'Din wen then? Di' ya?'

I noticed Conka out of the corner of my eye, laughing at me. Why didn't this loony just fuck off?

'Din wen then? Di' ya?' she said, elbowing me now.

And why do these weirdos always have appalling West Country accents? 'No,' I answered. I thought if I kept it brief there was a hope that she wouldn't want to chat any longer, but, alas, there's no stopping some people.

'Gotto train up bit, you know. Eat right too.' She grinned at me, revealing a selection of very stained teeth. 'You need to put a bit of weight on, you do,' she said, stepping dangerously close.

I felt like offering her a pint of slurry. Fortunately, the slowest barman on earth had finally got our drinks, so I paid him and rejoined Conka.

'You're a loony magnet, you are, Charlie,' Conka observed.

'Yeah, she just wanted a free drink, most probably.'

'Well, she didn't come up to me when I got the last lot. You definitely attract them, I'd say.'

'Well, what does that make you then – Einstein?'

'Who said I was attracted to you in the first place?'

'It doesn't have to be said,' I said, while returning her rather penetrating stare. 'Cheers, me dears.'

'Cheers, Charlie!'

We clinked our glasses and threw back our drinks, avoiding following up any innuendos. There was something there, a flirtation. I knew I was tipsy, but why was I thinking that my best mate was after me? Or was it me after her? Was I misreading the signs or was I unwittingly signwriting? Conka had encouraged me to go out with blokes, especially that time with Mr C, but maybe she'd only done it because she knew I'd humiliate my sex-starved self. She wanted to prove a point: cocks suck, and chasing them could turn any sane woman into a prize prick. I felt as if she was rubbing my face in it, but scarily I didn't care. If Bing, Mr C and a pubload of rank gits was anything to go by, then, yes, perhaps I had been looking in all the wrong places. Conka seemed to be taking me over, and I didn't know what I wanted.

'I wonder how little Miss Horny's getting on with Dr G, eh?' Conka said.

As we finished our drinks and got our coats on, the barman was ringing the bell and all the interesting people were rushing to get their last orders. I hadn't seen the punters so lively all night. This must be the high point of their evening, I thought. The 'last order squash'. It'd take that barman until opening time tomorrow to serve them all at his so-slow-it-hurt pace.

Tasha's heart missed a beat when the doorbell rang. She'd managed to persuade Sarah to have a shower and go to bed – that way she could have the doctor all to herself once he'd finished the examination. She'd got the kids into their beds and tidied up downstairs. She reaffirmed and checked her face. She felt pretty good, especially since she'd had her hair replaited. She gave her lips a final application, took a deep breath and answered the door.

'Hi, Doctor. Come in.' She spoke in a breathy voice.

He looked stunning. She'd remembered him exactly. His smell engulfed her as he came in from the cold.

'Good evening, Tasha,' he said.

She loved his formal tone. His body language was shouting at her, his voice soft but commanding. And he'd remembered her name.

'Your patient's upstairs,' Tasha told him. 'Follow me.'

She allowed her arm to brush his as she went past him and up the stairs. She climbed slowly, delighted to feel his eyes travelling up and down her legs. She could sense him eating her up, tasting every quivering muscle. She was almost fainting by the time they got to Sarah's room.

'Sarah,' Tasha cooed, 'the doctor's here now.'

Sarah rolled over. The doctor took off his coat and opened his bag.

'Hi,' Sarah said flatly. She was pretty wiped out.

Tasha decided to leave them to it and went downstairs. It wasn't long before she heard him coming down.

'Would you like a drink?' Taska asked.

'No. I'm really sorry but I'm already running very late.'

Tasha's heart sank. He was putting his coat on and was nearly out of the door already.

'Oh, well,' she said, not knowing what to do with herself. 'I guess I'll see you around.'

The doctor stood still and looked directly at her. She knew there was something strong between them. Surely he couldn't be immune to it. You could almost see their auras merging. She fiddled nervously with her plaits.

'Look,' he began. 'I'd love to see you again – I mean away from patients and hospitals . . .'

Tasha was so relieved. 'Oh, that would be great.'

'Well, I'd better be off, then.' He offered her his hand.

Tasha started to panic: he'd opened the door, suggested they see each other again but had not yet attempted to make an arrangement.

'Before you go,' she said quickly. 'I was wondering if you could just look at my eye. It's been incredibly irritable today and I'm not sure why.'

It was an oldie but goldie, and it worked. 'Certainly,' he said.

Phew! She'd stalled him. Surreptitiously, she poked herself in the eye as they walked into the living room.

'Come and stand under this light,' he instructed.

Tasha shuddered at his commanding tone. She staggered over and allowed him to hold her chin with one hand and lift the lid off her eye with the other.

'It does look sore. Have you been using any new cosmetics or facial creams lately?'

'I never use anything that isn't one hundred and twenty per cent natural,' she said, putting unnecessary stress on the word 'natural'.

The doctor cleared his throat. Her sexual prowess was slicing through his stiff white coat.

'I suggest you sluice it with salt water, then see how it is in the morning.' He let go of her chin.

'Sluice it?' she repeated, again making the word 'sluice' triple X-rated.

'Yes.' He coughed again. 'I'd better be off now.'

But this time he didn't walk straight to the door. They stood staring at one another for a second longer.

'Look, it's my birthday on Thursday. I'll give you my number. Call me if you feel like coming to the celebrations,' Tasha suggested hastily.

'That would be great.'

She scribbled down her number. 'Thanks, Doc. I'll see you soon.'

'Please call me Craig,' he said, as he went to the door. 'I hope your eye improves. Goodbye, Tasha.'

''Bye, Craig.'

As we marched – we never walked slowly – back to Sarah's, we made predictions about Tasha's level of success with the doctor. Conka reckoned dinner in the next few days, I gambled on breakfast tomorrow: Tasha usually worked fast and I knew she'd want instant satisfaction.

Sarah was in bed and Tasha had that smug look on her face. She'd definitely got a result of some kind, that much was sure. Conka and I sat down in front of her, like story-time at school, waiting for her to reveal all.

'I was so cool,' she began, 'I – rather, we really connected, and I mean *big-time.*'

She widened her eyes when she said 'big-time', suggesting that this wasn't something her fanny was talking about but something much more powerful, something uncannily unavoidable, something with Fate's dirty great fingerprints all over it. Conka and I continued our silent stares while Tasha relished the memory.

She stroked her throat when she spoke again. 'He's got such an amazing energy – really pure.'

'Wow, Tash, what about his wallet, then?' Conka tried to bring her back down to earth, or at least somewhere a bit nearer, and to the crux of the story.

What life-enhancing quality was this man going to bring to Tasha's life, or was it only going to be sexually fulfilling? Tasha smiled dreamily as she allowed herself to drift back into more romantic recent recollections.

'Well, is he going to take you out or what?' Conka asked, as she threw a cushion on to Tasha's lap.

20

They were in their usual spoons position. Trevor awoke with his morning glory. Sharon awoke with the familiar nudging on her bottom. She felt his enormous hands encompass her breasts, while he let his dick do the 'guiding in' by itself. They made slow, moving love and Sharon felt like crying when she came. Then they heard those steps – the steps you know are bound to come. You just wish they'd stay in bed, a bit longer, just *for once*.

'Mum! We haven't got any cereal.' Liam bounded in, just as Trevor was pulling out.

'Oh, God, here we go.' Sharon sniffed. She flopped down on the pillow, pulling the duvet over her head.

'Come on, Liam. Let's go and get some eggs and bacon.' Trevor fumbled under the duvet for his boxers, while Sharon lay next to him, not quite believing what she was hearing. Trevor was behaving like a new man all over again. Weird. Within five minutes he'd pulled on his jeans and trainers and had gone. Sharon felt sure he must be guilty of something. He'd decorated, moved furniture, even *cleaned*, and now he was taking Liam out to buy breakfast – letting her lie in – and he hadn't even asked her for money. This was impossible, unheard of. What the fuck was wrong?

She vaguely heard them come back in, but wasn't quite ready to wake up yet. She half snoozed and half listened to them fussing in the kitchen, cooking breakfast. She smiled to herself. Trevor always made really insane breakfasts, and, although he said eggs and bacon, he didn't mean it. That was one of the things she loved about him. She thought he was eccentric, different. Smells wafted through to the bedroom, good smells. Even though breakfast would be odd, it would still be delicious. It was smelling a bit Greek today.

Liam walked in, trying desperately not to spill the coffee, and slopping it all over the place.

'Be careful, Liam,' Sharon said, taking the cup from him. 'Thanks, Peanut. Can you go and ask Trevor for a ciggie?'

'Oh, Mum, you're disgusting. You shouldn't smoke.' Liam walked out of the room.

'Go on!' Sharon called after him.

She drank her coffee and waited for her cigarette, then noticed half of one in the ashtray so smoked that instead. Then she got up and joined the others in her newly improved living room. It looked stunning. Trevor had bought flowers and put them in her long blue vase on the table, now positioned in front of the window.

The table was covered in plates. He'd fried some hash browns, garlic, strips of turkey and bacon; there were olives, tomato and cheese salad, onion and lettuce salad, and more coffee.

'Trevor, this is wonderful.'

'It was Liam too.'

Sharon grinned at the pair of them: they looked so pleased with themselves. 'It's a shame I'm not hungry,' she said cruelly, before bursting out laughing, ''cause I'm *starving*.'

They sat down and enjoyed their feast. There was no way Sharon was going to ask what the fuck it was he felt guilty about, not just yet. Trevor suggested a visit to a museum, followed by a picnic in the park. This was just the kind of day Sharon dreamed about. She just prayed she'd be able to restrain herself from ruining it.

Back from Sarah's, Conka went to bed that night with her mind racing. She'd found the entire weekend most bizarre – in a good way. For a start she was already a much improved driver: buying the car had been the first opportunity well taken. Driving to and from Sarah's had been the second: it was like having ten lessons in one – brilliant. She loved her Cortina, and life would be so much easier from now on. Third, although Sarah had had the miscarriage, it still had been a great weekend and a good idea to go there, making a change from stinky central London.

Weird pub, though, that they'd ended up in, and Charlie had been drunk and strange. It was a nice, warm sort of strange but she seemed to be on some hidden agenda that Conka couldn't quite fathom. She appreciated that Charlie was slightly disturbed from her recent bad dates, but there was something else.

As Conka lay on her back, watching car lights prowl her bedroom ceiling, listening to the various shouts and sirens that punctured the constant traffic drone, it dawned on her. Charlie had been flirting with her! Nah, Conka thought. Charlie *was* a flirt, but with women? There again, Charlie had got so disillusioned with the fellas recently, maybe it was exactly that: Charlie had turned gay and Conka was now the object of her desires.

'Ha!' Conka laughed aloud. 'Why not? Why not indeed?'

She stretched out in her bed and ran her hands down her flat tummy and on to her hips – all firm, skin soft. She felt pretty chuffed at the thought of Charlie finding her sexually desirable. In fact, she wouldn't blame Charlie if she had fallen for her. Charlie was quite the long-leggy-lovely herself. But Conka wasn't a skirt-lifter – at least not as far as she knew. But perhaps she should try it for a laugh. It might be a turn-on. If Charlie was willing to bend, why shouldn't she? The more she thought about it, the more saucy she found it. Then she wondered why she hadn't tried it already; probably because it wasn't really her.

For the meantime, she decided to try it in her dreams. She shut her eyes, told her brain who to have dirty dreams about, and promptly fell asleep.

Despite the bitterly cold bursts of gusty winds, Liam and Sharon had enjoyed the day. It had been just the three of them, all day, alone – how Sharon liked it best – no interruptions, no disturbances, no interfering busybodies. Sharon was happy as she could see where her man was. Liam was happy too as he got to play loads of football. Trevor was good like that; even he seemed happy. She thought of the others still at Sarah's, and was glad not to be there. The idea of four single mothers forming a band was utterly naïve.

As the wind picked up some more and the sky got darker, they decided to go home.

Sharon didn't want the day to end. 'Let's stop and have a drink somewhere, shall we?' she suggested.

'Yeah, why not?' Trevor said, smiling. He had such a handsome smile.

They gathered their belongings and headed homewards via the

Half Moon. Sharon felt great. It had been a beautiful day and the three of them were strolling along holding hands.

Then Liam began to play up a bit, especially in the pub. It was at times like these that Sharon wished she could just drop him off somewhere and enjoy the rest of the evening alone with her man. It would be different if Liam was Trevor's son. Very different. Trevor was pretty quiet, which seemed to enhance Liam's voice all the more. She stared at Liam. Why was he so bloody loud? She felt like gagging him. She could see Trevor's agitation building up with Liam's every comment. When he spilled his drink, Trevor's face became so tense that Sharon knew it was time to go home.

The flat looked a mess. The remains of breakfast were limp and tired on the plates they'd left on the table that morning. A fat fly buzzed noisily around as Sharon began to tidy up. Trevor sat on the sofa and kicked off his trainers. The temperature seemed to plummet. Although he'd put the telly on, and Liam was noisily fart-arsing around, it was suddenly very quiet. He asked her to get a beer. She looked in the fridge, but there was none.

She went back into the living room, smiling nervously. 'Uh, we haven't got any. Sorry.'

Trevor answered with a stony glare and put his feet pointedly on the sofa. He wasn't going anywhere. Sharon grabbed her coat and left quickly. Maybe she was just being paranoid and imagining things. Trevor hadn't actually said anything, and she hadn't done anything, as far as she knew. As Sharon walked back from the shop, four-pack in hand, she convinced herself that Trevor was more than likely just wiped out. He'd been on the go all day, and they hadn't exactly had an early night. She was about to go in when she saw a familiar-looking girl cycle past. She knew her. Fuck, it was that *Tiffany*! Sharon remembered that she'd thought Trevor had been behaving guiltily. She'd fucking well straighten this thing out once and for all.

She came in ready for a show-down. But as she walked in, Liam and Trevor laughed aloud at something on the telly. Perhaps she'd leave it for now. She gave Trevor a beer and went to fix some tea. No doubt, Liam would soon be screaming for food, and Trevor didn't look like he'd be making any new-man dinners tonight. Besides, she wanted to think about this whole Tiffany situation.

She lit a fag, cracked open a beer and stared out of the small window down to the street below. The pig-buses were blocking up the roads again. Maybe one of them could knock that Tiffany off her stupid bike. Sharon had tried cycling recently and had been shocked at her lungs. They had not been able to cope, not one bit. Maybe she had Aids? God, had it come to that? She gulped down the cold beer. It felt good. No wonder Trevor had looked upset when she told him they didn't have any.

Suddenly she remembered what she was supposed to be doing and flicked the kettle on for about the third time. She'd make some pasta.

'Mum! I'm hungry!' Liam shouted.

'Yes, I *know*!' Sharon shouted back.

'Is there any more beer?' It was Trevor's turn.

'Yes. Hang on . . .'

Sharon had only just started hers. She couldn't believe how fast he could drink. She poured the water into the pan and handed Trevor another tin.

'There's a great match on tonight,' he said to her, winking.

'Oh, Mum, please let me stay up for it – I've been good all day . . .'

They were both grinning at her. She knew damn well they were going to watch it, no matter what she said. The sound of the water boiling distracted her.

'Only if you're good,' she called as she went back to the kitchen.

'Yes, yes, yes!'

She could hear Liam chanting. Trevor wasn't exactly calming him down, either. They're both a couple of bloody football hooligans, she thought, as she put the kettle on again. Maybe tonight wouldn't be show-down night, after all.

She lit another cigarette.

The boring football had finished and Liam had gone, at last, to bed. He was exhausted. Sharon turned the telly off and looked at Trevor.

'What d'you go and do that for?' he hissed.

'Because I want to talk.'

'I was watching that. Turn it on!'

Sharon hesitated, 'I just want to ask you one question.'

Trevor pushed past her and turned the telly back on. 'Look, Sharon, we've had a great day. Let's just chill out and watch this. Come on, darling, look at those beautiful dolphins.' He stared at the picture. 'They're supposed to be more intelligent than humans.'

Sharon went to run a bath. There was now no doubt in her mind that he was hiding something. He was refusing to talk. That's why he'd encouraged Liam to stay up late – so they wouldn't have any time alone. He was covering something up. As she lowered herself into the steaming bath she began to cry. Trevor didn't notice her tears when he came in to pee. Sharon added more hot water, and stayed in the bath for hours. Finally, she heard Trevor slope off to bed. She knew she had a sleepless night ahead of her.

After Sarah's unfortunate miscarriage, I welcomed the relative normality of Monday morning. I like Monday mornings, just like I like New Year's Eve. It's a fresh start, a clean slate, time to forget about last week's mistakes and upsets, time to move on, to take a deep breath and face the world with renewed vigour.

Sharon's dreadful on a Monday morning. She reckons I'm an 'eternal optimist'. I guess I am, in a way, or maybe just a weekly optimist as, by Tuesday, I'm almost as depressed as her again. Almost, but not quite. But, then, I never get quite as inebriated as Sharon either. Except on New Year's Eve. That's the one night I go completely barmy: phoning-people-in-foreign-countries barmy. For some reason I forget about such trivialities as phone bills: I suddenly want to wish all those sexy acquaintances I once met briefly from LA a fan-fucking-tastic New Year and tell them all how much I really do love them and that this year I really will make it over and that this is *the year*, right?

Anyway, this Monday represented a new chance and a new beginning. Bing had made my blood boil but, hey, that was last week and I'd decided that if I bumped into him in the street, I would greet him calmly and politely. I was over it. And maybe on to something new with the lovely enigmatic Conka.

With the delicate Bing matter cleared up – thanks to Sarah and Conka's extreme diversionary tactics at the weekend – I wanted to concentrate on matters of a more pressingly urgent nature: the rest of my life; money; work; the band; sex life; Conka *et moi*. Would Conka and I adopt, impregnate, or stick with the two we already had? Would we be mega-lesbo rock stars? This was madness! I was not a lesbian and, as far as I could see, neither was Conka. Mind you, we did have such a great time together.

But what about Sharon? I found her sexy too, with her agonising vulnerability. Maybe I was in the closet but just didn't know it. Sharon annoyed me way too much, though. I hoped she was up for the band as I reckoned she'd be a great asset. It was hard to tell from the rehearsal if she was actually any good, but she definitely looked the part.

Although Sarah's miscarriage had ensured that our rehearsal went out the window, we had played enough to convince me that we were not entirely hopeless. The band idea niggled at me: it was a possible escape route out of Brokesville. But it would require dedication and concentration, and that would be hard to achieve, especially from Babe Sharon.

I was pleased to see her show up at the school in her usual harassed way this Monday morning. She was only two minutes late, but she made a big deal of the buses being slow and the drivers being rude. Then she burst into tears. 'He's such a bastard, Charlie. He doesn't love me, he *can't* love me. I just can't go on any more.'

We went for coffee at Mario's, the tiny Italian greasy-Joe's breakfast-served-all-day gaff, where the Don Cappuccino thought we were beautiful and that all young men these days were poofs or drug addicts and no wonder we were always complaining. Mario told us that, although he was fifty-eight, he could still go crazy – 'you know whad I min?' He hated his grumpy wife. He pulled faces behind her back and they communicated by throwing things at each other. It sometimes got a bit messy in there when they were having a big old communication session. But we liked it and the coffee was good, so who cares about flying eggs?

We squeezed in and sat down on the narrow wooden benches. Mario was busy doing a few customers takeaway breakies, which meant we wouldn't get served for ages. Besides, he always ignored his regulars. Builders came in asking for atrocious sounding orders, like the two-egg, four-bacon, double-fried-bread sandwich and some chips. Yuck! It was only nine fifteen. The local bank clerks and estate agents were ordering their individual coffees, toasts and marmalades, so there was no way Mario was going to do two simple coffees.

We lit our fags and I gave Sharon a look that said, 'I really don't want to talk about Trevor. You know what I think.'

'I know you really don't want to talk about Trevor, Charlie, but I don't know what to do.' She bit her bottom lip hard in an attempt to stop the tears streaming down her face but she was too tired. I remembered being that tired after arguments all night long, then having to get up early and deal with the boy. Being a mum every day: no rest, no space, no recovery time. Every day an emotional battle, every day walking on broken glass in fear of the struggle, the battle that chips away at you, slowly but surely wearing you down, confusing your truths as you know them. I remembered how exhausting it was. When you're that tired, crying is sometimes the only thing you can do – you don't even have the energy to kill yourself. I couldn't turn my back on her.

We talked for an exhausting hour. 'Look, Sharon, it's simple,' I said at last. 'Who is the most important person to you?'

She looked surprised by my interruption. 'Liam, of course. And I know it isn't doing him any good seeing me like this, and that Trevor –'

'Shut up a minute, will you? It's simple. Forget about Trevor refusing to talk to you. *Liam* is alive and well, you are alive . . . just, and that's all that's really important. Fuck the rest of this bollocks. There are people walking ten miles a day just to get water in parts of Africa. Do you think they spend years wondering whether some pea-brained fart loves them or not? Who gives a shit? You could die tomorrow, and have you enjoyed today? Or

133

yesterday? You've got to have a bit of fun, Shassa. You've got to laugh again. If this is love and it gets you down so much, then I don't think love suits you. You've got to get a bit more of a superficial life, dear. Actually, you've just got to get any life that doesn't revolve around Trevor. Take the band, for instance, we could make a go of it, you know, and it doesn't have to lead anywhere as long as we're enjoying ourselves and being creative. But what if it did lead somewhere?'

Sharon smiled at my ridiculous optimism.

'It could be our escape. We'd never have to go to the launderette again, or sign on, or accept drinks from twats. We could get the boys piano lessons and a big house in the country. We could donate to charity. It'd be fantastic, and if we got there by ourselves, no one would be able to take it away from us. It would be ours, a paid achievement –'

'Charlie?'

But I'd slipped into Fantasy Land: I was accepting the award, and the camera flashes were making me flinch. I had to shield my eyes with my free hand, the other rendered useless, weighed down by my enormous trophy. The applause was deafening. Conka was clapping and cheering me. I saw people wearing T-shirts with my serious face looking out strongly at the world, contorted and stretched across their breasts. This made me feel slightly embarrassed and a little coy but, none the less, I was touched by my fans' enthusiasm and took time out to chat to them. There would be rallies and demonstrations . . .

'Charlie? Charlie, will you answer me?'

'Sorry. What was the question again?'

'Have you got anything to smoke at home?'

'Yeah.'

'Shall we go?'

'Yeah, yeah. Sorry, come on.'

I paid for our cappuccinos, took a small amount of flak from Mario and headed for the bus stop. 'So, see you and Liam at mine after school? We'll have a puff, and then try to write a little number or two?' I said.

'Why not? Sounds great.'

134

21

I went back to my flat and stared at the mounting pile of unpaid bills. How was I supposed to cope with this lot? A wave of anger swept over me as I thought of Luke's dad swanning around America, giving some poor idiot the 'I'm a dad, you know. I love my son, but she doesn't let me see him. God, I love that boy' routine, reaping sympathy and drinks out of his plight. He's a fucking human parasite! I'd let him see Luke all right, but it would be slightly tricky sending him to the States every other weekend and one night a week. What was on my mind was money, and it pissed me off that the prize delinquent never bloody sent any. Especially today, when suddenly it got to me again. Sharon's depression was infectious.

I adjourned to the bathroom, a bill-free zone, and stared at myself in the mirror. I looked older but still had some spots. That pissed me off too. Don't you ever grow out of the buggers? Do you have to be totally wrinkled before you can have clear skin? Do spots make you look young? I tried to regain some of my enthusiasm for the band. Who the fuck was I trying to kid? I was a dead man's makeup artist. What the fuck made me think I could be a pop star?

I put on some more foundation and thought how depressing Sharon was. We had to get out of this hellish situation. I put on some black eyeliner, something I don't normally wear, and tried a few Robert Smith faces. I knew I was capable of giving it some, if I had a chance. Conka knew it too. What else could I do? Cry? Fucking great help crying is. I blinked away my tears and looked even worse. Black eyeliner runs a treat when wet, and my spots and nose looked as if they'd glow in the dark.

I slapped my cheeks and tried to think what Conka would do if she felt like this. The trouble was, I couldn't imagine her feeling like this. She was always so flipping happy. Why couldn't I be like that? But she did treat herself. I remembered our caravanning holiday and decided to give myself a mini-facial. Mini-facials and whistling, I find, are two things that stop me from wallowing in self-absorbic-sorry-for-mesellie acid. And the thought of whistling while wearing a face mask tickled me enough to put on an okay-there's-a-lickel-smile-in-me-*just* face.

I whistled 'Always Look On The Bright Side Of Life' while I boiled the kettle. It was such a stupid song it cheered me up.

I steamed my face, which maade me cough so much I thought I was going to chuck, but it felt pretty good. After a quick squeeze, I slapped on my Dead Sea mask. There were no more tears: the mask was too expensive to ruin with such things. I scrubbed my delicates and went out to hang them up. I managed a little whistle, softly through my setting mouth, as I pegged my greying silks up on the line outside.

'Morning!' came a voice from over the wall.

'Hello!' I replied, peering over the line.

It was a neighbour, a Muslim, who was always very nice to me and didn't mind too much when my drunk friends mistook his house for mine on their return from off-licence runs. We were always very polite to one another and invited each other to our parties, but neither of us ever went. We knew we were worlds apart: at his parties the women sat on chairs making shrill tongue rolls from behind their veils, but at my parties the women tended to get outrageously drunk, fling themselves all over the place and sometimes take off most of their clothing. I used to see him play cards with his mates at night in his front room. In the summer there'd be a couple of mattresses in the back yard and they'd sleep under the stars. I thought that was really a cool thing to do in the middle of the city; unusual. We respected one another's culture.

'How are you today, then?' I asked. He seemed particularly happy.

'Very well thank you.' He was laughing. 'Very well indeed.' He could hardly contain himself. 'And what about you?'

Then I realised what he'd been so giggly about; my stupid black face. How embarrassing! I ducked behind the washing-line, getting my beauty efforts out of sight.

'Oh, I'm fine, thanks,' I shouted, from behind the washing. 'Beautiful day, eh?'

'Oh, yes. It is a very beautiful day today indeed.'

I walked Groucho-style back down into my flat. Life could be fucking ridiculous sometimes.

I felt altogether much better leaving the flat the second time around. Then I bumped into Sharon. She looked distraught. 'Do you want to come to Soho with me?' I asked. Then, linking my arm through hers, I said, 'You're coming.'

I needed to get Tasha a birthday present and a large vibrator was what I had in mind. I wanted to get her off the scent of the cocky docky, who I reckoned was a bottle of bee-stings disguised as cough tincture if ever there was one. I'd get her a vibrator big enough to make a donkey feel ashamed. I explained this in a loud clear voice on the busy but silent tube, and Sharon duly found it impossible to remain miserable.

We wandered around the Brewers and Berwicks of Soho, gazing in the windows, past seedy doorways, debating whether any of the girls ever enjoyed their line of work. None of them looked very happy, but can you look alluring and happy at the same time? Sharon thought not.

We turned into Old *Campt*on Street and the Ann Summers shop beckoned. They'd have what I was looking for.

This was a first time for me. I'd never been in a sex shop before – not even with a friend at the age of sixteen. Never. Sharon apparently had come to this very shop with Trevor when they first met and spunked a load of money on frilly underwear that had long since been ripped off and chucked away.

'You know the quality of the garments isn't that great,' she whispered in my ear, as we walked in.

This sex shop was pretty much how I'd expected it. It was all trashy, and red and pink, with lots of frills and frou-frous. A gay guy was smooching around assisting a seventeen-stone dyke in the handcuff section, and a large friendly blonde, with lashings of pink lipstick over half her face and enormous false eyelashes, was ready to serve us at the furry till. There was a well-dressed businessman sorting out a nurse's outfit, a fat monk sizing up the torture equipment, Sharon and me.

Sharon went straight to the vibrator section.

'Blimey, you certainly know your way around here,' I said, joining her.

I looked at the wide and narrow variety of fake cocks before me. 'Don't you just love it, Sharon?' I said. 'Lots of cocks all neatly lined up, on display, with price tags and no men attached to them. Superb, isn't it?'

'Argh! Look at that.' Sharon pointed to a flourescent pink one.

'Guess who that reminds me of,' I said, wondering whether Bing had inspired the designer of that particular vibrator. I launched into a hummed chorus of our first hit record.

'Charlie, that's disgusting.'

'No. What's disgusting is that.' I glared at the offensive pink thing. 'That is blatant misrepresentation. It should have a sign that says 'enlarged times 10' on it. What a turn-out, though. Mad place, this cock shop, isn't it?'

'Well, you've got to get her a big 'un. Tasha's forever going on about size.'

'Believe me, I intend to,' I said.

'You know, she even went as far as photographic evidence on one occasion. She was so impressed she couldn't believe it herself.'

'What? She showed you the picture?' I asked, incredulously.

'Polaroid, yep. Good-looking guy. Fucking massive packet.'

That pissed me off a bit, Tasha hadn't shown me the photo. I went back to the job in hand. Sharon had already got it down to a shortlist of two. It was a choice between an *enormous*, straight, proud, realistically shaped black one, and a *very, very large*, but not quite agony (like the black one), beautifully cut, slightly curved one, *with balls*. An added attraction, maybe.

As we pondered betwixt the two, another customer came into the shop. A man in a mac, how perfect was that? The pervy in the dirty bloody mac snivelled and shuffled around with his glasses falling off his dribbling nose and his top lip curling up, showing his yellow teeth, excited and quivering in anticipation.

'He'd cream himself, if you told him off,' Sharon said quietly.

He looked over at us. We smiled at him then I winked. He grabbed a free catalogue and legged it out of the shop.

We decided to get the big black one, which won on

'plausibility'. It was astonishingly expensive – but worth every penny, as it turned out.

We went straight to school to pick up the kids, and Sharon and Liam came back to mine. The boys went into the garden to play. I made the tea while Sharon sprawled on the sofa. I gave her a half-smoked joint to light. She wasn't a big smoker (when she had to pay for it), but had a puff when she came to my flat, and always seemed to relax a bit. She was unbearable when she had too much nervous energy. She pulled hard on the joint and her eyes instantly became larger and moist.

'Oh, no. Now I'm stoned.'

'It's good for you to relax for once. Let's just write a bloody song and forget about the rest of the world.'

Sharon laughed at my idealism. 'You can't just do it. You've got to get in the mood – loosen up and all that.'

I grabbed the Ann Summers bag and shoved it in her face. 'Have another look at that. That'll cheer you up!'

'It looks even more enormous now we're out of the shop.'

'Okay, Sharon? In the mood now?'

'Well, not really,' Sharon said.

'Let's just do it, baby,' I said, taking off my jumper. 'Come on, gorgeous . . .'

She looked shocked.

'But, Charlie?'

'Don't worry,' I said softly. 'We can carry on without the others.'

Sharon went pale.

'Are you all right?' I asked, looking for a pen and some paper.

Sharon stood up and got her things together quickly.

'Sharon? You going already?'

'Yep. Sorry, I'm too stoned for this. *Liam! Come on! Now!*'

Liam tore down the hallway and they were gone within seconds. I couldn't believe it. Talk about shit rehearsals and strange behaviour! She must be going through it worse than I'd originally thought.

Five minutes later, the phone rang.

'Oh, Charlie. You're not going to believe this . . .'

It was a distraught Sharon. My eyes started rolling. 'I couldn't believe the way you guys just legged it out of here –'

'Listen, I've got a court summons for not having a TV licence. I could go to jail.'

She started to sob. Fucking TV licence people don't realise what terror they instil in people. *My* phone was virtually shaking from Sharon's hysterics.

'Sharon! Sharon, don't cry. Just come over. Can you do that?'

'Okay.' She sniffed, sounding about five.

This was bad. The TV licence people have always frightened the shit out of me. Ever since they had those ads on the box where the van drives around with its detector satellite spinning on the top and shifty-looking men in the back with headphones and lie-detectors strapped about their persons, this has been one law that I can confidently say I've never broken.

When she and Liam arrived, I got a brown-paper bag and talked Sharon through some breathing exercises. We made a list of 'things to do' and 'people to ring'. Finally her panic subsided. I offered her the best advice I could think of, which mainly involved staying calm. I told her to be happy and that we'd have a really good time at Tasha's birthday party.

'This is her present, remember!' I said, whipping the vibrator out of the bag and waving it around in a crude, childish way.

'Charlie! Put that bloody thing away! If Liam gets his eyes on that –'

'It's fine. They're outside looking for snails to race.'

She looked so upset I put it back in the bag. I told her I loved her and tried to get her into the idea of song-writing again. Apart from robbing a bank, there wasn't much else I could do.

'Let's exorcise some demons.' I put the pen in her hand and the pad on her lap.

I thought another joint would be a good idea – good for getting 'in the mood'. Sharon looked at me in bewilderment for a moment, frowned then starting writing furiously. I rolled and smoked, passed the joint to Sharon and read over her shoulder. It was good, it rhymed – I liked songs that rhymed a bit – it was angry and alive, it chewed and spat.

'That's really great, Sharon. Did you just make that up?'

'Oh, it's dead easy to write songs. Anyone can do it. I just pour them out like water.'

'Wow, that's really great! You've got a talent. And not everyone can do this.'

She knew, all right. She just wanted this special part of her to be loudly appreciated, and I didn't mind providing her with that service. 'It's really great. I've never been able to write a song that quick.'

She looked at me a bit guiltily. 'I didn't actually write that song just now. Well, I kind of did in places, when I couldn't remember how the original went. But I wrote the original too, you see, but that was about seven years ago. Blimey, seven years. No wonder I can't remember it exactly.'

'Well, it's great anyway, Sharon. If you could write one like that now, I think we could have a platinum in our hands.'

'You really do live in Fantasy Land, don't you?'

'Get back to your drawing-board, Wendy. Time's a sprinter.'

I watched the children play outside, allowing the undiscovered genius to write away – this time not quite so fast. The boys were quiet for once, which made a pleasant change.

I guess I did live in Fantasy Land, to a degree. I had always thought of myself as a realist, but everyone said I had a funny way of going about things. Maybe they meant I had a screw loose but didn't have the heart to tell me. I could genuinely see this band taking off. I knew it was mad, and I did catch myself running leaps and bounds ahead of where we actually were on the success front. Maybe Sharon was sane and I was mad, when I had always thought it was the other way round.

The children were engrossed. They were watchable kids, and would ensure an end to my internal debate. Oh, no! They were only force feeding the snails with marijuana leaves off George's plant.

'Don't pick those leaves!' I shouted, running outside as Liam grabbed another handful.

'What else is there?' he yelled back, ripping off some more leaves.

He had a point. My garden/cement yard would definitely win

the Most Barren competition. George's plant was pretty much all the greenery there was.

'Oh, go on, Sharon. Tell him not to pick any more. It's such a waste. George is going to be furious,' I said to Sharon, as she came out.

'There's going to be a load of stoned snails wandering around the garden,' she pointed out unhelpfully, and started to impersonate a stoned snail, if you can imagine such a thing. I knew that she was stoned herself, but this play-acting gave me cause for concern. It was fucking funny, though, especially when she went on to do the 'vocal stoned snail' with really bad munchies. She made an incredibly gormless face, rolled her eyes back into her skull and relaxed her cheeks so that her tongue practically fell out of her mouth, which she moved in a more carp-like manner than a carp (if you've ever seen a carp's mouth move, you'd understand. I haven't, and I'm just guessing, by the way.) She even made a 'snail' noise.

'Oh, no! They love the weed. Look, the snails are going back for more!' Sharon pointed to them in disbelief.

Sad but true. Our English snails are no better than the Australian koala who apparently gets the koala equivalent of stoned on eucalyptus leaves from a particular type of eucalyptus tree (ever heard of skunk-eucalyptus?), which is why they don't bother eating anything else, or even drinking anything else. They just eat these leaves – they can't even be bothered to go and get a glass of water. They just sit 'n' munch up in the trees, chatting about their last bad leaf. If reincarnation is true, then can I come back as a koala, please?

We went back inside, I made some tea and we tried our luck at writing songs again. We decided to write alternate words. The theme was Single Mums.

'Babysitters . . .' Sharon began.

'Head lice . . .' I sang.

'Bailiffs.'

'Bad quiffs.'

'CSA, PTA.'

'Up the school, in the hall.'

'Fed up.'

'Had enough.'

'On our own.'

'In the home.'

'I'm on my way.'

'It's a brighter day.'

'There's a clearer way.'

'I'm on my way.'

'Runny noses.'

'Broken homeses.'

'Oh, no, and there's a little bit more.'

'CAB, help for free.'

'Had a fight, saw the light.'

'Now, I'm free – I'm so happy.'

'Oh, oh, and there's a little bit more.'

'I'm on my way, it's a brighter day, I'm on my way!!'

We collapsed on the sofa, worn out by our use of lung and brain – organs we generally abused. But I liked the words – Sharon was quite inspirational – and I thought it could be developed into a kicking song. Sharon's eyes shone with exhilaration. She looked beautiful, and there was life in her face again. Her white blonde hair was falling over her eyes. She made a half-hearted attempt to blow it out of the way, but she'd run out of puff. She shut her eyes and smiled.

Moments like these, when Sharon was more alive and happy than I'd seen her in a long time, demolished the doubts I sometimes had about the ridiculousness of the band. We were good. It was good.

'Did you write that down?' I asked.

I knew I'd be crap at remembering it. I took the pad from her hands and, sure enough, she'd managed to get most of it – it just wasn't much. We hadn't even started and we were behaving as if we'd just finished three intense weeks in a residential recording studio. I jumped up, slapping Sharon on the thigh.

'Oi! What did you do that for?'

'Come on, Sharon. We can't just collapse after one tiny little effort. Let's do some more.'

But that session, too, was destined to come to an early end. Liam and Luke were bored with each other's company and

Liam interrupted us constantly. I had to fight him for the Ann Summers bag. He very nearly got it open, the little git. He pushed Luke, then ran out. Luke cried, and Sharon left, apologising, chasing Liam down the street.

22

Sharon didn't know what to do. Where the hell was she going to get the TV money from? She thought about doing another course – you could sometimes get grants. But she seemed to owe money everywhere and she needed a fortune. She shoved the TV licence court summons under some old magazines in the corner by the stereo with the other offensive papers. She wanted it out of her sight. She glanced down at her records. Records. She still had a record collection and a record player. That was money. But no CDs, or CD player. She hadn't been inclined to buy any music, not for a long time. She just hadn't had the spare cash. Her collection was probably worth quite a bit. But if she sold that – well, there'd be nothing of her old life left, nothing whatsoever.

She pulled out one of her old favourites. Madness. Those days of Brighton and mopeds, idealism in her youth. She used to have such good fun. She missed that. Charlie came close to fun, but it was nothing like it used to be. Besides, Charlie had seemed to be about to jump her earlier on and that wasn't her idea of fun. She turned the volume up and tried to get in the mood for Tasha's birthday dinner. She needed to find something she felt like wearing.

Everything she dragged out of the wardrobe was old and worn out. She hated the whole sorry lot.

Madness came to an end.

'Hiya!'

She heard the door go and Trevor's familiar stomp up the stairs. 'Anyone home?'

She didn't feel like answering his dumb question. He'd find out quick enough. The place was so sodding small.

'Hi there, Liam.'

'Hi, Trevor,' Liam called.

Sharon heard them discuss some match or other.

'Is Mum in?' Trevor asked.

Sharon felt angry immediately. She wasn't going to fucking well leave Liam, aged seven, on his own, was she?

'Yeah, she's in her room.'

She heard him clump nearer. Angrily she pulled at a dress stuck in the cupboard. It ripped. 'SHIT!' She felt like crying.

'Hi, darling,' Trevor said.

Sharon just wanted him to piss off. What use was he?

Trevor looked at the bedroom. There were clothes everywhere. 'Well, I won't be decorating in here for a while, eh?'

'Don't start on at me now,' Sharon snapped.

'Hang on, all I said was –'

'I heard what you said. What's the point in decorating, Trevor? And if you've got so much money to fling around, then give me the phone money and the rest.'

'God, you don't appreciate anything I do, do you?'

'What? What do you *do*, Trevor?'

'I fucking spend all of my dole on getting this place ready for you, buying food – remember breakfast – visits to the museum –'

'Big fucking deal, Trevor. I don't know how many coffees, toasts and eggs I've fucking made for you. You do it once in a blue moon and then shove it down my throat about how much you had to fucking spend!'

'Well, that's the last time –'

'I don't care. I've got bills coming out of my ears. I'm in severe debt and now a court summons for the TV licence and *no money*!' Sharon started to cry.

Trevor softened. 'Fuck them. They're not going to do anything. You never watch telly anyway, just tell them that.'

'Oh, Trev . . . What am I going to do?'

Trevor knelt down beside her. 'I've got a job, darling.'

'What?'

'I start next week. It's not much money, but it'll be something.'

'What is it?'

He stroked a strand of wet hair away from her face. She was so beautiful. He felt himself go hard.

'Trev?'

'Um . . . driving. A van. A friend of a friend needs some help, they need a driver and you are looking at their new man.'

'So will you be able to give me some money?'

'Well, not until Friday next week. They don't pay at the end of the day, baby.'

Sharon chewed her bottom lip. Trevor pushed the door shut and put his arms around her.

She leant against his chest. He may not have money, she thought, but this feels so good. She shut her eyes and started pressing into him. His hands fell down to the backs of her thighs, massaging all the way. Hitching up her skirt, he gently parted her legs and hooked his fingers under her knickers. She undid his shirt, took off hers and shuddered as their skin touched. Immediately he pulled her breast free of her bra and sucked hard on her nipple, thrusting his finger deeper inside.

As she struggled to get his trousers undone, she put her hand into his pocket and felt something strange. 'Trev? Trev, what's this?'

She pushed Trevor off and pulled a wrap out of his pocket. 'Trevor! Where did you get this?' She unfolded the packet and dabbed her finger in the white powder.

Trevor grinned. 'I thought you'd like my little surprise.'

She did.

Every year Tasha has organised something a little special for her birthday. I'm not big on birthdays, but ever since I've known Tasha she's stretched her birthday celebrations for sometimes as long as six weeks and over two or more continents.

We were to meet at an Italian bar where we were to have a meal that was solely for 'special friends' of the 'closer nature'. Of course, Dr You-know-who would be sitting in the prime place, next to the birthday girl. Then we'd go on to another bar in Soho, where we would meet the rest of the party, maybe adding up to thirty in all. Then on to a nightclub or two.

But Tasha also insisted on meeting me for coffee in the daytime. Well, I couldn't exactly say, 'No, piss off. How much attention do you need, you greedy girl?' could I? Not that I wanted to. I did want to try and find some more work, though, but that would have to wait. Anyway, Tasha would get the chance to try out her present. What a special way to celebrate.

We met up at around two thirty in one of our favourite cafés. It was upstairs, above a bike shop, run by a motley crew of likeable testosterone from different parts of the southern hemisphere, Italy and France. They played really great music really loudly, and were flirtatious in a charming way. Of course, we loved it there. It was slightly on the expensive side and offered unusual sandwich combinations that often sounded better than they tasted. However, the coffee was excellent.

I felt Tasha's present throb in its bag against my leg. It wasn't switched on – that might give it away. It was just calling very loudly, and I couldn't listen to anything she was saying. I think she was going on about the doctor. Apparently, they'd got in a few good hours on the blower over the past couple of days, and were building up a really understanding friendship. One thing was for sure though: my leg was fast developing a friendship with the hunky vibey under the table. I couldn't wait to give it to her. I reached down to separate my leg and its would-be new friend.

'Happy birthday, darling!' I squeaked, bursting into laughter as I handed *him* over.

'Oh, wow! Thanks, Charlie!'

Tasha leant across the table and gave me a meaningful hug and kiss. I thought she should wait until she'd opened it before thanking me. She might not like it. Or it might just be a brick-in-a-box, for all she knew. Anyway, after wiping away the trace of a tear, we reordered our ruffled feathers and sat down again.

I had wrapped him very carefully. Our coffee arrived after she'd taken it out of the box and unravelled the first layer. I was grinning so much that Tasha was getting suspicious – especially as the winking waiter was hovering to see what it was, and I was going red. Tasha gave it a squeeze through the paper.

'Oh, oh. *Uh-oh!* I think I know what this is –' She was feeling the gift up and down, looking at me for confirmation that it was indeed what she had thought. 'And I think I'll wait until I get home to open it.'

'Oh, no! H'open him now. It's the birthday. *Si*, you 'ave to!' Giuliano, the Italian waiter, had no idea what was in that wrapper. He would have been shocked, a good, hard-working Catholic boy like him.

'Yeah, maybe you *should* wait, Tasha,' I said.

'Can we have the bill, please?' she asked.

'Tasha! We've only just got our coffee.'

'So you no h'open him now?'

We shook our heads apologetically.

'Ah, you crazy, you no want the bill? Nut now?'

'In a while, thanks,' I said.

He smiled and backed off into the kitchen, winking at Tasha as he turned away.

'God, Tash, they love you in here, don't they?'

'I'm telling you, I specialise in Italians. Craig is half Italian. They *do* like me, and me them.' She eyed up Giuliano's rear. 'And is this really what I think it is?'

'If your mind is as dirty as your laundry, then yes, my friend.'

Her eyes widened in excitement, as she gave the hulk another rather sexual rub and squeeze.

'Okay, Tasha, steady on, darling. Wait until you're in the privacy of your own home. I can see that he's already a success.'

After naming him Giorgio, we continued with our coffee talk. Tasha was ranting on about this flipping doctor. He was getting her all wound up about her dream project: a farm in France, where they'd grow organic foods and run a retreat, a creative-spiritual centre. Their combined healing skills and his qualifications would enable company bookings. They were thinking big, hippie, rosy-posy and love-happy. She was on cloud fucking nine hundred. She didn't mention the band once. She had the next twenty-three years well sorted out and the single-mother brigade did not feature in it, not one iota.

Conka was late getting to the school. I waited with her mini-double, Helena, and Luke at the gates. They were going on about some new fad they wanted from the newsagent's. This seemed to be a large part of my relationship with Luke, I noted: his persistent asking for stuff and my pleading with him to stop begging and whingeing the whole goddamned time. I really

148

would have to address this problem of ours instead of trying to solve everyone else's worries.

The kids picked up all kinds of needs and wants from school. Every week there was another kind of sticker or popper they had to have. It was pointless crap as well, and totally worthless, except for the X-Men cards. I have to admit the artwork on them was something else. I didn't mind so much when he asked for those.

Conka seemed slightly harassed as she came marching down the road to meet us. She looked cold and her nose was bright red. Before anyone else could get a word in, Helena started begging to go to the frigging shop. Conka said yes quickly, which meant that she had something to tell me that was worth paying the kids for a quiet life. Interesting. We bundled into the newsagent's and bought the fips and gips they wanted, then headed towards the bus stop.

'What happened, then, Conks? Good day?'

'Pretty funny, really. Quite eventful, I suppose. You're not going to believe this, but you know my friend Elsa?'

I nodded. Elsa was Conka's catering partner.

'Well, you know she's got that great big stupid Dobermann?'

Yeah, I knew. Conka and I had met him with Elsa a couple of weeks ago in the street. The dog had left a lasting impression on my mind. It looked really terrifying. It was big for its breed and the average Dobermann comes up pretty big. It dribbled profusely, as well as seeming totally uncomfortable, which was slightly unnerving. Yeah, I knew that Dobey.

'Me and Elsa was taking David out for a walk across the back woods, right?'

I'd forgotten the dog had a stupid name. David. Huh!

'Well, we was walking along, gassing away, when we realised we hadn't seen David in a while. So, anyways, we start calling him and calling him and splitting up and walking all over the place, and it was freezing fucking cold today, in those woods. Do you know where I mean?'

'Yeah, yeah. Some places are always freezing, no matter what time of the year it is and that place is one of them.'

'Absolutely, Charl. So I'm freezing my nuts off and there is no bloody sign of him. I mean, he's not an obedient dog at the best of times, but he normally comes back – eventually. But today he wasn't coming back. We've been looking for him all this time, but to no avail. None, *nada*. That's why I was flipping late at the school.'

'Oh, no!' I was a good listener.

'Well, I says to Elsa I had to go. What I was worried about was him having a flipping heart-attack and kicking the bucket, and us finding some big fuck-off-dead Dobermann dog. I mean, he's pretty old and that's not an unlikely scenario. So I tells her I've got to come and get Helena and that she should call the cops.'

'You're kidding? So, you didn't find David, then?'

'Nah, my friend. We had to abandon the search. We were looking for close to two hours – well, an hour, maybe. It was so fucking cold though, I'm frozen all the way to my bones, you know?' She screwed up her nose.

I liked her nose. It was big and pudgy, but sweet. It made you want to squeeze it. I *really* felt like squeezing it when she screwed it up like that.

'Tragedy, innit?'

'Will she be upset if the dog is dead?'

'Elsa? She'd be devastated, mate, totally bleeding devastated. She's been married to that dog for the past eight years.'

'So she's a dogsbian?'

'Nah. Wouldn't it be a dogosexual?'

I laughed.

'It's not funny, Charlie,' Conka said, frowning.

We got on the bus in silence, out of respect for the dog. It seemed pretty gloomy.

'You ever had any dogs down the morgue, then, Char?' Conka asked.

I looked at her in disbelief, but she seemed serious. 'No, not really.'

A slow smile grew on Conka's face. 'You mean, some of 'em look like dogs after you've finished with them!'

'You haven't got a clue how beautiful a dead face can be.'

Conka looked at me devilishly. 'I want to see one,' she said.

'Oh, do you now?' I teased.

'I could be the manicurist. I'm good with nails.'

'I suppose it wouldn't hurt,' I conceded. It was a pretty lonely job.

'Great. That's settled, then. When's your next job?'

'Not until next week.'

'When? Monday? Thursday? Tuesday?'

'Thursday,' I mumbled. 'Although they don't know for sure.'

'How come?' Conka asked, not letting up.

'Because,' I said slowly, 'she hasn't died yet.'

Conka laughed. 'You mean you've been booked for a job on a dead woman and she hasn't even died yet?'

'Keep your voice down,' I hissed, noticing the entire bus turn and look at us. 'Some people do it that way. She's been dying for about three weeks apparently, so she should go soon.'

'Have you met her?'

'Of course not. Now shut up.'

'What are you gonna wear tonight to Tasha's do, then?' she asked, changing the subject cleverly.

I hadn't a clue.

'Let's go back to yours and we'll get ready together,' Conka suggested.

Once back at mine, we decided to don our Afros. As we got ready, the kids laughed and climbed up the hallway wall. Putting on a wig really gets you in a good mood for going out, I can tell you, especially when you've got two mad five-year-olds pissing themselves every time they look at you. Of course we smoked a couple of truly silly ciggies, which added to our frivolity. We didn't do the whole brown-body-paint thing though this time. Rather than being Brazilian trannies, we merely leant towards the seventies. We ended up looking quite saucy.

The buzzer went. Sharon jumped. She was nervous from the coke.

'Who's that?' Trevor asked.

Sharon went to the intercom praying it wasn't the bailiffs. 'Hello?'

'Hi!'

Phew! it was Liam's friend from school, Sam, and his mother. He was staying the night with her.

Sharon got his pyjamas. 'Come on, Liam. Let's go.'

Trevor heard Liam object, Sharon insist, the soft voice of Sam's mum, and then the door close. 'So, how come Liam's staying with her?'

''Cause I'm going out, and I didn't know if you'd be back from the pub in time to babysit or not. Let's face it, Trevor, you're not normally in till half eleven.'

'Great! So if I was back in time, I'd be your fucking babysitter!'

Trevor stamped out of the bedroom, flicked on the television and sat in his usual spot on the sofa.

Right, Sharon thought, I'd better get ready. She remembered her hipsters. They were very tight – she used to be tiny – and probably wouldn't fit her any more. They squeezed on. She found an old but sweet short top that tied around her boobs. She used to feel sexy in this particular outfit, but now she felt way too old. She took off the hipsters, put on her short suede skirt and some high boots. She went into the living room to do her makeup. She could feel Trevor staring at her. She'd make him wish he'd treated her right. She sat with her legs teasingly apart – she knew his weak spots.

'Where are you going, then?'

'Tasha's birthday party.'

'What – like that? Where is it? A singles bar in Soho?'

Sharon ignored him and pencilled in her eyebrows.

'Aren't I invited?'

'I didn't think you'd want to come . . . I thought you hated my friends.'

'I said, aren't I invited?' Trevor stood up and turned off the television.

'To Tasha's?'

'If that is where you're going.' Trevor was now about a foot away from her face and she could smell the beer on his breath.

'Yes. Yes, of course.'

'Good. I'll just get my jacket.'

Part Three

A Live Performance and
a Visit to the Dead

23

Tasha waved to Conka and me as soon as we arrived at the restaurant. With her zillions of plaits in a load of ribbons, no wonder the doctor was all over her. Tasha looked brilliant and very sexy. He, on the other hand, didn't look nearly as sexy out of his stethoscope and white coat. Quite a disappointment, in fact. I preferred a funkier man myself. Tasha and I had never had the same taste in men, but the cocky-docky verged on the slime-ball.

As Tasha showed us where to sit, she managed to tell me quietly that she'd done it with Giorgio. Fantastic! She hadn't yet slept with the doctor, just as she hadn't yet tried talking to Giorgio. I hoped secretly that Giorgio would put the doctor to shame. There was definitely something about him I didn't like. But, hey, it was birthday night and no overt cynicism was allowed. Just as well, really, as both Conka and I were dying to lay into Sharon when she showed up with Trevor.

They both looked off their faces and Sharon immediately went to the ladies'. Trevor walked over adamantly. He had that look on his face that said, 'I should have had a personal invite, as I am with Sharon, you know. But I didn't get one, so now I'm here just to *spite* you all. Okay?'

Well, walking into a roomful of people who can't stand you does tend to create a bit of an atmosphere. What made it worse was that they were the last to arrive and there was only one chair left at the table. No one moved too quickly to get another one, either. It was only when Trevor sat in the chair that had been 'saved' for Sharon next to the doctor that another was found.

Sharon looked amazing, but she couldn't relax all evening. Trevor and the doctor hit it off big-time, though, which worried me even more. Maybe they were in collaboration and out to confuse single mothers. I could tell that Sharon didn't trust the doctor. She kept giving me sneaky sideways glances when he and

Trevor were in the thick of some debate, proudly demonstrating their intellect in peacock performances. I noticed how both men held their women's upper thighs territorially throughout their conversation. I wondered what it'd be like if John Boring Bloody Major delivered a speech while rubbing Norma up, or the Queen and Phil. Sharon and Trevor: what a bad combo.

I'd never seen Trevor and Sharon in a situation as apparently normal as this before. In fact, I'd never seen the two of them having a good time together which, according to Sharon, they did sometimes. The vibe between them was more like your regular Hitchcock than anything even close to love. It reminded me of my relationship with Luke's dad and the rare occasions that we'd tried to go out together. We always had a shit time. That should really be a sign, shouldn't it? If you're not laughing or dancing or eating great food and enjoying good conversation, then you're having a crap time, simple as that. And if you're uptight about an argument you know is inevitable, you're definitely having a rubbish time.

A live band clambered on to the small stage, which was situated near our table. Conka nodded at them. 'That could be us,' she mouthed to me.

I winked at her. We had the spirit, Tasha and Sharon the sex appeal. Our band was destined for success. Conka poured me another tequila from the hefty bottle that we'd had the forethought to bring with us. The Afros were warm and by the time we'd worked our way through half the tequila they were positively roasting. Bubbles of sweat popped out all over Conka's forehead, and the dewy beads on my upper lip kept plopping into my drink. Still, it saved me licking the salt.

Conka and I tended to behave like a double act when we were wigged up. We performed. We knew what the other was thinking. For example, she knew I was dying to slag off the doctor, and I knew that she wanted to sing Happy Birthday to Tasha onstage. We had the kind of telepathic relationship a couple would die for. Maybe we should give it a try. If the sex worked, we'd be a kicking couple. It'd be fun for the kids, and easier for us in many ways. Plus, I could call off my search for suitable, capable, detached, fun-loving testos. Conka had the ability to make me feel anything was possible. Conka was worth dragging a screaming Sharon onstage for. She gave me the power and I was going to use it.

Conka had already okayed it with the band to borrow the guitars and their drummer. She threw the bass on to the objecting Sharon, got a guitar strapped on to herself, thrust a mike in my hands, and adjusted her mike stand.

'Ready?' she asked.

Neither Sharon nor I was in a fit condition to reply. Sharon looked terrified and I *was* terrified, as well as having to concentrate very hard on standing up straight.

Conka began playing, and Sharon quickly came in with the bass. It seemed like she'd suddenly got into it. She kept up with Conka and the drummer. This was good and gave me a surge of confidence as we began to sing.

Apart from my voice cracking a couple of times on the high 'birthday' bits, I sang really well. Conka's voice did the trick, though. Give her a mike and she's Tina Turner. Tasha stood up and cried openly. She can be so American sometimes. We'd finished the song and I was just getting ready to sit down again when I heard Conka call to Tasha to join us – and, to my astonishment, Sharon egging Conka on to play 'Bing Banged My Lula'.

'All right, Charlie?' Conka called.

I was sweating badly by now. My wig was itching the crap out of me, and I really didn't know if I could carry on. Sharon and Conka had heaps more experience. I shook my head, desperate and unable to answer. But Conka's attention was firmly set upon reminding the other two how 'Bing Banged' went. Before I knew it, they had started to play. I heard Conka sing the first couple of lines. I still couldn't move. I was aware that my mouth was stuck half open. At last she realised I was going through serious stage-fright, locked her eyes into mine and hypnotised me into singing again.

'Bing went wrong, with a big bong,' I heard myself sing.

'Bing banged, Bing banged my lula,

Bing banged, Bing banged my lula . . .'

My confidence slowly returned. Sharon was strumming away

coolly. She still looked amazing. It was Tasha who sounded terrible. As we sang, I noticed the real band motion to Conka to get us off, and Conka ignoring them. At our table, Trevor was standing up and looking very pissed off. Sharon must have clocked him too, as she slowly stopped playing. The band and Trevor stormed the stage simultaneously in a cunning pincer movement and our impromptu gig was forced to an early end.

Trevor tried to drag Sharon home immediately, but somehow the doctor managed to defuse the situation. You could feel the rage emanate off Trevor.

Sharon was laughing. She'd got off on our musical experience. She loved showing off and coke gave her the confidence to do so. 'Did you enjoy that then, Craig?' she purred.

Trevor clenched his jaw.

'It was very good,' Craig clipped.

'What happened to you?' Conka asked me, as she refilled my glass.

'Bit of nerves, I reckon,' I answered, too engrossed in Sharon's outrageous flirting with the doctor to bother dissecting my performance.

I passed Sharon my glass, the contents of which she downed readily.

'Guys, that was so great. I loved it. This is the best birthday, *ever*,' Tasha said, leaning over our chairs. 'Thank you so much. What do you think of Craig?' she whispered in my ear.

'Nice, yeah,' was all I managed to come up with.

Fortunately, Tasha didn't hang about for a more in-depth opinion as by now she was sitting on his lap.

'I bet he's loving that,' Conka said, nudging me.

'Bastard,' I replied.

'Yeah, he's a tosser, inne?' Conka agreed, giggling.

After some more drinks and dances, I was ready to go home. Trevor and Sharon had left a while back and I was getting bored. Conka gave me the nod, we put some money on the table, said our slurred goodbyes and left.

We went outside the restaurant to wait for a cab. It was suddenly quiet and cold. A cab drew up, took a closer look at us and sped off.

'You *bastard!*' Conka shouted after it.

'Maybe we should take our wigs off, Conks,' I suggested. We did look a bit weird.

'You can. I'm not gonna. I'll fucking freeze.'

'But we'll really freeze if we have to stand out here all night. I don't think I *should* take off my wig, considering how much I sweated tonight.' Conka still wasn't making any move to remove hers. 'But I will, just so we can get home. All right?' I said heroically.

The next cab stopped and we were on our way.

Conka took my hand. 'Well done, Charlie. You did really good tonight.'

'I couldn't have done it without you, though, Conks.'

She kept hold of me. Her hand felt soft and warm; mine was cold and clammy. Just as I thought she might be about to kiss me – not just to congratulate me on my musical début – the cabbie slammed on the brakes and we landed heavily on the floor. It fucking hurt my arse and made me think that perhaps Fate had decided that I wasn't yet ready for my Conka-romp.

I asked the driver to drop Conka off at her house, telling Conka that Luke was in my bed, the babysitter in the other, and that I'd see her in the morning. We kissed goodbye on the lips and Conka winked at me as the cab pulled away. There was no doubt that we loved each other, whatever.

Trevor shouted so much when they left the restaurant that Sharon stormed off on her own. She assumed he'd come after her like he always did, but this time he didn't. She was soon regretting it as she had hardly any money. He'd been the one looking after the cash, so no wonder he hadn't chased after her. Bastard! She found her way to a mini-cab office and negotiated her fare home. She was exhausted and the coke was wearing off.

She was about to fall asleep when the phone rang. She leapt out of bed but, as soon as she switched on the light, it stopped. He's checking I'm in, she thought, as she stared at the street below. She saw him walk up the road – the way he had gone when he went to that Tiffany's.

Sharon sat down in the kitchen on her stool – her lookout post

– next to the curtain. She lit a cigarette, and sighed deeply. She couldn't even cry any more. Maybe she was wrong? Maybe things would improve once he started work? Trevor, to be fair, had been pulling his weight recently. But money was what she needed. She wondered where he could have gone. Why did he have to do this to her *now*? She hated coming down like this on her own. She couldn't remember feeling this depressed in a long time.

Trevor had had enough. He was going round to Tiffany's. He had felt vaguely repentant the last time. Tiffany had been great, but something had pulled him back to Sharon. She just knew how to – well, you know . . . no one had a mouth and tongue like Sharon. But didn't she do a beautiful job of shaming him in public? Fucking bitch with her ridiculous single-mother mates.

Not only had Sharon become impossible to go out with she also never fucking appreciated anything he did. He was wrong when he was wrong, and wrong when he was right. She couldn't stop whingeing about money, except when she was doing some rock-and-roll number. He didn't even feel like starting this fucking job with Tiffany's brother any more. The bloke got on his nerves as it was. He stopped by the off-licence and bought a few beers. Fuck Sharon! He could get Tiffany to suck his dick.

He called Tiffany on her mobile from the next pay-phone. He wasn't going to, but he did. She was in her car on the way to pick someone up about five minutes away.

'Stay there. I know exactly where you are. Five minutes, ya? Okay, sweetie?'

'Okay, Tiffany.'

Trevor glugged back his beer and opened another. He thought about Sharon. He knew she was in. He wondered if she'd come to her senses yet. He thought about going back.

'Trevor! Over here!' Tiffany shouted from her Golf.

That was fucking quick, Trevor thought, as he waited for the traffic to clear so he could cross. Tiffany looked good in her racing-green car. She waved at him until he managed to join her.

'All right, Tiff?' Trevor said, as he climbed in.

'Oh, *don't* call her that, *please*,' came Jeremy's annoying voice from the back.

'Hello, Jeremy,' Trevor grunted.

'Ready for Monday, Trevor? Tiffany tells me you've more muscle than you show.'

'Shut up, Jeremy,' Tiffany snapped. 'How are you?'

'Fine. Who were you going to pick up?'

'Eleanor,' Tiffany answered. 'We're going for very late cocktails at a private party in Kensington Gardens – d'you fancy it?'

'I'm not really dressed for it.'

'Oh, go on. Don't be a bore.' Jeremy nudged the back of Trevor's seat. 'You look fine. Besides, you can be our token bit of rough. Go on, Trevie, there'll be plenty of booze and beautiful people. You never know, it might turn out to be an orgy!'

'Jeremy! Will you shut up?'

'Oh, come on, Tiffany, don't you fancy Eleanor any more? You've always been so nice to all my girlfriends.' Jeremy fell about in hysterics. 'Your face, Trevor –'

'Fuck off!' Trevor turned to look at him. He felt like punching his hooked nose right into the back of his skull.

'Ooh, temper! How about a nice little line, Trevor?' Jeremy winked. 'Park here, Tiffany. We'll stop off at Eleanor's and rack them out.'

'That's the first good idea you've had in ages, brother dear.'

They walked up some grandiose steps to a large walnut door. A bright security sensor light lit them up. Eleanor let them in. She looked too tanned and her floral perfume stifled Trevor. The large door clicked shut quietly behind them. They walked through the enormous hall and into her apartment.

Trevor looked around: Eleanor's Notting Hill pad was made for doing drugs in. Every surface was smooth, clean and hard. There was a steel bar, jutting into a lounge that had Turkish floor cushions all over the place. Trevor thought that the pick-and-mix effect of cultures and décor was ridiculous.

Jeremy racked out four large lines on the bar. Trevor watched Tiffany snort it up professionally, nice and clean, no fall-out from her nose. Eleanor, next. Yep, her nose worked just as well. She handed him the brass straw, designed specifically for snorting cocaine. Even that detail had been thought about. Trevor gladly snorted up the larger of the two remaining lines, and passed the straw to Jeremy.

'Anyone for voddy?' Eleanor called.

'Go on, then,' Jeremy sniffed. 'We're already three hours late. But, okay, just a quick one. Then we'll really have to get going.'

Eleanor brought in a silver tray with a bottle of vodka, a bowl of ice, a jug of cranberry juice and four identical tall blue glasses. Something about all this got on Trevor's nerves. Sharon didn't have any matching glasses – you were lucky if you could find one without a crack or chip – but this, everything nice, clean, the best vodka, the best cocaine, even the ice, this pomp fucked him off. He went to the bathroom.

It was warm with a thick cream carpet underfoot, and mirrors everywhere. He looked at himself while he peed, his piss splashing out over the bowl. He was pretty handsome, and only twenty-eight. He *should* be going out and having fun – it wasn't him with the kid, after all. He wasn't doing anything wrong. Was it so bad not to want to go by fucking pushbike everywhere? He enjoyed being driven around in Tiffany's car; he enjoyed her company. It was really only Jeremy that put him off. Even Eleanor Rigby was okay. He zipped up his flies and spashed his face. Yeah, he was good-looking all right, he thought, as he combed back his hair.

They were looking pretty cosy, shoes off, holding drinks, by the time Trevor came down.

'Do you want another line, sweetie?' Tiffany asked. She took him by the hand and led him to the lowered den in the far corner of the lounge where there were yet more floor cushions, strewn around a suitably hard, smooth-surfaced table.

'Why don't you take your shoes off, Trevor?' she said, while carefully setting up more lines. 'You'll be more comfortable.'

She smiled at him and beckoned him to join her on the floor. She was pretty sexy too, Trevor thought, as he kicked off his trainers and sat down. They did another line and Tiffany took off her shirt. She had a kind of Indian bra on, and loads of thin, beaded necklaces. Her tits were minute though, and she was skinny on top. She looked quite flushed, no doubt from the coke. Trevor was getting too hot himself and took off his tracksuit top.

'Don't you just *love* it here? I always think it's like an opium den,' Tiffany said, as she wriggled up to him.

Trevor thought it was nothing like one, but who gave a shit? He put his arm round her and they started kissing. Her lips seemed small and tight compared to Sharon's, but her hand was doing nicely. Trevor was aware that Jeremy and Eleanor were getting more and more naked in the other part of the room.

'What about the roof-garden thing?' Trevor asked, in between kisses.

'Oh, we've missed that now. We should have been there ages ago. It would have been naff anyway. This is much better.'

She was rubbing his leg. It felt good, but he wanted her to grab his balls. He wasn't really getting turned on. He didn't like the others being so close. He heard a phone ring.

It was Jeremy's mobile. 'Yep, I'll be right there.' He was getting dressed as he spoke. 'Yep, I know where that is . . . Okay, 'bye.' He bounced over to the den.

'Tiffany, can I have the car keys? I've got to go and snort something out,' Jeremy said, laughing. 'Stay here and keep Eleanor company, okay? See you later, Trevor. By the way, here are the keys for the Transit. It's parked up at Tiffany's. You'll need to be there *early* on Monday.'

He gave Trevor a set of keys and took some others from Tiffany. He licked his finger, swiped it over the table, picking up some crumbs of cocaine, then rubbed his gums. He gave Eleanor an affectionate tap on the bottom and sped out. Trevor noticed how ugly Tiffany's feet were as she came and sat down again.

'Do you guys need a refill over there?' Eleanor called, after Jeremy had gone.

'Yes please, darling,' Tiffany said, grinning at Trevor. 'And how about another of these?'

Trevor was as high as a kite already, but it felt good and it was a pretty cool situation. 'Go on then, you devil,' he said, causing Tiffany to squeal with delight.

Eleanor had joined them on the cushions and was nestling close to Tiffany. Trevor noticed their breasts touch when she leant over to do her line. Eleanor's were massive.

'So what was Jeremy on about in the car, then?' Trevor asked.

'Oh, ignore him. He's just a silly schoolboy. Gosh, it is warm over here, isn't it?' Eleanor said, taking off her top.

Her sumptuous breasts were begging to be freed from the tight purple bra that imprisoned them. Her belly rolled in Rubenesque splendour. Trevor noticed Tiffany's other hand rub Eleanor's thigh, the same way she'd been rubbing his. He gulped back his drink. He kept thinking of Sharon, he just couldn't help it. He hoped she was okay. He knew how bad she could get when she was coming down.

Eleanor poured some more drinks, allowing her semi-naked breasts to rub over Tiffany. Tiffany unhooked her bra strap, freeing her friend's splendid form.

'Ooh, Tiffany, you naughty little girl!' Eleanor cried, in mock-horror.

As Eleanor reclined, Tiffany's hand played with her breasts, kneading them like spongy dough. They kissed, snogged.

Trevor still didn't feel like it. 'Look, I'll see you later.'

'Don't go.' Tiffany turned her attention to him. 'Can't you stay an incey bit longer?'

He wanted to. He wanted to fuck the pair of them stupid all night. He had nothing to feel guilty about. But he knew he couldn't get it up right there and then – too much coke or something. 'Nah. I've gotta do something. Boy, I wish I could stay – you girls . . . Well, I'll be off.'

'Don't you want another line?' Tiffany called as he got to the door.

'No thanks, darling. I'll see you soon.'

When he got in Sharon was still up, sitting transfixed on the kitchen stool.

'Where the fuck have you been?' she asked, choking back the tears.

Here we go, Trevor thought, here we fucking go. He should have fucking well stayed with those posh dykes. 'If you must know, I've been with the guy I'm working for next week.'

'At this time of night?'

'*Yes, Sharon,* at this time of night. We had to wait for someone else to bring back the van and he needed to give me the keys. Jeremy couldn't make it at any other time.'

Sharon knew he was lying. 'Huh. You think I'm a fucking idiot, don't you?' She lit yet another fag.

Trevor took out the Transit keys and threw them on the table. 'I'm trying, okay?' he said, more gently.

Sharon stared at the keys on the table. Trevor went into the lounge. They looked like van keys, all right. Sharon certainly hadn't seen them before, but something still felt wrong. There again, he was finally going to give her some money, and she really needed it, that was for sure. She heard Trevor cough. Maybe she *was* just paranoid and jealous about nothing after all. She hurried into the living room.

'I'm sorry, Trev. I didn't know, you just left . . .' She broke down in tears again.

Trevor put his arms around her. 'You waltzed off. You behaved like the loony.'

'I'm so sorry, Trev,' Sharon sobbed.

'Look, you said you needed some money and I'm trying, okay? This guy I'm going to be working with is a total arsehole. It's a shit job, but I'm doing it. Fuck Sharon, I'm trying! And it's not some stupid pie in the sky band either. Jeremy, my boss – well let's just say, I can't stand the guy. I'd *much* rather be here with you.'

They kissed and he felt her melt into his arms. He carried her to the bedroom and stroked her hair until she fell asleep.

24

Around eleven the next morning I rang Tasha to see if she felt like going to the launderette. I suggested a post-birthday-party-mortem while our whites washed whiter. My hangover wasn't too fierce. I tend to be all right if I stick to the one drink, and even though tequila is pretty rough, Conka's hand-holding moment combined with arse-ache from hell had sobered me up enough to remind me to drink a pint of water and swallow a couple of aspirins before bed. I find that always helps.

The same could not be said for Tasha. She'd gone for it in a big way and still felt pissed. She was up for the launderette outing, though, so I picked her up ten minutes later.

Well, as soon as I saw her, I knew. The uncontrollable grin wiped across her face and that dazed look in her eyes said it all, but just to make sure I got the point, she was walking like she'd just been on a four-hour hack. She'd have put John Wayne to shame.

'Well, hello,' I said, as I opened the boot for her to sling her washing in.

'Hiya,' she replied sweetly.

'Has Giorgio been put to shame, or did you stay up all night talking to him?'

Tasha managed a feeble giggle as we got in the car. 'Oh, God, Charlie! You're not going to *believe* it.'

Tasha tried to stare right into my face to emphasise the *unbelievableness* of it all, but I kept my eyes firmly on the road. She refrained from talking to me until our arrival at the launderette. For the remainder of the journey she resorted to noisy, breathy sounds, as if exhaling loudly could communicate the enormity of how great it all was. He'd rendered her pretty daft.

We unloaded, sorted, loaded, fumbled with washing-powder and coins, bagged our baskets, got takeaway coffees and sat down on the bench opposite our machines. We were finally ready for our forty-minute chat.

Tasha's tired but happy eyes locked into mine to ensure my total concentration. She began her detailed description of the evening, starting from the hand-on-leg episode in the bar. This was going to be a fully detailed number.

I got comfortable and ready to listen to her thoughts on the evening, even the ones that included the doctor. She was hungry for him, she had launched into maximum-warp-drive-flirt all evening, leading on to a full-on sexual pig-out and was now ready to digest with me. Well, I wasn't getting any, I'd missed my chance, so I might as well listen to her story.

She told me how she had asked the universe to bring her someone like the doc; how they had interactive auras and loads of other spiritual shit, which meant that the chemistry between

166

them, which could go back as far as four hundred years and many eras ago, was so strong it was electrifying. When he rubbed her thigh, she stained her kegs – by him just doing that. This girl was on fire.

He'd been everything she'd ever wanted a man to be: a gentleman, but not a wet pushover fart; flirtatious, but *only* with her – I should bleeding well hope so too; financially obliging, but not annoyingly flash with the cash. This man had it all, baby, and when it came to performance in the sack, he was an anatomical genius. Tasha was stunned. Poor old Giorgio, there's not much call for second-hand vibrators. I'd want a new one, wouldn't you?

After Conka and I had left, Tasha and about five other survivors had apparently carried on to the Rub-a-Dub Club, which throbbed drum and bass, occasionally burped a bit of dub, and heaved with sweat and steam. I was happy to have missed what seemed close to a hideous nightmare.

It was time to do the unload-load thing again: dry time. Drying took more effort than washing. You had to feed the machine constantly with an infernal diet of fiddly twenty-pence pieces, as well as taking stuff out and folding it up. With all this action, the intensity of the conversation was reduced, while the subject matter became funnier.

Tasha began describing the more intimate details of the doc's personal anatomy. As she was talking fairly quietly, my attention waned and I became aware of a youngish man on the other bench. I noticed his ears poised in our direction and that he hadn't turned the page of his newspaper for quite some time. Tasha began to talk a bit louder to regain my attention.

'It's just as well I've got A BIG MOUTH!' she blurted out at full volume, at which point the newspaper dropped down from the man's face as he took a frightened glance at the pair of us.

'Oh dear. That came out a bit loud, eh?' she whispered.

'Just a tad, dear.'

The man reburied his head in his paper. I think we put him off women for life.

'Hey, Tash, you've got to come over after school. Conka and I are going to have a mini band practice. I want to ride on the spirit of last night, babes.'

'You must be joking. I'm still pissed now. By then, I'll be totally hung over.'

'Oh, come on. You need to practise your harmonies.'

'Is Sharon coming?'

'No. She said she was up all night arguing. Surprise, surprise. But that doesn't mean you shouldn't come.'

'You know, it was so great yesterday, it really showed me how we could work as a proper band. And being sung Happy Birthday to like that – well, it was so cool, thank you so much. You know, I'd really love to come and rehearse, but I honestly don't think I'll be any use.'

I wanted to work on the music and it would be much better if Tasha could be there, but she was not to be persuaded. I forgave her flakiness this time, but warned her that we might have to play on tour when we felt like that. There were bound to be hundreds of occasions when we'd get really sloshed after a gig then have to travel and play the next night. Touring was no picnic.

Tasha just smiled. She loved the rock chick in me, and so did I.

As usual I met Conka at the school. We got the kids and went home. She had good news. 'David showed up.'

'So the Dobey ain't dead?'

'Nope, thank God.'

'Fabtastic. What happened, then?'

'He showed up in a bingo hall in Acton, five flipping miles from where we lost him. He just trotted in, apparently. He's so friendly, he'd never hurt anyone, but he bounces up to people and tries to lick them all over. You can imagine what that did to the oldies in the bingo hall . . .'

'Were there any recorded heart-attacks?'

'None as yet. The oldies called the police and stood on their chairs until they arrived – imagine them all standing on their bingo forms. I love old people, they really are fucking mad. They probably loved it really too. A bit of unexpected excitement is always a laugh, know what I mean, Char? Can you imagine, that's gonna be their Christmas story for the next ten years, maybe until death, who knows? But they're going to love spinning that one, for sure, Charl – I'm telling you. Although they would have been scared. I mean, you don't expect to run into a Dobey when you go bingo, do you?'

'Certainly not Conks, for sure.'

'Well, he had a dog tag on him and the police had contacted Elsa by about seven last night.'

'God! It's nice to hear a story with a happy ending. Mother and dog are doing fine, I take it?'

'Never felt better. An emotional reunion, but a healthy one at that.'

'Great news, Conks. Great news, *mon amie*.'

Conka began to strum the guitar that lived at my house. 'I think we should write a song, Chassy baby.' She strummed a few dangerous chords. 'A song about a darned garn Dobey, who we thought was dead, turned up later, made some faces so red, the darned garn Dobey, who we took for dead . . .' she sang, and played in rock 'n' roll style.

I jotted down some of the dead-dog lyrics Conka was spouting so prolifically, while trying to sing along with the chorus that was swiftly developing.

'The darned garrrn Dobey, whom we took for dead,
He was wild and roaming, but he certainly weren't dead,
He took to bingo, like copper 'n' lead,
He played his collar, he was losing his head,
Old David Dobey, barked out loud,
On to the tables, leapt the crowd.
In came John, Jack to his mates,
A copper with guts, too many chilli plates.
Oh too many chilli plates! Chilli plates!
Still,
The cops came in, and caught him straight,
No more bingo – too darned late.
The darned garn Dobey, whom we took for dead,
Took to bingo, like copper to lead,
The darned garn Dobey, he weren't dead.
David the Dobey – he's alive,
Woah David Dobey – he survives, cause . . .
That darned garn Dobey, he ain't dead!'

The children sang with us, and we got louder and sillier as we sang the evening away. At around bedtime, Conka took Helena home. Nothing had been said about our hand-holding episode. Phew! A lot, however, had been said about the funeral home. Conka was getting insanely excited at the prospect of going.

I was pleasantly worn out from singing and partying the night before, so I flopped into bed shortly after Luke was asleep. Singing made me feel A okay about life, I thought, as I lay there feeling pretty fruity, waiting for King Slumber to come and kidnap me.

25

Conka looked serene in her sober, dark blue outfit. I was dressed in my usual long black skirt and black turtleneck. Our booking was at nine fifteen, so we dropped the kids off at school and went straight there, skipping our usual dose of caffeine at Mario's.

'She died, then?' Conka asked on the way.

'No. We're doing her while she's still alive, stupid.'

'All right, Charlie, calm down. So, what do you normally do with the hands?'

'You just do a usual manicure – clean them, file them. I don't normally bother with buffing. It's not as effective on dead hands for some reason. Then you give them a coat of clear. I've got all the materials in my box.'

'Blimey,' Conka said.

I think she was getting nervous. She'd never been so 'hands on' with a dead person before. It was pretty strange. I just hoped she wouldn't be chucking up.

'Are you sure you're okay about this?' I asked, as we got out of the car.

'I'm fantastic, Charlie. Stomach of steel, don't you worry.'

We entered the funeral parlour through the usual front door.

Matthew, the guy who ran the place, came to greet us. 'Good morning, Charlie. Hello there,' he said to Conka.

Matthew was about thirty-five, short and plump with fluffy reddy-pink hair. He'd bought the business about six years ago and was still very eager. 'We've got a lovely old dear today.' He pulled the warm apologetic face he adopted when talking about the deceased.

I think he thought it made him seem more sympathetic, but it actually looked as if he was about to burst out laughing. I knew he wasn't, but Conka obviously didn't: she was pulling mock-shock faces at me every time I caught her eye.

'This is Conka, my assistant for the morning. She's a manicurist,' I said quickly.

'How very pleasant to meet you.' Matthew shook her hand. 'Well, you know the ropes, Charlie. Do you ladies want a tea or anything?'

'Have you got any coffee?' Conka asked.

'I believe so.'

'We'll have two coffees, then, please. Both white with one sugar. Ta.'

I looked at Conka in disbelief. And there was me wondering if she was nervous. So far she'd taken it more in her stride than I'd ever done and I'd been going there at least four years. I never had a single coffee.

'I'll have Mary bring it to you,' Matthew said, as we walked towards the cool store.

'Well done, Conka,' I said, as I pulled the stiff out of its fridge.

I watched Conka as she looked at the body. I'm sure it freaked her out. It still freaks me out and I've seen loads – you never really get used to it.

A nervous giggle escaped her. 'This is fucking mad, Char. Mad,' she said.

I let Conka take a closer look before I began. The woman must have been in her seventies or eighties. She was a little thing with long thin silver hair, dressed in black. I pushed up my sleeves and put on my polythene gloves. Conka backed away a bit. I always start with the hair, so I lifted the upper half of the body to wedge the pillow below the shoulders so I could brush and tie it back. As I was shoving the pillow under, the corpse let rip an almighty burp.

'*Fuck! Fuck! Fucking hell!*' Conka screamed, leaping backwards and turning completely white.

She was jumping around the small room, staring at the body in total disbelief. '*Jesus*, Charlie. *Fuck!* For fuck's sake, what was that?'

I was laughing my head off. I was used to bodies farting and burping. The fresher ones especially do it when you move them around.

'It's just trapped gas finally working its way out,' I explained, between gulps of laughter.

Of course it had terrified me the first time, but, unlike Conka, I'd been warned.

Conka began to laugh too. 'You bastard, Charlie. Fucking hell, I've never been so scared in all my life.'

We were still giggling when Mary, Matthew's God-fearing wife, came in with the coffee. You could see the hot air waft up from the cups, but you couldn't smell the coffee. Nothing could conquer the chemical smell in that room. We took the coffee from Mary, she crossed herself and left the room, which gave us more cause for giggling.

'What are they like?' Conka asked.

'Now, come on, Conks, we've got to take it seriously,' I said, even though I was having more fun at the funeral home than I'd ever had before. I took another slurp of coffee and started on the hair again.

'Come on, jump to it. We haven't got all day, you know,' I said to Conka. 'You'll find all the nail stuff in the bottom tray.'

Conka took out the implements and approached the body slowly. She went to touch the hand.

'*Pah!*' I shouted, just as she touched it.

Conka leapt back with a scream.

'Shh! We'll get into trouble!'

'Well, stop making me jump,' Conka hissed.

Just then Matthew walked in. Conka made a dive for the hand and started filing away manically.

'Everything all right in here?' he said, smiling in his benevolent manner.

'Fine, thanks. Conka just jumped when the body passed wind,' I explained.

'Okay. I'll leave you to it, then,' Matthew said, retreating.

'I see you've got over your phobia, Conks.'

She was still in the throes of full-on filing. 'Well, as you said, we haven't got all day,' Conka said.

I finished dressing the hair and laid the body down, carefully holding everything in place. I started the makeup, beginning with the foundation. She wouldn't need much. There's not much you can do with a dead woman's skin tone. Generally I just use masses of blusher.

''Ere take a look at this.' Conka pointed to one of the hands. 'If I'm not mistaken, that's your genuine 1920s white gold Zvinderstein band. They're worth quite a bit.'

'Well, you know your antiques. I wouldn't have a bleeding clue.' I dabbed on some more rouge.

'It'd be a real shame to bury treasure like that, though.'

'You'd be amazed what some of them go down with, especially the Catholics. They reckon they'll pass it on to God or something,' I said.

'What? They don't give 'em to the relatives or nothing?'

'Nah. It's a shame, I suppose.'

'Why don't we nick it, Charlie?'

'No way, Conka.' I couldn't believe she'd even asked.

'If we pull this scarf here round her hands, who's going to fiddle with it?' Conka started pulling at the ring.

'Stop it! No, we can't, Conka!'

'Look, when you say goodbye to your dead loved one, you're in too much grief to notice if they've got their hands covered up or not.'

'Conka, that is not the point. You can't steal from the dead. How would you like it?'

'I'd love it, mate. What use would any of it be to me? I don't see what the problem is.'

Christ, she'd nearly got the flipping ring off her now. I had to stop her. 'Don't, Conka, please. Some relatives actually kiss the hand. Some may even want to kiss the ring, you never know. I'd lose my job, 'cos they'd know it was us.'

Conka looked at me with disappointment and pushed the ring back on. 'I thought we were a team, Charlie,' she said.

'We are, Conks. I'm sorry. It's only a ring.'

'Precisely.'

We carried on in silence. The already chilled, chemical air seemed to get colder and more acrid. I couldn't work out why Conka had wanted that ring so badly. Surely not just for the cash? I felt terrible and desperately wanted her forgiveness. I wished she'd crack a joke or something but she'd gone really quiet. I avoided eye-contact while I continued to work. I glanced now and then to check on what she was doing with the hands and, I suppose, to make sure she didn't swipe the ring regardless. I chided myself for being so suspicious and knew that she wouldn't really nick it. But this was the only job I'd managed to hold on to, and I needed it. When I noticed that Conka was applying orange nail varnish instead of clear, I decided against saying anything. Besides, it didn't look too bad.

About half an hour later we'd finished and were ready to go. Mr Matthews did his inspection and was his usual grateful self.

'Thanks a lot, Matthew. I'll send you the invoice as normal. 'Bye,' I said.

'Right. I'll be off then too, Charlie,' Conka said, as soon as we were outside.

'You don't want to go for a coffee, then?' I asked.

'No. I've got zillions of things to do today, ta. I'll see you later.'

'Okay then, 'bye,' I said, feeling flat.

'Oh, when do we get paid?' Conka asked, as I turned to go.

I stopped in my tracks. I couldn't believe she wanted me to pay her now. I didn't know quite what to say.

'I'm only getting my usual fee, Conka. I won't be getting any more for you, I'm afraid,' I stuttered eventually.

'Oh.' Conka looked even more pissed off. 'Well, I guess you can just buy me a bag of weed, or something. Never mind. See ya, then.'

I watched her stride off. I felt as if I'd done something very wrong but couldn't put my finger on it. But I knew I had been right in not taking the ring.

Three hours later I was back at the school, waiting for the kids with a bedraggled Sharon. I'd looked everywhere for Conka, but hadn't found her. She wasn't at any of her usuals. Sharon hadn't seen her either. It pissed me off, not knowing where she was, I wanted to clear things up.

Then I saw her. She looked stunning. Not only was she dressed in a very smart trouser suit – God knows where she procured that – but there was something else about her that was different, a haughtiness I'd not noticed before. 'Wow! Conka, you look amazing.'

'What are you all tarted up for, Conks?' Sharon asked.

'I've got a job.'

Neither Sharon nor I could hide our surprise. 'What?' we asked in unison.

Conka rearranged her suit collar and brushed some invisible fluff from her sleeve, deliberately ignoring us.

'Come on, tell us,' I pleaded.

Conka stopped fussing, gave her lips a lavish lick, and began. 'I thought it was 'bout time I got a job so I got the paper the other day, spent a couple of hours making a few phone calls, went on three interviews over the past couple of days, went back to one this afternoon, got offered the job, accepted it on the spot and I start tomorrow. And this morning's manicure session,' she continued, turning all her attention on me, 'proved to me that I won't be wanting to follow up a career with the dead, Charlie.'

With that she walked off to find Helena, leaving Sharon and me standing open-mouthed. Not only had she got a *job*, for fuck's sake, but she'd also made my job sound like the crappiest thing in the world.

'You took her down the morgue?' Sharon asked in disbelief.

'Yes.' I was still watching the vanishing Conka. 'Hey! Conka, wait! Congratulations!' I called, running after her. 'Hey, Conka! Wait for me.'

Conka had always seemed busy enough running around car-boot sales and markets, selling and buying. It seemed like really fucking hard work to me. She was a good dealer and I thought she made all-right money, but maybe I'd been wrong about that. Maybe that was why she was so pissed off about the ring, but just hadn't let on how broke she was.

I guess it'd got to her as well. We were unlikely to be making our mega-bucks from the band just yet, so there was no reason why Conka shouldn't get a job. We'd done that computer course together a few months back precisely to enable us to get work. But I didn't realise we were going to get actual, real jobs. Weird! And, for Chrissakes, *someone* had to do the stiffs. It must have freaked her out more than she was letting on. Still, she'd gone and got a job, and she'd made it look so easy. Apart from the funeral home, I hadn't had a makeup job in weeks. I should look for a more normal job, but my typing was crap compared to hers. She'd probably be using a computer as well. She'd be surfing the flaming Net before long. I couldn't bear it.

Once we'd got the kids, we regrouped by the gates. Conka chatted excitedly – thankfully, the deathly morning's doldrums seemed forgotten – telling us more about her new career. It was perfect for a mother. It was within school hours and was okay pay. She used her sister's name so she could continue to claim all her benefits. Her sister lived abroad, so she neither claimed nor paid any national insurance contribution, and as Conka's new employers would deduct it at source, Conka felt that everyone (herself, her sister, her employer and the government) would be happy, especially as after the deductions, the wage was not nearly enough to survive on.

It was Conka's first office job and she was pretty fired up about it. She would indeed be using a computer, and doing accounts. I was pleased for her, and put down the morning's freezer treatment to pre-interview nerves combined with stiff-burp phobia. Sharon hardly spoke at all. In fact, she looked as if she was about to burst into tears. Recently she had bawled her eyes out while waiting for Liam at the school gates. His class was late back from a school trip and she'd convinced herself that the bus had crashed.

Today, Sharon looked like she had one brewing and Conka's news just seemed to bring it nearer to the surface. I was anxious to get myself back into Conka's good books, and a band practice was what I had in mind.

'So when shall we have another rehearsal, girls?' I said brightly. 'I spoke to the smitten kitten earlier in the day and she let it slip that the cocky-docky was on duty almost constantly for the next three days and nights, so she has no excuse to miss it. How about Friday?'

'Sounds possible, but where?' Sharon said.

We finally agreed to meet at Sharon's on Friday night then maybe descend on Sarah during the weekend. Conka thought we should just organise a gig, but there was no way we were ready for that. I, more realistically, just prayed that no one would flake and cancel.

26

Tasha lay awake, watching him sleep. He was beautiful. They'd made the most amazing love about five times, and it had just got better and better. They'd travelled into another dimension, and had spent almost the entire day in her bed. But she was going to have to get up soon. It was almost time to pick Daniella up from nursery. She didn't feel like moving. She wanted this magical moment to last for ever. She'd found her soul-mate at long last, and this would be their last chance to be together for at least three days as Craig had some heavy shifts coming up.

She decided to ring the nursery and ask them to keep Daniella for an extra hour. She'd make some excuse – they didn't usually mind. She spoke quietly into the phone that lay next to the bed, then lay back with a sigh of relief. She watched Craig's chest rise up and down. He had smooth Mediterranean skin with quite a covering of chest hair. She wondered if that meant he'd be bald by the time he was forty. He was thirty-two, a good age. Well, perfect, really – older than her but not by too much. They could age gracefully together.

Tasha reflected on the bits of conversation they'd managed to grab in between kisses, cuddles, nibbling, licking, sucking . . . She couldn't believe how good it was. She'd never had it that good before. At one point she'd been literally screaming. God knows what the neighbours had thought.

Soon there wouldn't be any neighbours. They'd discussed France again. He wanted it as badly as she did. They were going to buy an old run-down farm; one they could find in the south-west quite cheap, with a fair amount of land and absolutely no neighbours. Heaven had come to earth. There would be no more trying to make ends meet, no more searching, no more recriminations for not working, she'd be doing a job, living her love, living the land. She felt that their love itself was more than enough to survive on. The doctor rolled on to his side. Tasha wished he'd wake up. She wanted more.

The phone rang, and Tasha put a pillow over it quickly. Craig didn't stir. The muffled ring continued. She found it very intrusive – she'd let the answerphone pick up. She could hear Charlie's voice, she was saying something about the band, but it could wait. The band? What band? It seemed funny to her now. She still wanted to do it, but now she'd met Craig things were different. She was realising far deeper desires and ambitions. Charlie and Conka wouldn't understand anyway. They couldn't appreciate fully how much you could get from a relationship with a man. They'd been hurt in the past and were now on a crusade to encourage everyone to be on their own. Charlie couldn't really see much beyond the band, and still had a lot of growing to do. Probably she craved a romance subconsciously, but she'd never admit it, not now she was this new nineties woman.

Still Charlie and Conka meant well, and Tasha enjoyed writing music and singing. She hoped she'd be able to help them write some cool songs, but nothing was going to get in the way of her new love and life. She looked at Craig's face. He was serene, and better-looking than anyone she'd previously been out with. They would be a pretty sexy couple. People hate it when you're this happy, she thought, and hoped they wouldn't get too much grief. She knew that Richard, Daniella's father, would give her some, but she'd find a way to get round it. He was picking Daniella up this evening, but she wouldn't mention France just yet. She'd have to think carefully about how to phrase that one.

It was time to wake Craig. She kissed his arm and whispered in his ear. He stirred as she smoothed back his hair.

'I've gotta go and get Daniella. It's four o'clock. Help yourself to the shower, darling.' She kissed him on the mouth, and dragged herself away.

*

In the beginning Trevor had enjoyed living with Sharon, but recently she hadn't let up. The flat was a mess yet again, and Trevor was in no mood to clean up. He flicked on the television and waited for her.

About half an hour later, he heard Liam tear up the stairs – that boy had too much energy – with Sharon shouting something after him.

'Hi, Trev,' Liam said, as he threw himself on the sofa next to him.

'All right, Liam? Have a good day?'

'Yeah, not bad.' Liam sniffed deliberately in his I'm-a-tough-grown-up-kid kind of way.

Trevor sniffed back. He'd go along with it. Liam could be pretty funny sometimes.

Sharon shuffled in. 'Thanks for tidying up, Trev,' she snapped, as she walked through to the kitchen.

He could hear her swearing under her breath at the mess she found in the kitchen. He had made a curry for their dinner, but why should he do all the washing up as well?

'Thanks, Trev,' Sharon shouted sarcastically again.

Trevor got up. Enough was fucking enough. He chewed the insides of his cheeks, contorting his mouth, lips and face as he walked into the kitchen.

He came right up to Sharon so that his face was about an inch away from hers. 'One more fucking complaint,' he hissed through his clenched teeth, 'it'll just take *one*, Sharon,' he poked her shoulder with every word, as if to imprint them on her, 'just one more, Sharon, and you're not getting anything, NOTHING – do you understand?'

Sharon bit her lip. A hot tear escaped and crawled down her face. She blinked but that just sent more tears cascading down.

Trevor softened, she was so beautiful, so sexy. He smudged away some mascara that had run down her cheek. Sharon jumped when his thumb touched her face. 'It's all right, darlin'. Come on. Hey,' he soothed, 'I'll tidy up in here, you do the lounge and then we'll have some dinner and a lovely evening.'

'But, Trev –'

'No buts, Sharon.' He threw her a glare to remind her of how ugly he'd been a couple of moments earlier. 'Let's go.'

Sharon joined Liam on the sofa. She needed to think. Maybe she should cancel everyone tonight. She lit a cigarette.

'*Mum!*' Liam started coughing and waving his arms around.

'Oh, all right! All right, Liam.' Sharon got up and went to the table. Liam was such a pain in the arse when it came to smoking: he couldn't hate it *that* much. She cleared the stuff off the surface while she thought about the band practice. Trevor would laugh at her if she told him. She didn't want to cancel it, though. She really felt like getting together with that lot, and after all it was her flat and Trevor wasn't paying any rent. God, he was on to such a good thing with her, so he should cook fucking dinner once in a while.

Trevor's meal, although basic, was delicious and all three of them had eaten well. He'd cleaned the kitchen as well. There were just a few things left to soak, but Sharon could deal with those tomorrow.

She looked at Liam fooling around with Trevor on the sofa. He was a great replacement-father figure sometimes, and certainly better than Liam's real dad, who was currently one of Her Majesty's guests. Trevor and Liam could be cute together.

She remembered that her three friends were due at any minute now. She frowned as she worried about warning Trevor. He'd probably get really angry and leave, even though he had been so nice lately. There was no way he would sit indoors with Charlie and Conka, that was for sure, let alone listen to them and their music. He wouldn't mind Tasha, probably . . .

Trevor came over and had a cigarette with her at the table.

'Mum, when's Luke coming?' Liam asked suddenly.

Sharon glanced towards Trevor. Goosebumps prickled her forearms.

'Mum?' Liam asked again.

She wished he'd be quiet. Trevor was beginning to do that cheek-chewing thing. He did that when he was stopping himself from shouting.

'Aren't you going to *answer him*?' Trevor screamed.

He slammed his hand on the table, causing the ashtray to empty itself everywhere.

'Any time now. They're coming soon, Liam,' she said slowly and carefully.

'So much for a nice night in.' Trevor stood up and put on his jacket.

'Trevor, don't go, please. I didn't know you were even going to be here tonight. It's Friday, for God's sake –'

But Trevor was at the door. He had places to go but he'd wanted to stay with her tonight. She was still shouting after him. 'When are you *ever* here on a *Friday* night?'

Sharon heard the front door slam downstairs. Why did her friends coming over have to cause such dramas? Why couldn't he just chill out a bit? He abused his right to walk out on things, but she couldn't do that. She had Liam. Trevor just couldn't wait to have an excuse to go and piss up with his mates at the pub. Sharon sniffed.

'MUM!' Liam yelled.

Oh no, not again.

'MUM!'

What now, she thought. Oh God, what now?

By the time I arrived Sharon's tears had been nicely subdued with half a bottle of brandy. Conka was already there, Helena-free, and was strumming on the guitar while puffing on a joint.

Tasha was the last to show up. 'Hiya! Sorry, I'm late, guys, but I had to wait for Daniella's father to pick her up. He was a frigging hour late!'

Conka stopped playing her guitar. 'But he's gonna take her off for the weekend, right?'

'It really pisses me off how he always does this, though,' Tasha complained.

Sharon and I looked at each other.

'The whole weekend?' Sharon mouthed to me.

I shrugged. 'You mean he takes her for *whole* weekends, Tash?' I asked.

'Yeah. But why does he say six when he means eight?'

At that point the three of us loudly voiced our envy of her freedom and extra help. Tasha soon shut up – especially as Liam and Luke were now embarking on a voyage to Decibel Heaven.

The boys seemed to wind each other up more at Sharon's house than at mine and, right now, they were driving us up the wall. Eventually Sharon and I worked out a couple of bribes we could use to shut them up for half an hour. They both had those typical boy things: football sticker albums. This meant buying about three million packets of stickers, which repeated the same few nerdy players over and over again which you couldn't swap for crap. Getting players like Ian Beautiful Wright (my personal favourite whom I love and worship), Cantona, Shearer and Pearce was like digging for gold. I should know. I was the mug that ended up sticking them in. We duly promised them five packets each.

We smoked a couple of joints, cracked open the first wine box and gradually settled down. We had the night ahead of us, so we gave Sharon and Tasha fifteen minutes to spill their guts about their men, then began our rehearsal. All further romanticising, complaining or fantasising about men was forbidden, unless it was in the context of a song. We were here to write songs, to change our lives. Drink and drugs were permitted.

I couldn't believe it. We'd done it! We'd all got together, with the instruments we needed and without too many children. It was Friday night and the girls were in, being musically creative. I loved it. I loved being a musician. I sang my lungs off.

We started with 'Bing Bang', as it was now shortened to: its 'working title' for those in the music biz. It was a good one to get us going. Conka and I had practised it loads and Conka began to harmonise sweetly with my voice. I was now a lot more confident with my vocals, and as I knew the song thoroughly, was singing formidably. For once, I wasn't put off when Conka sang different notes.

Unsurprisingly, the brandy, wine and joints helped us relax. The boys had finally collapsed in Liam's bedroom, so we shut the door and kicked back.

'One, two, three, four!' Conka counted us in.

Sharon plodded around on the bass, for moments sounding

brilliant, then losing the rhythm and fluffing severely, thus giving her an excuse to start waffling on again. Conka did her best to shut her up, and got everyone together again. Tasha was fumbling around on the keyboards and coming in with some interesting high harmonies. She kept trying to turn everything into a love song, though. The love vibe from the cocky-docky was infiltrating everything.

'Tasha, the "I love you" bit don't work.' Conka rolled her eyes at me. 'Let's start again from "Bing Bang".'

'Hang on, hang on,' Sharon slurred. 'I've lost me frets again!'

'You haven't *got any*, stupid,' I said. Our rehearsal was rapidly sliding now.

'I know. I want some,' Sharon whined.

'You're fretful enough, gal. Now, come on, one, two, three, four!' Conka tried again.

We managed to get about half-way through when Sharon mucked it up again. But there were moments when it worked. I could see potential, and had a lot of hope. Then again, it could have been the alcohol talking.

Sharon drank faster than the rest of us, although she didn't smoke as much. The drunker she got the less she played, and the more she talked. We could only ignore her for a certain amount of time – after which we all threw in the towel and got heavily wrecked.

27

As I slowly regained consciousness, to axemen bungee-jumping with pneumatic drills and chain-saws in my skull, I realised I couldn't remember where I was. Or, more to the point, whose bed I was in. Even worse, who I was in bed with. I became more and more aware of the warmth of this other body and of human breathing *very* nearby. Uh-oh.

Opening one eye required patience and supreme effort; opening two was out of the question. I chose to open the one that vaguely worked. Focusing was the next step. Unfortunately, I must have skipped the getting-ready-for-bed stage and had failed to remove my makeup. This greatly hindered my focusing as I first had to co-ordinate a hand and eye operation to rub away the black chewy film that blinded me.

My brain took a while finding my hands. I must have crashed in one position and stayed in it. Everywhere seemed dead. I was seriously *crap* on booze. This was hell! I think I moved a finger. I felt a few tingles. Brain had made contact with hand and hand was finally responding. Brain was getting confused signals: was hand trapped? Or was hand severely hung over and making excuses? Brain desperately searched for the other hand. Brain was sure there *used* to be one. Brain aborted the search and returned to hand one. More tingles were coming through. Brain was becoming sure that hand was trapped. I managed a few blinks with my open eye, which kind of cleared away the gunk.

I began to work out what it was, so close to my face. A female breast was sighing up and down softly. Not a bad thing to have practically in your eye, but it took me a while to figure out how it got there and to whom it belonged. As I watched the smooth skin rise up and down, I felt soothed and the flaying axemen in my brain eased up a bit.

I could tell that Conka was out cold. Her breathing was gentle and regular. I lay motionless as I tried to remember the course of events that had led me to be in this unusual position. This was Sharon's house, I was in Sharon's bedroom, lying on Sharon's bed and this was Conka's breast. That was the bit that worried me the most.

Moving any part of me was still out of the question, but my brain was starting to make contact with other parts of my body. It reckoned on one totally dead arm, the other partially dead, two tingly legs, which felt radically entwined with Conka's, a very dodgy stomach and back. Why had I mixed my drinks yet again?

I wondered if we were both in the nude. I managed a pathetic turn of my head and looked down. Thank God! I was semi-dressed. I definitely had my T-shirt and knickers on, and I was almost sure I had socks on, but I couldn't quite see my feet. That would have to be confirmed later.

Conka was cradling me in her arms. I was turned into her body, as she lay slightly above me. She had almost taken off her

T-shirt, but hadn't managed to get it over her head, so her neck must have been pretty warm. The hand that was working now checked if she had her knickers on. Yep. Her knickers were there. Phew! That was good – at least I could now be fairly sure that I hadn't made mad passionate love, *lesbian love*, and forgotten all about it. I felt sure I would have remembered.

But the boob bit continued to worry me. What *had* happened? And why were we cuddling each other so intensely? I normally sleep alone – even if I am sharing a bed with someone, if you know what I mean. But we were well wrapped up. Our legs and arms were all over the place, my hand was *very* close to Conka's bum, and her tit was *dangerously* close to my mouth. All I'd have to do was stick out my tongue and I'd be licking her nipple. Had that happened? How would I feel if it had?

Conka stirred and I took the opportunity to begin to unravel myself from her arms and thighs. Fuck – my arm was *dead*. I could feel a coughing fit coming on and in my current position that was potentially disastrous.

I had to re-position myself, and fast, as my lungs were ready to expel some of the poison I'd smoked into them last night. I pulled my legs out from underneath and in between Conka's. The live arm grabbed the dead one and I went for the big old roll-over.

Once separated, I suffered the inevitable, horribly loud and painful coughing fit that served to shift only a small percentage of last night's debris and merely disturb the rest enough to leave me with a constant tickle. I lay for a while, battling with my lungs, the agony inside my head and the bizarre situation I'd woken up in. I just couldn't quite remember; every time I retraced events, I'd get to a certain point and lose track.

A whole section was totally blank. Unfortunately, as always, the 'blank' was the bit I was most interested in. But I was in too much pain to try to deduce any more. I had to face the fact that alcohol destroys brain cells and it must have munched through a fair amount of memory ones last night. There was no point in fighting it, so I closed my eyes and prayed for the sandman.

But there was no returning to the lublie land of slumber for me, none at all. I hoped I might be able to squeeze in a sneaky snooze.

Instead I began to feel shivery, which I quickly added to my long list of ailments.

I could vaguely hear the boys playing in Liam's bedroom. I pulled the covers up over Conka's tit and groaned.

'Luke . . .' I was hoping he would hear my barely audible moans. 'Luke . . . water . . .' I groaned louder.

Conka moaned and moved. She rolled over on to her side, turning her back on me. Maybe she didn't feel as bad as I did and would be able to get some water.

'Conks, are you awake? Please? *Conka*,' I pleaded.

She rolled back so that we were facing each other. She opened her eyes and smiled at me. 'Please?' she echoed, giggling.

'Conks . . . please . . . water . . . Conka!'

She looked at me again. This time she saw the agony in my face and began laughing even louder.

'Ha! *You* were the one who insisted on the tequila and brandy slammers. I told you it was suicidal, you turd-brain. Ha, ha!'

She knew I hadn't the strength to respond to her taunts. I could only groan and pull faces. But eventually she showed some compassion and got up to get some water. She pulled her T-shirt on properly. She did it naturally, without saying anything – not even anything about any sex we may have had. I hoped that meant there was nothing of any significance to remember. It also dawned on me that as she was capable enough to fetch water she couldn't have drunk as much as I had and therefore would be able to remember getting to bed. Maybe she'd even remember getting into that strange cuddling position I'd woken up in. She bounced back in with a pint glass of water. Where did she get her energy from? I took the glass from her and drank the lot. Then before I could glean any further information, I had to rush to the bathroom and chuck it up again. Shite.

This drinking-and-throwing-up routine went on for a further two hours with no break for inquisitions. After which, the throwing up subsided and I managed to keep the water down. At that point, I risked a few aspirins; talking was still a no-no.

Sharon was feeling much the same, only not quite as sick. Thank Christ for Conka. She positioned us on the sofa, under a cover, in front of mindless Saturday morning telly and provided us with a constant supply of water and tea. After we were out of the critical stage, she gave us peace by taking the boys out for an hour or so. She went to get a load of vegetables, to make us one of her famous soups. What a *great* mate.

It was freezing outside but Conka was glad to be out of that smelly flat. She hated the stink of stale smoke and dead alcohol first thing in the morning. Sharon's living room smelt almost as bad as that flipping morgue. She had flung open a couple of windows and got out as quickly as she could. Although she'd not drunk nearly as much as the others, she still felt vaguely hung over and this kind of weather zapped away any residual fog lurking in the brain. She zipped up her jacket and walked quickly; the boys ran ahead. By the time she'd picked up Helena and bought the food they'd all be starving, she thought. She'd make a beautiful soup and get a load of fresh bread.

Conka smiled to herself as she reflected on the night before. It hadn't taken long for the rehearsal to collapse – although some of the music had sounded fabulous. But Sharon had just wanted to moan all night, Tasha couldn't think about anything except her new man and Charlie just went on and on all night about how independence was the most important thing and how cocks (and doctors) were rubbish. She'd got outrageously drunk, danced when she could no longer speak, collapsed when she could no longer dance and when Conka finally helped her to bed, she had wept, begging Conka's forgiveness. Then she slurred, 'I really love you, Con'a, you're sush a great friend, I'm so sorry,' about fifty times before curling next to her like a puppy and crashing out. Conka grinned. There was no doubt about it: Charlie had definitely given her the green light. If her dreams were anything to go by, she might just give it a go.

While Conka was out, Sharon and I tried to piece ourselves and the night together. Sharon's memory was worse than mine: she could hardly remember my name, and she certainly had no idea how any of us got to bed.

'Well, are you a lesbo, Charlie?'

'Come on, Sharon. You know I'm not,' I answered, somewhat surprised by her seriousness.

Sharon chewed her thumb. 'Answer me this, then,' she began slowly, clearly fighting severe head pains. 'Were you after me . . . with Tasha's vibrator that day or not?'

It took me a while to work out exactly what she was on about. The penny eventually dropped, 'Fuck off! No! You're nuts! I think you're gorgeous, Sharon but, uh-oh, no way. You'd be a crap girlfriend.'

'Thanks a lot.' After a few deep breaths trying to overcome more spasms of pains, she said, 'Perhaps you're bi.'

She might have had a point. 'Well, I'm practically ambidextrous . . . I'm fed up with men . . . but you can't knock a great shag,' I sighed.

'Nah, guess not.'

We watched telly in silence for a while to recover from this strenuous conversation. I wanted to find out more. Finally, Sharon gave me her opinion: she reckoned Conka was possibly in love with me. She said she behaved differently – in a more masculine manner – around me. I didn't think there was anything very masculine about Conka's tit this morning and had to disagree about this particular observation. I pointed out to her that people generally do behave differently around different people. Some people inspire you in some ways and some in others. I didn't find Conka masculine in any way at all.

'You're in love with her, aren't you?' Sharon accused.

'God, how would I know?'

Maybe I *was* in love with Conka, but hadn't let it register. Maybe I was just in love with the *idea* of being in love. Why was it so important to feel loved and to love? Did we only survive on the nourishment provided by the permanent quest for love? Were these consuming emotions an integral failure in our makeup? Could we ever ignore them? Conka seemed able to, even if she was in love with me. Surely it was possible to have a life void of such romantic emotions and yet still lead a full and happy existence?

Yet I couldn't even get shagged. Every other sentence of mine was 'I hate men'. Something was definitely awry. The fact that a decent man was so seemingly impossible to find meant that I shouldn't rule out any alternatives.

I was open-minded and Conka was certainly *great* to be around. She made me feel good, and she made me feel like a real singer. I'd been thinking more about her than anyone else recently and was finding her physically more and more attractive. Maybe in my drunken state I had dropped my guard and jumped her? Maybe that was what I truly wanted? Fuck, my head hurt.

'Charlie?' Sharon gently touched my hand. 'Charlie, you *can* talk to me, you know.'

'What about Tasha, eh?' I said.

'Yeah, she's gone, hasn't she?' Sharon grinned insipidly.

'Oh, come on, Sharon, it's ridiculous! She doesn't even know him!'

'I think it's really romantic. Anyway, don't you believe in love at first sight?'

'I don't believe in love full stop,' I snapped back. 'It hasn't done much for you either, eh?'

Sharon stuck her fingers up at me.

I'd had enough. Every time I had thought I'd been in love in the past, either my life had been put on hold or it had been entirely fucked up. Had I missed something in all those romantic novels, where the two handsome lovers gallop off into the distance and live happily ever after? There was never any mention of their struggle and arguments over their council-tax payment or the gas bill.

My maths teacher and I used to have eternal arguments over the need for maths. Why had she never mentioned *anything* that could have been vaguely useful to me as an adult? I couldn't see the point in finding the 'log' of 52. But I could have done with some tax-saving tips or even 'how to read your bank statement'. No one tells you anything. All you get told are the really *stupid* things. What are we supposed to learn from Henry 'the Chopper' VIII? How to get rid of your wife?

No one told me about how men will fuck you over if you're a gullible idiot and happen to fall in love with a really dodgy one. No one told me how much interest the Government charges if you're late with your tax payments. No one mentioned *bailiffs* outside the Robin Hood context. What about dentist's bills? Cellulite? Extortionate television-licence fees? Hangover cures? (Now *that* would have been useful.) Direct-debit payment plans? Communication skills? Mortgage advisers? Wrinkles? Subsidence and damp problems? Periods and white trousers? The car breaking down *just* when you need it most? No one said *anything*.

Someone could have at least mentioned that just surviving is fucking difficult. Especially on days when the world felt like it didn't give a flying fuck about tiny, spotty, shitty, broke you. And then there was the headache the size of Liverpool. I looked at Sharon, the romantic, depressed fool. She looked about as glum as a human could. At least Conka was always chirpy.

'So, Sharon,' I began, 'would you say that I was as different when I'm around Conka as, say, she is when she's around me?'

Sharon gave me a blank look. I repeated my question.

'I think that different people bring out different things in different people,' she answered finally.

'That's roughly what I said earlier on. Can't you think of anything more original and enlightening?'

'No. Sorry.'

We stared at the appalling crap on the telly. She obviously wasn't in the mood for talking. She was probably worrying about Trevor – he was all she'd spoken about all day: 'Why isn't he here? Why didn't he come back?' Whinge, whinge, whinge. She had hardly heard a word I'd said.

'What would you think, Sharon, if I told you I *was* in love with Conka?'

'Oh, fuck off, Charlie, you love a man as much as I do.'

'I do?'

The buzzer went, signifying the return of the breast, the potential off-screen lover, the laughter and, of course, our lively, lovely, NOISY sons. Sharon and I tried to stare the other into getting up and answering the intercom.

'You're nearest,' I said.

The buzzer farted again.

'Oh! You go, Charlie, please.' Another fart. Conka was getting impatient. 'You're the one that's in love with her.'

I got up, not without pain. 'ALL RIGHT!' I shouted on my way past Sharon's ear. God, she can be *so* lazy.

28

A cold chill came into the room with Conka and the boys. Plus one: Helena, whom I adore but who can also be really noisy.

'It's bloody cold out there today, girls, even me eyelashes are frozen,' Conka stated, as she came in with the shopping. 'I've got some veggies and I'm gonna make us a healthy heart-warming soup, so you two relax and get better.'

I couldn't believe our luck: soup was the perfect thing to have as it's easily abosrbed, and having someone to make it for us was bliss.

Conka stormed straight to the kitchen. I badly wanted to talk to her. I still felt disturbed by the tit fiasco this am, but Conka was behaving as it were any other ordinary day. I couldn't believe her calmness – or was it simply a lack of feeling for me? I hoped not. I had to talk to her but there were too many kids around and my head hurt. I was still too hung over for any surprises anyway.

Luke disappeared downstairs with Helena, to play on the Nintendo with Liam in his bedroom. Sharon and I continued to stare at the telly, while Conka sang as she made soup. Eventually she came out of the kitchen and plopped herself between us on the sofa: joint break.

The smell of the cooking had followed Conka into the room. I couldn't work out whether I liked it or not. I had always liked the smell of garlic, but today just when I thought I might be feeling a hunger pain, it turned out to be another wave of ghastliness, followed by a swift and desperate dash to the bathroom. Conka shook her head in despair: she was her usual bubbly self. Fucking annoying – sometimes.

She rolled and smoked a lethal-smelling joint. I couldn't stomach a ciggie, let alone a joint. The broth brewed steadily away, and the scents wafted in thicker and heavier. It smelt like shampoo and I began to dread Conka serving it up. There was no chance of Luke eating it. Woose! I ran to the bathroom.

I think Sharon thought it smelt peculiar as well. When I came back in she gave me a couple of sideways glances and twitched her nose. Jesus, it fucking stank! It was really making me feel bad – just when I was beginning to feel nearly normal too. Conka was yabbing on about how bloody-good-for-you it was going to be, but my stomach was begging me not to do it.

Things seemed to click into slow motion. The sound went distorted, then mute. I watched Conka's lips move, as she rose and made the dreaded move into the kitchen. Help! I looked at Sharon, she looked at me, we both looked towards the kitchen. Utter terror would be putting it mildly. Neither of us could speak.

Conka returned, arms laden with a tray of steaming soup and hot bread. Panicsville! The bread looked and smelt delicious; the soup, revolting. It had this brown sludgy foam floating on the top, which compounded with the shampooey smell, made me feel even more ill. Even Conka began to look a bit worried, but she carried on regardless, passing around the plates and bowls. When she shouted at the kids to come and eat, the fluff was knocked out of my congealed ears. The boys ignored Conka's calls and disobediently but wisely stayed downstairs, not enticed by the cooking smells when there was a computer game to play.

'Mummy, I want to get to the next lebel!' Luke called up to me.

'Okay. Don't worry for now.' I shouted back. Crikey, that really was loud.

Helena came up, grabbed a large chunk of the delicious looking bread and ran away again. Nice work, kid. Conka huffed vaguely, giving me her most challenging look, as she offered me a bowl. I took it quickly, crumbling under her powerful stare, then passed it to Sharon who received it vacantly. She hadn't realised that she was about to eat 'shampoo soup' and was once again running on automatic.

Conka passed me a bowl. There was no getting rid of it this time. 'Oh, thanks,' I lied.

I stared at it. It stared at me. It couldn't have looked more revolting: murky brown sludge with soapy lighter brown froth, slightly sinking on the surface, and the *smell* – well – simply vile. How could *this* make anyone feel better?

Sharon was spooning it slowly into her mouth, oblivious to any unusual taste sensations she might have been experiencing. She seemed all right, so far, although she was pulling a slightly disgusted, pained face with every mouthful. Conka began to plough through it ruthlessly. I played with my bread, breaking off little pieces and rolling them around between my thumb and forefinger before planting them delicately on my tongue. I was consciously playing for time, delaying for as long as possible that first, inevitable mouthful of slurry.

Conka kept glancing at me out of the corner of her eye, impatient for me to take my first spoonful. Sharon had slowed up. Her taste buds must have finally alerted her to the abomination in her mouth. Conka was still going strong. I couldn't take it for much longer. I put my spoon in my bowl, disturbing the foam into a multitude of stringy bogies, which caused me to retch instantly. That was it. Enough is enough. I was too sick.

'Conka,' I blurted out. 'What the fuck did you put in this soup?'

Conka looked at me, with a smile in her eye. 'Well, to be honest it does taste a bit strange – it's good though, full of great veggies, you know,' she answered.

'Yeah – but why has it gone like this? And what's with the weird smell?'

'Oh fuck, Conka, what's in this soup?' Sharon interrupted. 'Oh my God, I think I'm gonna die. Oh no . . .'

'Shut up, Sharon.' Conka and I said together.

We could all see that Conka had eaten a lot more than Sharon had and was, so far, not doubling over, frothing at the mouth or generally *dying*. Sharon though was writhing around on the floor holding her stomach and moaning louder than a grizzly bear on acid. A typical over-reaction, as per usual. I tried nudging her bum with my foot to try and shut her up but it didn't work, so I gave her a gentle but sturdy kick in the arse.

'Ow! What the fuck do you think you're doing?'

'Oh sorry, that foot has been out of control for weeks.' I kicked it back with my other foot. 'I was hoping to take your warped mind off your belly for a couple of minutes so you shut the fuck up and let us try and work out if we – rather you and Conka – should be rushing to the hospital.'

As soon as she heard the word hospital, Sharon shut it.

'Did you wash the saucepan thoroughly? Or did you just think it was clean?' I examined a spoonful of soup at close range again, and took another whiff – I just couldn't place that synthetic stench.

'It did look clean, I think,' Conka replied, scratching her chin thoughtfully.

'Oh, my God! You didn't use the red saucepan, did you?' Sharon asked stupidly.

We all stared at the red saucepan sitting cockily on the table. 'You did?'

'Well? Come on, tell us!' Conka shouted. She'd had enough of Sharon's suspense policy.

It was fucking obvious to *everyone* that we wanted to know *what* made the saucepan so dangerous – except of course its colour. Yet Sharon was still staring at it: a horrified, fixed, terrified stare, as if the pan were a tiger about to shred her alive.

'Trevor! It's fucking Trevor!' she screamed suddenly. 'He's fucking poisoned me. BASTARD! I can't believe it.' She ran to the bathroom.

Conka and I burst out laughing – there was no stopping hypochondriac extraordinaire Sharon. As usual, she was over-reacting to her heart's content.

'What do you think could have been in it, Conks?'

'Haven't got a bloody clue, mate.'

We took a second inquisitive sniff.

Conka turned into Sherlock Holmes. 'It smells like hair dye or bleach or something. Let's take a look in the kitchen for some clues.'

We rummaged around in the bin, looking for some incriminating evidence, but to no avail.

'I don't know what the bleeding hell it could be,' Conka said, before marching into the bathroom.

I followed.

'What was in the pan, doll?' Conka asked gently between Sharon's gasps.

Sharon looked up at us, tears streaming down her face and dribble on her chin. A sorry sight indeed.

'He told me he'd washed that pan, fucking LIAR! He soaked it

194

in Flash. I told him to make sure he rinsed it out properly. I bet he didn't.'

I put my arm around her to try to placate her. She had really taken it badly. 'Sharon, it was an accident. Come on ... he doesn't want to poison you.'

'Charlie, you don't understand.'

'No, I suppose I don't, but I don't think it was deliberate.'

'Just let me wash my face, and I'll be with you in a minute.' Sharon tried to smile. She obviously wanted to bawl in private.

We left her to continue her wailing.

'Well, that'll clean out me pipes,' Conka concluded.

We started to giggle, slightly dimming the sound emitting from the bathroom. The giggles rapidly turned into full-on hysterics. Conka's healthy heart-warming soup had turned out to be a vile, poisonous mother-fucker.

Eventually Conka and I decided to make tracks homewards. We tidied up. I was, thankfully, feeling relatively normal again. I retrieved Luke. He and Liam had lost patience with each other and Luke was eager to go. We left Sharon zoning out on the sofa with Liam crawling all over the kitchen looking for something to eat.

'What a bloody disaster,' Conka said, as we walked down the stairs with the kids.

'Yeah, some rehearsal, eh?'

We rolled our eyes at each other. We'd been doing that a lot lately. In fact, we'd been doing a lot of rolling in general, what with joints and a few other interesting little things.

We were about to part company, when I realised I still hadn't discovered why I had woken up with Conka's tit in my face. I didn't want to go home without finding out, but I was still terrified to ask. I dithered around, then plunged straight to the point.

'Conks, do you remember what it was we did just before we went to bed?'

She gave me one of those seductive, cheeky looks again. Oh man, something *had* happened, I couldn't remember what and Conka wasn't going to tell me. She definitely had something up her sleeve.

I stood there speechless, while she leant over to my ear. I

thought she was going to tell me something. Instead she kissed me really loudly and walked off with Helena skipping and giggling beside her.

29

Sharon was fed up with being told she was overreacting and she had wanted Charlie and Conka to leave long before they did. After Conka's soup fiasco she'd sat on the bathroom floor sobbing, and wondering about Trevor.

Sharon needed to talk to someone – she needed to work it through – and she'd given up on Charlie, Tasha and Conka. So she rang Sarah instead who was having problems with her twenty-two-year-old, who had a cocaine habit. This scared Sharon into being a little less self-absorbed and therefore not quite so upset.

Sharon told Sarah about the saucepan affair. Sarah didn't think it *was* beyond the realms of possibility that Trevor might have been trying to poison Sharon, which for some bizarre reason cheered Sharon up. As far as Sarah was concerned, *nothing* could be ruled out – she'd had men try a lot worse.

They'd gone on to talk about the revenges Sarah had taken on her various assailants. Once she had systematically cut through the crotch in every pair of her ex's trousers – then she'd got so scared of his retaliation that she had sat up all night sewing them up again. Still in need of revenge, though, she devised another cunning plan: she left the lid off the full-to-the-brim-with-real-stinkers nappy bucket and placed it in his wardrobe until his clothes stank. Foolproof and satisfying. However, the tactic she had adopted with her latest ex-husband was just to be unbearably nice whenever he came round or rang. She was getting good at this and as a result now had limited credit-card use.

'They just don't know what to do when you're really nice to them, Sharon – you should try it.'

Sarah's words resounded in Sharon's head all Sunday. She trusted Sarah. She was older, maybe wiser. Actually she wasn't much wiser. It wasn't that long ago that Sarah had been so nice to her ex that she'd fallen pregnant. That would be a disaster. Anyway this *nice* tactic was one Sharon hadn't tried before. She decided she wasn't going to interrogate Trevor if and when he returned. She'd try not to care where he'd been. The point to remember was that he would be back here with his arms around her and that he would soon be earning that all-important money.

Trevor had not expected the welcome he got when he returned to Sharon's on Sunday evening. It pissed him off, not having his own place. He wished he didn't need to come back to get his frigging clothes.

He had spent Friday night down the pub with a mate and crashed at his. He planned to go home then, but instead allowed himself to be dragged into helping a friend who was DJ-ing at a rave in Bognor Regis of all places. He'd rung Sharon, but that bitch Charlie had answered so he'd hung up and called Tiffany instead.

Tiffany was up for it and joined him at Jamie's, this time without her incestuous entourage. Still, after loading Jamie's car with millions of fucking records, he'd at least got to ride down there in Tiff's lar-vel-lie Golf. The gig was good but Trevor ended up doing way too many drugs – at one point he thought that Tiffany's arse was a bouncy castle. His head pounded. He was now ready to get cleaned up and he wasn't in the mood for any of Sharon's whingeing. He braced himself for a row.

Sharon was vaguely watching the telly when she heard him come in. She reminded herself to be nice.

'Hi, darling,' she whispered.

Trevor almost fell over with shock. He'd come in with that challenging look on his face – there wouldn't have been any point in interrogating him anyway, as he obviously had his story well worked out already. Sharon watched him take a quick glance around the place, making sure her friends had gone.

'Hi,' he muttered.

So far, so good, Sharon thought. But this was going to be hard: Trevor had *party* and *sleaze* written all over his face. She'd thrown him, though. First point to her.

*

Although the place seemed clean, Trevor noticed a strange lingering smell, a mixture of garlic and fuck-knows-what – window-cleaner? He glanced at the bin and managed to identify a couple of empty wine boxes, which were badly obscured by a load of brown stuff. They'd obviously had some party. There were empty bottles of brandy and tequila by the rubbish. He knew what Sharon was like on tequila – and he hadn't been there. Shit! There were cigarette papers all over the place too. What a fucking tart, Trevor thought.

Don't get caught up in any arguments, Sharon reminded herself as he came back in. He just wants to put you off asking him where he's been. She couldn't believe how manipulative he was. She could see now why being nice worked for Sarah.

Trevor was getting pissed off with her fucking irritating attitude. What game was she playing?

'Have you been *fucking* around?' he sneered, grabbing Sharon by the elbows and bringing her close to him. 'I'll fucking *smell* it on you, if you have.'

Be nice, Sharon reminded herself. This was difficult. She liked Trevor's jealousy, though: it showed he still cared. She still had power. She bit her lip – she wanted to tell him the truth – but it turned her on to watch him panic like this.

'Go on then,' she teased, 'smell it on me.'

She pushed her thigh between his legs, so that her hips were pressed against his. Sure enough, she felt it move slowly: he was getting hard and there was nothing he could do to stop himself.

Monday. By the time Sharon got up Trevor had left for work. He'd even left her a note. 'Gone to work, darling. Thanks for last night . . . See you later, xxx.' How nice! Sharon was about to call Sarah to tell her how well it was all going when the buzzer went. She looked out of her window and saw two men in long black macs. They buzzed again and she darted away from the window as they looked up.

'Come on, Liam, we've got to sneak out of here. Get your shoes.'

'But, Mum, I haven't had any breakfast.'

The buzzer sounded a third time.

'Please, Peanut, we've got to get out of here.'

'What's happening Mum?'

'Shush. Follow me. Come on, and remember we're not who we really are.'

Once out and away from their building, via next door's garden, they headed up the road towards Charlie's.

Before Luke and I were ready to leave for school, the buzzer went.

'Who the hell is that?' Luke asked, sounding more like a grumpy fifty-five-year-old than his innocent five.

'Don't swear!'

But Luke had already picked up the intercom and was shouting 'go away!' He was growing up so damned quick.

A distraught Sharon and an unkempt Liam were standing at the door.

'Charlie! Oh my God, things are really bad.' She walked straight in.

'Mum, I'm hungry! Mum!' Liam the Terrible had started.

'I can't believe how bad things have got. I'm in so much trouble, Charlie.'

'Mum!' Liam interrupted, in his loudest football hooligan bellow. 'Mum! I'm starving!'

It was at times like this that I really disliked that boy.

'Oh, Charlie, do you mind if I give him some breakfast?' Sharon stuttered, and she helped herself as Liam yapped around her like some irritating Jack Russell.

'Mum, I don't want it like that, you idiot!' Liam yelled.

'Don't you talk to your mother like that.' I was objecting now. 'Not in my house. I won't have it.'

I was turning into General Charlo. Liam gave me his worst scowl, but shut up and got stuck into his breakie while Sharon searched the premises for a ciggie.

'What causes this felonious intrusion?' I asked, handing her a cigarette.

Sharon looked at me strangely, then lit her fag. 'They've come, Charlie.'

Why did she *always* talk in riddles? She sat on the sofa, slowly shaking her head, nearly burning her fringe with her ciggie, just like my gran used to before she died, waiting for me to say, 'Who?'

'I had to leave the house surreptitiously this morning. I had to pretend to be someone else.'

The riddle became more complicated: one day her house loses Sharon and another Sharon wants to lose her house. What was it with Sharon, her house and her riddles?

'Those fucking TV-licence bastards. First, they sent a recorded bloody court summons and now they're sending fucking bailiffs. They not only *made* me buy a licence, they now want me to pay some kind of fine or I could face imprisonment, Charlie. It's terrible, I don't know what to do.'

She burst into tears. She just couldn't keep the floodgates shut. Liam rolled his eyes at his mother: unsympathetic git. Mind you, she was like this so often I couldn't really blame him. I decided to take the boys to school, leaving Sharon on the sofa, to wail and wallow for a few private moments.

Tasha moved her sofa and plants the way Craig had suggested; like her, he was sensitive to the positioning of things in the home environment. He lived in digs near to the hospital, so they spent most of their time at hers. She wanted him to feel that it was as much his home as hers: she had given him some keys. She checked her feng shui book and was delighted to find that Craig was a natural. She had had it wrong in her living room all along and not even realised – no wonder she hadn't liked sitting in there.

When she heard him arrive, she sat down, cross-legged, on the meditation mat they had bought together, closed her eyes and waited. She wanted him to catch her meditating. To her delight, he used his keys and was calling her name softly as he came up. Tasha concentrated on keeping her eyes shut and, although bursting with excitement, managed to remain in her yogic position. She felt him come nearer. The cool air still lingered around him. She felt herself grinning, so opened her eyes. His beautiful face was just inches from hers.

'Hello,' he said, very quietly.

Tasha leant forward to kiss him, but instead he put his finger to her lips, commanding her silently to stay where she was.

'I want to try something different, darling. And now that you've done the necessary with the plants we can face each other and feel the electricity between us without even touching.'

As he spoke he removed his shoes and coat, putting them down just out in the hallway.

'I want to take a voyage to the astral plane with you – I want us to ascend the heights of karmic pleasure. We don't have to be bound by our earthly bodies.'

Tasha's heart was racing with excitement: she hadn't known that men like him even existed. She felt more and more in love every time she saw him. She followed his every movement, until he sat down opposite her.

'Okay?' he asked.

Tasha nodded.

'Let's close our eyes – actually, wait, I think we should take off our clothes, yeah?'

Tasha nodded, hypnotised by his eyes. They stood up and silently stripped. She couldn't believe how sexy she was feeling and they still hadn't even touched. Once naked, they resumed their sitting position – cross legged, opposite one another.

'Okay?'

Tasha nodded.

'Let's synchronise our breathing.'

They exhaled together, eyes locked on one another's.

'Okay, now let our subconsciouses merge.'

They exhaled loudly and allowed their gazes to roam around and over each other's bumps and curves. Tasha's eyes flicked up to his and saw his eyes resting on her pussy. She virtually came: this was incredible. She stared at his manhood, willing it to grow and throb. It did. He held his hand outstretched to hers, their palms almost touching. She could hear music. She closed her eyes and fell deeper into this symphony of love. Tasha had never felt so alive and so happy: Craig was so beautiful, she had finally met her match. There was a loud ring in her body and she had an almighty orgasm. She opened her eyes just in time to see his semen bubble over – and they hadn't even touched.

'Wow,' they said together.

'This is love.' Tasha sighed.

Not wanting to rush straight back to the miserable Sharon, I went via Tasha's, hoping to have a quick chat. To no avail. I buzzed and knocked, but was ignored – that doctor was probably giving her a big one from behind, up against the kitchen sink, most likely. Lucky bitch.

By the time I got back, Sharon had calmed down a bit, but still looked red and puffy around her eyes. The tears welled again as soon as she saw me. But at least she wasn't howling and wailing as hysterically as before and could talk without taking great big gulps of air between each sentence.

'I'm so broke, Charlie, I don't know what to do. I can't cope any more, I really can't.'

She sobbed quietly. If she'd had a tether then she would have been at the end of it. She was in a mess and she'd come to me for help, which made me think that she must be even less coherent than I'd previously supposed.

I certainly couldn't bail her out financially, but I supposed I could show some compassion. She knew we could relate emotionally. She was reaching rock bottom and I knew she had to go all the way down before she could even hope to come up. I made her tea and gave her some biscuits, which she could only nibble at half-heartedly. It was all the comfort I could offer.

I didn't know what to do. I'm not a trained psychiatrist. I knew what she was feeling and that it was total shit. I also knew it would take at least a year, if not two, to sort her whole life out and that's if she really concentrated on it. But she'd allowed everything to slip so far.

Initially she didn't believe I'd ever been half as weak as she was feeling, until I told her that it took me four years to leave Luke's father.

'How long were you with him?' she asked.

'Five years,' I lied; it had been nearer four and a half.

Then she began to believe me. She'd seen me over the past year or so. I didn't put up with any shit from men, *at all*, and had become a strong advocate of the 'leave 'em, if they're not up to scratch, you're better off on your own' policy. I could understand why it was hard for her to see me as a weak, love-needy, dope-on-a-rope. But when I had convinced her of my past, she calmed down somewhat.

'I can't believe you took four years to leave him, Charlie.'

'Yeah, well, we don't choose to be single mums, do we? I wanted my son to have a proper family, whatever the fuck that is, and I did a five stretch. Not bad when it's with someone you really can't stand.'

'That's amazing – you don't even give them five minutes, these days.'

I wanted her to slim down her excuses for staying with Trevor. The desperate love-search demon had dug its ugly claws into Sharon and it had to rip her to shreds before it would spit her out, all mangled, chewed, broke and bitter.

'Look, Sharon,' I said decisively. 'I know you think nothing else could possibly go wrong –' I stopped and thought I should start again. 'Look, Sharon, I know that everything in your life feels like a total mess, but don't try and sort it all out at once. It's impossible. Don't panic. You've got to try to remember there was happiness before Trevor, just as there will be after. Trevor is incapable of helping you and therefore he must go. It worked for me. I had one hell of a mess to clear up, mind you, but I did it. You can too.'

Sharon started to cry again. Shit. I knew there was nothing I could say that would make her feel even the slightest bit better. She was feeling crap and had every right to do so. There was not one thing in her life that was good. Not a sausage. I put my arm around her and allowed her to sob her guts out on my shoulder. The only other thing that could go wrong for her now would be a death in the family, but I decided not to point that depressing fact out to her. Especially as her 'family' basically consisted of Liam and herself.

What to do? At times like these, rolling a joint or pouring a drink were the only feasible options I could think of. As I didn't have either in the house, I rang George, my trusty neighbour, to see if he could supply me with either of the above.

Within five minutes he was round, spliff in hand. He rolled a joint, we passed it around, each taking long, hard pulls. A couple of minutes later, the atmosphere seemed less tense.

George relaxed and began talking. 'Look, whatever it is, it ain't all that bad,' he said, winking cheekily at me 'Not when you've got a spliff in your hand.'

God, George was incorrigible. Sharon was too stoned to despair of us – I loved the way she got instantly wrecked. We sat chatting about not a lot really and, when George took his leave, an altogether lighter atmosphere remained.

I began to go through a few of the theories that had helped me when I'd had my really shit time. 'Basically Sharon, rule number one is to remember that things can only get *better*. Rule number two is to deal with everything as honestly and as swiftly as possible, although you should incorporate white lies when necessary – especially when talking to the state.'

'I could go to the doctor and get a recommendation for psychiatric help – that might help me get out of a few things,' Sharon suggested.

'Great! Perfect,' I said, encouragingly. I couldn't object to that. Madness was certainly an option and one that was easy to believe in Sharon's case. Who was to say whether it was a white lie or not? 'We'll write it down, Sharon, that'll make it easier.'

We made a couple of lists of letters, appointments to be made and other shit she would have to sort out. I assured her that once she'd begun it wouldn't be nearly as daunting as it seemed now.

We were having about our tenth cup of tea when I realised it was time to get the boys: we'd talked and smoked the whole day away. But Sharon was together enough now to come with me and collect Liam herself.

I was pretty exhausted and was relieved to say goodbye to her at the school gate. I gave her a hug, kissed her cheek loudly and wished her luck. This all seemed a bit dramatic but, fuck it, I really hoped she wasn't going to get that upset again.

30

Trevor had got the van early. He looked down into Tiffany's basement, but the curtains were drawn. He didn't especially feel like calling in anyway. Sharon had looked so beautiful this morning – he'd left her a note and vaguely hoped things would come good between them. Tiffany was just a distraction.

He'd got the van going pretty quick and the drive had not taken long. He had been parked outside Jeremy's for about half an hour and had already smoked most of his packet of ten Marlboros. He thought how strange it was that Jeremy begged him to go to fancy places with him half the time, and then didn't so much as ask him in for a cup of tea when he wasn't ready to leave. It annoyed him from the start.

When he finally got in the van Jeremy made no apologies for keeping Trevor waiting. He was obviously extremely hung over: he looked terrible and was wearing sunglasses, even though it was overcast and dull. His hair looked greasier than Trevor had seen it before and his lips were chapped and red as if he had the beginnings of a cold sore. Trevor reminded himself to check Tiffany's mouth – he didn't want to be catching any tell-tale viruses.

'There's the first address,' Jeremy said, shoving a piece of paper in Trevor's hand. 'Do you know how to get there or am I going to have to be the navigator?' He yawned.

Trevor recognised the name of the town – somewhere in the south-east. 'Yeah, go to sleep, flower,' Trevor answered. 'It'll take at least three hours.'

He was amazed when Jeremy let his head flop back and did exactly that. Thank fuck he wasn't going to have to listen to that piece of shit for a while. Trevor knew his route and let his mind wander while he drove to Ramsgate. He kept thinking of Sharon and Tiffany: Tiffany was offering him a lot. She said he could move in with her if he didn't have anywhere else to stay. He'd have to bear that in mind. But he wanted to stay with Sharon: it was just that she was putting him off a bit, these days. Her place was handy but recently Trevor had found her state of mind almost scary; she never used to be like that. Now she'd want his money too, and he wouldn't even have this stupid job if it wasn't for Tiffany. Trevor put the radio on.

Nearly at Ramsgate; it was time to rouse the flower.

'Jeremy, we're nearly there.'

'Oh, God, my head. Where are we?' Jeremy said, as he rubbed his eyes open and yawned.

'Stop yawning, will yer?' Trevor said.

Jeremy yawned loudly a couple more times. Trevor tutted.

'Oooh, he's all grumpy. Get up too early this morning, did we?' Jeremy jibed.

The little shit was more pleasant when he was hung over and curt, Trevor thought. 'What are we picking up anyway, flower?'

'Parts, darling, washing-machine parts. That's all you need to know. Don't call me flower, darling.'

'Don't darling me, flower, or I'll pluck every one of your petals off.'

Trevor looked at Jeremy: he was unscrewing a small vial and was about to spoon a toot up his nose. 'Want some?' he asked.

He can offer me a toot but he can't offer me a cup of tea, Trevor thought. 'Yeah, go on,' he said.

Jeremy passed him the vial while they stopped at some lights.

'You never answered me, flower.' Trevor sniffed. 'What are we picking up?'

'Just drive,' Jeremy answered.

Well, whatever it was, it certainly made Jeremy behave strangely. He was silent for the remainder of the journey. Trevor was ordered to lift and load a ton of boxes, then drive back and deliver to a lock-up in Hackney. Jeremy didn't travel back with him, but gave him a large enough line to make the journey go pretty quickly anyway.

He was wiped out by the time he got home.

Conka was getting bored at work. The accounts didn't tally for about the fifth time. Each time she went through it, it came out different. It wasn't consistently over or under. Not funny. Mrs

Uptight-Sumo-Arithmetic was breathing down her neck the whole time, which didn't make things any easier.

'Oh, for Christ's sake! Not again!' Conka sighed, now totally exasperated.

She felt Mrs Uptight smile to herself. She had been here since the beginning. She'd never taken a day off. When she had tried to, a business disaster had happened – this place simply couldn't function without her, she said. Conka thought it was the other way round: Mrs Uptight wouldn't be able to function without this business: she'd be totally bleeding lost. She loved it when Conka fucked up: it meant she was needed and important. Conka had initially found it all quite funny, but it was now beginning to bore her tits off. Wayne, the boss, was great when Mrs Uptight wasn't around, but when she was, well, he was just as much of a twat as she was.

Mrs Uptight however was far worse when Wayne wasn't there. When he was, she behaved slightly sweeter. She didn't want him to see her as the full on bitch she really was. Conka reckoned Mrs Uptight was in love with him and had been from the *beginning*. She looked at him in that dopey way. Wayne, it seemed, was incapable of any feelings towards anything other than his stomach and cheap booze. He wasn't married and Mrs Uptight had divorced years ago. Mr Uptight had apparently left shortly after they married and she'd never considered it since.

'Which it?' Conka had asked cheekily.

'Well, marriage of course.'

'So you would still consider the other it, then?' Conka asked, very seriously.

Mrs Uptight took a moment to register what Conka meant. As it dawned on her, she turned a rosy kind of burgundy. 'I think you'd better carry on with those time sheets,' she snapped. 'And stop this idle tittle tattle now, will you?' Her eyebrow arched higher and higher throughout this mini redressing. 'We are not here to discuss anything other than business, Conka. Business, dear. You are now in the business world. And you mustn't forget that. The business world, dear.'

She was giving Conka her sternest stare. Conka wanted to

bleeding business world her. Where was her sense of humour? Anyway, after that little discussion, Mrs Uptight had never relaxed around Conka again. In fact, she'd watch and wait for Conka to fuck up. Sometimes she'd stoop low and deliberately hide a receipt or invoice. She'd done that today and it was really getting on Conka's nerves. Conka couldn't bear to give her that satisfaction and she was determined to get the books balanced. Fuck Mrs Uptight. Conka continued with her calculations.

'Well, your dream's come true,' she said at last, smiling inanely at Mrs Uptight.

'What, dear? Doesn't it add up?'

'No, actually, it does,' Conka answered triumphantly.

She had realised where something was missing: she'd remembered Mrs Uptight signing an invoice for one of their builders and Conka had noticed her deliberately place it in the wrong tray. She had noticed the amount imprinted on Mrs Uptight's pad – now left on Conka's desk – where she could easily see the figures she needed.

'Do you want me to check it for you, dear?' she croaked.

'If you want, but it might be easier if you just get me the invoice from Bob's schedule,' Conka said, wetting herself inside.

A car beeped loudly outside.

'Well, it should be in the yellow tray,' Mrs Uptight said, as she fumbled in her handbag, getting ready to leave. 'If it's not in there then maybe Wayne put it in the green tray by mistake. Have a look. I've got a business lunch. See you later.'

With that she clacked out of the office in her ridiculous heels – they must be so uncomfortable. Conka noticed that she always wore the same style but in different colours. Even Barbie had better taste! Conka's feet were aching in her relatively flat shoes: she was used to trainers. She looked out of the window to make sure Mrs Uptight was really going and noticed a handsome man outside in a dark blue convertible Jag.

'Nice,' Conka said aloud. 'Very nice.'

She heard the front door slam and watched Mrs Uptight clack down the street. She was just about to kick off her shoes when she saw her walk towards the car.

'I don't fucking believe it,' Conka said.

Mrs Uptight said something to the gorge-geezer in the car and then looked up. Conka dived to the floor. When she heard the rumble of the engine, she dared another peek. She glimpsed Mrs Uptight in the passenger seat as the car pulled away.

'Oo-er, missus,' Conka said.

She sat down and put her feet up. She put her hands behind her head and swung back on her chair. She'd grab forty winks.

About five minutes later the phone rang. Conka leapt into action. 'Seven nine two, five eight four threeee,' she sang. She liked holding the last note just a bit longer than normal – it made her smile. It really wound Mrs Uptight up too.

'Hello. Great Days?'

'Great Days in great ways,' Conka sang in her best operatic.

'Er, this is Mr Davenport, I'm ringing in regard to the September despatch . . .'

Conka let the client gabble on for a while before she interrupted. 'Excuse me, but can you give me your number? I'm not in a position to deal with that particular detail. I'll have to get the boss to call you back on that one. All right?' She sang the all right.

'Well, I say. You're very chirpy, aren't you? You new there?'

'Chirpy cheep cheep, I am,' Conka said, in her huskiest voice. She couldn't resist a phone flirt.

'I've not spoken to you before.'

'Nah. I bet you always get that Mrs Upton. She's always here. She was here before here was here, if you know what I mean?'

'Oh, that'll be her, yes.'

'Never mind, eh? There's no use getting upset now, is there?'

'Well, I – wasn't getting upset – really . . .'

'No, but she can be really grumpy, eh?' Conka interrupted.

'I suppose . . .'

'Anyway, I'm here now and you'd better give me your number, before you get me in any more trouble. You're quite a *distraction*, you know.'

Conka put her hand over the mouthpiece to allow herself a gulp of laughing air. He was silent. Conka resumed in her husky voice. 'Er, Mr Davenpour. What was your number, darling? Shall I take a little message for you?'

Mr Davenport coughed and reminded himself and her why he had rung in the first place. He gave Conka his name and number.

'Thank you . . . it was lovely talking to you. Maybe I can meet you next time I have to pass your way?'

'Ooo, Mr Davenport, you sound ever so nice. 'Byeeee,' she sang. Conka laughed. Another satisfied customer, she thought.

Conka was a bit late, so I hung around with Helena and Luke at the school gates until she came striding up. She looked really good. She was Miss Office Worker now, and sported a smart pair of chocolate brown trousers with a co-ordinating jacket, which she'd framed in a long black cashmere coat neatly finished with a black poloneck underneath. Her dark hair was coiffed and shiny, and she'd put on just enough makeup to enhance the laughter in her eyes. She had dabbed a touch of rouge on her lips, to make them look that little bit fuller and more kissed than usual. She even had smart black leather gloves and real shoes instead of her reliable but skanky trainers.

'Hello, Smarty-pants. Did you have a good day at the office, dear?' I inquired.

We air-kissed each other hello, near the cheeks in an overdone fashion manner.

'Oh, darling, I've been tewwibbly busy, it's been wush, wush, wush, all day long. I'm simply exhausted.'

Helena giggled and looked at her in awe: she was proud of how well her mum brushed up. She swung on Conka's arm, listening carefully to every word. Luke was doing the opposite: not listening to anyone. Instead he asked me continuously for a cake from the shop. He was always so hungry when he came out of school these days. Daily we went through the same routine of me asking Luke what he'd had for school lunch and him telling me that he couldn't remember. Occasionally he'd make something up just to shut me up, but he never told me what he'd eaten. It got on my nerves.

Conka and Helena came home with us: yet more tea making

for me. I made a brew and told Conka about Sharon. She rolled her eyes.

'She's got to snap herself out of that one and *soon*. She's boring everyone.'

I agreed with her. 'I know. I couldn't easily go through another day like today – I feel so drained. I want to get on with my ambitions. Time has this dreadful habit of slipping gently away and, before you know it, you're eighty eight and suddenly remembering all those things you'd meant to do with your life,' I said.

'Yeah, and by then your body's fallen apart and no one's interested in what you might be wanting to do 'cause no one's ever got enough time,' Conka stated, in her new business manner.

I looked at her with deep admiration: she seemed to have all the answers. Where are you supposed to get your time from? Is this just something else someone's forgotten to tell me?

Conka began to tell me about her life at the office. I could just envisage her there: she couldn't take anything seriously. I knew she'd spend her time working out where she could get a little nap in or put her feet up for five minutes. She was very good to herself. Not that she wouldn't work hard: she'd put her hours in. But unless she was getting paid an absolute fortune, which she wasn't, she'd always manage to have a surreptitious little skive at some point in the day.

'Yeah, I'm answering the phones, sending faxes, doing a bit of filing and all that malarkey,' Conka said, as she picked up her guitar. 'It's a doddle, Charlie. I could do it standing on my beautiful head, mate. I think I'll enjoy it for a while, then get bored, no doubt, but there's a couple of real characters working there.'

She strummed playfully on the guitar while she was talking to me. 'Yeah, yeah, yeah,' she sang.

Conka's visit, so immediately after Sharon's, drastically highlighted the difference between them. Conka was full and happy, alive and kicking. The atmospheres they created in my house were black and white. Still, I felt I might have helped Sharon today, even if it was just by being there when there was no one else.

'Have you got faith in our band, Conka?' I asked.

'Of course!' she answered quickly. 'And it'd be good for Sharon – remember how much she loved it at Tasha's birthday?'

'Oh, yes,' I said. *I* still believed in the single-mum brigade.

Conka was pushing for another live performance. She insisted it would be the best plan. I finally agreed when she said she could get some labels to the gig. That could mean money, so I was keen, very keen, but still too nervous. We decided to aim for another rehearsal, maybe at Sarah's again: enough time had passed now since the pregnancy incident and Sarah would probably be glad to see us all – it had been a while.

Luke and Helena played their Italian Game (whatever that was) in Luke's room, while Conka and I had a sing. I still hadn't got any more information out of her about our previous Friday night and was increasingly curious, but too shy to come out with it. Conka must have read my mind and looked at me rather seductively. I allowed my gaze to rest on hers, rather than retreating immediately away, as I had in the past.

The vision of her breast sighing softly in front of my mouth and eyes flashed before me. I felt myself get more and more turned on by it. The more I thought about it, the wetter I got and the longer I lingered in her stare. I felt sure that it hadn't had quite this effect on me at the time.

Eventually my gaze drifted away from Conka's: she was losing herself in a sexy melody while I fantasised away. I shut my eyes and allowed myself to be carried away with the music and the memory of the vision. I licked my lips, tasted her hard nipple. I cupped her breast in my hand to press its fullness into my face. I felt expectant flutters, quivering inside me, that were turning into a compelling desire. I wanted to caress her strong body, to taste her and make her come, touch her with my fingers, pushing deep into that place inside, that wonderfully sensitive, fluttering place. I knew I'd find it in Conka. I could find her butterfly.

But Conka was on an altogether different vibe. She had locked herself into the riff she'd stumbled upon and was humming a melody to it. I snapped myself out of my fantasy and hummed along with her.

*

Sharon was finding Trevor's behaviour more and more intriguing. He was coming home later and later and not saying *anything*. They hadn't made love recently either. She knew he was working and was probably more tired than usual, but something very weird was going on, she was sure of it. She could tell he'd been doing something else as well as working. Maybe he'd been shagging someone after work or the person he delivered to. What *was* he up to? Sharon needed to know. She couldn't seem to get away from it. It was driving her mad. She wished she could stop her head from asking all these questions: she tried to make herself believe what everyone else seemed to believe, that Trevor was just working. Things were bound to be a bit different.

She found it torture keeping her mouth shut: every time she saw him she felt her lips contort as she tried not to spit out accusing questions. The whole world seemed to be against her, although Liam had been great over the past few days. He was in bed now, pretty early for him. Sharon smiled to herself as she smoked her cigarette at her lookout post. What a flipping week.

They'd managed to avoid the bailiffs or the court summoners or whoever they were nearly all week and tomorrow Trevor was going to give her some money. Sharon had to remind herself that things were looking up. Charlie was right, she shouldn't take life so fucking seriously. She stayed on her stool, smoking and thinking. She wanted to wait up for Trevor tonight. She wanted to *enjoy* his company again.

Later that evening, I rang Tasha to pin her down for the rehearsal. She'd spent every spare moment with the doc. What a surprise. This girl's sexual appetite was not to be scoffed at.

Ready for something like a *Playboy* story, I was shocked to discover that they spent a lot of time staring at each other and that they had the most amazing sex without even touching each other. Sounded terrible to me.

Tasha was so into this guy that it seemed pointless even to mention the band to her. I had to allow her a full ten minutes to go on about him before she'd even begin to listen to me. She was certainly feeling like she was *in love*. I winced when she said that.

How could she do this to us? She genuinely believed that this was the real one. But it *always* feels like the real one! Why should this one be any different from the rest? How could you tell a real one from a fake one? I felt like I'd lost another comrade to the other side. I knew it'd be ten times harder to pin her down now than it had been before, and it hadn't been exactly easy then. Tasha continued to describe her astral night. I didn't say much. Maybe I was wrong about myself and Conka. Maybe I was groping around for any wayward piece of life. Tasha was reminding me how fab a cock can be – and that's just looking at it. Maybe I was jealous of the fact that she had a man – a doctor – in her life, and I was merely having strange lesbian fantasies.

I wondered whose bed I'd rather be in. I couldn't work it out – I just knew it wasn't mine. Perhaps the band idea *was* stupid and childish. It was all becoming a bit too much of an effort from my side: organising this lot was harder than organising a batch of headless chickens. But remaining a headless chicken was an even more frightening prospect, and no one had come up with a better idea. I concluded that I'd stick with it a while longer and try to persuade Tasha along to another rehearsal. 'Go on, Tash, you know you'll enjoy it,' I pleaded. 'Conks and I have written a very funny song about a Dobermann – you'll love it.'

'I know what I *do* love,' she mused.

God, it was going to be hard distracting her. She was hooked.

'Yeah, yeah, Tasha, you've made it very plain what you love, how much you love it and how often you love it. I'm completely clear on that one. I love it too and I'm not knocking it. I just think the band would give us something that men can't.'

'Oh, I know,' she said, with renewed enthusiasm, which surprised me.

I was expecting more of a fight than that. She was keener than I'd realised.

We agreed on a time but left the venue to be decided. I immediately rang Conka with the good news and to suggest she rang Sharon – I didn't want to risk it: I had things to get on with that night. I ran my long hot bath and allowed myself to wallow in fantasy, wetness and warmth.

31

As anticipated, organising the next practice was a real test of my devotion to the band. Tasha and Conka were reluctant to go all the way to Sarah's, which would take pretty much the whole weekend – Conka, because she wanted to do a market stall in Portobello on the Sunday, and Tasha for obvious 'medical' reasons. Sharon was nowhere to be found.

I had resigned myself to the annoying fact that Sharon probably wouldn't make it, but I was still looking forward to getting a lot done with the other two. Conka wasn't trying to get out of it: she just wanted to be professional and book a rehearsal room for a couple of hours, not fart around like a bunch of third-formers all weekend. It did seem the more adult approach, just as 'rehearsal' sounded more professional than 'band practice'.

Tasha, although claiming enthusiasm, was developing a habit of ducking out at the last minute. She'd say either that she was too ill, or she was too tied up with Daniella, but we knew it was an excuse to bunk off or bonk off. Now she was saying she was busy all day Saturday and could only make it for a couple of hours on Sunday. I told her that Conka wanted to do it on Saturday and couldn't do Sunday. Then I had to ring Conka back, then Tasha, then Conka.

'Seven nine two, five eight four threeeee,' Conka sang. 'Great Days in great ways. How can I help?'

'Hello, Conks?' I shouted. 'You're so funny! Do they know you answer the phone like that?'

'Oh, hi there, Charlie. How are you?' Evidently Conka was having quite a good time at this new job of hers.

'I'm still trying to organise this flipping rehearsal,' I said.

'Hey, you know I've got access to just about everything here?'

'Yeah?'

'Well, I reckon we should make a video,' Conka said in a hushed tone.

'What *kind* of video, Conks?' I asked.

'A *music* video, of course. "Bing Bang" would be perfect for it.'

'Oh, right,' I said.

'Yeah, it'd be brilliant. You and I could do it, it's practically recorded already and I can get use of loads of stuff. If the others aren't up for it, then it doesn't matter, we should do it anyway and then release it. We could wear our Afros, knickers and small tight T-shirts with Bing written on one and Bang on the other . . .'

'What would we have on our feet?' I was picturing it, and it was looking pretty funky so far.

'Clogs, mate.'

'Clogs? You mean platforms, right?' Clogs ruined it for me.

'Yeah. Platforms, clogs – great big fuckers anyway.'

We continued talking for a further twenty minutes making plans and exchanging ideas, until Conka's boss got back. We said goodbye and I felt great that another member of the band had as much foresight, enthusiasm and interest as me.

Conka had given me a couple of names and numbers of studios she'd worked in with Elsa. After about three hours of negotiation, I eventually managed to arrange a practice in rehearsal rooms around the back of Harrow Road for the coming Saturday. Thankfully I'd got the rooms for free: there wasn't an abundance of rock 'n' rollers wanting to record/rehearse from midday to three on a Saturday afternoon. I then made Tasha promise that she'd be there. She promised that she'd be there with a smile on her face. I told her I wasn't worried about the smile.

Next: Conka. She was pleased with the result – she liked anything if it was free, and I knew I could count on her to be there. Things were looking good.

Fame assured, I decided to walk to the school that afternoon. I left myself plenty of time to go the more scenic route. My thoughts charged around in their usual haphazard way as I ambled along. I wondered whether any of the other parents knew of my near miss with Mr C. I seriously hoped not; in hindsight he was so incredibly revolting. It was amazing where desperation led you. I looked at everyone walking past and wondered how each of them coped with this ridiculous life.

I wanted to see Sharon. I'd left a few messages on her machine, but hadn't heard from her since the television-licence thing. I wanted to know if she was all right. I turned the corner and bumped into another mistake. Bing. Marvellous. I wasn't really in the mood for him and his caustic quips.

'All right.'

Ugh, that *drawl*! How could I even have contemplated it? Still, it was a polite opening and it'd be rude to stand there in silence all day.

'Hello, how are you?' I replied magnanimously.

'Fine, yeah. I've just seen your mad friend, Sharon.'

'Bingo! Where was she?'

'Just down there.'

He pointed in the direction I was going.

'Thanks, see you,' I shouted, as I ran to find her, much relieved to get away from Bing so quickly.

Sure enough, I soon spotted the familiar figure, the blonde head cocked to one side, eyes down, shoulders hunched, arms crossed, a thumb being chewed. I quickened my pace and caught up with her.

She was startled to see me.

'Where did you spring from?' she asked.

'Highland,' I replied, as I fell into step with her.

We walked in silence for a while. She tried a feeble smile whenever I made any of my frivolous comments to try to break the ice. I felt that whatever I said would make her cry. It took all of her strength to get out of her house and go to the school: she couldn't handle talking to other people as well. She didn't even want to risk catching the bus for fear of bursting into tears when trying to buy her ticket. I knew how she felt; it wasn't so long ago that I had been in a similar mental state.

'You know we've managed to book rehearsal rooms on Saturday for a couple of hours – in case you're up for it. Of course, none of us are expecting you to come, we all appreciate what's going on at the moment . . . but if you do want to take your mind off things . . .'

God, it was difficult saying anything. I felt like everything I said was the wrong thing. But I ploughed on.

We were getting closer to the school, but as we had been walking at a fair old pace, we were far too early to just hang around at the gates. We went to Mario's.

Mario was always value for money, and his Italian passion shone brightly through the grease and grime of his grotty Bush café. He could tell Sharon was a little down in the mouth so paid her extra special attention, by putting extra marmalade with her toast and extra chocolate on her cappuccino. She didn't notice – she was oblivious to most things.

I carried on talking at her for a while, about the band and the video. It was the only thing I could talk about that contained zero-upset value; I had to keep her bobbing gently along, with no surprise waves. I felt like her temporary life-jacket, but that was part of the tragedy. I was only *temporary*.

We had one another, we were all good friends and, although we had our differences, we could count on each other. In fact we were all far more dependable than any of the dirty, rotten, stinking males that any of us had been daft enough to have tolerated in our lives. We worked like a rota: we helped each other out. But we didn't spend nights wrapped around one another, except when completely pissed, doing those things that only a man and a woman do so well together, listening to a craving, a need, allowing a man to be inside you, an intimacy that's perfect in its moment. We couldn't give that to one another, at least not to Sharon. Maybe Conka and I could – given that we'd slept together, sort of.

Sharon stared at my cigarette while I spoke. Her glassy stare was unbearable, way too intense. Who said I could handle this? I know I said I related to this, but every time I saw Sharon, she had deteriorated some more. I was exhausted just by sitting opposite her.

'Oh, come on, Sharon,' I said, somewhat aggressively.

She looked up, surprised by my change of tone. I'd had enough and felt a wave of anger towards her. There was no turning back now.

'You've got to snap the *fuck* out of it,' I hissed. 'There is simply no point in getting this upset the whole time. No one's dead, it's not that fucking tragic.'

I saw the tears well up in her doleful eyes. 'No! Don't start fucking crying, again. *No*, Sharon!' I screamed. I couldn't take it for one second longer. 'You're boring the fucking tits off

218

everyone, with the same ongoing, tedious, fucking ridiculous saga. Life isn't easy for anyone, Sharon, so stop feeling so goddamned sorry for yourself and just get the fuck on with it. Accept that it's hard, life's a bitch and all that shite. We are all on our own, we are all lonely fuckwits at the end of the day. You're born alone, you die alone, you may as well live alone and just go out every so often and have a fucking ball, and not get so fucking upset about it. There's no point in going under, Sharon. Everyone dies, but not everyone really *lives*. And you've got plenty of life in you yet, girl. Torturing yourself is a fuck of a tiring way to live and, if you ask me, it's about time you gave it up. Misery is optional, you know.'

She continued to stare at me, amazed by my outburst. I had calmed down considerably by the end of my tirade.

'What are you talking about, Charlie?'

'Staring. You stare too much without speaking. It's heavy, that's all. I just wish you'd say something.'

'Can't get a fucking word in, can I?' Sharon said, and smiled.

'Wow, Sharon, you're smiling now! Insult a few people! Go on, it really cheers you up. I think we've found your personal cure. Go on, insult Mario, he won't mind.'

'Well if he won't mind, there wouldn't be much point in doing it, would there?'

Sharon puffed heavily on her ciggie. Then she smiled again. Phew, this 'rough' approach could be working.

'I was actually feeling all right today, Charlie,' she said.

Oh, my God, I had just given her one of my toughest talking-tos to date and she was feeling all right.

'But I am worried about something –'

'You don't have to make something up,' I interrupted.

'No, I'm not making anything up. It's a puzzle, that's all.'

As always, I thought.

'You see Trevor's working . . .'

Well, Trevor *working* was a puzzle to me too.

'He's doing a driving job, which means he'll be able to give me some money by Friday. The thing is, he's been behaving really weird . . .'

Here we go, I thought.

'Well, he would be acting *weird*, wouldn't he?' I said.

Sharon hadn't made the obvious connection.

'He's working, right?'

Sharon nodded. I shrugged my shoulders and said no more.

'I see what you mean, but I know something strange is going on.'

She was about to explain the jealous feelings and a load of other unfounded bollocks. I had to put her off the scent.

'Please, Shassa. Why not just insult people? It'll make you feel better – it's so much funnier than playing detective about a bleeding temporary van driver.'

Sharon frowned at me. I frowned back.

'Hey, Mario!' she called. She beckoned him over and gave me a knowing look. I felt the giggles well up inside me, anticipating the humour of what she was about to do. Mario glided to our table, winking at the mute young Italian waiter, who nodded approvingly.

'Yes, my ladies. Wha' do I do for you?'

Now that was asking for it.

'Mario, you do absolutely *nothing* for me, *at all*. Nor would you if you were the last man on earth. I'd rather shag my toast,' Sharon said.

I was howling. She'd said the whole lot dead seriously, while staring right into his eyes. Poor guy. I think only his charming wife would have said something like that to him before. Mario scowled in cartoon fashion as he huffed off, not sharp enough to retaliate in any other way.

'Shassa, that was monumental. How do you feel?'

She was grinning broadly, as well as looking a bit guilty. I pointed out to her that Mario more than likely deserved every word he got: how would Sharon like it if she knew her husband was behaving like Mario did with all his female customers?

'All men are shits,' she said as we got up to pay.

The irrepressible Mario blew us both a kiss and wiggled his tongue at Sharon, while we handed over our money. 'Hey, you know you really swear too much, you know it's no ladylike,' he said.

'Listen, Mario, if I can't fucking do it, then at least I can fucking say it. So fuck off.'

'All men are shits,' Sharon reiterated to Mario, as she took her change.

'I couldn't agree more,' he said, in perfect English.

All men are shits. I agreed with Sharon so much that the idea of having a more permanent female partner was becoming extremely attractive. One woman in particular was on my mind.

I was thinking about her for the remainder of the walk to the school. I was always thinking about her, these days, and wondering. Sharon was now in quite good spirits and even talking about coming to the rehearsal, but I couldn't listen to her any more. My mind was on my own worries. I felt I was really falling in love with Conka. And I still hadn't done anything about it.

To my delight, we ran into the woman herself at the school gates. She was on time for once – since she'd started her job, she'd often been turning up a few minutes late. I felt my heart quicken when she beamed at me; she added so much zest and humour to my life. She was beautiful.

'How ya doing, sunshine?' she said, as she kissed me hello.

I shuddered as her peck rippled through me.

'And how's our Shassa, then?' she added, giving Sharon's arm a quick squeeze.

Sharon managed a pathetic smile.

Luke burst into tears as soon as he saw me. He told me he hadn't had anyone to play with either at break or at lunchtime. I asked him why he didn't play with Helena at school. He looked at me as if I was a complete idiot and told me that in his class girls and boys don't even *talk* to each other. Great. There was another thing that I should have brought up in that parent-teacher meeting.

But Luke was seriously down. How could anyone *not* want to play with him? My heart sank. I couldn't deal with Luke being depressed too. What was going on in this sad world?

Despite my obsessive pull towards Conka, I decided to go to the movies with Luke, on our own, give him some extra special treatment.

We mooched off together, hand in hand, leaving Conka and Sharon at the school, still fussing over coats and book-bags and the like.

After credit-carding the movies, I decided to go the whole way and end the evening with a slap-up meal. My credit card was fat and that's all that mattered. Besides, I kidded myself, soon I'll have so much money from the music that I won't know what to do with it. May as well spend some of it now. I took Luke to my favourite Italian, which happened to accept Visa. Luke loved the pasta there and I treated myself to a smooth, comforting glass of red wine. Both the food, the wine and the company were excellent. Luke had enjoyed the film and was chatting pleasantly away.

Here was a boy, *my son*, who was going to grow up into a *man*. That's God's little joke for you. I remembered how my grandmother always used to hark on about what a beautiful baby my father was. She could never come to terms with the fact that he grew up into a *man*; I was beginning to understand what she'd been on about for all those years. What made men so awful? What lessons could I give Luke? There weren't any men in my life that I could think of who I would like Luke to look up to and learn from. I prayed that he would turn out all right. I decided to have another glass of wine.

As I looked around at the other diners, my thoughts drifted back to Conka. I imagined being there with her. I knew we'd be laughing if we were there together. Maybe I'd come back with her. The other diners were mainly couples, lovers, I supposed. Some were laughing in flirtatious flurries. One couple was deadly quiet, not even looking at each other – perhaps they were getting divorced? Others were talking intensely to each other. Each pair had their own definite intimacy. An intimacy I envied. Tasha reckoned she and the doctor were like that: they communicated in a private, unspoken language.

There was a table of four men, probably on an extended business meeting. They were all suited up, their pot bellies lurking purposefully around the table. They had an obscene air of money about them, of too much rich food and loads of whisky. Nice.

Then there was a table with an adult family. All five looked the same, even the husband and wife, who must have been either attracted to their mirror images, or with each other so long that they'd begun to look like one another; they bore an uncanny and unnatural resemblance to each other. The whole family did. They were all tall and skinny, with large bulbous noses and thin lips, and they all wore really bad-taste glasses. No wonder they went out *en famille*.

There weren't any other lone mothers with their kids, or lesbian couples. I felt like a freak again. No matter how I looked at things, I always seemed not to fit in. And, no matter where I looked, there wasn't one man in the restaurant that I'd have liked Luke to grow up to be like.

Luke had finished wiping ice-cream all over his face and I was ready to curl up in my hiding-place, out of sight of the rest of the world and its disappointments. We got the bill and went home.

I let Luke sleep in my bed that night – we both needed the extra comfort. It paid. The first thing that Luke said to me the following morning was, 'I love you, Mummy.'

32

Tasha gave her daughter a gentle kiss as she put her to bed. Even Daniella seemed calmer and happier than normal. Craig was having a wonderful effect on their lives. She would be glad to leave this flat, this whole area; they'd both benefit from living in less-polluted climes. As she drew the curtains she looked down to the street below, at the people passing by. Her attention was drawn to a car across the street blaring loud music. She was just about to turn away when she realised Trevor was talking to its owner.

'Oh, no,' she said, as she watched him get in and kiss his female companion.

Tasha couldn't believe it, but perhaps the driver was just a mate. What was she going to tell her friend? Sharon had seemed a bit better over the past couple of days. At least, she was more worried by outside bad vibrations, some TV-licence bastards, or bailiffs, arseholes anyway, than about Trevor. Tasha decided not to be sure. She'd seen him from the back; he wasn't necessarily Trevor. No. Tasha was not sure at all. She didn't like the idea of rocking an already unstable boat. She would soon forget she'd seen anyone looking even remotely like Trevor getting into any vehicle, kissing anyone at all.

Besides, Tasha had her beautiful Craig to think about now. Over the last few days they had spent a lot of time together. They'd had an enchanting time. He made Tasha so happy. There was no doubt in her mind that this man really loved her.

The climax for her was when Craig got down on his knees and held her around her legs while burying his face in her belly, proclaiming his lifelong unearthly love for her. She had stroked his hair and wept as she too declared undying love. They discussed marriage. *Marriage.* The word sang prettily in Tasha's head. They would unite their souls. They didn't want a traditional wedding. Tasha wasn't into legalising things – besides, she'd never really believed in the traditional vows. With a pagan wedding they would get to write their own. Tasha had a white-witch friend who would know the recipe of paganesque marriage rituals. She smiled to herself as she pictured Craig and herself, adorned with daisy chains, jumping over the broomstick together.

Tasha sighed a happy sigh as she felt her heart plunge into another world, their own intimate, trusting, wonderful world. They had found one another and not been frightened to admit it. They were in love, they were a *whole,* a double identity merged into one. They felt safe with one another; the world was there for them to enjoy. He was so passionate; she was passionate. Her body felt swollen from her love; she couldn't imagine a love bigger than this. It was an enviable relationship: complete trust. Tasha was *so happy*! She couldn't wait for her new life to begin. She lay down next to Daniella and fell asleep with a contented smile.

Trevor knew he was on a drug run. It was fucking obvious right from the start: Jeremy was always sweating buckets, either from being really nervous or completely wired. Trevor just hadn't got him to admit to it yet. He was pathetic when it came to acting naturally as well: whenever Trevor asked Jeremy anything about the supposed washing-machine parts, Jeremy would scream at him to stop asking so many bloody questions. Trevor knew that, if he played his cards right, he could probably ask for quite a bit more than Jeremy was hoping to pay him. Jeremy was snorting a couple of hundred quid a day as it was and could certainly afford it.

Jeremy never came in the van any more, which was good for Trevor: it confirmed that whatever he was transporting was either drug- or bomb-related. It had to be the former and he thought he'd ask Jeremy for danger money. He'd wait until the end of the week, by which time he would have sussed out all the drops and pick-ups. Trevor had meticulously recorded every place he had had to visit over the last four days.

Tiffany kept showing up here and there. When they had run into each other today, she had suggested lunch. Trevor had had a couple of hours to kill – he got round London so fast he always was ahead of his schedule – so, why not? Tiffany had paid, making lunch an even more delicious accompaniment to the two bottles of wine they guzzled. Trevor's next pick-up was right around the corner from Tiffany's, and he felt a bit horny after lunch, after the wine and especially after the snog they'd had in Tiff's car. Once inside the house, Trevor put one hand up her skirt and the other on her breasts. It didn't take much to get her going. She let him hike up her skirt and pull down her panties, no problem. He lifted her on to him – she was pretty wet – she clutched him like a monkey and they fell back on the sofa. Tiffany's arse was made for spanking – it made a great noise – so he walloped and fucked her and she loved it. She was coming all over the place and rode him like some fucking jockey. Trevor pulled her off and came all over his stomach. Fuck, work wasn't too bad, after all.

Tiffany fussed all over the place, making tea, racking out lines, running a bath. She can't have had a good fuck since I last did her, Trevor thought, as he allowed himself to be placed in the bath and sponged down.

'All right, Tiffany, I can manage now,' Trevor said, taking her hand away from his dick and out of the bath. He wanted to wash himself in peace. 'Thanks, darling,' he said.

Tiffany smiled as she backed out.

'What time is it?' Trevor shouted to her.

'Seven,' Tiffany called. 'What time do you have to be there?'

'Oh, not until eight thirty. Have you got any food?'

'Bits and pieces, but I can order a pizza.'

Tiffany had come back into the bathroom. She still hadn't got properly dressed: she was wearing his T-shirt and nothing else.

'Do you mind taking that off?' Trevor said. 'I'll need it in a minute,' he said, vaguely trying to hide his annoyance. This was her house, full of thousands of her fucking clothes, and she has to put on *his* T-shirt. Fucking women.

'Oh, sorry.' Tiffany giggled.

She stood right in front of him with her back to him and peeled off his T-shirt. Her bum still had red patches on it from his slapping. Actually it looked revolting. It was really fucking huge from this angle. Trevor shut his eyes and ducked under the water.

'No pizza,' he said, on his way down.

By the time the contact had arrived and Trevor had made his delivery it was already eleven, and Jeremy wanted him to start at seven the following morning – he would definitely be asking for a raise now, he thought, as he went back to Sharon's.

He was cream-crackered by the time he got in. He was surprised to see Sharon. She'd had a bath and was naked under her floaty see-through dressing-gown. Her hair was half up and half down – she looked very sexy like that.

'Hi, darling,' Sharon said.

Trevor went to her and folded her in his arms. 'Sorry I'm late. It was the pick-up . . .'

As they kissed, Sharon became aware of two things: alcohol on his breath and someone else's perfume on his shirt. She pulled away from him. She'd stop herself asking any questions until tomorrow – and then only after he'd given her some money. Trevor was still holding her. She tried to move away. He grabbed her arse. He gently squeezed and began to push himself against her. But she pushed him away, she couldn't get into it. She felt terrible. How could he be having an affair and be this horny after her? Maybe he wasn't, she chided herself. She didn't know. She was tired and he was being pushy.

'No, Trevor, not now.'

'Baby doll, your pussy doesn't want a little visit?' He stroked her while he spoke.

It turned her on, but there were too many strange smells.

'No, Trevor, not now,' she said.

She took his hand away from her and went to bed. He was here and he wanted her: she'd be able to sleep – a bit.

Conka was convinced that sexual energy could be turned into something useful, rather than aggression and frustration. Apart from her naughty dreams, and passing out on a bed with Charlie, she'd not had any sex in nearly eight months now and she wasn't bothered. She had been at her part-time job, cleaning out her mum's cupboards, doing the stall and looking after Helena whenever she wasn't at school. She was pretty pleased with herself. A nice saving was growing steadily in the bank – she'd certainly have enough to take Helena on a great holiday and send Marge to Spain. Conka had been busy, but at work she had time to think about other things. That's when she had worked out the eight months.

Conka knew that Charlie was obsessed with her. She was intrigued. She had never done it with a woman and Charlie would be the one to experiment with – she was quite sexy. She was receptive to all of Conka's ideas – she'd liked the one about the video – she was a good driving instructor and a great puffing partner. Conka would go along with the music side of things for now and maybe dabble in a sexual experiment or two. What harm could it do?

Conka saw Wayne sneak a smile at her through his glass door, when Mrs Uptight's back was turned. Conka wondered about the gorge-geezer in the Jag; when she'd asked if it was her son Mrs Uptight merely threw her a glare so vindictive that Conka deduced it must have been her lover. Hats off to Mrs Uptight.

The remainder of the day went by remarkably fast, and Conka

had plenty of energy to discuss more video ideas with Charlie later that evening.

Trevor awoke with his usual throbbing splendour, but Sharon wasn't having any of it. As soon as he prodded her she'd leapt out of bed. She was kind of nice to him, though, before he left for work. She made him tea and they left the house together. She seemed a bit tense, but she still kissed him goodbye.

Trevor watched her and Liam walk hand in hand to the bus stop. He tasted Sharon's lips lingering on his: her mouth was so full and tender. He had a burning desire to chase after her and ask her to forgive him – he felt suddenly that she had the power to absolve him from everything, his life and himself. He didn't want to go to work and he was already an hour and a half late. Jeremy had said seven, but Trevor was buggered if he was going to wait outside Jeremy's for a fucking hour again. No one does *anything* that early – especially not when they've got half of Columbia up their nose. Still, he should hurry: he shouldn't fuck things up now. It was Friday, pay-day, and he was more than ready to get some fucking money.

As he anticipated, Jeremy's house was as dead as doornails. Trevor buzzed and a few moments later a groggy Jeremy answered. 'Trevor?'

'Yes, flower.'

'I'll be down in a minute, I've just got to get dressed. Won't be long. What time is it?'

'Eight forty-five.'

'What?' Jeremy squealed.

'I said, *eight forty-five*!' Trevor shouted into the mouthpiece.

'*Why the bloody hell weren't you here at seven?*' Jeremy was furious.

'I was, flower. And I buzzed. I just couldn't keep my finger on the bell long enough.'

Trevor laughed when he saw a dishevelled Jeremy come down. He bundled into the van and gave Trevor the address.

Two and a half hours later they arrived in a remote village somewhere near Huntingdon. Jeremy was panicking about being late. His mobile phone wasn't charged and he hadn't stopped telling Trevor to go faster all the way there. Trevor much preferred it when they travelled separately. Jeremy offered Trevor a toot, which he gladly accepted. He had refused a lot of times, but today he felt like getting nicely off his face.

They made a relatively smooth pick-up, not too much hanging around, then straight back to London, this time to an address in Kilburn. They made their delivery. Trevor waited in the van while Jeremy did his business. Jeremy returned, they did a line then went to a café for some lunch.

'So you'll be paying me today, eh, Jeremy?'

'Yes, all right, Trevor. I hadn't forgotten.' Jeremy glared at him.

Trevor didn't give a shit: they were in a greasy spoon and Jeremy could keep his evasive standards to himself.

'How much were you intending to pay me, then?' Trevor asked.

Jeremy frowned and leant forward over the table. 'I'm intending to pay you what I've always intended to pay you, nothing more and nothing less,' he hissed. 'Now be quiet and let me eat in peace.'

Trevor stared at him. The arrogant little shit.

'What's in the boxes, Jeremy?' he asked quite loudly.

Jeremy ignored him and continued stuffing in his mashed potatoes.

'I said, *what's in the boxes, Jeremy?*' Trevor poured his tea over Jeremy's mash.

'What the bloody hell did you do that for?' Jeremy fumed.

'Don't ignore me, Jeremy. If you want me to stop asking such innocent questions, then you'd better pay me well.' Trevor spoke slowly so that the flower could understand. 'Kilburn is quite an Irish place, don't you know? I want to make sure I'm not carting around a load of Semtex. If I was, then I think I should be paid properly.'

Jeremy smiled a relieved smile. 'No, no, no, don't worry, Trevor, there's no chance of you blowing up in smithereens.' He laughed at the thought. 'You silly man, it's just washing-machine parts. That's all.'

His laugh ground to a frown as he realised Trevor's fork was pinning his to the table.

'Trevor, let go of my fork. Come on, let's eat now, eh?'

'That village we visited this morning,' Trevor continued, 'nice little cottage industry, that one. There was a very strong smell of *ammonia* when we got to the farm, didn't you think?' Trevor stabbed his fork harder into the table and stared at Jeremy. 'I know what you need to clean drugs, to doctor them, to do all of that. I *know* the smells, Jeremy, and that place stank. So, I'll ask you again, how much are you intending to pay me?'

Jeremy was silent for a moment. 'All right, darling, I'll give you an extra two, making it four hundred altogether.'

'You are joking, I take it?' Trevor sneered.

'No, I'm deadly serious,' Jeremy said, snatching his fork away from Trevor's, 'and you'd better not push your luck.'

'A thousand. I want a thousand.'

Jeremy fell about laughing. 'Five hundred, and that's as high as I go,' he said, in a fake American accent.

Trevor was not impressed. He sat staring at Jeremy, chewing the sides of his mouth. Jeremy giggled nervously. 'Five hundred, Trevor,' he repeated, more seriously.

'Eight hundred, or I'll go home now and make a few phone calls.'

'Don't threaten me, Trevor. You don't know what you'd be getting into. I'll give you six fifty. You can take it or fucking leave it.' Jeremy stood up and threw a tenner on the table. 'If you don't join me in the van in five minutes, I'll take it that you've gone to make your phone calls. Tiffany *will* be disappointed to get your dick in the post. If you come to the van, you'll get your six fifty and you'll shut your fucking mouth. This is not up for discussion any longer.'

With that, Jeremy turned and left the café.

Trevor thought for a moment. Six fifty was more than he'd hoped for. He thought he'd muck around and start high, but he'd surprised himself when a thousand came out of his mouth. What a result, he thought, as he paid the waitress.

The next stop was the place near Tiffany's. Trevor wondered if she'd show up again. He didn't feel like seeing her today at all. He just wanted to get his money and go home. He wanted Sharon. He missed her. He'd hardly seen her all week. Sure enough, Jeremy suggested waiting at Tiffany's until it was time for the last delivery.

'No. I think we should head on over there and chance it. Besides, the traffic is going to be murder soon,' Trevor said. He just couldn't face the thought of hanging out at Tiffany's. The idea of her made him feel sick.

'I suppose it will be. You don't want to call round for a quick nose up?'

'No, Jeremy, I don't. You've got your vial, let's use that.'

'Okay. You're the one driving. Tiffany will be disappointed.'

Trevor had to bully Jeremy into getting the cash. He'd wanted to pay him the rest on Monday, but Trevor told him to suck his fat one. In the end Jeremy gave him five fifty and a generous gramme. Trevor was well pleased. He'd be able to cut and sell half of the gramme and make an extra sixty easily. Nice one.

Part Four

**Badly Bruised Hopes,
Hearts and Faces**

33

I had a wedding to do, which cheered me up. The bills were getting on top of me again, especially as I had been credit-carding better and faster than any other sane, broke person I knew of. Everyone seemed in good spirits. I hadn't had much work recently and they would pay me well. Luckily, the bride and her mother were funny too. They were Welsh and very excited. Their lilted, lively accents sounded like music to my ears — especially when they broke into actual song, which they did frequently.

The bride was beautiful: her skin was of that immaculate creamy porcelain type, which looked all the more dramatic against her jet-black lustrous hair. She had dark blue eyes that looked enormous and magical once I'd finished making them up. Her lips were soft, full and pink, and seemed to be in a permanent smile. She was so ridiculously happy and full of love that you just wanted to hug and kiss her. I hoped she wouldn't be disappointed — for some reason my cynicism waned and I found myself really wanting this marriage to work. They paid me in cash, with a hefty tip, which put me in an even better mood and made me believe a little more in the theory that you have to spend to earn.

At the school I ran into Conka who was even more lively than usual. She'd walked into surprise but inappropriate greetings of happy birthday at work. She had almost put her foot in it, she told me, but had remembered that it was, in fact, her sister's birthday and that was who her employers thought she was. She had no other choice than to go along with it. In explaining away her obvious surprise, she told them that she always kept her birthday fairly quiet and never normally celebrated it.

'Well it's bloody marvellous I think, and no harm done. I mean, when they gave me the bottle of perfume, I did feel a bit guilty. Mrs Uptight didn't think I deserved it. But I only felt guilty for a moment. 'Cause I've already earned a bonus, mate, I'm telling you. Apparently, because of me, Mr Davenport has doubled his usual order and told everyone that I have an excellent phone manner.'

'Oo er, Mrs.'

'Yeah, well, it takes ten per cent talent and ninety per cent personality, don' it? Then they took me out to lunch. We had a couple of glasses of wine and pudding. Lunch and presents: gorgeous, eh? Made the day a darn sight more interesting as well. You've got to enjoy life – otherwise, what's the point?'

I couldn't agree with her more.

'The great thing is that they reminded me it was my sister's birthday, so I rang her when they were out on a delivery. I would have completely forgotten otherwise. They did look at me kind of strangely though, when we were talking about my age.'

Conka was thirty two but looked and behaved a lot younger.

'I think Mrs Uptight's jealous that I look this good for thirty eight!'

'You really don't look thirty eight at all – nowhere near,' I said.

'Yeah, well, it's like the time I had to explain to them how the fuck I got the nickname Conka when me name's Janet.'

'Who's Janet?'

'My sister. Or me, innit?'

I couldn't stop laughing. Conka invited me to a celebratory spliff session. It was her sister's birthday after all, and she was feeling flash with the cash, seeing as she got paid today and it was Friday. Boy, did we *love* our Fridays. We stopped off and purchased a nice bud or two, then went back to mine for a Friday night smoke-off.

Conka was quick off the draw to roll a big green one. I put the kettle on – well, what else do I do? The kids had water and Jammy Dodgers while we mums relished our Earl Grey and skunk. Fantastic!

The kids ran into Luke's bedroom to play leaving Conka and me to carry on on our own.

Conka picked up the guitar and began her gentle strum-style warm-up. She hummed softly while I sat listening, rolling a joint, getting lost in my own stoned world. I was vaguely listening to the children, catching the odd word here and there. Helena was definitely the bossy one and Luke the follower. I loved the way they had all these funny names for their games. I couldn't work out why this one was called the 'disco' game – maybe because they spoke with rough London accents, shouted a lot and generally pretended to be about sixteen – I don't know – although I did overhear them trying a cover version of an Oasis number.

Conka began to play 'Blue Sky', so I had to join in. I stood up and sang loudly along; this was about the only song to which I knew nearly all the words. I was crap at remembering words to songs, even the ones I'd recently co-written; those people who can remember all the words to songs they hear only once or twice really get on my nerves. Luke's like that, little git. Still, I enjoyed singing along to this one and gave my lungs a good old workout. I reckon singing is great therapy. It really makes you feel good: it gets the oxygen flying around the body and brain. You can't get too depressed when you sing: you have to feel at least vaguely all right to be *able* to sing – it must be good for you.

That mother and bride, especially the bride, were so happy they sang all the time – they had really made me feel good. I made Conka play 'Blue Sky' over and over again. Each time she'd change how she played it, so I'd attempt to sing it in the appropriate style. We did Spanish, opera, jazz (I was quite good at that one), rock and roll, country-and-western. After about the eighteenth rendition, Conka had had enough.

'Are you going out tonight?' I asked her, somewhat tentatively.

'Yes, I was actually, Char, if that's okay with you?'

She looked at me strangely. I felt uncomfortable, pissed off, even. Why had she asked that? I was about to question her, but the kids had re-emerged from Luke's room. Conka flopped on the sofa and casually asked me if I minded Helena staying the night.

'*What?*' I said, not hiding my surprise.

Conka stared at me, like it was really shit of me to be so surprised.

'Oh, yes, oh, please, Charlie . . . please can I?' Helena said, jumping up and down.

'No, not if it's a problem for Charlie, Helena,' Conka intervened, still looking at me in a rather cold, challenging way.

I didn't know what I'd done – maybe it was pay-back time for

237

going on my Bing date with Sharon instead of her. Or perhaps she'd never forgiven me for whatever happened the night of the boob incident. She seemed angry with me. It felt horrible. And, on top of that, she was making me feel guilty.

'It's all right, Helena, I'll take you to Marge's,' she said, grabbing her coat.

'No, no. It's not a problem – not at all. I was just surprised.'

'*Please*,' Helena whined, in her most desperate way.

'Yes, of course you can,' I quickly said.

The kids cheered up and ran back into Luke's bedroom for a game of 'kittens'. Conka sat down again. She clocked my distress and explained that her Dobermann-mate, Elsa, had rung her that day at work and had asked her to do vocals tonight. She said she wasn't going to miss being on Elsa's new album.

'I'm doing BVs, get a bit of wedge for it, you know.'

Conka looked at me and saw that I wasn't happy. Elsa had been the one with whom she'd run the canteen at the computer centre. They had sung there as well. I suddenly hated fucking Elsa. Whose band was Conka supposed to be in? And what the fuck were BVs? Bacterium Vaginitus?

'You get a oner for backing vocals these days,' Conka explained. 'It's at them rehearsal studios we'll be using too.'

'Great,' I said, as sincerely as possible.

As if telling me where she was going was going to make me feel any better. I don't know quite what I'd assumed was going to happen that night but I certainly hadn't expected this. Conka looked at her watch. I felt a pain in my heart as she stood up to go.

'You off, then?' I asked feebly.

'Yeah. I was supposed to be there half an hour ago, actually.'

Conka left, taking all of the spliff with her. I felt as if the wind had been knocked out of my sails. There I was, only moments ago, harping on about how great singing made you feel, but now I felt like shit.

I went to find Luke and Helena, to see if there was anything I could shout at them about, but his room was okay. In fact, I think they'd tidied it a bit – it never normally looked *that* good.

I left them alone and ran myself a bath. I put in about twenty drops of lavender oil, as it's supposed to be so fucking great at calming and relaxing you, and locked the door. The smell and steam filled the bathroom. It felt like a sauna as I undressed. I stood before the mirror and, even though it was steamed up, I stared into it as I always do when I take off my makeup.

I felt around the bottles for my Vaseline, scooped a couple of blobs in my fingers then rubbed it on my eyes.

'JESUS! CHRIIIIST!' I screamed, fumbling furiously around for the cold-water tap or something to get this stuff off.

I couldn't open my eyes and the burning was making me feel sick. I finally found the cold tap and rinsed my eyes.

'*No!*' I shouted.

Somehow the water made it even worse. Wiping the tortuous stuff off was the only thing that worked. My eyes burnt like fury. The kids had mucked around with my stuff and had put the Vaseline lid on the Vicks' vapour rub.

'I need this like a fucking *hole in the head*!' I yelled at the top of my voice. I couldn't even read the side of the pot to see what to do in case it accidentally goes in your eyes.

I knew there was no way the kids were going to come anywhere near me now – I'd shouted so much – so I decided to tell them off later.

The bath calmed me down. My eyes watered torrentially – or was I crying? I felt vaguely melancholic and sorry for myself. I missed Conka. I felt jealous of Elsa. I wanted to be doing BVs as well. Why was I the idiot left at home alone? I allowed the tears to stream down my face. I was really fucking tired.

Sharon had been a bag of nerves all day. She was sure she was followed at one point by one of those horrible bailiffs. She'd run into the library and hidden in the thriller section. She ended up staying there the whole day. She hadn't intended to, it was just that she started reading a Stephen King and couldn't put it down. Of course that made her even more nervous. She'd intended to see the doctor and get a sick note today, to help her plead her case. But by the time she'd got to the surgery it had shut. Fucking typical. They always closed early on Fridays, she should have remembered that. Now she'd have to wait until Monday. What a twit.

She walked to the school, too jittery to stand at the bus stop and with plenty of time and energy to burn. She still got there early, which was just as well, as Liam's class was let out a bit before three thirty. They left immediately so Sharon didn't get to see Charlie or Conka. Liam wasn't happy – in fact, he was in an ugly argumentative mood. He badly wanted the new Man U strip. Muhammed had it, why couldn't he? He wasn't going to be palmed off with anything other than the real licensed thing either. He answered back to everything Sharon said. He couldn't understand how broke she was, and Sharon supposed that was probably good. He kept on and on – she was really fed up with him, he always wanted something expensive. Sharon hated this fucking pressure.

She decided to go straight to the Natural History Museum. Entry was free after four thirty and by the time they got there it would be about that. It was one place Liam never seemed to get bored of. He still argued all the way there, saying he hated it, but Sharon knew he'd like it once they were there and, besides, she really didn't want to go home: she wanted to stay out as long as possible. She didn't want to be sitting at her lookout post for too long: she knew that was always where she gravitated to in the flat. Her stool.

'Mum? Are we here?' Liam asked.

'Oh, yeah, quick, Peanut, here we go.'

They jumped off the bus and sprinted to the museum. Sharon let Liam charge around the massive place. He loved it. He raced up and down the stairs, stopping every so often to growl at the stuffed bears or pull a face at the monkeys mouldering away in their glass cabinets. Sharon found herself writing bad poetry in her head.

> The monkey was caught,
> The monkey was dead,
> They pointed the gun and shot the lead.
> The monkey laughed,

The monkey cried,
But the monkey's soul
Never died.
He was gutted and sprayed,
Stuffed and sewn.
In a see-through glass case,
He now moulds alone.

By about six they had finished a Chinese takeaway and Liam was
begging to go home. They dawdled back, Liam leaning heavily
into his mother as he held her round her waist. They were
walking as if they were joined at the thigh, giggling as they tried to
stay in time with each other.

Suddenly Sharon felt sick as they arrived at her door. They
went in, unnoticed, Sharon thought, by any hovering bailiffs.
Liam went straight to his room and she to the kitchen. She put the
kettle on, lit a cigarette and looked out.

The house was completely quiet when Trevor came in. 'Hello?'
he called. He noticed a light coming from the kitchen, but the rest
of the place was in darkness.

'Hi, what's up?'

Sharon was sitting on the stool in the kitchen, looking pretty
tired. It was about ten thirty. Liam was in bed.

'Hi,' she eventually said.

'What are you doing in the dark?' Trevor asked, as he flicked
the lights on in the lounge.

Sharon followed him in there: she wondered if he had it. He
bent over the sofa and put some music on.

'We are going to party, darling,' he said, as he took out the
wrap.

Sharon's heart sank.

'Oh, no, Trevor, don't tell me you've spent all your money on
that. Please don't say that.'

Trevor went over to Sharon and held her. 'Don't worry,
darling. Let's just say this just fell off the back of a lorry. This is
for you.' He handed her a wad of folded notes.

Sharon smiled. He'd come through. He hadn't let her down, after all. She sat down and counted the money.

'Oh, Trevor, thanks, darling, this is great. There's a hundred and fifty there. Did you save any for yourself?'

'Enough, he gave me two hundred and I figured you need it more than I do.'

'Oh, Trev . . .'

They kissed, undressed, tooted, drank and made love. And then they did it all over again. And again. And then they slept very well.

I woke up bright and early after a night of vivid, lively dreams. They were all confused and mashed up and I couldn't begin to tell you about them, but they left me feeling ready for a great day and a *fantastic* rehearsal. It was a sunny Saturday morning and I was determined to make it a good one. We really had to get kicking now, before this life-changing ambition dissipated entirely.

I rang Tasha to confirm her presence. She was there, she said. I checked in with Conka. She was ready to rock 'n' roll and had already asked her mother to have the kids. Things were looking *good*. I dialled Sharon's number but hung up before anyone answered. I didn't want to get down again: I figured it would be better to call her from the studio, later on.

By now the kids were ready to go for a walk so I got dressed in my funkiest clothes.

'If you're going to be a pop star, you've got to have style,' I explained to the kids, as the three of us skipped out of the house and merrily down the road.

I could feel it in my bones: today was going to be a good one.

When the phone rang Sharon got up. Whoever it was rang off as soon as she got there. Her head felt heavy and it was pretty late. Liam was up and watching telly. Sharon hadn't heard him. Trevor was still snoring loudly. She flicked the kettle on and decided to do some cleaning; she wanted to have a positive day, however hard her head tried to torture her. She cleared up last night's debris and made herself and Liam some toast. She was happy to realise that she felt hungry for the first time in ages.

242

Maybe they'd go to the park. It looked like it was going to be a nice day.

While she was in the bath, she heard Trevor get up. She positioned her legs in the most flattering way and waited for him to come in for his morning pee.

'Hi there, darling,' she cooed, when he appeared.

Trevor grunted in response. He peed, flushed the loo and left without looking at her. Great. So much for nice legs or a nice day. She was about to cry, but she remembered her promise. Not today, Sharon, not today. Don't let it happen today, she said quietly to herself, over and over again, while she rubbed her feet with a pumice stone. By the time she came out of the bathroom, her feet were raw and Trevor had gone. Sharon burst into tears and ran back into the bathroom. Liam kicked over the coffee table and went to his bedroom.

'Yeah I understand, I'll tell her ... next week? Definitely? ... Okay, see ya then, 'bye.' Conka put the phone down. 'Oh, shit, Marge, Charlie ain't going to be too thrilled. Elsa's gone and nicked our studio space. I told her she was fucking about too much last night.'

'Oh, don't worry, you can do somesing else ... There is always somesing to do,' Marge said affectionately.

The sound of Helena's voice came nearer.

'Ah, here they are,' Marge said.

As soon as she opened the door the kids flew straight past Marge and into the garden at the back.

'Come in. You want some tea and cake?'

'Yes, please, Marge,' I said, giving her a kiss. She always had excellent cakes.

'How's Conka?' I asked, kissing her hello.

'Fine thanks, Chas. And yourself?'

'Oh, I'm ready for a kicking rehearsal, baby.'

I punched the air in true rock 'n' roll style. Conka didn't seem quite so enthusiastic.

'I'm afraid I've got some bad news for you. They've just this minute cancelled the studio,' she said solemnly.

243

'That can't be true. I phoned yesterday and he said it was still fine,' I said.

I couldn't believe it. I had been so looking forward to doing this. The kids would be looked after, three out of four members of the band were definitely going to be there and we had a professional studio. I had spent many long exasperating hours on the phone organising this and now it was being swept from under my feet. Unfortunately Conka didn't look as if she was joking.

'It should have been available, but I was there last night with Elsa and they were fucking about for ages. When you've got money to burn I guess you can take a bit more time,' Conka said.

'So *Elsa*'s got our time?'

'It doesn't really matter who's got it, does it? The point is that they are paying and we aren't, which is why they can cancel us at the last minute. Unlucky, that's all.'

She was so flipping calm. I was pacing. Fucking Elsa.

'Don't worry, Charlie, you can do somesing else today, there are all ways going to be knack-backs,' Marge said, giving me a cup of tea.

'Thanks, Marge.'

So much for feelings in my arthritic fucking bones. I would never trust my instincts again. This was crap. Why was it so difficult to do something as seemingly simple as rehearse? How were we ever going to get anywhere? I have to say I felt like crying. This band idea had become a means of escape for me, a way forward. But I knew we'd have to work hard at it, and that without money nothing was assured. Conka told me that she had reserved the studio for us next Saturday, but that was another week away. Time was racing by. I wanted to improve my life soon enough to live it. Conka looked at me and started that slow-grow grin of hers. I was fed up and tried not to smile back.

'What?' I snapped.

'Why don't we make the video? We've got the eight-track version of "Bing Bang". I think we should do it . . . today,' Conka said, smiling.

'Yes!' I leapt up, overjoyed. 'What a fantastic idea! Yes! Yes! Conka, you're brilliant.'

'Come on, we'll leave the kids here, go to yours and get

organised ... Is it all right to leave them with you for a bit, Marge?'

'Yes, yes. Off you go, girls. Enjoy yourselves,' Marge said, as she ushered us out of the house, giving us some cake wrapped in kitchen roll. 'Take it, it's good for you.'

We yelled goodbye into the garden, hopefully Luke and Helena heard us, then sped back to mine. Once back, I played my messages and flipping Tasha had cancelled too.

'Did you hear that, Conks?'

'Yep. She ain't interested, Char. She's fallen in bonk with that doctor and that's it. You may as well rule her out,' Conka stated.

'But she looks so good. And she was so enthusiastic – it was her that was pushing for it right from the start, remember. Perhaps she really is ill today. Shall I give her a ring?' I asked, not really knowing what to think.

'Let's have a smoke and you and me will sort it out, my friend. Don't worry 'bout it. If you ring she won't pick up anyway.'

That was true. Since Tasha had met Craig she had little time for us. Conka was right, we should just get on with it, regardless of the other two. It was bound to be easier that way, anyway.

'I was telling my mate Gabriel down at the studios 'bout us lot last night. He's a fantastic engineer – could be really handy later on, you know,' Conka said.

'Oh, yeah?'

'Yeah, you shouldn't get so worried, Charlie – I described what we were trying to do, who we were, what we looked like, etc., etc., and he reckoned we was in with a chance. So chill out.'

'Cool,' I said.

'Yeah, very cool. We can get some diamond guys working with us if we play our cards right – Gabriel is one of the best.'

That made me feel much better: it was nice to know that people outside the band could believe in us too. Conka rolled a joint while I wrote down our strategy. If we were going to make a pop video, we needed to be organised and I was the right man for the job. We grabbed my makeup box, my video camera, the costumes and Afros, went via Marge's to pick up the kids and finally headed for Sarah's.

*

'Sarah, you've got to hold the camera stiller than that,' I shouted across the park. 'We'll run to you, you stay there.'

I was pulling Conka back to our original starting-point, both of us stumbling over the various termite hills and rabbit-holes. We looked great, though I say it myself, even though we were freezing, and wearing next to nothing. We had nice big white knickers and white T-shirts on, with 'BING' written on mine and 'BANG' on Conka's. Thank God it wasn't raining. It was still April but the spring sun shone on us and, what with being wigged out and so excited, we soon got warm. We had huge platform shoes and our makeup was brilliantly over the top. With every passing dog-walker, we had our money's worth of hysterics. Even the deer stared at us.

'Okay, girls?' Sarah shouted. 'Are you ready?'

'Yes!' I bellowed, as Conka and I turned our backs to the camera.

'Cue sound!'

'Bing Banged My Lula' sang out from Luke's tinny stereo. Conka and I began our routine.

'Hang on!' Sarah shouted, 'There's a fly in the lens . . . Okay, let's take it from the top!'

'Bing bang, bing banged my lula!' we sang excitedly.

'Excellent!' Sarah shouted. 'It's a certain hit. Absolutely brilliant! Well done!'

'Don't you reckon the record companies will pay attention when they get a stunning video through the post rather than the usual boring cassette tape, then, Sarah?' Conka said, grinning knowingly.

'Oh, yes, you'll go down a storm,' Sarah said enthusiastically. 'The first all-single-mother band. I love it! What's the band's name, anyway?'

I looked at Conka, this was something I hadn't considered yet.

'THE HERB GIRLS!' Conka shouted.

'Excellent,' I said. Conka always had the answer. 'Which Herb are you going to be then, Conks?'

'Well, you could be Saucy Herb and I'll be Skunky Herb,' she said.

It was so exciting, I had to hug her.

'Okay, Herbs,' Sarah shouted. 'Let's go again from the top! Ready?'

'Ready!' Conka and I shouted in unison.

I loved this. I was definitely meant to be dancing and singing. This was the life. While we danced and sang, the children ran around and Sarah shot the video. After about three hours, a lot of falling over, laughing and fluffing, we eventually ran out of tape. My feet were in agony but I didn't care: it had been a beautiful day.

Sharon had calmed herself and went back to join Liam. He wasn't in the living room and the coffee table was everywhere.

'*Liam!*' Sharon screamed.

She began to panic, thinking that he had gone too. Thankfully, she heard his door creak open. She went to his room.

'Liam?'

'*What?*' Liam shouted.

'Come on, Peanut, don't be like that. Shall we go out?'

'Where?'

'I don't know, I'll think of something. Just get ready – please, Peanut.'

Sharon went upstairs and got herself together. She couldn't bear being hemmed in with Liam all day, not with him in that terrible mood. She rang Tasha, but her machine was on. Then she remembered they were rehearsing. Maybe she'd pop to the studio and see them there. She knew roughly where it was.

They left the house and got a bus in the general direction of the studio. Liam brought his ball and they stopped in a small park so he could play. It was two in the afternoon by the time Sharon found the studio and talked her way in. It was a weird place, dark and dingy. She knocked on various doors, but couldn't find Tasha, Conka or Charlie anywhere – no one had seen any of them. The last door swung open at Sharon's first knock.

An older man, sitting in a chair facing the door, an acoustic guitar on his lap, smiled at them. 'Hello, Sharon. Hello, little boy. My name's Gabriel. Please come in.'

Sharon felt a mixture of fear, surprise, apprehension and excitement as she found herself drawn in.

Liam giggled nervously and held his mother's hand tightly. This man was weird. 'Do you know 'im?' he whispered.

Sharon squeezed his hand, unable to speak. Gabriel: nice name. He seemed familiar, but she couldn't place him. She wasn't sure if she knew him or not. She was surprised when he'd said her name. How'd he know that? He was incredibly calm and kind. He motioned to the other chair in the room, a swivelling office chair, comfortable. The whole place was very high tech, everything painted in matt black, yet it wasn't cold. Gabriel was dressed head to toe in black, black jeans with a loose black silk shirt. He had silver hair and a faded bronze beard. He sat comfortably with his legs crossed, perched in his chair, exuding peace. Sharon could almost see his generosity and wisdom. She completely trusted this man, she was never normally like that with strangers. She felt so much better. It was so strange but suddenly everything, all her problems, Trevor, *everything* was all right. Gabriel stood up. He was quite small, elfin almost. He opened a cupboard and took out a small wooden box.

'What's your name?' he asked Liam.

Liam looked at his mum.

'It's okay,' she said.

'Liam,' he said quietly.

Gabriel bent down to Liam's level and offered him the box.

'See if you can work out the puzzle. I'm going to talk to your mummy.'

'What's in it?' Liam asked, cynical of any toy other than electronic games.

'It's better than any computer game you've ever played.'

Liam took it, sat down on the floor near to Sharon and was quickly absorbed.

Gabriel sat opposite her and put his hand gently on her shoulder. 'I understand,' he said softly.

When those words caressed Sharon's ears, she began to sob, from her gut. Her whole body wept. She didn't know how long she cried, or if she'd ever cried like that before. She felt all the anger, the jealousy, the rage, every emotion pour out. In floods.

34

By the time he came home, Trevor was ready for an argument. He knew she'd be in a foul mood, probably crying, and Liam would be annoying. Trevor was going to tell her he was leaving. Tiffany was offering him a fuck of a lot more than Sharon. He'd really tried with her, but she drove him mad; he couldn't take it any more. Besides, he reminded himself, he was too young to be tied to any kid who wasn't his.

He'd given her some cash; that was all he could do. He looked up to the flat. It was in darkness. Fuck, that meant Sharon was on a gloomy one and sitting on her stool, smoking her head off. Oh, happy days. Well, he was going to put an end to all this depressing shite. He gulped a mouthful of vodka from the half-bottle he'd bought earlier. It had gone warm in his jacket pocket and tasted revolting. He coughed and spluttered as he climbed the stairs.

'Hi,' he called, as he walked past Liam's bedroom.

The door was open and Liam wasn't in there. Must mean he's in our bed, Trevor thought. He went through to the lounge and noticed that the coffee-table was overturned. There was crap everywhere.

'*Sharon!*' he shouted.

He glanced in the kitchen: no Sharon. In the bathroom: no Sharon. He kicked open the bedroom door. Why the fuck hadn't she answered him? No Sharon. Where the hell was she? It was eleven o'fuckingclock. He rang Charlie; he got a machine. He kicked the coffee table and swallowed the rest of the warm vodka.

Five minutes later, he heard them come up the stairs. Liam was laughing.

'You've got to go straight to bed now, Peanut,' Trevor heard Sharon say as they came in.

'Oh, Mum, when can we see Gabriel again?'

'Soon, darling,' Sharon answered.

'And who is *Gabriel*, Sharon? An angel, perhaps?' Trevor roared down to them.

Sharon took a deep breath. She hadn't expected him to come back. She'd almost got over him. Well, she felt she had got over a lot of things today.

'Yes, actually he is,' she said.

Trevor felt rage swell in his stomach. He heard her voice again.

'Go to bed now, Peanut, I'll see you in the morning. Night, darling.'

Sharon closed Liam's door softly and slowly came up the stairs. She noticed herself shaking. She went straight into the bathroom and washed her face. She stalled as long as she could. She knew she'd have to face him eventually. She took a deep breath, opened the door and *bang*! A burning pain in her eye, then ... black.

'*Mum!*' Liam bellowed from his room.

'Get back in bed! She's in the bath!' Trevor shouted, before Liam could come up and see Sharon slumped on the floor.

'I want a glass of water!' Liam called.

Trevor slowly put down the plank, staring at her all the while; he hadn't meant to do it.

'*Mum!*'

'Stay there! I'll bring you one,' Trevor said, dragging Sharon into the bedroom, 'you little shit.'

Conka had thoroughly enjoyed the weekend. They had ended up staying at Sarah's until Sunday evening, which meant that Conka had abandoned her stall. But she figured she was working all week at Great Days, so forgave herself for missing one Sunday. She'd enjoyed making the video: she knew they'd be able to do something with it. She and Charlie were a winning team. Besides, it was great to seal their joint humour in celluloid – that was all they did seal it with, though. Conka hadn't expected anything to happen at Sarah's, but Charlie had looked as sweet as cherries in her 'Bing Bang' outfit. But all this had resulted in Conka waking up this morning feeling unusually sexually frustrated. She definitely needed a bunk up. She'd have to sort it out.

She dropped Helena off and walked to work, stopping for a delicious cappuccino on the way. She got to work bang on time.

Fuck, she'd forgotten the keys – *again*. And she was supposed to be opening up. Oh, well. She'd forgotten the keys every single time they'd given them to her. Conka laughed. It killed Mrs Uptight when she rolled up at ten and saw Conka waiting, smiling, on the steps. 'The whole point of you having keys is so that business can start at half past nine, dear,' she'd say. Mrs Uptight had given her the exact same speech on every occasion; today would be no exception. 'This is a business responsibility. We have to be able to count on you. I don't know what Wayne will say.'

Well, Wayne never said much, especially as Conka always smiled so broadly at him, no matter what was coming out of his mouth, it really put him off. Sure enough Mrs Uptight arrived at ten, was predictably furious and gave Conka the speech she'd heard enough times before.

'Maybe, if you reprimanded me in another way, Mrs Upton,' Conka suggested, as she followed her into the office, 'maybe I wouldn't forget next time.'

But Mrs Uptight was in a queen-size strop and refused to make any further comments. By the end of the day, some of her bad mood had rubbed off on Conka. Then there was more trouble at the school.

Another child, Timmy, had kicked Helena in the shin and thumped her in the eye. This was the third time it had happened. By the time Helena had stopped crying enough to tell Conka how she'd got the bad scratch on her face, Conka was livid. She waited for Timmy then spotted his father.

'Excuse me!' Conka said loudly.

Timmy's father hoped she wasn't addressing him.

'Excuse me,' she said again, 'are you Timmy's father?' Conka turned Helena so that he could see what his son had done. '*That* is what your son did,' she said, pointing to Helena's scratch, 'and I'm not very happy about it.'

'Did it happen at play-time?' Timmy's father asked nervously.

'I don't give a flying monkey where it happened. It *happened*, your son did this and that's bad enough.'

'It's just that this school doesn't monitor the children nearly enough at play-time. That's when all the trouble happens.'

Conka couldn't believe he was trying to blame the school.

'You know what I think, I think it's the parents' fault. I don't know many boys who would do that to a girl – he should know it's something you just don't do.'

She was furious.

'Well, we're going to see the school about it.'

'I don't care who you see. I'm telling you, if this happens again, I will do the same to you, personally. You're lucky Helena's father doesn't know about it,' Conka said.

'Know about what?' Edwin said, from behind Conka.

Conka turned around to face him. He was picking up his other two kids.

'It's all right, Ed, I've dealt with it now,' she said, noticing Timmy and his father scuttle away.

'Can I go Daddy's?' Helena asked.

'Garn, Mum, can you come and get her at about six?' Edwin was grinning at her. He was the first person she'd seen smile all day. 'You're looking very posh, these days. Have you got a job?' he asked.

'That is none of your business, dear,' she said with a cocky half-smile.

'Did his kid do that?' Edwin said, noticing Helena's scratch.

'Oh, Mummy, let me go with them, *please*,' Helena begged.

'Yeah, but I told him he'd be sorry if it happens again and he'll be sorry if he has to deal with you,' Conka said. Helena was still pulling for her answer. 'Go on, then,' Conka said to her.

Helena squealed in delight. She seemed to have forgotten about that scratch quickly enough. Conka hadn't seen her so enthusiastic to go to her dad's in a long time.

'Well, maybe I should go and have words with them anyway,' he said, looking in the direction of Timmy and his father, who were now nearly out of sight.

'I'd rather you didn't. I've spoken to him now. If there's any more trouble, you can deal with it. Anyways, Ed, I'll see you later. I'll pick her up at six, yeah?'

'Yeah. See you then.'

Conka went home, had a good old soak in the bath, put on some nice comfy clothes and watched a bit of telly. It was soon time to go to Edwin's.

The kids were upstairs playing on the PlayStation and he was mucking around with music in the lounge. Helena was nowhere near ready to come home. Conka noticed a bag of weed on the table.

'Do you want a cup of tea?' Edwin asked.

'Go on, then, a quick one.'

'What? You want a *quick one*, do ya?' Edwin said, smiling.

'Yeah, Edwin, a quick cup of tea, okay?' Conka said, raising a questioning eyebrow.

'As opposed to a slow one.'

Conka couldn't believe his flirting. But then she remembered how they used to flirt, yonks ago, before Helena was born, before all of it.

'Where's Stacey?' Conka asked. Stacey was Edwin's third woman.

'Away.'

Edwin went to make the tea. Conka looked around. She'd not come this far into his home before. They'd got on all right recently for some strange reason. She thought it was maybe because Edwin had finally realised that he couldn't hurt her any more. He was powerless against her. Besides, if he so much as laid a finger on her, then not only would he never see Helena again, but he'd get all his limbs broken – she'd make sure of that. He had Fat Slag Stacey to beat up now.

'All right if I roll one up?' Conka called to him.

'Sure, go ahead.'

She already had. She lit the joint and relaxed on the sofa. He brought in the tea.

'It's all right here, innit?' she said, passing him the spliff.

'Yeah, come and have a look round.'

He showed her the kitchen, the downstairs toilet and then upstairs. There were three bedrooms; one was full of all his junk.

'Yeah, I've got to sort that room out.'

In the next room, the kids were absorbed in their computer game.

'Hello, Helena. Hi, guys. Are you feeling better now, Helena?' Conka asked.

'Hi,' they all answered, without moving.

'My God! They love that, don't they?' Conka said.

'Yeah,' Edwin said, as he closed the kids' door. 'That's our bedroom and this is the bathroom.'

Conka glanced into their bedroom. It was too flowery for her liking. She followed him into the bathroom. There was a big sash window with smoked glass on the lower half, clear at the top. She stood up on her toes to see out.

'Nice view,' she said.

She looked at the bathroom. It was a nice one: big free-standing bath, wooden loo seat, loads of plants, a few brightly coloured plastic toys. 'You've done well. That's a great bath,' she said.

'Did you see the towels?' Edwin said, unfolding a large blue one and laying it on the floor. 'It's really soft. Try it.'

Conka sat on the towel next to him. 'Yeah, spongy,' she said.

'Lie down and I'll give you a massage.'

'Great,' Conka said.

She took off her shoes and sweatshirt. He locked the door. She had a vest top on underneath and tracksuit bottoms. She lay on her front and allowed him to roll up her vest and slip it off over her head. He gave great massage. She'd forgotten how good he was. He massaged her bum, turning her round so that he could pull down her trousers. He pushed his fingers inside and made her nice and wet. He pulled off his clothes and, before she could change her mind, had got a condom on and was pushing it in. *That* felt good.

Conka lay back and let him do all the work. He didn't give her maintenance so he might as well be useful for something. She decided she'd be crap in bed or, in this case, on the nice fluffy towel. He was a gymnastic fuck and she got what she needed. He ran a bath and she got him to do it to her again in there. This time from behind. It was just what she needed. But she didn't want to hang about.

He followed her out of the bath. As they dried and got themselves dressed he said, 'So, if you need any shelves putting up, or anything like that –'

'I'm all right, fanks,' Conka cut him short.

'Well, is it all right for me to pop round?'

'No, Edwin,' Conka said seriously. 'Nothing's changed.'

She left the bathroom and went to get Helena.

'Oh, Mummy, can I stay the night, please?' she implored.

'No,' Conka answered firmly. 'Get your book-bag and say 'bye to ya dad.'

Helena saw the don't-mess-with-me-now look on her mother's face and did as she was told.

'See you, then,' Edwin said, as they left.

Conka went home and rang Charlie. She had been negotiating all day for some free time at an editing suite in Soho, to cut their pop video. She was very excited.

'He said we'd definitely be all right for a couple of hours on Thursday. It's going to be brilliant, I can't wait. You've got to get out of work.'

Conka decided against telling Charlie about what had happened with Edwin. Maybe another day.

Tuesday. There was no way Trevor was going to look after Liam for another day, not after yesterday. They'd all overslept and Trevor had foolishly thought Liam would be good if he was let off school; he couldn't have been more wrong. Liam had been a fucking nightmare, refusing to do anything Trevor said. The little git wouldn't even be bribed into telling Trevor anything about that Gabriel cunt either. Sharon was too ill to get up, so he'd missed work and looked after the pair of them – all day. He wasn't going to do it again today. He rang Charlie; the bitch wasn't there. Someone answered at Conka's.

'Yes! One minute . . . I get her.'

Trevor heard the phone being placed down and footsteps in the background. Conka finally came to the phone. 'Hi,' she said.

'Hi, it's Trevor. I was just wondering if you could take Liam to school?'

'Why can't Sharon take him?' she asked.

'She's got the flu . . . I'll drop him at your mum's, yeah?' Trevor said.

'Okay, then, but tell Sharon she owes me one.'

'Thanks.'

'Who's picking him up?'

'If you don't mind?'

'Yeah, all right, but I'll drop him home straight after school, tell Sharon.'

'Okay.'

Sharon opened her eyes slowly. The last couple of times she'd tried, it had hurt so much she'd had to give up. She had no idea what had happened. She wanted to remember, but her head was thumping. Trevor brought in a cup of tea, he was so sweet, she'd been vaguely aware of him taking care of her.

'I've dropped Liam at Conka's. She's taking him to school and will pick him up and bring him home . . . I'm afraid I've got to go to work. I'll get the boot if I take another day off. Will you be okay?' Trevor said softly.

Sharon managed a weak smile.

'Maybe you'll be well enough to talk about it tonight. Look I've really got to go. I'll try and come home early,' he said kissing her hand.

'Thanks,' Sharon whispered.

She heard the door slam and he was gone. She closed her eyes – they didn't hurt so much like that – and tried to think, but she must have fallen back to sleep. She dreamt the same dream again – she kept dreaming about this man, who seemed to know her really well, even though she didn't know him. She recognised him from somewhere, but it wasn't like he was a friend or something. He was an older guy, maybe he was famous. Anyway, in her dream he would tell her that he understood, and then not say anything else. Sharon couldn't work out what it was that he understood, but every time she tried to ask him, her mouth refused to say the right words and she found herself asking him if she could play with the puzzle in the box – that confused her all the more, because she couldn't see a box in the dream. The continuing sequence of the dream never changed, but she enjoyed it, however much it frustrated her. She really felt good in this man's company.

*

256

Sharon's bladder woke her up. She badly needed to pee. She moved slowly to minimise the pounding in her head. As she got to the bathroom doorway she shivered: her whole body was prickly with goosebumps. She paused, took a deep breath and just made it to the toilet. She threw up in the basin while she sat on the loo. She finished on the loo then washed her hands and face. The bathroom looked different somehow, darker. She opened the door and again was taken aback by the cold shiver that speared through her body.

Sharon went through to the kitchen and found a watch. It was three o'clock. Liam would be home soon. She made herself some tea, had a cigarette and sat down. As she looked out the window she heard his voice again, 'I understand', he said. Sharon jumped up and looked round but no one was there. She looked in the bedroom and downstairs in Liam's room, but no, she'd imagined it: playback from her dream.

She sat down in the lounge, held her mirror to her face and checked her bruises. She'd taken quite a fall. She put some makeup on her nose. There wasn't much she could do about the swelling, but the colour she could improve. Her eyes were harder to make up, especially the left one: it still stung so badly. She tried brushing her hair, but could only skim over the top; she had a throbbing bruise at the back of her head – that's where she'd landed. She'd apparently walked out of the bedroom straight into the fucking plank she'd been asking Trevor to move for God knows how long. Typical! On the day he moves it, she collides smack bang into it, bangs her head on the corner of the door-frame, gets knocked out cold, both her eyes swell up and she gets a great big nose as well. She did a pretty good makeover repair job, though, and went to get dressed. She found a tenner on the bedside table – Trevor had thoughtfully left it for her to order pizza.

A few minutes later the buzzer went.

'Hello, Sharon?' Conka said.

'Hi there, come up . . .'

'Actually, Sharon, if you don't mind, I've got a zillion things to do and I don't particularly want to get the flu . . .'

The intercom was a bit crackly, but Sharon was sure she heard Conka saying that she didn't want to catch flu.

'What are you talking about?' Sharon said.

'I'll send Liam up, I can't stop – okay?'

'Are you sure you can't come up?' Sharon asked.

She really felt like the company, even if it was Conka.

'No, thanks. I'm a germ-free zone and I intend to stay that way. I'll see you later.'

'Thanks, Conka.'

She heard the door downstairs slam and Liam come up.

'Hi, Peanut,' she said, as Liam walked in.

He ignored her, kicked off his trainers, flicked on the telly and plonked himself on the sofa.

'I'm hungry,' he said.

Jeremy had fallen for Trevor's story about his mother, which was pretty ironic since he hadn't seen the drunken bitch for over fifteen years. But he used the mother excuse every now and then, and people seemed to like him more for it. 'Is she any better?' Jeremy had asked, as soon as he saw him.

Trevor thought he was talking about Sharon for a minute, then realised that the flower was showing a surprising level of concern for his mum.

'Oh, it was a standard hip-replacement operation. She just gets silly when it comes to hospitals – you know what they're like,' Trevor said.

Jeremy smiled in agreement. 'Isn't she a bit young for a hip replacement?' he asked. 'I thought they only did that when you were ancient.'

Trevor could feel his mouth twitch. 'Well, she is pretty ancient, Jeremy. She had me very late.'

'Oh, sorry,' Jeremy said, going red around the ears. 'Come on, we'd better go, it's that one near Huntingdon again – you know, the cottage industry one. Trevor, I do think it was good of you, though, to have taken your mother. I wasn't mocking, you know.'

'Nah, I know. Thanks anyway,' Trevor said. 'It's tiring – that's all.'

'Yes, I suppose it is. Would this make you feel any better?' Jeremy asked, taking out his vial.

'Maybe. Thanks, flower.'

Trevor drove while Jeremy got more and more off his face in the passenger seat next to him. For once, Trevor found him pretty amusing. Jeremy asked loads of questions about his childhood and Trevor told him a pack of lies. The flower believed it all. Plus, he didn't put up any significant resistance to Trevor leaving early.

By the time Trevor got home, Sharon was up and looking much better. He wanted to find out who the fuck this Gabriel was.

'Hi, darling,' she said. 'Do you want some pizza? I saved some for you.'

'No thanks, I'm not hungry.' Trevor sniffed. 'How are you feeling? You look a lot better.'

'Yeah, I'm feeling much better. My head has stopped pounding but I've taken about fifteen paracetamol, so it's not really surprising. My face is very sore still.'

'Can you remember anything yet?' Trevor asked.

'Not really.'

'What. Nothing at all?'

'Well, I think I can remember seeing the wood come at me, but I see it as if I was coming out of the bathroom and you said it was the bedroom.'

'It *was* the bedroom,' Trevor snapped.

Sharon looked at him: he seemed sweaty.

'I know it was, darling. That's what I mean. I don't yet remember it properly. But don't worry, I'm sure it'll come back to me.'

'Yeah,' Trevor said.

'Mum!' Liam screamed, from his bedroom.

Trevor rolled his eyes and turned up the telly. Sharon apologised and went downstairs.

By the time Liam was in bed, Trevor was also feeling pretty wiped out. He decided to leave the quizzing about Gabriel until tomorrow. Besides, the football was on. Sharon came in complaining of tiredness.

'Well, go to bed. It's obvious, innit?' Trevor growled.

Trevor stayed up to watch the match. She was asleep by the time he went to bed.

35

I couldn't believe how helpful everyone was being with the video. It was as if people were throwing open the doors for me. Wonderful. I had no idea that the response to my half-bluff, half-truth would be like that. Saturday's cancellation made me think that you really did need money to get anything off the ground. But that wasn't necessarily so: I was getting to use equipment worth thousands of pounds for nothing, all because this guy liked our initiative. We were making a pop video for *nada* – and it was going to be great.

I couldn't wait to tell Conka. The footage we had watched on television at Sarah's had been wild. That put me in a great mood. All of it did. We were finally getting somewhere. The band idea was turning into something tangible. We were laying the foundations for a fabulous new life. I felt like celebrating already. I felt like a celebrity already. Dodging the *paparazzi*, I drove Luke to school.

Conka had already left for work and I decided to hang around for Sharon – I felt like telling her all the good news. I must have missed her, though, when I popped to the post office. I was only gone five minutes and I hung around a bit more when I got back, but she never showed.

I thought I'd try Tasha instead. I rang her from a payphone and nearly ran out of change as her machine droned on and on. She'd left an unfriendly message for Daniella's father. There followed about a thousand bleeps – presumably his retort. By the time the last one sounded, I had about two seconds left for a brief message: 'Coffee. Charlie. Ring. Have you seen Sharon?'

But the machine had already cut me off. I figured that was a sign for me to go home, clean out my makeup box – and stop drinking so much frigging coffee. Maybe I'd also call in at the funeral director's – it'd been a while since I'd had any work from them. People couldn't have stopped dying.

*

'Don't you think you should sometimes pick it up, Tash, or at least listen to it?' Craig asked, as he relit the joint.

'I find the phone so intrusive, baby. I don't like it when I'm disturbed by that annoying thing – I like communicating in other ways,' she answered, as she kissed her way down his torso.

Tasha hadn't ever imagined that so much sex – so much *amazing* sex – could ever be humanly possible. But that was part of what she loved about her relationship: *none* of it seemed human. She lay watching the purple and orange light bounce around her room while the wind tinkled her crystals. He was in the shower. He was singing. He must be in heaven too, she thought. She idly pressed the play button and decided to wade through her stream of messages.

The first was from Sharon. 'Hi, Tash, I hope you're well and all that. Tasha, I really need to talk to you – something very strange has happened. Call me.' Click.

The next was from Richard: 'It's me. Look, Daniella has told me she's going to live in France. What's going on? We need to discuss some other things you've been telling her. What's her obsession with witches? Tasha, it's not healthy – she's only three, for Christ's sake. Call me back and let me know if seven tomorrow evening is all right for you, 'bye.' Click.

The next was also from Richard. 'Yes, it's me again. Who the *fuck* is *Craig*?' Click.

Next Tasha's mum: 'Hi, darling, I hope you and Craig are doing good – it was so wonderful to meet him on Sunday. Thanks, darling, he's really great. 'Bye. Oh, I nearly forgot, I'm going to book a weekend course in transcendental meditation. I thought maybe you'd like to join me. Don't worry about money. If you want to come, I can cover it. 'Bye, darling – oh, call me and let me know. 'Bye.' Click.

Then Sharon again. This time she was crying: 'Tash – call me – please.' Click. Tasha played it again. She could hear something else in the background – maybe another voice, not Trevor, maybe the telly. It sounded weird but she couldn't put her finger on it, so carried on listening to the rest of her messages.

'This is Mrs Carshalton from Thames Water. Can you please call me regarding your outstanding debt. You must get in touch or we may be forced to cut you off. Goodbye. You can get me on the same number, extension forty five. Thank you.' Click.

There was one more message. 'Coffee. Charlie. Ring. Have you –' Click. That was the last of the messages.

'Fucking hell,' Tasha said.

What the hell had Daniella told her father? And the sodding water company had not only caught up with her but were now threatening to cut her off as well.

'Fuck. Fuck. Fuck. And what the fuck is going on with Sharon?'

'Who's Sharon?' Craig asked, as he came back in, wet hair falling in his eyes.

'Don't you remember? You met her at my birthday,' Tasha said.

'Oh, I remember – what's his name? Oh, yes, Trevor, his girlfriend. Honey, have you got any razors? I should really shave,' the doctor said, rubbing his bristles.

'Yeah, handsome. Follow me.'

Sharon wished she'd been up to going to the school. She missed seeing her friends and she couldn't get in touch with anyone on the phone. She'd left a couple of messages on Tasha's machine, but Tasha hadn't rung back. She knew Sarah was away all week. She decided to have a bath. She liked a bath. Liam was back from school so quickly it seemed. Once she'd dealt with him, she spent the evening crying, smoking, waiting for Trevor and taking painkillers. Her head wouldn't give up the thumping and her left ear hadn't stopped ringing for two days. She accidentally fell asleep in the kitchen, until she slid off the stool, banged her elbow and woke herself up. She then went to bed. Trevor hadn't come back. It was four in the morning.

Thursday.

'Seven nine two five eight four threeeee. Great Days in great ways! Can I take your name, please, caller?' Conka sang.

Mrs Uptight frowned at her. She'd only just told her off for singing, but it'd become a habit that Conka was enjoying too much to break. It had become the best bit for her at work. The phone was the only thing she could muck around with: the rest of it was too fucking straight and boring.

'Hello, Conka, it's Mr Davenport.'

'Oh, hellooee, Mr Davenport! How are you?' Conka answered, in her huskiest voice.

Mrs Uptight leapt up when she heard Mr Davenport's name and was frantically miming to Conka to pass him to her.

'Oh, I'm fine, thank you, Conka. And yourself?' Mr Davenport asked.

'Oh, I couldn't be better, thanks. I think Mrs Upton would like a word, if you'd just hold the –'

'No, hold on, Conka. It's you I want to speak to.'

'Oh, Mr Davenport, how can I help?' Conka said. She put her hand over the mouthpiece. 'It's all right, Mrs Upton, he wants to speak to me, relax. Yes, Mr Davenport?' Conka continued.

Mrs Uptight flapped her hands even more, indicating big trouble if Conka didn't pass him to her. But she'd have to wait. He was telling Conka about some cheap flights to Spain he could get hold of.

'I can get you three for next Wednesday, forty quid each,' he said.

'You're joking. I only needed the one for me mum,' Conka said.

'Look, you don't have to let me know today. Give me a ring on my mobile if you want them. You can let me know as late as Monday, but the sooner the better. Either way, just let me know. We'll arrange to meet up somewhere half-way.'

'Oh, thank you, Mr Davenport, that's really great. I'll call you soon. I'd better pass you over to you-know-who, before she throws herself out the window. Look, I really appreciate that offer – don't give the tickets to anyone else, yeah? I'll get back to you real soon on that one. Thanks again. Hold on a sec and I'll transfer you.'

'Take care, Conka.'

Mrs Uptight creamed herself on the phone to Mr Davenport; Conka'd never seen her suck up to a client so much and was convinced it was Mr Davenport's compliments about her phone manner that had suddenly made Mrs Uptight bother – and the increase in his order. She was such a pain in the arse, Conka thought, as she watched Mrs Uptight dribble down the phone.

But Mr Davenport's offer had set Conka thinking. Since she'd bonked Edwin, he managed to bump into her everywhere, sniffing around like a dog. It fucked Conka right off. She was beginning to think she should take those tickets if only to get away from him for a while. He didn't look as if he'd ever be moving anywhere. Also, since her massage, she'd made a few inquiries. Sure enough, he'd been bashing Stacey, fucking around. Stacey had had enough and was staying at her mum's. So if Helena stayed over, Edwin would be looking after her on his own. The thought made Conka shudder and she decided Helena wouldn't be spending any nights while Fat Slag Stacey wasn't there.

The phone rang again.

'Seven nine two, five eight four threeeee.'

'Hi – Conks, it's me. Is it a go situation?'

Conka looked over to Mrs Uptight.

'I don't know, Charlie.'

'Come on, you know you want to. The editing suite can't wait. It's going to be really good fun – just say you've got a migraine.' I pleaded.

'She's on the phone,' Conka whispered.

'So just sneak off – she won't notice – I'll meet you at the tube in five minutes. Come on, Conka, you'd make me if it was you.'

'Fuck it,' she interrupted. 'Five minutes, Charlie.'

Trevor spent a restless night at Tiffany's, followed by driving to the wrong fucking addresses all day. Jeremy called him 'brother', which was even more piss-annoying than 'darling'. Neither of them was black, for fuck's sake. That Gabriel character was niggling him: he decided to go back to Sharon's to see if she'd got her memory back. He'd get some more of his stuff to take back to Tiffany's while he was at it.

He stopped at the pub for a few pints and got back around ten thirty. Liam was in bed and Sharon was in a fucking mess. She threw herself on him when he walked in.

'Where have you been? Why didn't you call me? Oh, Trev, thank God you're all right,' Sharon said, crying.

Trevor went over to her – why was she so fuckable? He held her in his arms and let her sob.

'How's ya head?' he asked.

'Okay.' She sniffed.

Trevor wondered whether her performance was genuine or not. 'Have you remembered what happened yet?' he asked.

'Not really, but I suppose it doesn't really matter,' Sharon said, sitting down on the sofa. 'My bruises have really healed well. There's still ringing in my ear, though, which is annoying.'

Trevor sat next to her.

'Do you remember what you did on Saturday?'

Sharon looked surprised. Trevor's tone was clipped and cold.

'Do you remember or not?'

Sharon had searched her memory for days now. It was blank. She hated it. Every time she tried to think she found herself remembering her dream.

'I don't know, Trevor, I really don't,' she stammered.

She could feel the tears well up in her eyes. She wanted him to be nice. Why was he staring at her like that? It was her that had taken the fall; she hadn't done anything wrong.

'Who's Gabriel?' he said eventually.

Sharon went cold. That was the man in her dream, she was sure of it.

'Have I been talking in my sleep?' she asked.

Trevor leapt up in anger and kicked the coffee table. Sharon screamed. 'What, Trevor? Stop it!' she shouted. 'I don't know who he is – I promise.'

Trevor calmed down a fraction, but he was still pacing up and down. He wanted to knock her down. 'What do you know?' he sneered. 'You couldn't even remember your fucking name four days ago.'

'Oh, Trevor, I can't take this any more,' Sharon sobbed.

'Well, nor can I.'

'What do you mean?' Sharon stopped crying.

'I mean I can't take it either,' Trevor said quietly. 'I mean – I'm leaving, Sharon.'

'No! Please, Trevor, don't go, we can work this out. Please. I need you, please . . .'

Sharon broke down in a pathetic heap on the sofa.

Trevor wanted to go, he wanted to get away from all this. Life was so much easier at Tiffany's: there wasn't this kind of pressure. Sharon looked up at him, her eyes red from crying, her nose still slightly swollen, yet she looked so incredibly beautiful, soft and vulnerable. Trevor tried to tear himself away from her gaze. He wanted to get the rest of his clothes and get the fuck out of there – but he was getting lost in her eyes again. He felt himself begin to cry. He wanted her, he wanted her, he fucking wanted her. He allowed the tears to fall hotly down his cheeks. He couldn't leave tonight. He wanted her to love him. He fucking wanted her and he hated himself for it. Sharon came over to him and put her arms around him. She held him strongly, yet with a gentle tenderness, as she rocked him soothingly. He didn't know how long they were like that, but when they moved, they kissed and became closer. Soon they were rediscovering each other's bodies, skin softly sliding against skin, and then they got closer still.

Sharon woke up feeling much better. Trevor had woken her with a kiss and a cup of tea before he left for work. Things felt like they could *finally* be getting back to normal. She and Liam left for school early so that they could go to McDonald's for breakfast: she felt like treating Liam, who loved the breakfasts there. She rang Tasha on the way and arranged to meet for a coffee after dropping the kids off.

She saw Conka at the school, dropping Luke and Helena.

'Hi, there.'

'Hello. How's Sharon, then?' Conka asked her.

'Oh, much better now, thanks. Where's Charlie?' Sharon said.

'She's got a job this morning,' Conka said, noticing the traces of bruising around Sharon's nose. 'How's Trevor?'

'Oh, he's wonderful, thanks, yeah, he's really been taking care of me,' Sharon said. Conka looked surprised. 'And he's got a job and he gave me a hundred and fifty quid last week.'

Conka was shocked. Sharon was normally bitching about this man.

'Great, well, I've got to work. I'll see you later – Oh, by the way, we're rehearsing tomorrow, in case you're interested,' Conka said, as she turned to rush off.

Conka thought it through. Sharon was definitely covering up for Trevor. She remembered how she used to do the same for Edwin when he bashed her up. She used to come out with excuses: she'd fallen down the stairs, walked into the door – huh, and got the flu. It was only when she'd been in hospital a couple of times with broken ribs, a cracked skull and fuck knows what else that she fucking woke up. Maybe that's what it would take with Sharon. She'd thought that Sharon was on top of that, though. Obviously she had been wrong.

Fucking Edwin, Trevor, men – Conka was above the whole fucking lot of them, they were all a load of tossers. Conka was destined to fly many miles higher. Huh, she and Charlie had managed, with a liddle help from the best editor in town, to cut a fucking sweet video in less than four hours. Conka had loved it. What a result.

Mrs Uptight was ready for a good old telling-off session when Conka walked in. It was written all over her face: she was really geared up. Conka hadn't given it much thought yesterday. She'd just got up and left when Mrs Uptight was on the phone. She had rung a couple of hours later, to tell her about her migraine and Mrs Uptight had said it was fine and she'd see Conka at the office in the morning.

But as Conka came in to work, she could tell it wasn't fine. Mrs Uptight had *lied* to her: Lecture-bloody-boring-City was coming her way.

'Good morning, Mrs Upton,' Conka said, as she took off her jacket.

'Good morning,' she answered, watching Conka with disdain as she sat at her desk. 'Well?' she asked. 'How's the migraine?'

'Oh *much* better, thank you,' Conka said, before turning away and opening her ledger.

'Well, Conka, I have to say . . .'

Yes, you bloody do, don't you? Conka thought.

'. . . that I am disappointed with you.'

'*Disappointed?*' Not half as much as Mr Uptight was when he first fucked you, thought Conka.

'And I did speak to Wayne about it.'

Oh, my God, *she spoke to Wayne*, big fucking deal.

'This is a warning, Conka.'

Otherwise known as a loud wet fart, Conka thought.

'Do you understand? You can't just walk out on *business*, dear, migraine or no migraine.'

Well, *no migraine*, in my case, Conka thought. Then the phone rang.

'Hello, Great Days,' Conka said, sullenly.

'Conka? Is that you? Mr Davenport here.'

'Oh, helloee, nice to hear from you. How are you?' Conka said.

'Well, I'm fine, thank you, but *you* don't sound your usual self.'

'Well, you know . . .'

'Is old Mrs Upton giving you a hard time?'

'You've got it in one,' Conka answered, smiling.

'Oh, don't you worry about her. Anyway, I just thought I'd mention that these tickets for Wednesday are one way only.'

'I thought they were cheap.'

'Well, they still are, cheeky. But I wanted you to know that I can get you returns just as easily – and as cheap. But it'll have to be last-minute again, so you'll have to do that from Spain. I'll give you a number for that. It's my brother, he lives there.'

'Oh, my sister lives there too. Where does your brother live?' Conka asked, ignoring Mrs Uptight's scowls and personal-calls face. Conka would let her speak to him in a minute: Mr Davenport would soon shut her up.

'He lives in a village not far from Alicante,' Mr Davenport said.

'Wicked! My sister lives round there!'

'Well, all the more reason to go, wouldn't you say?'

Conka hadn't intended to go: it was her mother she wanted to send. But since Mr Davenport had mentioned it, she had given it some thought and it seemed pretty enticing. She would wait and see how the rehearsal went tomorrow, though, and decide after that. But then she wondered what she was doing in this crap country, anyway.

'You know what Mr Davenport,' Conka began, while Mrs

Uptight leapt out of her seat, 'I want them, please.' At forty quid each, she thought, she might as well take them even if she sold the two for her and Helena. 'Will that be all right?'

'No problem at all, Conka.'

'Thanks.'

'Listen, call me on my mobile on Saturday and we can meet up,' Mr Davenport said.

'Great, I will. That's wonderful. Hey, do you mind –'

'Not saying anything to Mrs Upton?' Mr Davenport interrupted. 'I understand. Don't worry, I'll deal with the battleaxe. Actually, I do need to speak to her as well. Speak to you on Saturday?'

'Yeah, that's great. Thanks again. I'll pass you over. Hold the line please, caller.'

Tasha had meant to get back to Sharon a couple of days ago, but what with Craig, her mother, Thames Water, Daniella's dad – well, she was glad when Sharon rang this morning and arranged to meet up. Tasha was looking forward to seeing her: she'd not seen any of them for a while.

'Perfect timing,' Tasha said, as they met outside the Portuguese place. 'How are you?' She kissed Sharon's cheek. 'I've got so much to tell you. So much has happened.'

Sharon smiled. Tasha looked radiant.

They went in, ordered some coffee and then settled down for a big old chinwag. Tasha began: she told Sharon all about Craig, the pagan wedding plans, Richard and the grief he was giving her.

'You know he cut Daniella's hair? I was furious, it looks awful. Anyway, I've told him about the France idea – it's not going to happen until Craig has finished his residency – so that's at least another nine months, but I had to tell Richard because Daniella said something. But he'll come round.'

Sharon had been listening attentively to everything Tasha had been saying. It sounded like Tasha had found the kind of love she'd experienced last night with Trevor.

'Yeah, he'll come round by then, probably,' she said.

'Anyway, what about *you*? What's been happening with you,

Sharon? What was so *strange* that you had to tell me?' Tasha asked.

'What?' Sharon was puzzled.

'Don't you remember? You left me a message saying something about something strange. I can't remember, exactly.'

'Oh, it was my dream!' Sharon said. 'I've been having this recurring dream. There was a man – actually it was really weird, 'cause Trevor told me his name last night.'

'What?' Tasha asked. Sharon wasn't making any sense.

'Yeah, he told me – I don't know how he knew but Trevor just came straight out with it. It was really strange.'

'Oh, Craig seems to know things about me too. It is a bit strange, I know what you mean. It's like we don't even have to talk sometimes, *amazing* – oh my God! I'm so *in love*!' Tasha said, rolling her eyes and breathing deeply.

'Oh, I can see, you look radiant.'

'Do I? Oh, thanks, Sharon. You look pretty good too.' Tasha grinned soppily.

Sharon didn't think so. She was just wearing more makeup than usual to cover her now yellow nose. She looked for a fag. The guy at the table next to them was smoking and she suddenly felt she needed one. Tasha didn't have any.

'Excuse me, I couldn't bum a fag off you, could I, please?' Sharon asked.

'Sure. No problem. Here,' he said, offering her a cigarette then a light.

'Thanks,' Sharon said, puffing hard. 'Have you seen Charlie at all?' she asked Tasha.

'No, actually, I was really bad and didn't go to Sarah's with them on Saturday,' Tasha said, pulling a guilty face, 'and I've kind of been avoiding – well, not really *avoiding*, I've just been so busy doing other stuff, know what I mean?' She giggled.

'Oh, yes, I know what you mean, you sex maniac!' Sharon said.

But something was odd. Sharon wished she could remember. What the fuck was it? Tasha had said something. Sarah's . . . that was it!

'But I thought they were going to rehearse in a studio . . .'

270

She trailed off as suddenly it all started coming back to her. The studio, she'd gone to the studio and they weren't there . . .

'No, it got cancelled so they had to do it at Sarah's. Oh, my god, Craig was so funny with my mum. She really loves him – you know how fantastic doctors are in parents' eyes. I'll tell you more about that in a minute. I've got to tell you about the sex,' Tasha said.

But Sharon wasn't really listening: she was trying to hold on to that memory before it deserted her again. She was in the studio, looking for Charlie.

'But that's why I didn't go to Sarah's. Mum hadn't yet met him,' Tasha continued.

Sharon looked at her, speechless. There was a thread of that memory there and she couldn't hold on to it any longer, with Tasha's torrent of words about Craig and her mum. The memory's thread frayed and was getting thinner. Sharon tried to tell Tasha to shut up, but she didn't want to concentrate on anything other than the studio. They weren't there. Then what? It had gone: one thread, broken.

'Sharon?' Tasha asked. 'Sharon, are you okay?'

'Yeah, yeah. I'm fine. Shall we go?' Sharon said.

She wanted to go home, so she could be alone, to try to find the rest of that memory.

'Yeah, I've got to go anyway,' Tasha said, getting her jacket on. 'I'm going to go to the rehearsal tomorrow, Sharon. Do you wanna come? It'll be a laugh.'

'Yeah, maybe I will,' Sharon said.

36

When Trevor got to work he found a scrawled note on the door: 'Darling, had to go and babysit Tiffany last night – thanks to you. Pick me up there. Jeremy.'

Trevor got back in the van. He felt like going back to Sharon; he felt like making love to her again, the same way they had last night. But if he did that, well, Sharon probably wouldn't want to anyway, she'd be bitching for his wages. Besides, if he didn't go to work today, then there wouldn't be any wages. He couldn't convince Jeremy and Tiffany for ever – they were getting funny about his story of his mother's neurosis about the phone as it was. No doubt they'd start ringing Sharon soon, if he wasn't careful. Also, if Trevor didn't take Tiffany up on the offer of a room, there'd be no job. Tiffany was getting impatient. She just had to sneeze and Jeremy would fuss all over her. If she said sack Trevor, Jeremy would. Then Sharon would hate him 'cause he didn't have a job, and therefore no money. The situation was fucking impossible. He decided he'd better go and see what was going on at Tiffany's – Jeremy had said they'd be busy today.

Trevor parked and rang Tiffany's bell. Eleanor came to the door.

'Hi. Is Jeremy in, please?' Trevor asked.

'Hello, Trevor, how are you?' Eleanor said, leaning into him and giving him a big kiss on the lips.

'Fine, thanks, Eleanor,' Trevor said, wiping his mouth.

'Come in, sweet one, come in. Tiffany's here,' she cooed.

Trevor followed her into the flat. He could hear Jeremy fussing in the bathroom as he walked past. Tiffany was smoking a cigarette.

'Hi,' Trevor said.

'Hi,' Tiffany replied, flatly, not smiling for once.

'I ended up staying at my mum's last night – she was kind of upset,' Trevor explained.

'Well, thanks for calling,' Tiffany said, as she got up to get some juice.

'Sorry, Tiffany. I'll make it up to you.'

'Why don't you just move in, tonight?' she said, giving him a glass of juice.

'Yeah, maybe I will. Don't pressure me, though, darling,' he said, grinning.

He kissed her lips and she smiled back at him.

'No time for that,' Jeremy said, as he came in, combing his hair. 'Come on, Trevor, we've got a busy one. See you later, girls. Be good.'

''Bye, Trevor,' Tiffany said, as Trevor got up to go. 'I'll see you tonight, won't I?'

'Yeah, 'bye,' Trevor mumbled as he left.

Saturday. When Sharon opened her eyes and saw he still wasn't there, she realised it was well and truly over. Nothing had changed. She'd been an idiot; he was a bastard and had probably shacked up with some other stupid slut. She should have known when she saw his face. He wouldn't have been so quick to accuse her if he hadn't been doing the dirty himself. It had come back to her slowly, all of it, when she was alone in the flat, yesterday.

She remembered that strange meeting with that psychic guy, Gabriel, who had told her loads of things. Some things made sense, others didn't – at least, not yet. She remembered coming home late and Trevor being there. She remembered putting Liam to bed and then she saw his face, his anger: he'd assumed she'd been fucking Gabriel because he'd been fucking around himself. What a bastard! She was going to explain all about Gabriel, but then she washed her face and the accident happened. There was still something odd about that. Had it been an accident? She thought she remembered seeing the plank, but now she wasn't sure. And Conka seemed to think she had had flu. It didn't make sense. Sharon wanted to see Gabriel again and talk to him some more. He had told her to be careful about something, something to do with hospitals – she was glad she didn't go to one the other day. Or maybe it was something to do with Tasha's Craig? He worked at a hospital. She definitely wanted to find out more. And she wanted something to take her mind off Trevor. How could he do this to her? She began to cry. *Why* did he have to do this? No, she checked herself, she mustn't cry any more, she'd cried enough. She would go and see the girls and Gabriel and everything would all be all right. She wanted to sort her fucking life out once and for all. Gabriel would help.

Sharon had asked Liam about the puzzle. She was curious about what had absorbed him so completely. Unfortunately, Liam didn't remember, but he wasn't being very communicative at the moment. All he could talk about was bloody football. He was having a big treat with one of his mates today: his friend and his mother were taking him to see Man U against Liverpool. Liam would be entertained for the whole day. They were picking him up early and not dropping him off until nine this evening. Bliss. Liam was very excited.

Fuck Trevor, Sharon thought. Once Liam had been picked up, she'd go to the studio, have a good laugh with the girls and see if she could find Gabriel. She'd also quiz them all about this flu rumour and see if she could make any more sense of her accident. She wasn't convinced by Trevor's story; they might help her work it out. As she splashed her face in the bathroom basin, she heard the buzzer. Liam raced to get it.

'Mack . . . yeah, I'll be right down. 'Bye, Mum!' Liam shouted.

'Hang on, Liam! Let me say goodbye! Liam!' Sharon called after him. 'I love you!' she shouted down the stairs, but he had already gone.

I had expected the studio to be much bigger than it was. It was dark and smelt stale from the thousands of combustibles smoked in it over the years. It was in a padded basement, long and narrow, stretching underneath some ice factory or something. Boilers and exposed pipes were positioned along the hallway, mostly at head height, ready and willing to bash passers-by. I got hit twice on the way to our designated room.

It was the smallest, narrowest and hottest in the whole building – the kind of room estate agents describe as 'third bedroom/ study', knowing that it's really only a cupboard. But this was rock 'n' roll, and I wasn't going to be the one complaining. We've done the video. Let's do some music!

Conka didn't seem to mind the turgid heat. She instantly took off her layers until she was in her sports bra-vest and her jeans, and got straight to work setting up the equipment while I sat and watched. She was so cool: she knew her way around this gear and I would have to get my head round it. But I was crap with anything electrical and decided to let her sort it for now.

Tasha arrived shortly after us and was also in good spirits. She and the doctor were getting on famously. The love bug had got her and there was no stopping it now. Her eyes and face shone with that just-shagged-will-be-shagging-later look. They obviously had an outstanding molecular chemistry that bound them between the sheets.

While Conka tuned her guitar, Tasha continued to tell me about her plans with the doctor.

'You know, we may even have a pagan wedding.'

'What? Get hitched?' I asked, stunned by this revelation.

'Well, we wouldn't actually be getting married in the traditional sense. It would be more of a spiritual union, a celebration of souls. We're gonna write our own vows and get blessed by the fairies. Oh, it's gonna be so beautiful – I can't wait. Besides, if we got legally married, I'd lose a lot of my benefits, which I can't afford to do.'

Conka wasn't saying anything, but I could tell what she was thinking by the faces she made. She thought Tasha was in Cloud Cuckoo Land; I knew she'd find the idea of a pagan wedding absolutely ludiChristmas. Also, if they were *so* in love and as he was a doctor, not an unemployed skank, what would it matter if she did lose her benefits? He should be able to share his pay check and help her out, surely.

Neither of us had *any* faith in *any* kind of marriage, and this pagan-wedding deal sounded more like a get-out clause for the smooth bastard. Still, cynicism aside, Tasha was bouncy and happy – even if she was totally off her trolley. Besides, a pagan wedding would be an excuse for a good old knees-up, if nothing else.

'I think that's great, Tasha, if you're happy. Congratulations, I suppose,' I said, giving her a hug and a kiss.

She seemed very happy and in love. She had a bed partner who was saying he was madly in love with her and they were tying the broomstick. I suppose I was jealous: she had found a potentially supportive partner, who would come into her life and share her responsibilities, who was so mad about her he was going to let the fairies do a little dance all over his medicated body. And I was still on my own, indulging in desperate fantasies about my best friend. I didn't even know if Conka was even slightly interested in me, let alone *in love*. Just what kind of sick bastard was I? And why couldn't I have Tasha's unswerving faith in the love of males? Or would she end up arse-over-tit, scrambling around alone in the dark, crying the whole time, frantically trying to get her head, heart and soul together again a few months down the road?

I looked at her, while she continued relating her plans. She's gone, I thought. We'd been seeing less and less of each other since she'd met the doctor and her interest in the band had waned considerably. She still had good intentions, but I don't think she really understood how serious I was. The band felt like a hobby she enjoyed, but no more. Everything revolved around the doctor's schedule; we came second.

'Hey, guys, I'm still gonna be there for you,' Tasha assured us, reading my mind.

'Yeah, yeah, Tasha, we know,' I said, as convincingly as possible.

I decided to make the most of today, regardless of whether Tasha was going to be off or not. She was here now and that was all that mattered. Her assurances were sweet, but both Conka and I knew that Tasha was incapable of holding an erection down when she was in love, let alone anything else. But there was no point in saying anything now.

Sharon was putting the finishing touches to her makeup when the buzzer sounded again. 'Hello?' she said tentatively, praying it wasn't going to be the bailiffs.

'Hi,' Trevor said.

Sharon's heart sank. What the fuck did he want?

'I've come to pick up my things.'

'Good. Come up,' Sharon said, coldly.

He could take his things and leave. She started to bag up his filthy clothes still strewn everywhere.

Good? She had said, '*Good*', when he said he'd get his things. Fucking tart, Trevor thought, as he climbed the stairs. He pulled his jumper up round his neck. He didn't want Sharon seeing Tiffany's territorial claims. Tiffany had got suspicious when he said he was coming to his mum's to get his things and had planted a hickey on his neck just to make sure. Nice try, but Sharon wouldn't notice. Sharon had sounded *glad* to get rid of him. She'd been fucking that Gabriel guy, after all, huh. She was probably

276

seeing him today. 'What a fucking tart!' he sneered at her when he came in.

He stared at her: she hadn't been crying; she wasn't waiting for him. She was all made up and ready to go. She *was* meeting him today. The fucking tart had her little skirt and boots on. He could see right through her stupid plans. He took a step closer. He wanted to punch her.

'I want to explain to you about Gabriel. I've remembered,' Sharon began, backing away from him slightly. 'It's not what you think.'

Trevor bit his cheek. He wondered exactly how much Sharon did remember. 'You fucked him and you're going to go and fuck him now!' he hissed.

'No, Trevor, I didn't and I'm not. Anyway, it doesn't matter now, does it? There's no trust with us. Let's face it, we can't go on like this, can we?' Sharon fought back the tears.

She didn't know why, but she loved him so much. This was so fucking hard. She'd been all right when he wasn't there. She tried to think of Gabriel, the girls, but now he was putting the rest of his stuff in the bags – now he was actually going. She felt her heart pull hard and the tears come.

Trevor threw down the bag and clenched his fists. He couldn't believe her. 'What do you mean "It doesn't matter anyway"? You fucked him! You tart!' he shouted, watching her crumble before him.

She sat limply on the chair, her head in her hands, her body silently shaking. Her skirt had ridden up and Trevor could see her peach against her white knickers.

'I'm moving out,' he said.

'I know, it's probably for the best, eh?' she said, looking at him with those eyes.

He wanted her – just one last time. He sat next to her and put his hand on her leg. She put her hand on his. He took out his wallet and gave her fifty quid.

'There you go, that'll help a bit,' he said.

'Oh, Trevor, thanks, darling.'

He did care. She looked at him. He was tired from working. She wanted to tell him to go, but it came out wrong.

'Do you have to go?' she said.

'Not yet,' he said, as he pushed his hand up her thigh.

She let her legs fall open as he pushed his fingers around her knickers, and then inside. He kissed her neck, then her breasts. Sharon couldn't fight any more. She didn't know who this man was, she didn't know who she was. She closed her eyes and saw old images of the young Trevor, so full of promises. She saw him with that Tiffany. She saw monkeys, guitars, swirling colours, she saw herself on stage at Tasha's party, laughing and singing, she saw herself before that, when she was happy, really happy, before everything, running around Brighton playing in a band. That was all so far away. She had no control any more, her mind and body were no longer hers. She was aware of hot tears tumbling down her face. She didn't care where they came from. Nothing mattered any more.

'All right, girls, let's start with "Bing Bang"!' Conka yelled, twanging her guitar.

We loved that one, especially since we'd done the video. Actually that was still the only one we all knew. Tasha didn't seem too worried when we'd told her we'd done the video without her; she was doctor delirious and had no other feelings. But she normally sang well – well, wellish – on 'Bing Bang', so we began.

Conka played her guitar faultlessly, but Tasha was all over the place.

'All right, Tash. Why don't you forget about playing for now and concentrate on the singing instead? You can always learn the guitar part after,' Conka suggested.

Tasha was too happy to be put out and could see that her guitar-playing needed some work. She began to harmonise with me. 'Bing Bang' was sounding pretty good, even though Tasha was singing too high, so we decided to go on and teach her the Dobermann song.

'What this song really needs is a good old slap bass. Why don't you phone Sharon, Charlie, just in case she can make it?' Conka suggested. 'Tell her to bring my bass. It's at my mum's – she can pick it up on the way,' she called, as I left to find a phone.

*

Trevor was on his back on the sofa and Sharon was on top. His hands felt huge around her hips as he moved her up and down. She was aware of lifting his hand and sucking his thumb. She then kissed her way up his arm, biting and sucking while he moved her up and down. She was coming over and over again and her eyes were squeezed shut in the agonising pleasure.

'I'm coming, baby,' Trevor whispered. 'Is it safe?'

'No ... no ... don't come inside.'

'Oh, my God! Fuck! Fuck your pussy! I'm coming, get off – fuck. *Get off*!' he said, as he threw her back, just in time.

Bang. Black.

'Oh, baby, was that your head? I'm sorry. I didn't realise the wall was so close. Wow, you were really going for it.'

Sharon was slumped on top of him, straddling his stomach; he could feel her juices dribbling on to him.

'You really came some, eh?' he said.

Oh, great. She'd gone all silent on him.

'Sharon? You know I do love you, it's just that we can't live together. Babe, do you understand?' he asked, stroking away the hair from her face. 'Sharon! Sharon! Oh, my God! *Sharon!*' he screamed.

On the way to phone Sharon I got lost. I'd seen the phones on the way in but somehow I couldn't find them again. I asked some strange but interesting-looking guy all dressed in black where the phones were. He was very sweet and I wanted to stop and chat but reminded myself that we were here to rehearse, I must be professional and just get the fiddle on with it. He gave me directions and I rang Sharon. Her answer-machine was on, but I shouted down the phone, anyway, just in case she was there.

'*Sharon!* Are you *there*?'

'Hello ... Charlie?' Trevor sounded scared.

'Yes.'

'It's Trevor.' He sounded really weird.

'I know, hi. Is Sharon there, please?'

'Yes, yes, Sharon's been – God! Look, can you come back to Sharon's to meet Liam? I think he's being dropped off at about nine tonight. I've got to take Sharon to the hospital,' he blurted out.

'WHAT?'

'Can you be here or not? I've got to go. She's unconscious – knocked out. There's no time to explain now! Well?'

'Yes. Okay, Trevor.'

He had already hung up. I felt all the blood drain from my face. What the fuck had he done to her now? I walked in a trance, until I whacked my head on one of those fucking pipes, back to the others. They instantly saw my concern.

'What's happened?' Tasha asked.

'I don't know,' I said as I sat down, rubbing my head. 'It's Sharon. Trevor's taking her to hospital.'

'Why? What's happened?' Tasha asked.

'I don't know. All he said was that she was unconscious and could I be there for Liam at nine tonight.'

'Unconscious!' Conka reiterated in alarm.

'Yes. Unconscious. The bastard finally went too far, I reckon,' I said slowly.

'Fucking tosser. After he threw the shoe at her that time, I told her to fucking leave him,' Conka said.

'Who *hasn't* told her to leave him?' I wryly pointed out.

'Wow, that's mad – she seemed really happy and in love as well. What do you think went on?' Tasha said.

We sat debating the Sharon and Trevor fiasco for a while, then despondently started to pack our things away. I had a strong feeling that this band was not meant to be.

Conka and I dropped Tasha off at her house on our way back to mine. We were all pretty quiet in the car. None of us knew what to say. Even the car with its worrying noises was quieter than usual. When I said goodbye to Tasha, I felt incredibly sad. I felt as if I would never see her again in the same way, as if an era was over. Everything had changed. The last-ditch attempt to secure our combined lives had failed. She was now one half of a couple, a couple that had nothing to do with a gaggle of single mothers. Yes, she had something beautiful, romantic, enviable, but something that inevitably took her away from us. It excluded us, it was personal, private, delicious, repulsive and precious.

But what if it suddenly disappeared? Could she *seriously* trust a man again? She was madly in love with this doctor, and if he let her down she would be devastated, lost. I hoped she'd never be battered down by the lonely monster again; the monster that laughs at you for being a stupid mug while you're banging your head against the wall, shouting at the only person near to you: your child.

I had wanted something more, something that was ours alone, our own self-sufficient high. I'd fantasised about a kind of happiness that would provide us with great cash benefits but, most importantly, a happiness that didn't rely on a man's dick.

If Tasha's castles in the air came crashing down, would we still be there with our weathered shoulders? More than likely. We were good at being there. Great. Oh, and buying one another the odd vibrator. Anyway, Tasha was radiantly happy. I really should be exuberant for her and get over it. Sharon was much more of a concern. What the fuck had happened to Sharon?

37

Thank God Liam had enjoyed a busy football day. He was somewhat calmer than usual. He became very grown-up when I told him that we were going to the hospital to meet his granny and to see how his mum was. His initial reaction was anger – he said he hated his granny – swiftly followed by fear and concern. For the first time ever he continued to hold my hand even after we had crossed the road. He was too big and proud to burst into tears.

I'd arranged to meet Sharon's mother at the hospital. I had only met her a couple of times before: like Sharon, she was tall and slim with hair dyed pale blonde. She was a man's woman, beautiful in her day, but now pretty weak and useless.

Once we'd parked the car and were walking towards the hospital Liam quietly held my hand. I could feel his trepidation. The hospital was as confusing as ever, but we eventually found the Roderick Jacobs wing. We waited for a few minutes while a nurse called Julie went to find Sharon's mother.

Mrs Dubrowski made no effort to hide her worry as she walked towards us, leaning heavily on a nurse and clutching a soggy tissue to her red nose. I could see where Sharon got it from. She gave Liam an over-the-top hug he didn't appreciate, then the nurse sat us all down and offered us tea. Tea. That had to be a bad sign. They normally ignored you. Offering tea had to mean something *terrible* was up.

The nurse quickly reassured Liam that his mother was going to be all right, but that she'd had a rather nasty bang on the head. She asked him if he'd like some cake and found another nurse to take him to the canteen.

Christ, now there was cake. Things were obviously worse than Nurse Julie had been making out. Once Liam was out of sight, she turned to us with an altogether more serious face. I was terrified.

'Sharon has suffered a fairly nasty bang on her head. One would normally recover quite easily, but . . .'

Here it comes, I thought. *Fucking* Trevor.

'. . . on top of another injury, and in Sharon's current state of mind, we are obliged to keep her in for a few days, maybe even weeks. We think she has suffered quite a severe nervous breakdown. We have to wait for the psychiatric evaluation, which may take some time, depending on how well Sharon is, which in turn, means that the social services may well have to be called in.'

She looked at us for a few moments, allowing us to understand everything so far. But I didn't understand a fucking word of it. All I wanted to know was if Trevor was going to get done for this, or would it just go unnoticed.

'How did it happen? Where's Trevor?' I asked.

Julie looked slightly surprised by my reaction and my aggressive tone.

'Well, he's in there with her. He hasn't left her since he brought her in four hours ago. And as far as how it happened . . .' when Julie said this, Mrs Dubrowski began crying loudly again '. . . well, apparently they were, you know, *copulating*.'

I huffed in disbelief. Copulating.

'You believe that, do you?' I sneered arrogantly. 'Why do you think he's not left her side? He doesn't want her saying anything when he's out of the room, that's why. I can tell you –'

Julie interrupted, 'There is evidence that they were indeed engaged in consensual lovemaking when the accident happened.'

I looked at her in disrespectful disbelief.

'I assure you,' Julie continued tersely. Mrs Dubrowski wailed again. 'I won't go into the details right now.'

'Why do you have to call in the social services? What's that all about?' I asked.

'Look, calm down, dear. Let me answer your questions. We may need to call in the social services because of Liam. Sharon is clearly unable to look after him right now and maybe not be able to for some time.'

'Oh, no,' I said quietly.

Until now I hadn't realised how ill Sharon was.

'Yeah, but you'll have Liam, won't you, Gran?' I said hastily, nudging Mrs Dubrowski.

'Well, I'd have to check with my husband but I suppose it'd be all right. How long would it be for, though? We were supposed to be going on that coach tour at the end of May –'

'Mrs Dubrowski!' I interrupted. 'I wouldn't worry about any fucking coach trip if I was you, not with your daughter lying in a hospital bed.'

As soon as I spoke, I regretted it. I made her burst into tears again and Nurse Julie was looking at me like I was some kind of robo-bitch or something.

'I didn't mean it like that,' Mrs Dubrowski whimpered. 'I love my Sharon, it's just her father can be a bit of a bully when his holiday plans get mucked up. That's all.'

She made a defiant sniff at the end of her little speech.

Julie continued to explain. 'You see, if there isn't a member of the family willing and able to take care of Liam while Sharon's here, then we have no choice.'

'You can take care of him, *can't you*?' I hissed to Mrs Dubrowski.

She looked back at me in fear, as if I was about to bite her head off again. She didn't have a fucking clue. I spoke slowly.

'They will take Liam away from Sharon and put him in a *home*, if you don't.'

I was begging her to understand. If Julie spent much more time with Sharon's mum, then she'd refer *her* to the psychiatrist as well, and Liam wouldn't stand a fucking chance.

'Oh, no, dear, I'll take care of him,' Mrs Dubrowski said.

Phew. Mrs D had finally clicked. Thank you, thank you. I nodded at her, encouraging her to go on. She rubbed her hands together, searching for the words to convince Julie that there'd be no need to call in the social services, after all.

'I'm sure my husband will be more than happy to have his grandson around for a while,' she went on.

Julie wasn't convinced.

'It'd do them both good.'

Julie still wasn't happy.

'Look, I don't care what he says, Liam is my grandson too and he's coming home with me. No one can take care of him as well as his granny can, and that's what I intend to do.'

Now Julie had heard what she needed to. 'Here comes Liam now,' she said. 'I think it'd be better if he didn't know how bad his mummy is. If we can try and be brave when we go and see her I think that'd help him a lot.'

We nodded, standing up and straightening ourselves out.

'Right then, do you want to go and see Mummy now?' Julie asked.

'Okay,' Liam whispered.

I'd never seen him so meek. His granny took his hand and, in a show of strength, walked ahead of us, chatting to Liam all the way.

Trevor looked worse than Sharon, who was sleeping peacefully next to him. He didn't see us coming and was watching Sharon intently, holding her hand. She had apparently come out of the concussion fairly quickly, but was incoherent, disorientated and alarmed. She had panicked about Liam and become violent when she realised she was in hospital. At this point she had had to be restrained and heavily sedated.

Liam broke free from his gran as soon as he saw Trevor, who

stood up and shook himself out of his reverie. Liam bounded towards him.

'Is she asleep?' Liam asked, looking at his mother. 'Well, she looks all right to me.'

'Don't sound so disappointed, Liam,' Julie teased, trying to make light of the situation.

'Hi, Trevor,' I said, once we were at the bedside.

He nodded to me; I didn't blame him for not talking. He looked pale and worried. He'd chewed his lips until they'd bled and done a pretty good job on his nails as well. I noticed an impressive hickey on his neck, that must have been the evidence Julie was talking about – they were more than likely Sharon's toothmarks. Trevor was obviously as needy of her as she was of him. Maybe I'd been too harsh when I'd judged him in the past. I could feel his anger towards me: I deserved it. How could I have undermined this devout display of adoration?

I fought back the tears. I hated seeing her there like that, sedated by drugs she had not willingly administered herself.

I stayed for a while to help Julie and Mrs Dubrowski sort out with Trevor the arrangements and forms. Trevor wasn't saying much, except to Liam. They were having a subdued, private chat. Maybe Trevor wasn't so bad.

I felt so useless. Sharon wasn't expected to wake up for some time and as neither Trevor nor Liam were particularly keen on me, I decided to leave.

As I bent over and kissed Sharon goodbye on the forehead, a heavy tear fell from my eye and landed softly on her hair. I carefully stroked it away, kissed her again and left.

Sharon slowly became aware of some voices nearby. It sounded like her mum. She opened her eyes and could see some people near her feet. She wanted Liam. Where was Liam? Her eyes refused to focus. Her mouth wouldn't open. She wanted some water. She needed to tell Liam she loved him. Nothing worked. She shut her eyes in a vain effort to concentrate more on making her mouth work. Nothing worked. She saw the monkey. She was the monkey. She opened her eyes in horror. She could see more clearly: she was in a bed with sheets. Where was Liam? She tried to listen to the voices. It was her mother . . .

'. . . but, Trevor, I could stay with you and Liam at the flat. You don't have to go. It'd be better for Liam, unless you want to come and stay with –'

Trevor couldn't listen to Mrs Dubrowski's drivel for a moment longer. Sharon would probably turn out like this – he could see resemblances already. Sharon, beautiful Sharon. What had happened? She was a mess. He was a mess. If he stayed, the mess would get bigger. He was too young for all this, for fuck's sake. Liam pulled on his sleeve. The kid wasn't even his son, he didn't even like him much. He couldn't take care of them. What was he? Some kind of fucking idiot?

'Please, Trev.' Liam tugged again. 'Please don't go, Trev,' he whined. 'We could watch *Match of the Day* tonight.'

'No, Liam, I'm sorry but I think it's better for your mum if I just let you two get on with it,' Trevor said.

'But, Trevor?' Liam said, staring at him, still holding his arm.

Trevor looked at Sharon and thought of Tiffany, who had everything – everything except Sharon's eyes and her sexiness, oh, and her madness. Sharon had changed, especially since she'd been mates with that Charlie. She thought she could be in a band, for fuck's sake. They'd wanted to make it big – it was laughable. Trevor knew it was that lot who had started the whole thing about money as well – Sharon never used to go on about it nearly as much until she started hanging around that sad, desperate bunch. What was it with these fucking single mothers? They were so anti-men. No one was good enough. They had no idea what it was like living with her – and Liam was a fucking nightmare. Yeah, she'd definitely changed. It was no wonder, really. Sharon was so easily influenced.

He wanted her back the way she was, but he didn't want the shit that came with it. He'd done his best, anyone could see that. He looked at the mother. Sharon didn't stand a flipping chance. Mrs Dubrowski was totally pathetic. As for Liam – well, he wasn't his kid. He didn't even know Sharon had a kid when they first started going out. She'd wanted to trap him first. How she managed to hide it for so long was pretty amazing really. Liam was still tugging on his arm.

'Get off!' Trevor snapped, shaking his arm.

Liam was shocked. He stopped tugging, looked at Trevor, then sank his teeth as hard as he could into Trevor's forearm.

'ARGH! Shit! Fuck off, you little bastard!' Trevor shrieked.

'Trevor! Liam!' Mrs Dubrowski started now.

That was enough. He had to get the fuck out of there. He took one last look at Sharon, he knew he wouldn't be seeing her again and, while Mrs Dubrowski was arguing with her uncontrollable, fucking cannibalistic grandson, he left to find a phone.

'*Liam!*' Mrs Dubrowski screamed, as Liam sank his teeth into her hand. 'My hand! Nurse! Nurse! Help!'

Sharon felt Liam land on her. Liam, my Peanut, oh, Liam, she wanted to hug him but still nothing worked. She could feel his sobs shake the bed. She wanted to tell him how much she loved him, how sorry she was, Liam, Liam, my baby. She saw her mother come over.

'Nurse! She's got her eyes open! Nurse!' Mrs Dubrowski screamed.

Sharon tried to speak. Liam's face was suddenly on top of hers. He was looking straight into her eyes. She managed to blink. Liam blinked back and she blinked again. Then he was pulled off. She wanted to scream – she wanted Liam. But she fell asleep. Monkey dreams.

A nurse had finally arrived and, with Mrs Dubrowski, they managed to prise Liam off his mum.

'Come on, darling,' Mrs Dubrowski said, to the shaking Liam, 'let's go home now ... Where's Trevor?'

'NO! I HATE YOU!' Liam screamed. 'I DON'T WANT TO GO! MUMMY! MUMMY! THEY'RE TAKING ME AWAY! TREVOR!'

'I think he's left, Pet. He'll probably see us later,' Mrs Dubrowski said, looking round desperately for any sign of Trevor.

'MUMMY! MUMMY!'

'Come on, dear,' Mrs Dubrowski spoke softly to the broken Liam.

38

I was bawling as I walked across the car park. I hated myself and the world. I'd lost Sharon, and Sharon had lost so much more.

When I eventually found my car, some toffee-nosed bitch had blocked me in. I beeped my horn and she waddled over, looking like a duck. She was on her fucking glitzy mobile phone.

'Ya, darling, I'm here now – in the car park ... Uh, the hospital. Ya ...'

I beeped again.

'So sorry,' she said, a tad sarcastically.

I felt a surge of hatred and an overwhelming desire to drive straight into her stupid racing-green Golf. Instead, I stopped at the off-licence on the way home and bought a large bottle of vodka and some orange juice.

Conka was waiting for me at mine, having put the kids to bed and tidied the place up. She'd lit a couple of candles and the place looked quite inviting. I crept into Luke's bedroom and gave him a kiss good night. Both kids were in deep sleeps – there'd be no disturbances from them tonight. I closed their door and found Conka fixing a couple of strong drinks and a joint in the living room.

We clinked our glasses and skulled them straight down. There was an urgency to get pissed.

I told Conka the news from the hospital. 'Apparently Sharon was on top, and Trevor thought she had her cap in. So when she told him that it wasn't safe, he was about to come and so he pulled her off. She went flying forward and banged her head on a nail on the wall.'

'And got knocked out cold?' Conka asked, failing to hide her amusement.

'Cold,' I confirmed.

Conka started to laugh. But I didn't find it funny. She hadn't seen Sharon in the hospital.

'It's not fucking funny!'

'I'm sorry, Charlie, but it's bloody typical, ain't it? Knocked unconscious *shagging*. Can't he even do that right? Knocked out cold, eh? Sharon just loves a bunk-up. I was knocked out with a baseball bat once, and I was just trying to do the cooking. It's not fair.' Conka giggled. 'What about the nervous breakdown?' she asked more seriously.

'Oh, I don't know, Conks. It's all gone wrong, hasn't it? Fancy another?' I got up and fixed some more drinks.

'Will there be enough hot water for a bath?'

'Yeah, plenty. That's something that never runs out in this household. We may not have any milk, bread or cereal, but there's always plenty of hot water.'

'All right, all right, Char. I only wanted a lavender bath, not one in fucking porridge.'

We clinked our glasses again and smiled at each other. Then I put on some music and we danced.

Today had been a disaster. I felt as if I'd lost two friends, Sharon and Tasha, both to the hospital. I pulled heavily on the joint, spun myself around and danced some more. I was going to forget it all.

'Fuck the band!' I shouted above the music to Conka.

'Yeah, fuck the band, Char baby. And fuck you!'

'Yeah, fuck you too, baby!'

'Right on, Char. Fuck all of us!'

'Fuck all of you!' I shouted joyfully. It's good to swear sometimes.

'I'm gonna run us a bath. Why don't you do what you're best at, Char baby?' She slammed down her empty glass in front of me and nodded at the dope tin on her way past.

Us. She said she was going to run *us* a bath. Amazing! I carried on dancing, poured us some even stronger drinks and then sat down to roll an extra spesh Camberwell carrot, except I only used seven papers. Conka wafted back in, the strong scent of lavender accompanying her. She took her drink, staring at me all the time. I stared back. She giggled at the size of the joint, and sashayed back to the bathroom. I followed her.

'Hold that,' I said, giving Conka the joint. 'I'm just going to turn the music up.'

I leaned forward, cupped her face in my hands and gave her a generous kiss on the mouth, then went to do the music. I felt my lips with my fingers, and realised how soft Conka's mouth had been. Wanting more, I blinked and took a deep breath before re-entering the bathroom. It was finally going to happen. Conka knew it and I knew it.

She was practically undressed when I came back in. Bending over the bath, she was feeling its temperature, and her naked bum looked fantastic. I ran my hand up her thigh and over her belly, turning her around to face me. We kissed passionately. I let my hand wander up her front and find her breast. It felt delicious. I had to push up her T-shirt to kiss it. I couldn't resist her. Conka's body was tremendous – soft but strong and amazingly smooth. We stopped kissing and looked at each other.

'You're like a roll of Andrex, you are. Soft, strong and very very mong,' I said to her.

First there was a little twinkle in her eye, then an enormous smile stretched across Conka's face. Then we both laughed out loud.

'Well, I've never kissed a girl properly before. It was rather nice. Fancy a bath?' Conka said, leaping into the hot water.

We sat in the steaming bath, facing each other and drinking the rest of our ice cold vodkas. We didn't really say much. We just listened to the music playing in the other room and smoked the rest of our joint.

'What a laugh, eh?' Conka said finally.

'Yeah, Conks.'

I closed my eyes, but not for long. I was beginning to spin a bit. 'Sorry, Conkarooney, but I think I've gotta get out now. I need to lie down,' I slurred.

'Hang on a second, Charlie.' She grabbed my arm and started to give me a good scrub down. It felt really invigorating.

'Wow! That's delicious.'

'Here, let me do your back. That's it. Turn around – lovely jubbly. There's nothing like a good old back scrub. Them Greeks and Romans really knew what they were up to. They did this as part of their daily routine, except they did it in that ass's milk stuff.'

'Yeah, Conks. They knew all right.'

She rinsed me down with cool water from the tap. It felt extremely fresh. We kissed again while we dried each other off. Then we wrapped our towels around us and went to lie down in the bedroom.

'You know, I fantasised about you,' I admitted.

'Yeah, I know.' She replied, losing herself in my caresses.

We felt each other all over, and kissed and licked. It was heaven for both of us. We were both coming all over the place.

'Roll over,' Conka whispered in my ear.

I rolled on my side and she curled up behind me, feeling me deep inside, touching that part and playing with me. We moved in motion with one another, passion releasing passion until we slowed to a natural peaceful calm.

We lay still for a few moments, silent but for the sound of our quick breathing. Then Conka started giggling, which set me off. The two of us lay on our backs, laughing loudly. We were fucking pissed.

'You never did know what happened that night at Sharon's, did you?' Conka asked.

'What did happen?' I sat up, leaped on top of her and tickled her. 'Come on, tell me, or you will die.'

Conka wriggled underneath me, but was too floppy to get herself free. 'All right! All right, I'll tell you,' she screamed.

I stopped tickling her and let her get her breath back. She sat up in bed and looked at me with amusement, making the most of my curiosity. 'Not a lot, actually.'

'Oh man! Oh, how I suffered!' It had been that black hole that had kick-started this affair off. It had been a life changing blank and I'd never had one of those before. I had now officially entered the realms of lesbianism. Sure, I'd messed around with a couple of women before, but they had only been moments – beautiful ones, but nevertheless still only moments. This was different. Here was someone I could live with. Here was someone I was falling in love with. We trusted each other. We had fun together. We learned from one another. We inspired each other. Here was someone who made my life easier in a practical way. It'd be easier for both of us as far as the kids were concerned, and it'd be good fun for them too. They behaved like brother and sister anyway. Woah! I checked myself.

'What did happen?' I reminded her.

Conka was beginning another spliff-rolling process. 'Well, we walked into Sharon's bedroom arm in arm, and then fell on the bed – you know, sort of wrapped together. We tried French kissing.'

'Snogged? With tongues?' I was absolutely astonished that I couldn't remember anything as monumental as that.

'Nah – I'm just winding you up. You told me you loved me a zillion times, but we were so drunk it would have been impossible to do anything, to be honest. You were so floppy you were like a rag doll.' Conka laughed again at my memory loss.

'Well, fucking thanks. And what about now?'

Conka answered with her eyebrow-raised look, as if to say not much. I was shocked. I must remember to cut down on the amount I was smoking. Memory loss – that's a sign, you know. I'll probably forget to do it though. That's the problem, you see.

'Then you played with my tits and I played with yours,' she revealed.

We both howled with laughter. It seemed so stupid. Tit-playing. How old were we?

'And that was all?' I asked. 'Did I do this?'

I leaned over and sucked Conka's nipple, playing with it with my tongue. It became firm and erect. She tasted so good.

'Nah,' Conka answered. 'Nothing happened, Char. You were even drunker than you are now.'

'Fucking wind-up!' I let go of her breast and propped myself up on my elbow in that I'm ready for a big old bed time chat position. 'Am I the first woman you've ever done anything with, Conka?'

'Yeah. And me?'

'Nah. Done the lot, Conks baby.' I winked at her.

'Really, Charlie? Tell me.'

'What do you think with my shag-success rate? Actually, there was someone once. But I've never got quite as far with another bird as we just did,' I told her, grinning. I explained to her about another woman who I love, that I had kind of felt sexual about, but had never really tangled with, not in any serious way.

'Why don't you have a relationship with her, then?' Conka asked.

'She's married and she lives in America, and neither of us would probably want it anyway. We've always much preferred men.' Conka looked at me. 'Until I met you. I've been very confused recently.'

'I know,' Conka said.

We smoked the joint in silence. I lay on my back and stared at my ceiling. It needed decorating. Conka stroked my hair. I was beginning to feel a bit freaked out from the day's events. It came in waves: one moment I'd be absolutely fine and not concerned about anything other than enjoying the all important moment. Then, out of the blue, there'd be a huge wave that made me want to burst into stomach-wrenching wails. Conka had such strength, such courage and belief.

'You are a rock, you know,' I turned to look at her.

'Yeah. Rock of bleeding Gibraltar, I am.'

This time she turned away from me and looked pensively at my ceiling.

'It needs decorating, doesn't it,' I said.

'Doesn't everything? Once you start, you can't stop though. You know that? Once you've done a little bit, you see how bad the rest is. You either have to do the whole bloody lot or leave the fucking ceiling alone.'

'Right you are, Conks.'

'Charlie?' She sounded serious.

'Yes, babe?'

'I'm thinking of moving to Spain.'

'What?' Not another one going. Please not *this* one.

'You know my sister's living out there?'

'Yeah?'

'Well, the flat beneath her is available and, to be honest, I've had more than enough of Edwin and his fucking tantrums and of trying to make ends meet in this God forsaken polluted country. Everyone here is uptight, or really sick in the head. Work is boring me to bleeding tears. I've had it here, Char. They're so much more relaxed in Spain. I reckon it'd do Helena a load of good to live out there for a year or so.'

'A year or so?' I didn't think I could take it. I wished I hadn't drunk so much – or a lot more. I needed something to wash this down. I looked at her grinning face and felt my heart sigh a deep sigh.

'Conka, you are breaking my heart,' I said finally.

'Oh, come on, Charlie. You know as well as I do that what's happened between us here tonight only happened because we're pissed.' I felt utterly dejected. 'And because we both needed someone to love, someone to hold tonight. We needed to see what it was like.' Her voice had softened.

'Conka,' I stammered. 'It was fantastic . . . I mean . . . I . . . felt you come . . . and –'

Conka put her finger on my lips gently. She could see I was getting carried away again. 'It was nice, *very* nice. I came and you Conkered.' She giggled.

I couldn't laugh. I stared at the ceiling again. She stroked my face.

'You're beautiful, Charlie. But I'm a meat and two veg kind of girl in the end. And you ain't no vegan yourself. We can only do so much for one another, and after that you've got to look after number one. We both know that the band ain't gonna work –'

She saw the tears stream down my face. I couldn't remember feeling so lost – not in a long time. And no, I didn't know the band wasn't going to work.

'Don't cry,' Conka soothed. 'You're going to do brilliant things, and we'll see each other. Why don't you come to Spain too?'

I lay with my face buried in the pillow and sobbed. What would I do without her? Without the band? Without the girls? Admittedly we hadn't got very far but we definitely had potential. This was my exit from brokes-ville. What could I do now? More dead people? I *loved* singing, and I loved singing in harmony with Conka. I knew I wouldn't be able to sing in harmony with anyone else.

I went into the other room and swilled a large mouthful of

vodka straight from the bottle. I knew I was being dramatic but I was in shock, pissed and stoned. Oh, I could deal with it all right. Of course I could Fucking deal with it. Just like I dealt with everything else. On my own. On my FUCKING own.

'Don't worry, Conka. DON'T FUCKING WORRY AT ALL!' I shouted from the living room.

'I won't. I know you'll be fine, you old toss pot!' she shouted back.

I could hear her laughing. Maybe I should go and live in Spain as well. I loved Spain. 'I'm coming with you,' I yelled.

'You're fucking mad!'

I fell on the sofa and couldn't get up again. ''Night,' I called, but I think she had finally passed out.

39

I didn't feel *soo* bad in the morning. I think I must have still been slightly pissed. I let Conka sleep in while I gave the kids some breakfast and flobbed on the sofa. I mused over the previous night's events to the tinny sound of the Top Twenty, blaring from my small radio. Music jolts memories, I thought. Conka and I had our music, and now our bing had banged.

I wanted to preserve these past few months. The music on the chart show was shit though. Our 'Bing Band' was much better. There wasn't one song that made me say, 'Oh, yes, baby, that's the song that sums up how I feel. That's really it.'

I decided that a visit to Sarah's was well overdue. I rang her. She would be delighted to see me and Luke as soon as we could get there. She was very upset about Sharon.

'Why couldn't we see it coming? What about Liam? I should never have gone away. I knew I should have come to London to see her.'

'Yeah, me too, Sarah. But I'm just going to let Trevor and her mum sort it out now. I think that things would only get worse if I interfered again.'

'Oh, it's really terrible, Charlie.'

'I know, Sarah, it really sucks.' My head began to spin again. 'Look, I'll see you soon and we'll talk then. I've gotta go now.'

'You're definitely coming, then?' she said.

'Yes. 'Bye, Sarah.'

As soon as I put the phone down, it rang. 'Argh. Hello?'

There was a long pause before anyone answered.

'Hello, Charlie?'

It was Sharon's mum. My heart took a nosedive directly to my stomach. I immediately feared the worst.

'Hi, how's Sharon? Is she all right?'

'Yes, she's fine.' Mrs Dubrowski sniffed.

She was obviously finding this whole thing very difficult.

'Well, she's not too good, really, much the same as yesterday. Put it this way, she hasn't got any worse.'

'Has she woken up properly yet?' I asked.

'Oh, no, dear. No, no, no. She's got to stay in for a while – you know, for tests and all that. It's Trevor.'

I rolled my eyes. Now Sharon's mum was going to go on about him.

'What about the charming man?' I asked.

'Oh, I'm glad you liked him too – I always said to Sharon he was a nice boy. Shame, isn't it?'

'What about him, Mrs Dubrowski?' I said.

I felt worms of irritation wriggle through my veins: Sharon was so much like her mother.

'Well, dear, I don't know where he is and Liam keeps asking for him.'

I could hear a shout from Liam in the background.

'What? I thought Trevor was with you?'

'No, dear.'

'I don't bloody believe it. Well, he's not here.'

'Oh dear. Well, I wondered if you had a number for him or something?'

'No, I'm afraid I don't. What did he say to you when you last saw him?'

'Well, that's just it dear. He left the hospital yesterday without really saying much. Well, he did say he thought we'd be better off . . .' She trailed to a halt.

'Mrs Dubrowski? What did he say?'

'He must have been terribly upset – he looked dreadful – but, well, he didn't come back.'

The bastard. Goosepimples prickled my arms as I realised he'd gone, scarpered, done a bunk. Of course he'd bloody gone – gone to find another sucker, preferably one without a child.

'Charlie? Are you still there? Charlie?'

'Yes, I'm here . . .'

'It's just that I, you know, need to ask him one or two things about what's best for Liam – you know, where he's going to stay and –'

'Mrs Dubrowski wait.' I had to interrupt her. 'You're telling me that you haven't seen him since yesterday afternoon.' My head pounded. I squinted to try to conquer it enough to continue talking.

'No, dear, he left.'

'And he hasn't rung?'

'No.'

Fucker. Fucker. *Fucker!* That was it, then. The heat got too much and he couldn't take it. The weak, putrid shit.

'Charlie?' Mrs Dubrowski's voice epitomised pathos.

Why couldn't he have done the decent thing and at least told her he was going? Asshole.

'Charlie? Are you there, dear?'

'Sorry, sorry, I've got a really bad headache. Look, I don't think Trevor will be calling, Mrs Dubrowski,' I said, 'and he doesn't have a number and by the way, I never came close to liking him.' I could hear Mrs Dubrowski's breath quicken as she realised what I was saying. 'Mrs Dubrowski, are you all right?'

She sniffed loudly into the phone.

'Oh, I'll be all right, dear . . .' She paused as the buzzer sounded in the background.

'I'll get it, Gran!' Liam shouted.

'He was such a nice boy,' she spluttered.

Through her breathy gasps, I could hear Liam yelling and some male voices, none of which sounded like Trevor's. No wonder she was crying. Even anus-breath-Trev could have helped a bit – just for a couple of days. But, no, he had to go and milk another cow.

'Oh dear,' Mrs Dubrowski said, 'it's the police! I'd better go.'

'What?' I asked excitedly.

'They're gonna get Trevor!' Liam was singing in the background. 'They're gonna get Trevor!'

'Fantastic!' I said. 'Is what I'm hearing correct? Mrs Dubrowski?'

But Mrs Dubrowski had hung up. Despite my thundering migraine, I found a smile. At last Trevor was going to pay. I went to the kitchen to make some coffee. I just hoped they'd find him and bang him up – that way the bastard wouldn't be able to go back to Sharon, even if he wanted to. He deserved everything he got.

I woke Conka up with a hot, milky coffee, a kiss and a glass of cold water. She looked like she'd been shagging all night. I was impressed with myself.

'How are you today?' I asked.

'Oh, I'm fine.' She took a slurp of the water. 'What time is it?'

'About ten thirty,' I said, as I flopped on to the bed.

'Oh, well, I'd better get a move on. I've got to get organised.'

She got up and stumbled to the bathroom. I'd wanted a cuddle. Never mind. I followed her to the bathroom. The door was ajar so I leant against the wall in the hallway and shouted through the gap. I told her about Trevor and heard her pee. It seemed she wasn't that interested in my hot gossip.

'As long as they don't come pestering me!' she shouted, through the door. 'As far as I'm concerned, I've never met the tosser.'

'Well I thought maybe – just maybe – he'd go back just to make sure Liam and his batty gran were all right. Sharon always said Trevor got on quite well with Mrs D.'

Conka gave a sarcastic laugh. She knew all along that Trevor wasn't going to go back to Sharon's – it was fucking obvious, apparently. I heard a fart. I felt silly even mentioning Trevor. I attempted to talk to her, but then I heard the loo flush. She'd lost all interest. Spain was pretty much the only thing on her mind.

What about me? Hadn't she thought about that. I'd changed my career for her. I'd sung for her!

She brushed past me as she came out of the bathroom. For a few moments, I stayed where I was, feeling sick.

Ten minutes later, everyone was dressed and ready to go. Luke was excited to be going to Sarah's. I still felt fazed. I needed to escape too. Luke was tugging on my arm. 'All right, Luke, we're going.'

I would have to tear myself away from Conka at some point. I'd just have to get used to it. She was coping all right. I watched her brush Helena's hair. Yes, we'd had a great night. We'd had loads of great nights in the past, but to me this one had been different. But not to Conka: not different at all. To her it was just a fantastic one-off. She'd been curious and I'd helped her out. She'd just wanted to explore further within our friendship. Conka had got what she wanted. As always. That's what had made me fall in love with her in the first place: her cheek, her ability to know what she wanted. She would always get it – and bollocks to anyone who got in her way.

My fantasies, however, had taken me way beyond friendship. I had wanted Conka to be there for me. But now she was going without me, without even consulting me. She lived her own life and, oops, I'd forgotten. I'd wanted to jump on her train, instead of finding my own. I should have fucking known. Never trust a man, I thought, but what about a woman? What about yourself? I wouldn't be doing that again for a while.

In a way we were closer than we had ever been: we had cemented our friendship, our love for each other was solid and good, even though 'it' would probably never happen again. I'd discovered that, for Conka, it wasn't anything other than fun, while I'd been barking up an altogether different tree. She'd found out what it was like and concluded that she still preferred her wet dreams. But we had made love. I really felt that. Christ Almighty.

I told myself to think positive: life changes. Always. There was going to have to be a great big rethink all round. A huge one. I made myself realise that I wasn't in love with her, not *truly*, however much I had wanted to be. I couldn't imagine being in love with any other woman. Perhaps I wasn't destined for lesbianism after all. Shitting bollocks. What was my destiny, then? I couldn't be a rock star now, either. Crap. I should have called the band Crap Attack. It might have worked.

I was about to say something to Conka about our night when Luke urged me to hurry. Parting would be easier without words. It was easier on the head too. By now my temples were leaping out of my skull and my eyes were itching like fuck.

'Do you know roughly when you're going to Spain?' I asked her when we were at the door.

'Wednesday,' she said.

I shouldn't have been surprised, but it was so soon. I almost fell over.

'That soon?'

'Yeah, well, you know, the tickets are dirt cheap if you leave pretty much immediately and I've decided to go. There's not much point in hanging around waiting to leave, is there?'

'But what are you doing until Wednesday?' I stammered. 'Come to Sarah's with me now.'

'I can't, Charlie. I've got to get on, you know, get sorted and everything. You know how it is.'

She saw my face drop. 'I'll pop by on Tuesday, okay? I've gotta do it, you know.'

'I can always see your point, Conka,' I said, forcing myself to smile. 'See ya then, babe-o-rama,' I said, giving her a big hug and a loud smacker on the lips.

'*Ciao, bella,*' she shouted as she left.

''Bye, Helena!' I called. 'Hey, make sure you write to us. We'll be joining you out there sooner than you know it!'

'Of course,' Conka said, standing at the top of my steps.

She took one last, lingering look at me. I could feel the lump in my throat swell, preceding the sobs. In a final effort of humour and lesbianism, I flashed my tits at her. She smiled and blew me a kiss, before bouncing down the road with Helena running behind, struggling to keep up with her. Maybe Conka was crying too. Doubt it.

40

Trevor woke early that day. He'd drunk so much the night before he desperately needed the loo. He rolled over to give Sharon a cuddle, but his hand sank into the depths of Tiffany's arse and he remembered where he was.

'Hi, darling.' She was smiling at him.

Trevor could only moan in response. He rolled out of bed and somehow made it to the bathroom. As he came out he heard her call him again. Fucking Tiffany, she was so flipping chirpy. She got on his nerves.

'Trevor, baby?' she called, again.

'Shut it,' Trevor mumbled, as he went to the kitchen and got a beer.

She'd got what she'd wanted – he was here with her now, for good . . . well, at least for a while. There'd be no going back to Sharon now, even if she hadn't ended up in hospital. Yesterday was definitely going to be the end of it, for Trevor anyway. He'd forget about the few remaining clothes he had been going to collect: he could afford new ones now. Now that he wouldn't have anyone nagging him for his money, now that he wouldn't have an extra mouth to feed. He knew he wouldn't miss Liam, but he couldn't help feeling a bit sorry for him. Liam reminded him of himself when he was a kid. They both had fucked-up mothers and nowhere-to-be-seen fathers.

Trevor sat down and watched some morning telly on the small set in the kitchen. He smoked a cigarette and glugged back some more beer. He was just beginning to relax when he heard Tiffany call him. He didn't know how long he'd be able to put up with her. He'd save his money and move on. This time he really would. He and Sharon had thought they could save when they'd first got together but they couldn't have been more wrong. Now there were bailiffs chasing them down the street. No, he would move on and next time he wasn't going to fall for any romantic bullshit either.

He grabbed another beer from the fridge and went back to the bedroom.

'Hi, darling,' Tiffany cooed.

He lay on his back and watched Tiffany go down on him. She was all right, he supposed. She was just getting warmed up when the fucking buzzer went. Tiffany looked up at him. 'I'd better get it,' she said.

Trevor rolled his eyes and reached for a cigarette – if it was that freaking poof Jeremy he'd fucking kill him. Tiffany put on her dressing-gown and went to the door. She wasn't gone long: Trevor had just enough time to take one long drag on his fag before three policemen burst in. One stood with a panicked Tiffany in the doorway, while the other two literally jumped on top of him, treating him like he was the flipping Pink Panther or something. He was about to tell them to relax when he felt a sharp pain charge through his arm and shoulder.

'SHIT! FUCK!' Trevor screamed, as they wrenched his other arm too.

It fucking hurt and he wasn't even resisting.

'GET OFF HIM!' he heard Tiffany yell hoarsely, as the two bozos hoisted him out of bed.

'Do you want one last little line, you slimy little cokehead ponce?' the fat policeman hissed, as he deliberately stood on Trevor's bare foot.

'Oh, shit,' Trevor said quietly.

'Oh, shit, indeed,' the fat pig mimicked, grinning in Trevor's face.

Conka looked at her watch. Unless she was accidentally on Spanish time already and an hour early, he was late. She'd wait a bit longer, though. She wanted those tickets now: as well as being curious about Mr Davenport, she was keen to go. She was going to miss Charlie and Luke terribly, but not Edwin or Mrs Uptight, or Sharon or Tasha or Trevor. She *had* to get out, she'd had enough of that life.

Where the furry fuck was Mr Davenport? Conka really didn't feel like seeing any of them again – no way. She'd been there, done that. It'd been a big fucking mistake having that bunk up with Edwin that time as well. No, she was going to change her life, improve her environment, teach her child Spanish and forget about the whole bloody lot of them – except Charlie. Last night had been definitely one to remember.

Charlie had surprised her. The sex had been great. But somehow Conka's fantasy still beat the reality. Weirder things had happened, she supposed. She needed to get away from Charlie as much as she wanted to stay near her. She knew Charlie was a good mate, but it was probably a good thing to go away right now – you know, to let the dust settle. Charlie had had that look in her eye that meant more than Conka wanted. Charlie seemed really ready to do a whole lesbian-relationship thing. But it wouldn't have worked. Conka knew that; Charlie surely realised it too. Where *was* Mr Davenport?

She was just about to give up waiting and go to a travel agency when she saw a smallish guy in a dark grey suit walking towards her. She smiled at him and he came over.

'Conka?' he asked.

Conka smiled. 'Hellooee, Mr Davenport! How nice to meet you.'

He was a neatly presented, well-dressed, rich-looking gentleman. He had that trust-me-I'm-genuine expression written all over his face. No wonder he'd done well. He seemed like a man very much in control.

'And how very charming to meet you at long last! Let's go for a drink,' he said.

Conka was tempted by the drink and company but, after a brief calculation, concluded there'd be absolutely no point. She was imminently emigrating, for fuck's sake.

'I'd love to, but I really haven't got time. I'm not just going for two weeks, I'm going for at least a year so I've got zillions of things to do,' she explained, smiling.

Mr Davenport didn't seem surprised. 'Did you hand in your notice?' he asked.

'Take a wild guess,' Conka said, counting out her money.

'You're just what I expected.' Mr Davenport laughed. 'Don't worry about the money, Conka. Take the tickets and have a fantastic time. You're a good, hard-working mum and the first person that's brought a bit of sunshine into my life since my daughter stopped talking to me.'

Conka took the tickets and gave Mr Davenport a quick hug. She felt he wanted to make up for something that had happened in the past, but she figured she was helping him out enough by accepting his gift of three tickets to Alicante. He was a really nice guy, too old for her, but it was encouraging to meet a man so kind, indeed generous. She didn't need to know the rest.

'Look, are you sure you can't come for a drink – just a quick one?' Mr Davenport asked.

'Mr Davenport, you know as well as I do, there's no such thing as a quick one,' Conka said, grinning, 'at least, not in my book.'

Conka was not one to hang around and talk about a load of bollocks. He looked slightly forlorn. Conka liked him a lot.

'I'm sorry, I can't tell you how much I've got left to do,' she said gently.

He smiled at her. He didn't really mind.

'Have you got your brother's number, then?' Conka asked.

She took it down and was ready to say goodbye.

'Thanks, Mr Davenport,' Conka said, kissing his cheek, 'I really appreciate this.'

She started walking back. She had to get moving. She turned to take one last look at her sugar daddy.

'I'll send you a postcard!' she shouted. 'Give Mrs Upton a big snog for me, yeah?'

Mr Davenport waved, laughing, as he watched her stride into the distance.

'Goodbye, Conka,' he said.

The sodding car overheated twice on the way there. That was another thing: I needed to get a few things fixed on it – yet more expense. I knew I didn't drive it in a way that would make it last longer, but the fucker chose to overheat on a day when I really could have done with a smooth ride. Still, I guess that's life's helpful little way of taking your mind off more depressing things. Cheers. Needed that.

As the buildings got lower and the green bits greener, I felt a clammy weight lift slightly, as I left behind some of my disgust with the world in the dense pollution. I couldn't get there quickly enough. I needed Sarah's calm and reason. I needed her to cook me some dinner and make me feel a whole lot better. She always did. I counted with Luke the number of roundabouts that were left to go. We knew that route so well: I'd gone there so many times before, drained, exhausted, hung over, let down and disappointed. Sarah always washed it all away for me. What a friend.

Sarah greeted us with madness and mayhem: she was upset because she had accidentally run over a frog with the lawn mower. That immediately cheered me up. We farted around for a bit with the kids, their rabbits and the frog's remains then sat down for our usual Spanish coffee and spliff session.

I told her about Trevor's disappearance and then about the police looking for him and about my recent lesbian-love loss. She wasn't surprised: she'd had a similar experience herself in the past. It hadn't worked for her either.

Another spliff later, it began to sound so bad it was funny.

'So, basically, Sarah, Sharon's in a hospital, off her rocker, somewhere near her dopey mum, who's now chief carer for Liam, poor sod. Trevor's nowhere to be seen, the fucker. Tasha's planning some mad pagan wedding and is lost in the world of the fascinating doctor and the vision of his perfect penis. Conka tells me last night that she's moving to Spain on Wednesday. And I don't know whether I'm straight, gay or Liberal Democrat. Or none of the above. Maybe I'm a closet nun.'

'Umm,' Sarah said.

'Yep.'

We sat in silence for a bit. I was sure it was funny.

'It is funny, isn't it, Sarah?'

'What is?'

'All of it.'

'Yeah.'

We sat in silence for a while longer.

'Well, Labour have won,' Sarah eventually said.

I had totally forgotten about it.

'Shit, I can't believe I fucking missed it! Bollocks! Sarah, I didn't vote! Oh, I can't believe it. I really wanted the Lib Dems to get in. They're the only ones who understand us, they've got the best green policy, they've got – the – they're the only bisexuals, for fuck's sake.' I sighed.

'Yeah, well, I voted – obviously. It's a shame. The first thing Tony Blair mentioned was bringing us single mothers back to work – like we're out there on frigging holiday. It's scary, Charlie. What does he think I can do? I'm forty-nine, I have no qualifications and no savings. I just want to bring up my kids.'

'I could probably get you in with them at the funeral home,' I said, winking at her.

'What if they take my benefits away? How am I going to pay the rent? I can't count on *him*.'

'Don't worry. It's going to be all right,' I said. 'You know, I *know* them at the funeral home. I have some very important connections. I could easily swing it for you, darling, no problem. Dead people *never* complain about their makeup either. You'd probably be really great at it – you've always been good with your hands. You get to meet some people who were once really interesting. There's absolutely no chance of suffering from heat exhaustion. It's fun. It's a great place to try out new colours, hairstyles, all sorts of things really . . .' I said.

Sarah slapped me around the back of the head.

'Ow! At least you haven't lost an entire music career,' I whimpered.

'Don't be upset about the single-mothers' band, Charlie – you can't fucking sing anyway. You know you can't. You'll find something else to do.'

I shrugged my shoulders.

'You know you will. I have great faith in you,' she said, laughing.

I was about to shout at her when I heard, 'You've got to roll with it, you've got to take what you take,' blare out from the radio.

I leapt up and turned it on full volume. This was *my song*.

'You've got to say what you say, don't let anyone get in your way.'

Oasis: now *there*'s a band.